Praise for THE LIFE ROOM

"Eleanor Cahn is of two minds about her impending trip to Paris, the event that kicks off poet and editor Jill Bialosky's introspective second novel . . . Eleanor's quest is the search for her lost passion and . . . [Bialosky's] poet's gift for language is up to the task." —*Chicago Tribune*

"Rife with allusions as well as foreshadowed yet satisfying surprises, *The Life Room* is a novel that takes on the formidable task of laying bare the interior life of a conflicted woman." —*The Washington Post Express*

"[A] suspenseful tale . . . Bialosky explores the idea that needy people are often the most powerful and destabilizing. We're not sure why Eleanor wants to have an affair . . . but we believe she does—and with a kind of reckless illogic that would do Tolstoy proud." —*The New York Times Book Review*

"Luminous . . . In whip-smart, gorgeous prose, Bialosky explores the push-pull of passion and responsibility, and the intoxication of dangerous liaisons." —*DAME Magazine*

"*The Life Room,* Jill Bialosky's second novel, re-imagines Tolstoy's society-driven epic, *Anna Karenina,* as a bildungsroman. Though the plot parallels the sordid events surrounding the affair between the troubled Anna and the dashing Count Vronsky, the best moments in Bialosky's book concern the interior life of Eleanor Cahn, a literature professor, wife, and mother in her late thirties . . . engaging." —*Bookforum*

"Like Michael Cunningham's *The Hours* echoing *Mrs. Dalloway*, Jill Bialosky's new novel has a literary ghost rattling around in its walls. *Anna Karenina* haunts *The Life Room*. Instead of a single Vronsky, Eleanor faces several. Her resolute self-destruction, with love the prime weapon, gives this novel the feel of an on-coming train." —*Los Angeles Times*

"The premise of Bialosky's novel seems generic, but she uses this to advantage, highlighting symbolic and schematic elements to produce a study in self-examination that withholds emotional satisfaction from protagonist and reader alike, managing at once to frustrate and to entrance. One of Eleanor's ex-lovers says of his own novel, 'It has no plot. It's about desire,' and something similar is true of Bialosky's. She is adept at capturing the banal-ity of desire and the patterns of contemporary lives that are 'all angst with no transformation.'" —*The New Yorker*

"*The Life Room* avoids easy moralization . . . Tolstoy is the genius loci of this novel, but in its interiority, its examination of the in-tricate psyche—particularly the mechanisms of repression—it's more Henry James." —*The East Hampton Star*

"Bialosky's brightly burning novel of desire and aberration, and a woman's quest for deeper understanding, is remarkable for its insights into erotic compulsion and the unbearable awkward-ness and pain of flawed and failed love." —*Booklist*

"In her exquisite, carefully observed exploration of a modern woman's inner life, Jill Bialosky has written a novel that poses an essential question: how do we reconcile our passions—love, work, erotic life, children? *The Life Room* is an elegant, daring book, driven by internal suspense."

—Dani Shapiro, author of *Slow Motion* and *Black & White*

"Jill Bialosky pierces the heart here until the reader feels just exactly what it means to have it all—husband, children, success—and yet to be achingly alone, longing for passion. Through Bialosky's elegant prose and tremendous talents as a storyteller, desire reverberates across the pages to meet the reader's own."

—Martha McPhee, author of *L'America*

"What's most extraordinary about *The Life Room* is its unabashed honesty. In a novel that is daring and form-shifting and challenging in all the very best ways, Jill Bialosky still manages to keep it true to course. There is a texture in every sentence, but most importantly you emerge from the novel feeling as if you have met a life that has glanced against your own, and gratefully your world has been shifted. A lovely, genuine, deep work of art."

—Colum McCann , author of *Zoli*

"*The Life Room* is patient in its investigations of love and erotically charged. By the end of this story, readers will be convinced that Eleanor Cahn knows more about Anna Karenina, let alone the inventive despair of the human heart, than anyone they are likely to have met in literature in a very, very long time. This is a stunningly generous and finely crafted novel."

—Howard Norman, author of *Devotion*

"In this story—at once graceful and pulsating—Bialosky holds up the old question to a new light. What is the nature of erotic desire that it can potentially devastate a woman's work and personal life? Unflinching and beautifully written . . . A truly impressive feat."   —Elizabeth Strout, author of *Olive Kitteridge*

"Who am I and how should I live? For a woman with an eye turned in upon herself, such questions inevitably lead to this: What does a person owe to those she loves and who love her, and what does she owe to herself? The power of this novel lies in its scrupulous examination of an honest heart laid bare."

—Sigrid Nunez, author of *The Last of Her Kind*

THE LIFE ROOM

JILL BIALOSKY

THE LIFE ROOM

A Harvest Book
Harcourt, Inc.

Orlando   Austin   New York   San Diego   London

Requests for permission to make copies of any part of the work should be
submitted online at www.harcourt.com/contact or mailed to the following address:
Permissions Department, Houghton Mifflin Harcourt Publishing Company,
6277 Sea Harbor Drive, Orlando, Florida 32887-6777.

Illustration credits—Page 83: *The Bathers*. Oil on canvas, 64 × 80 cm. Fragonard,
Jean-Honore (1732–1806). The Louvre, Paris, France. Courtesy of Réunion des Musées
Nationaux/Art Resource, New York. Page 93: *Woman with a Pearl*. Oil on canvas.
Corot, Jean-Baptiste Camille (1796–1875). The Louvre, Paris, France. Courtesy of Réunion
des Musées Nationaux/Art Resource, New York. Page 103: *Dante and Virgil in Hell*; also
called *Dante's Boat*. 1822. Oil on canvas, 189 × 246 cm. Delacroix, Eugene (1798–1863). The
Louvre, Paris, France. Courtesy of Réunion des Musées Nationaux/Art Resource, New
York. Page 113: *Venus, Satyr and Cupid* (wrongly titled *Jupiter and Antiope*). Oil on canvas.
188 × 125. Correggio (Antonio Allegri) (1489–1534). The Louvre, Paris, France. Photograph
by R. G. Ojeda. Courtesy of Réunion des Musées Nationaux/Art Resource, New York.

Excerpts from this book were previously published in *Bomb* and *Open City*.

www.HarcourtBooks.com

The Library of Congress has cataloged the hardcover edition as follows:
Bialosky, Jill.
The life room/Jill Bialosky.—1st ed.
p.   cm.
1. Self-realization—Fiction.   I. Title.
PS3552.I19L54   2007
813'.54—dc22   2006038236
ISBN 978-0-15-101047-9
ISBN 978-0-15-603432-6 (pbk.)

Text set in Garamond MT
Designed by Cathy Riggs

Printed in the United States of America

First Harvest edition 2008
K J I H G F E D C B A

"Where am I? What am I doing? Why?"

—From *Anna Karenina* by Leo Tolstoy

THE LIFE ROOM

PART I

1

She had been born with different colored eyes. One blue and the other green. When she looked at herself in the mirror, she felt as if she were split down the center, divided, as if one part of her were competing with the other. She had heard that if a person has dissimilar eyes at birth, it is quite possible that the two eyes were subjected to different pressures within the womb.

Tonight she felt as if her blue eye was telling her to go to Paris and her green eye was telling her not to go. She had just been invited to give a paper on Tolstoy at an international conference on world literature at the Sorbonne and, of course, she had to go; it was an honor, something she had long hoped for. She loved the exhilaration that followed after presenting a paper. She imagined herself walking through the Parisian city streets and sitting in cafés, hearing stimulating lectures by academics she admired. She imagined she'd find both the quiet time and the inspiration she needed to begin turning the paper she had written on *Anna Karenina* into a full-length study. The thought of going filled her with guilty pleasure. But she did not want to think about leaving her family behind. She could not bear being separated from them. She knew it was irrational, yet she often experienced feelings that on one level seemed irrational and on another felt perfectly reasonable. Now she was in bed, glad that Michael had drifted off. She hadn't told him yet about Paris, not because she chose to keep secrets. She only wanted to keep her trip to herself for as long as possible, to revel in her accomplishment privately. She didn't want her own thoughts to escape before she'd had a chance to digest them.

Eleanor listened to the creaks in the wood, the bang of the radiator. The boys were sound asleep in the room across the hall from them, and Michael was breathing in lightly, making a whistling sound through his nose. Suddenly, Eleanor was so frightened by the thought of leaving them that she couldn't move. She said to herself, *It's okay. Nothing is going to happen to the boys or Michael if you go away. They'll be here waiting. Go see your boys.* She rose from the bed and moved into the room where the boys slept and slipped in next to Noah, the youngest, and held him. She fell asleep again, and when she awoke it was dawn. She crept down the drafty hall, folded her body underneath the sheet in the bed next to her husband, and fell back to sleep.

First it was Noah she heard rustle in the bed across the hall, the patter of his bare feet on the wood as he turned the corner to the bathroom, the creak of the toilet seat lifting—he remembered this time. She heard his small feet running back into his bedroom. Light began to filter through her open window, and the morning released its crisp smell into the air. It was the weekend, and time had slowed down just a morsel, so that she could feel everything around her more intensely. She watched the light slowly strengthen in the room, the colors of the walls shimmering. Soon she heard Noah and Nicholas. They were whispering in their beds, no doubt hatching a plan.

Michael was turned into the corner of the antique bed, the sheets reaching across his broad shoulders. She felt his hand reach across her middle. It was warm and she allowed him to pull her against him. She had awoken to his particular smell for over twelve years. And each morning she took it in newly, never tiring of the comfort and warmth of his body beside her. She nestled her head into the back of his neck. He wasn't quite awake, and it was in this half-conscious state that he always wanted to hold her first, as if he needed her body to rouse him before he took in any more of the world. This desire to see life through her eyes was what she found so endearing about him from the first day they met. She remembered how he had wanted to share every minute with her, so that going to the store to shop for dinner was an adventure. He took her by the hand through the aisles to the most secluded spot in the store where he could embrace her, until they felt an urgent desire to return to either her studio apartment or his. It did not matter whether they had much in common to talk about. She was in awe of all the ways in which he was different from her, so that together they seemed to make a neat package of contradictions.

If only she could hold this moment of reflection longer and stop time from moving forward. She was already aware of how quickly the morning would be consumed by the obligations that awaited her, but when the boys flew into the room, bounding on top of the bed with their plastic swords and reenacting a duel from *Star Wars,* she laughed. Michael continued to feign sleep while they poked him with their swords, then came to life in a roar. The boys came tumbling down on top of them, forcing Eleanor and Michael to make room for them.

"I was invited to Paris," she whispered, curling up against Michael's sleep-filled body after the boys had run out of their bedroom with their swords. To release her anxiety, she told Michael about her paper's acceptance in a voice intimate and private, wanting him to share in her enthusiasm.

"That's terrific," he said, turning over to look at her. "But Paris? For how long? Are you sure you want to go so far away without us?"

His reaction deflated the excitement she had been carrying around with her for nearly twenty-four hours and made her more anxious. In his reaction she read her own fears. She explained the significance of being asked to participate in the conference, how it would be an added asset to her vita, an important place to make connections. She did not want to tell him that lately—when she'd learned a colleague had just published a new book or someone she knew had gotten tenure — she felt panicked, as if time was racing by without her.

"But it's not something you have to do?" Michael said, yawning.

"If you don't want me to go, just say it," she said, rising from her pillow. She nearly hated this part of him that could not fully accept that she had ambitions separate from his. She had wanted him to encourage her to go, to tell her that they'd be fine without her, that it was an honor she couldn't refuse. "I haven't gone away for more than a weekend conference since Nicholas was born."

"Of course I want you to go." He pulled her closer to the warmth of his body as if claiming power over her. "If leaving us is what you want to do."

"I don't want to leave you."

"I know," Michael said, his voice still not quite awake.

2

Michael Gordon was a heart surgeon affiliated with a research hospital. He acted rather than pondered. He went in and fixed things. He cut open the chest, parted the walls of the thoracic cavity, inserted tubes to initiate heart-lung bypass, and then placed grafts into the blocked arteries. Often, after the boys were in bed, he looked at biopsies of animal heart muscle for a research project he was involved in on the regeneration of damaged hearts. Other times he reviewed laboratory results and images of carotid studies.

They had met at a wedding of mutual friends. Eleanor was an assistant professor at Columbia and Michael was doing his residency. They ended up in the lobby of the Plaza, both having ducked out before the dancing (they were at the age where it was depressing to be at a wedding if you were unattached), and shared a cab. "I noticed your eyes at dinner," Michael said. His were surrounded by tortoiseshell glasses. Eleanor had grown used to people staring at hers. The two different colors had a hypnotic effect, as if people wanted to be drawn in closer, to see more when they looked at her. Or perhaps people were drawn to the unfamiliar. "I don't think I've ever seen a person with that particular mutation. It's always been textbook." He looked at her more closely. Sometimes the bluer eye seemed softer, other times the green eye, so that it was often difficult to read her.

He had walked Eleanor to the door of her building, and they continued talking on the front steps. "Why did you want to be a heart surgeon?" She studied his cleanly shaven face, catching a whiff of his expensive cologne. She noticed his pressed Brooks Brothers suit and conservative tie; his stiff, practical leather shoes. She was used to academics, writers, and artists, who dressed more casually. She studied him more closely. His fingernails were cut short and square. His hands were rough from washing and scrubbing. He spoke in short sentences. He listened. He was tall and broad and athletic looking. His thick brown hair was slicked back off his face. He had nice sideburns, perfectly in line with his jawbone. He was handsome in a boyish way. It was 95°, one of those saunalike August days in New York. "Don't you want to undo your tie?" she said, looking at him as sweat dripped down his face. She had the urge to mess him up.

He told her about his training, how he had learned to distance himself from the organs in the body, to view them as pathology specimens. But once he'd held a still-beating heart in his hand. "The heart is the only organ that functions outside the body. It contains its own spontaneous activity. That's why poets and philosophers have proclaimed it the place in the body where we feel things." Sitting on the stoop, they were at eye level, but she could not quite see into his eyes through the lenses of his glasses, and this troubled her. He tucked his hand inside the lip of her blouse above her breast and rested it over her heart. It was beating so strongly she thought it was pulsing out of her chest into his hand. "This is what I do," he said. "This is what I take care of."

Every day there was something new to admire about him. Some people are perpetually late and others are perpetually on time. He was always at the proposed meeting place precisely when he said he would be there. He was a man of his word. He was organized and focused. He knew exactly what he wanted out of life. His constitution was as structurally sound as a building. She found in his presence that her inner clock began to steady. She didn't have to try to numb herself so that she would not feel so deeply. Michael was easy and soothing. He didn't question her constantly or demand so much of her attention. She felt she had more room to be herself. He liked to run, sometimes five or six miles in the park, and when he returned he was more energetic than when he had left. She wondered what he thought of when he ran, what absorbed his attention when it wasn't the activity at hand. Once she asked, and he said he counted his paces. They married a year after they'd met. They settled into their life together, and Eleanor learned to adjust to his practical, more reserved nature. It wasn't that he didn't look for the underside, it was that he put his feelings in perspective. His disposition had the effect of balancing out Eleanor's moodiness, but she found herself keeping some of her thoughts to herself. Sometimes she wished he would let go and be more spontaneous and adventurous.

Eleanor worried that eventually the novelty of the obsessive, passionate, emotional person that she was would wear off and he'd wish he'd married the more conventional girlfriend from medical school. "Eleanor, I'm with you," he said, exasperated when she forced the idea upon him. "I don't look back." In order to take his emotional temperature, she had to catch him off guard.

When he woke up in the morning, he checked his pager. At the hospital, he performed surgery or laparoscopic procedures guided by images on monitors. In his profession, there was no room for doubt. It was the ability to be exact that made one a good surgeon. He did not have an inner voice inside him competing for his attention. She was used to people who said one thing and did something else. Or people like her father, whose emotions overruled their intellect, who said what they meant but then could not follow through with their intentions. Michael was a new species to her, and she studied him as closely as he studied his pathology specimens.

Noah was clingy the night before she left for Paris. He prolonged his bedtime, asking to read a second book when she'd finished one, cuddling up next to her in his bed, stroking her hair. Once he'd finally fallen asleep, he awoke an hour later, complaining of a stomachache. She lay in bed with him until he quieted and fell back to sleep. Nicholas was impatient for attention. He looked at Eleanor with the angry scowl that had recently begun to dominate his expressions. "Do you still want me to read to you?" she asked. "You don't have to," he said. He was at that stage where he wanted more independence. Noah was an easier child by nature, and Nicholas was aware of it, and resented his brother because of it. Now that he was ten, he refused to let Eleanor lie down in bed next to him as she had done when he was small, and yet she knew he still wanted her to. Once Noah was asleep, she moved to the edge of Nicholas's bed. "I'll sit here until you're asleep," she said. "You don't have to, Mom." He no longer called her Mama or Mommy like he used to.

"I want to," Eleanor said.

After the boys were asleep she went to her study to review her paper. The phone rang. It was her mother wishing her a safe trip. "Stephen Mason's in Paris. I gave Carol the name of the hotel you're staying. I hope he'll look you up." "Why?" Eleanor asked, bewildered that her mother had given Stephen's mother the name of her hotel. "Because you're like family," her mother said. Eleanor hung up, and felt a little strange. She was surprised to learn that Stephen Mason was in Paris and that her mother had given his mother the name of her hotel. She pushed the thought away. It was too disturbing.

Michael was working in the kitchen. She thought again that she should cancel the trip. How could she leave her boys? She remembered the nights after her father had left. She was Nicholas's age then. How she had missed the feel of his lips on her skin when he cradled her in his lap; how she had missed the passionate, resounding music that came out of the piano at night when he had gotten home from work, too bottled up to speak. Even though he didn't believe in God, she knew God was inside him. She knew God had already forgiven him for his disbelief. God was his music. But she could never say those things to her father. She barely could keep track of what country he lived in.

She was selfish to go. No, of course she had to go—she was being silly. She left the study and went down the hall to check on the boys. They were sound asleep. She heard Michael's chair scrape the kitchen floor and the creak of the wooden floors as he walked down the hall. She heard him go into the bathroom to brush his teeth before bed. She felt them all drawing from her—*one more chapter, Mommy, one more page, one more kiss*—wanting her to make the world more animate, more alive, warmer, safer. What hollowness she would feel without them.

She went into the bedroom and thought about the conversation with her mother and the fact that Stephen would be in Paris. For a second she wondered if he would call her, and then dismissed it. Michael was in bed watching the evening news. It bothered her that he liked to watch TV in bed when at the end of the night she longed only for silence. But she refrained from asking him to turn it off. She felt him waiting for her to finish undressing, his eyes on her back after she took off her blouse and pulled the T-shirt she wore to bed over her head. She remembered the times before her sons were born, when she wasn't always so tired, when she was eager to slide into his arms, to slip her legs between his. She remembered how fascinated she had been by the completely other universe inside the body he inhabited.

She needed to finish packing, but stopped and looked at him. "Tell me the story again about the first time you felt a heart beating in your hand."

"It was pulsing and slippery. A thing of beauty, really. After I left the pathology lab, I couldn't stop thinking about what it takes to keep something alive. Everything is dependent upon something else in the body."

"But does it scare you? To have someone's destiny in your hands? For someone to be that dependent?"

"I don't think of it that way. As a physician you have to look for the symptoms and signs of failure. You attend to them the best you can. You have to trust when it's time to let go."

"But what if you're afraid?" The light from the TV created strange patterns on the dark, familiar walls.

"It's okay," he said. He looked at her with that look that said he wanted her to awaken something inside him. She was aware that part of her didn't want to get too close, as if she needed to prepare for their separation, and yet another part of her longed to be as close to him as she had felt when they first fell in love.

"Are you sure you're okay with me leaving?" she asked again.

"If you ask one more time I'm not going to let you go." He grabbed her arms and pulled her toward the bed.

"But I have to finish packing," she said playfully. She saw the disappointment in his face and a stirring of love for him pulled inside her. "I mean, after you're tired of me."

"I'm never tired of you. You know that. Is that why you're so frightened?"

"Daddy, how many times does the heart beat in your whole life?" Noah asked at breakfast the next morning. Michael attached his beeper to the waist of his pants, and then unsuccessfully attempted to pry his stethoscope away from Noah's sticky hand. Eleanor liked listening to his conversations with the boys, who brought out aspects of him that were still mysterious.

"The heart beats more than two and a half billion times in an average lifetime, Noah."

"Daddy, how much does it weigh?"

"It's about the size of a clenched fist and weighs about 9 to 11 ounces."

"What does it sound like?"

"Every heart has its own sound. You have to listen to its particular depth and rhythm."

Noah was still fussing with the stethoscope.

"It rests in a moistened chamber called the pericardial cavity, which is surrounded by the rib cage. The diaphragm, a tough layer of muscle, lies below. It's one of the miracles of nature, how sound and protected it is."

Noah hopped out of his chair and sat on her lap and put the stethoscope to her chest. "Mommy, is your heart protected?"

"You all protect it." She kissed the top of his head and squeezed him against her body. "When I'm with you it's like being in a sacred garden surrounded by a wall of comforting trees."

"If it's so comforting then why do you have to go to Paris?" Nicholas looked at her squarely.

This particular way he had of catching her off guard was something new. For a moment she could barely remember why she was going. She looked into Nicholas's face, his penetrating blue eyes, and felt her heart catch. She said nothing, only refilled his glass of juice.

The boys ran off to collect their backpacks. She looked at Michael checking his pager and simultaneously reading an article in a medical journal. She wished he would look up and hold her in his eyes. Instead, she reached over and touched his arm. He was wearing the blue tie with the yellow stripes she had bought him for his birthday and her favorite tweed sports jacket, and his hair was a little longer in the back, the way she liked it. Sometimes when she looked at him suited up for the hospital and thought about all those responsibilities he had, apart from her and their children, it still amazed her that she was his wife. She saw him suddenly in the way that he appeared to others, not clouded by the way they interacted as a couple. He was strong and confident, possessed a sharp mind and a clear sense of purpose.

His face was still buried in the journal. "It might be a good idea to get to the airport a little ahead of schedule so you can change some money. And remember to wear shoes that are easy to slip off for when you go through security. You'll call when you get to your hotel, won't you?" he said, looking up at her for a moment.

"Of course I will," she said, trying to regain her confidence about traveling alone. She looked at the three small rosebushes on the terrace. The bushes were covered with burlap sacks to keep them protected from the cold. They looked shriveled and cramped. She wanted to take off the sacks and expose their frail limbs to the elements, but it was unseasonably cold for early May and she was afraid she'd cause them undue harm.

"You won't forget us, will you?" Michael said, closing his journal and rising from the table. She saw the spark of vulnerability in his eye that she had seen when she had first fallen in love with him. It made her want to cancel the trip.

3

Eleanor found her seat near the window of the jet. She pictured Noah's face as they said good-bye. She had held him in her arms and told him she would call him every night. "Even when I'm away, you're here," she said, pointing to her heart. She brushed her lips against the top of his soft black hair. She thought of her father being separated from his parents in the ghetto and never seeing them again. She had learned to think that way in order to forgive him for leaving. She reminded herself that she'd be home in ten days. She was worrying too much.

Noah's hair reflected the light, and the top of his head felt hot to the touch. His skin was delicate, white as porcelain, his eyes a shade of blue she hadn't seen in another person. It was not quite the color of her one blue eye. It was more luminescent, clearer. He was the kind of child strangers stop on the street to admire. Nicholas was more intense looking, yet he was also striking. She was embarrassed by how much the beauty of her boys pleased her, how everything about her children was a consuming source of pleasure and delight. She thought about some of the other mothers at the boys' school, the mothers who were there every day at drop-off and pick-up, who observed every nuance, every lost tooth, with incredible intensity, and wondered why she was different, why she still had needs separate from her children's. She had imagined that personal dreams ended once children were born.

Noah had stubbornly pushed his face into her chest and tightened his arms around her neck. Michael had to pry his hands away, finger by finger. "Don't go, Mommy," he screamed, flailing his arms and legs. Nicholas stood outside the cab throwing a ball in the air and catching it with his mitt. "Aren't you going to give me a kiss?" Eleanor said, stooping down so that she was level with his eyes. He looked at her as if he could see straight through her. He was her defiant child, internal and closed off. He was her mirror.

"It's not like you're going away forever, Mom."

"You can be angry. It's okay. You'll see, I'll be back before you know it."

Eleanor grew sleepy. She tried not to think about the fact that the plane was suspended above the clouds and traveling over an endless ocean. She tried not to think about her children and her fears that the plane might go down. She had never feared flying until she had children. She thought of her last day of class before the trip and the lecture she'd given to her Russian lit class on how Tolstoy's personal views and internal world informed his fiction. Part of the lecture was research she had completed for the paper she was presenting in Paris. A. N. Wilson, in his biography of Tolstoy, wrote that Tolstoy had one of the most documented unhappy marriages in history. In the lecture Eleanor had explained that Tolstoy had multiple sexual liaisons, which he did not hide from his wife. In fact, when he was in his early forties, he gave his eighteen-year-old virgin fiancée his diaries, which were filled with his dark, sometimes vile sexual encounters and fantasies, to read on her birthday.

Marlee Reynolds, one of her favorite students, had thrown up her hand. "So, I mean, are you saying, Professor Cahn, that Tolstoy couldn't have written *Anna Karenina* if his marriage *hadn't* been conflicted?" Mark Zukovsky, who had been in her modern poetry seminar last semester, had that ironic look in his eye again. She steeled herself. His goal throughout the semester had been to argue with whatever point of view she put forward. "It takes 740 pages for Tolstoy to make his point. People fall in love. Love is irrational. It's just so obvious," he had said, rolling his eyes. "I don't get it."

"What don't you get, Mark?"

"I'm just saying it's not that complicated. I mean, Professor Cahn, you're married, aren't you?"

"I don't see how my personal life is relevant," she had said, organizing her papers in a neat stack against the podium to hide her annoyance.

"Well, did you ever wonder what might happen to you if someone like Vronsky walked into your life?"

Marlee cut in, showing off the purple polish on her nails as she raised her hand. "Mark, you're missing the point," she said. "Anna is far more complicated than Vronsky. If the novel were written by a woman, do you think she'd send her heroine to the grave? While Anna's adultery is in the foreground of the novel, her brother Stiva gets off rather easy, don't you think? It's as if Tolstoy is saying that women's emotions are greater or more extreme. Are even dangerous to their well-being."

Reflecting on the class filled Eleanor with pride. Her students were intelligent and provocative. Sometimes it was a challenge to stay a step ahead of them. What would happen at the conference if questions were raised in response to her paper that she was not prepared to answer? While she knew that the paper had merit, she also worried that she'd be found out—a fraud, not quite up to the position she'd achieved in life. She told herself there was no reason for her to feel insecure, and yet something she couldn't yet identify troubled her.

After a few sips of wine the anxiety began to dissipate. She relaxed, her body softened. Her mind drifted away from her paper to thoughts of Stephen Mason, a boy she had known in childhood. He had been in the back of her mind since her mother in Chicago called to say good-bye. But with all the rush of leaving, she hadn't had time to really think about it clearly. Her mother had mentioned that Stephen was also going to be in Paris writing a magazine piece. The last Eleanor had heard of him he was still living in Colorado. She was happy to hear he'd become a writer, as he'd wanted. Hearing about him had filled her with a jumble of excitement and anxiety, followed by a familiar lingering confusion. She'd told her mother she doubted he'd want to see her. "You two are like cousins. Don't be silly. Of course he will," her mother said. After she hung up, she told herself the odd feeling inside was about leaving for her trip.

4

The Masons lived in the house behind Eleanor's childhood home in a northern suburb of Chicago. From her upstairs window she could see into the window of Stephen's bedroom. Even after twenty-five years, mysterious, illogical memories still grew like weeds around a grave. Eleanor remembered the texture of light through her bedroom window, the branches of the tree in her yard almost touching the tree in his, the bent branches on the verge of breaking. She remembered the flashlights she and Stephen used to signal each other in the dark, like fireflies sending their own private code in the twilight.

Eleanor's mother was having company for Christmas. Ted and Carol Mason, an air of estrangement between them, came over with their son. When Eleanor's father still lived at home, the Masons and the Cahns had formed a tight foursome. But that year, when she was twelve, her father had been gone for three years.

She was a dreamy, sensual girl who painted her ceiling sparrow-egg blue so she could lie on her bed and cast her eye on beauty. She was also adventurous. Sometimes they played kick-the-can in the street with other neighborhood kids, or built intricate snow forts, or hung out in Stephen's backyard playhouse. Eleanor wore her red hair long. Her body had begun to fill out; she wasn't used to the way her growing chest made it difficult to sleep on her stomach, or the cramps in her abdomen once a month, or the longings. One eye could look bluer if she was wearing blue, or the other eye greener if she wore green, and sometimes, like her mood, they changed color for no particular reason. She had white skin and a long neck.

"Eleanor's upstairs," Eleanor's mother told Stephen, before he burst into her bedroom. She was reading on her bed. Stephen took the book out of her hand. His eyes were deep blue and his face chiseled. Even at twelve with long eyelashes, you could tell that he was going to grow up to be a heartbreaker. "You can't read on Christmas." He pulled out firecrackers from his pants pocket. "Watch this." He opened her bedroom window, lit one, and threw it outside; they watched it explode and then fall into the snow.

He gazed at her, his dress shirt pulled out of his dress pants, his hair uncombed, his face damp. Heat traveled up her neck and warmed her cheeks.

"Did you like the way that firecracker went off?" She looked at him. "You liked it," he said, knowingly. He tickled her in the ribs, pushing her to the floor. He pointed out her window toward his house. "I've been watching you. I know what you like."

It was a turning point, that moment when she realized there was no need to be afraid of her own powers. Stephen leaned closer, so that she felt his forehead graze her neck. She caught his dark, visceral scent. His soft lips touched her skin. He whispered her name so tenderly that later that night, after all the company had left, she wondered whether she had imagined it. He had always been rough, but she'd never seen this side of him. After he lifted himself away from her, he looked her in the eyes and boldly felt her chest. Bewildered that she had allowed him to touch her, she found herself without words. He slicked his wavy hair back and stood up to tuck in his shirt. She noticed the curve of his spine as he rose, the way his hair curled behind his ears, and the mole on the back of his left lobe. "I didn't embarrass you, did I?" he asked, turning back around.

"I'm not embarrassed," she said, a little defensively.

The encounter lasted less than a moment, but it seemed to define their history.

It was snowing that afternoon, falling over the bare, gnarled branches of the tree outside her bedroom window, the same tree whose branches touched the branches of the tree in Stephen's yard. As the snow continued to blanket the quiet streets, it enclosed the two of them more tightly inside Eleanor's room, separating them from the noisy conversation of their parents downstairs, so that all that was left was the two of them, as if they'd become their own secret family.

"I got suspended from school the other day," he said, proudly, before they went downstairs. "Got caught smoking a cigarette in the boys' bathroom." He paused. "Do you want to get caught doing something bad with me?"

She looked back at him, slightly perplexed, once again at a loss for words.

It wasn't until the night was almost over that the two talked again. Stephen followed Eleanor into the kitchen as she was bringing in a stack of dirty dishes.

"Do you know other divorced people?" He hiked himself onto one of the stools in front of the kitchen counter. "I mean, besides your parents?"

"No."

"Well, now you do." He paused. "My parents are getting one."

"My parents aren't really divorced. They're separated."

"Why am I telling you these things, Eleanor?" His blue eyes clouded with feeling.

"It's okay." She forced emotion into the smile she gave back to him.

"It's not a big deal. At least I won't have to hear them fighting anymore." His eye landed on the wet dish towel balled up on the counter. He picked it up.

"Do you miss your dad?" He looked into her eyes of different colors with such intensity she felt as if she was suddenly brought to life.

"He's been gone three years. You get used to it."

He played with the knob on the gas range. When he ignited the burner, the gas burst into flame. Seemingly enchanted by the power he held, he turned the knob, watched the flame go slack, then bloom into a dangerous blue flower. He took the dish towel. From his other hand, he danced the dish towel in front of the flame so that the fringe teased the fire, scorching the ends.

"You shouldn't do that."

"Are you scared?"

"Not really."

"Then I'll stop." He was a strange bird, but she liked him. He gave her back the dish towel, allowing their fingers to touch, before he went back into the living room.

The snow burned her fingers. The air burned her cheeks. Ice was frozen into her mittens. Two days after Christmas they wound up in a snowball fight on the lawn after Stephen slipped a handful of snow down the back of her coat. Their ski jackets and hats dusted with snow, they retreated inside the playhouse — a mini version of Stephen's house, white with black shutters — behind the Masons' garage to get warm. Stephen steamed up the window of the playhouse with his breath, and using his finger, he wrote their initials over the windowpane. He did not enclose the initials inside a heart. Still cold, they went inside Stephen's house, through the kitchen door. His parents were arguing upstairs.

"How come you don't touch me anymore?" Stephen's mother's voice wound down the stairs like agony, chilling the air between them. "I'm not like Elizabeth. I need to be touched."

Eleanor glanced at Stephen. He looked back at her somberly.

"Because I'm no longer in love with you," his father said. "Is this what you want? It's dead between us. Is that what you want to hear?"

"The kids are downstairs." His mother clearly had been crying. "For god's sake, lower your voice."

Stephen tapped Eleanor on the shoulder. "Let's play hide and seek. Count to ten and try to find me." In an instant he was gone.

She closed her eyes and counted out loud, thinking about what she'd overheard. She went to find Stephen. She looked underneath the couch in the living room, behind the cushioned chairs, inside the closets. The back door banged shut. Stephen had run back outside. She grabbed her ski jacket and followed. The dampness seeped uncomfortably into her skin. When she found him he was standing behind the playhouse door grinning, unmistakenly glad to be found.

He slouched to the ground. He looked sad. Stephen gazed around the four walls of the playhouse. In one corner was a spiderweb with a dead fly trapped inside. He perked up and looked at her. "I like being in here with you. Would you let me kiss you, Eleanor?"

His nose was dripping, and he was shivering. His hands were curled up in the sleeves of his sweater. He had run out of the house without his ski jacket. She watched him wipe his nose with his sleeve. "We're friends," she said, not quite sure what to say.

"What if I don't want to be your friend?"

"I won't let us not be friends." She reached over and kissed his cheek. His face brightened into a smile.

"Do you think you could really like me?"

"Maybe."

He looked at her intensely, and as she watched him she felt new feelings inside. He continued to look at her, fixated on her eyes until an icicle fell against the glass.

Then he turned on the record player and put on "Eleanor Rigby." The turntable was plugged into an extension cord that traveled to the playhouse through the Masons' garage. The record skipped, warped by the dampness. He picked up the needle and sang the refrain. *"Lives in a dream . . . Who is it for?* It's for me, isn't it, Eleanor?" he said, pinching the skin on her ribs. Candles dripped pools of wax on the old wooden crate they used for a table. He dipped his fingers into the burning wax. "Ouch," he said, smiling, as though he liked the feel of the burn.

"You want to see something?" He dug into the pocket of his jeans and pulled out a Swiss pocketknife. "My father gave it to me. He said I'm supposed to protect her."

"Protect who?"

"My mom."

"That means he still loves her."

"It means he's leaving." He looked at her again. "I like your eyes."

"They don't creep you out? Janis Talbot said I look like a cat."

"You're the cutest girl in the school. Can I tell you something? Sometimes I get this funny feeling. Like I'm going to jump out of my skin. I want to destroy things. Kick in a door.

Or burn up something. Do you ever feel that way?" He opened the blade of the pocketknife and began to saw it into the wooden crate they were using for a table.

"Kind of." She wasn't sure but didn't want to make him feel bad.

"You're it." He ran to hide as if in love with the idea of fleeing, being sought after, and being found.

She went back out to the yard to try to find him. She went to her house. He was nowhere. She decided to wait for him inside. She looked out the back window from the kitchen. The playhouse was on fire. Within minutes, fire engines encircled the block. When she went back outside Stephen was standing by the playhouse, watching it burn. His parents were consulting with the fire chief. The smell was like burning leaves, grainy and pungent. Smoke floated over the snow-crested hedges like neglect. Mrs. Mason pulled Stephen away from the fire and pressed him against her side. She wasn't a demonstrative person, and seeing her awkwardly holding Stephen brought tears to Eleanor's eyes.

"It's okay, Mom," Stephen said, pulling out of her grasp.

Eleanor tapped him on the shoulder. Her look said, *What happened?* He turned away. She tried to catch his eye again but the fire put him in a hypnotic trance. He ignored her. She thought about the cigar box where they kept their secret stash of cigarettes. Their pile of records. The privacy of their talks. How just minutes before they had seemed so close. She wished she had let him kiss her. She pulled on Stephen's shirtsleeve.

"Cut it out, Eleanor." He stared ahead, transfixed at the fire devouring the wood.

"But how did it happen?"

"Be quiet, Eleanor."

She felt like he had jabbed her in the stomach.

Beneath the snow, the fire chief found the chewed-away extension cord with exposed wires that Stephen had run from the garage into the playhouse. He said it was an accident waiting to happen. That night she was unable to sleep, thinking about Stephen, how she was drawn to him and frightened of him at the same time. She thought about the fire, his parents arguing, and the words she'd overheard, wondering if the reason her father had left was because he wasn't in love with her mother, and she felt strangely linked to Stephen and his own pain.

Stephen's father moved out the next day, to a home on the other side of town. A few months later Stephen moved in with him. His mother mysteriously left town. There was talk she'd had a breakdown. Once Stephen moved out, the shades were drawn over the window in his room. Empty of his bike, Frisbees, and baseball bats, the Masons' backyard looked like a graveyard. Eleanor found herself night after night seated by the window. Stephen's father eventually fell in love with a young French au pair named Sabine, and within a year she was installed in his new house.

When Stephen's mother returned to her house a year later, Eleanor's mother called her changed demeanor a nervous condition. Stephen continued to live with his father and Sabine. The idea of the newly in love couple gave the impression that life could be exotic and foreign even if you lived in a suburb of Chicago, but Eleanor overheard Carol Mason bitterly tell her mother that Stephen was treated like a third wheel.

Eleanor rarely saw Stephen since he moved. Once they ran into each other when he came by his mother's to visit. He acknowledged her with a quick nod of his head, as if he had revealed too much of himself and was embarrassed to be in her company.

Sometimes Eleanor caught a glimpse of him from the window of her house. She ducked in the shadows of her room to make sure he hadn't seen her. She didn't know why she did not want to be seen. As she watched him walk up his mother's porch stairs in his leather bomber jacket, a hot, distracted feeling consumed her. When he turned sixteen and began to drive, she sometimes saw his blue Pontiac parked in his mother's driveway. They never spoke. And yet, she often found herself looking through her window into his, as she had through all the years of her childhood.

5

She never told Stephen about why her father left, because she did not know herself. He lived in different cities, in hotel rooms and rented flats. Sometimes months would pass without a word from him, until a postcard arrived telling her about a particular piece of music to listen to. Dvořák meant he was nostalgic. Mahler if he were in torment. Schubert for when he was emotional. Mozart when he was happy. He rarely invited her to visit, never seemed to have a permanent home. Airports with their VIP lounges and complimentary tea and coffee, places for arrivals and departures, longings and regrets, were his second home.

"I have to leave," Eleanor's father had said to her, stroking her hair. "It's because I love you."

He did not talk about his past, but Eleanor had pieced together that he had lost his family during the war. He had been sent to an ammunition factory and then a camp in Munich. Eventually, when he was nineteen, he was sent to Chicago to live with Horowitz, a friend of his father's from the old country. Horowitz took care of him like a son. All he had left from his family was the mezuzah his mother had ripped off the door and put in his pocket when they were told to leave their homes. His father had wrapped bread in his prayer shawl and given it to him, but eventually even the prayer shawl was lost. *I have to go,* Joseph Cahn told his daughter. *Give me a kiss, Eleanor,* Joseph said, as if her kiss could save him.

He was the kind of tortured, handsome man women coveted, with deep-set eyes and a crooked nose and burnt auburn hair, a man who looked like he was going to cry when he laughed. Eleanor loved him more than anyone on earth. Eleanor's mother spoke of his sad eyes, his broad shoulders, the ridge down the center of his forehead, the way he walked in a room and drew all eyes toward him, and the way he got lost in his music when he played the piano. His mother had played the piano in Budapest and had given him lessons.

Horowitz sent him to music school in Chicago. Everyone thought he'd be famous. But after music school it was decided he needed to have a trade. "The burden is too great," he once told Eleanor. "To put so much pressure on the thing in the world you love most." Horowitz set him up in the dry-cleaning business. Joseph eventually owned four dry cleaners throughout the city. For some reason the laundry business failed, Horowitz died, there were other businesses, other schemes. There were so many stories about why he left that even Eleanor did not know which one was the truth. He was one of those men whose suffering could not be contained in one life; that's how she had chosen to see him.

Once, longing for his attention, she paraded into her father's study wearing a blue princess dress with a lace skirt and satin bodice, a crown of flowers on her head. Her mother had made the costume for her, hand sewing the sequins and ribbons. He was absorbed in a phone call. She sat quietly on the leather chair in the room and waited for him to finish the call. She imagined he would lift her in the air and kiss her, as all girls want their fathers to do, and anoint her Princess of Her Father's Heart. In her anticipation she felt warm and good and beautiful and it made the waiting easy (she would have waited all day). His voice grew more urgent and tense on the phone. "God damn it, Moshe, you're killing me," her father said. "You're burying me alive." She heard her father eventually place the receiver into the phone's cradle. He made little notes on a yellow legal pad on his desk. He rose from his swivel chair and placed his forehead against the glass of the window. She crept off the chair and put her hand in his. He didn't look at her. He continued looking out the window, his forehead kissing the glass. "Your father is in trouble, Eleanor. Go find your mother."

When he played the piano at night, he made the keys cry. His music transformed him into a person she didn't quite know. He demanded that the menorah go in front of the picture window in the living room on Hanukah. "I want those motherfuckers to know we're still alive. That we won." He bowed his head, lit the candles, and said the prayer. She looked at the menorah dripping wax, listening to the sound of her father's voice and feeling he was a part of her and she was a part of him, and they were not separate, as she feared. She sensed his pent-up fears, his desire to escape. She believed protecting him was one of her reasons to live. When the light went out of the menorah all at once, it was as if God's eyes had blinked.

"Let me tell you something, Eleanor. There's good and bad inside all of us. The bad part of me is fighting against the good. It's taking me away from you and your mother. I have no strength over it."

After her father left, her mother opened a tailor shop in

town; she had been Joseph's seamstress at the dry cleaner. She developed migraine headaches. They were severe enough that she spent days and nights in bed, until the cycle worked its way out of her system. But the migraines always returned. She spent her evenings, when she wasn't plagued by the headaches, with a pincushion bracelet attached to her wrist and straight pins slipped into her blouse, dipping her needle into a curtain or the hem of a woman's coat. She still looked shapely, possessing the kind of beauty that deepens over time. Eleanor thought it was a shame that her father could no longer see her mother in the way she intuited a woman needed to be seen by a man.

Eleanor walked quietly around the house. Sometimes she wanted to swipe her hands along the keyboard of her father's piano but she kept the top down, the keys locked inside their cage of wood. She kept the lights turned off because they intensified her mother's headaches. She read until her eyes stung. Her mother stayed in her bedroom with the shades drawn, curled into her pillow. When Eleanor heard her moaning in bed, she went in her mother's bedroom to bring her a drink of water and another one of her tablets. *I had a dream, Eleanor. Your father was eating my kugel. By New Year's he'll be home. Don't worry. It'll pass.*

Eleanor said her prayers before she went to sleep. She asked God to get rid of her mother's headaches. She asked him to watch over her father. She thought if she prayed hard enough her father might come home. She began to think that the mezuzah nailed into the side of the front entranceway of her house was a sign. She kissed her fingers and touched it every time she went in and out of the front door. If she forgot her homework and had to go back inside again, it was particularly annoying because that meant she kissed the mezuzah at least three times going back and forth, but she felt the compulsion to do so nevertheless. The mezuzah was the last thing her father had from his mother in Budapest. Eleanor thought that because he didn't take it with him, it meant he was coming back. She washed her hair every morning. She pressed her own skirts and blouses. She polished her father's piano. She was a straight-*A* student.

Once, when her mother was working, Eleanor went looking for some scotch tape in the French desk in her bedroom and came upon her mother's diary. What daughter doesn't want a glimpse of her mother's interior life? In the diary, with matchbooks taped to the bottom of pages, or a dried rose pressed between wax paper, Elizabeth recorded the restaurant where she and Eleanor's father had gone for dinner, what she ordered (Sole Bernadine), the color of her sweater suit with matching colored shoes (coral) that she wore to Joseph's recital. In one entry she had written,

> Joseph scares me. He can go all evening without saying a word. When he plays the piano it is as though he's in a trance. His eyes close, he smiles. I'm afraid of his hands. He wants us to get married at City Hall. When I told him I wanted to be married in front of God, he said, "There is no God."

"He has demons in his closet," her mother said to Eleanor the first night the two of them had sat alone at the table for dinner. Joseph's chair at the head of the table still reigned over their conversation despite the fact that it was empty. "He thinks that if he leaves us he'll escape them. Maybe it's better this way. I told him to go."

"You should be mad."

"You know what he's like. Is he a man you can be mad at? With those eyes."

"You shouldn't have let him."

"And let him destroy us?"

Elizabeth was strong and determined. Her terrible forgiveness had filled the rooms of Eleanor's childhood.

6

E leanor did not have a boyfriend until she was sixteen. For weeks they had watched each other circling around the ice-skating rink on the outskirts of town. She loved the cold air on her skin, the sense of openness as she skated, the way pockets of wind pushed her forward, the tall evergreens and pines surrounding the open ice, and the sounds of winter birds in the distance swooping through the trees. His dog was tied up on a long leash outside the gates. The dog barked with excitement each time his master, William Woods, skated by.

William scraped his blades into an abrupt hockey stop and a spray of crushed ice sprinkled Eleanor's face. He took her scarf and unraveled it as if it were a piece of ribbon, and then wrapped it around her neck again. "Your name is Eleanor, isn't it?" She nodded. His eye was black and blue. "I've been watching you. Here, take my hand. Let's skate faster. Hold my hand tighter. Come on. Faster. "

They stopped at the edge. She was panting. The wind was cold against their faces. She looked at him more closely. He was so unusual.

"Did you get in a fight?"

"Something like that."

His eyes, including the bruised one, were surrounded by long, black, curled-up eyelashes. His hair was thin and reached past his neck, where it was tied in a ponytail. A look of suffering weighed down his face when he wasn't aware she was looking, or was it just the black eye that made her feel that way? He was soft like a piece of fruit, with an edge of hard skin around him. His black-and-blue eye inspired in her an overpowering rush of compassion that would define their relationship.

"What happened?" Eleanor took off her gloves and gently touched the skin underneath his eye. The touch seemed to soften him.

"Nothing you need to worry about." His cheeks were red and chapped from the frozen wind. "Are you cold, Eleanor?" He put his arm around her. "Do you know what I was thinking when we were skating? You see this ice we're skating on? See how thick it is. Fish are swimming under us. Underneath a whole other world is going on. Let's keep skating."

William came from a family of six kids. He was the last son at home. His house was filled with the sound of his father watching television, the dishwasher running in the kitchen, two dogs and three cats circling the angles and curves of the overly decorated rooms. Behind the house was a barn where they kept horses.

"Don't worry," William said, the first time he brought her home. "Even when my parents are around, it'll just be the two of us. When I watch football he thinks I'm watching the game." He was referring to his father. "He thinks we're rooting for the same team. He thinks he can control me, but he can't. I can disappear into myself whenever I want."

Mr. Woods came into the den, and William introduced him to Eleanor. "Did your red hair come from a bottle or a can?" he said.

After he left, William turned to Eleanor. "We don't get along. He thinks I should care what kind of car a person drives and what college they're going to. He thinks things like that matter." Eleanor at first thought it commendable that Mr.

Woods had chosen to marry someone less attractive than he was. His wife's face was plain. She wore A-line skirts, sweaters, and heels, even when she was preparing dinner. But he did not treat his wife with consideration. He sat by himself in the den while she served him lunch.

"Let me tell you what I know, Eleanor," William said. "You can be inside yourself when people are filling up the air. Close your eyes. Picture it. Imagine we're still skating. Imagine we're holding hands."

Eleanor loved everything about William for no particular reason, confirming the theory that no one ever understands what drives us toward another person. The nature of attraction is a mystery. His thick lips with a dust of hair above the upper one, the way his eyes caught the light. The long strides of his walk. How looking at him produced a tingling feeling inside her. She liked boys who took up all the energy in the room, so she wouldn't be left with her anxieties and worries. He was contemplative (those long silences). She liked the poetic way he observed things. He read obscure books on Buddhism, philosophy, evolution, cuttlefish, as if to fill his mind with knowledge to make up for what he couldn't quite grasp in himself.

"It's all about keeping the balls in the air. You never watch your hands. If you watch them you'll get spooked. You have to trust that they'll come back," William said, juggling three tennis balls. He liked to juggle. He'd take the three yellow tennis balls and throw them into the air, first one ball, then the other, then the third until he found the balance, and it was in the balance where everything disappeared except for his desire to catch one ball, send the other one into the air, and then catch the other. William had a feeling for all things not directly of this world, like the air that circulated through the three balls when his rhythm was on.

He liked to play with his dog, Scout. All of his dog's affection laid in his one desire — to retrieve a ball and bring it back to his master, a young boy who had a mind for dogs. William needed balance, shape to his day, and the dog and the balls provided it. Everyone should have a dog named Scout who follows you everywhere as if he were completely dependent on you, to love and to cherish you. And William was a boy who knew how to cherish. He did not understand the reason for fathers. He said his father paid the bills, went to work, and came home angry. And his mother held tissue in her hands.

He took her into the woods behind his colonial house. He liked to take walks in the forest with the dogs trailing after him, their tags ringing against their necks. In the woods he relaxed and found union with the sky and the trees. "You like it here, don't you, Eleanor? Even though it's snowing. You look so pretty when you're cold. Come here, let me feel your cheeks. Why do you look so serious? You look like something terrible happened."

"No." She couldn't believe her luck. "It's because I'm so happy."

He collected butterflies and knew all the different species. He knew how to tell how old a tree was by the rings in its trunk. He could spend whole days alone, weeks, with the sole companionship of his dogs.

With soil still in their clothes and hair, William drove her home. Her mother was at work. The small house suddenly felt different now that William was in it with her. Everything was different. She no longer felt the emptiness of her father's leaving. "Where's your dad?" he asked.

"My dad doesn't live here anymore."

"You have this sad little frown on your face when you don't know anyone is looking. Your dad put it there."

"It's not his fault."

"Where is he?"

"He's trying to find himself."

"I wish my dad would leave."

One day as Eleanor and William stood kissing in front of her house, Stephen Mason waved to her from his car. She hadn't spoken to him in three years. William jerked her close to his hips by the belt loop of her jeans. She was embarrassed and tried to inch away, but William drew her closer.

Stephen looked at her severely. "Eleanor," he said. She saw him give William the once-over. "I need to talk to you."

"Okay," she said. She looked at William.

"I'm leaving," William said. "See you." He planted a long, purposeful kiss on her mouth before he disengaged. "Are you going to be okay?"

She nodded. "He used to live behind us when I was a kid."

William hopped in his truck and pulled away.

Confronted with Stephen's solid physical presence—he was dressed in a leather bomber jacket, blue jeans ripped at the knees, and leather Frye boots—she considered how ethereal William was in comparison, dressed in his crumpled flannel shirts and faded corduroys, with his eyes the color of the forest. They could still hear William's pickup round the corner.

"Can't he afford a new muffler?" He looked down at his boots and raised his eyes. "You have a boyfriend, Eleanor?"

She nodded.

"See this piece of paper?" He took out a crumpled receipt from his pocket and lit it with a cigarette lighter. The paper curled up in flame. He threw it to the ground and stomped out the fire with his boot. "This is how it makes me feel. Like I'm burning up inside."

She looked at him, slightly frightened. Something about him had changed and made her uneasy. His face broke into a grin and he started to laugh. "It was a joke, Eleanor."

"I have to go in," she said, turning toward her house.

Eleanor and William spent almost every day of high school together. She preferred being with him, away from her own silent house. In William's presence calm descended upon her. She could spend hours with him, simply holding his hand, collecting stones near the creek, taking long hikes in the woods, identifying constellations from his telescope. And yet, a part of her was restless. Eleanor's mother spent her time sewing, taking in hems, tucking and tacking, pinning her beautiful handmade clothes around the nude mannequin in the sewing room at home. But something about it was empty and depressing; the house had become a shrine for her absent husband. For as long as she could remember, Eleanor dreamed of moving to New York with the idea of doing something artistic—studying painting or literature or becoming a writer. When she was accepted to Columbia University for the fall, she knew she had to go.

"Here's how it's going to be," William said, when she told him she was leaving. "We're always going to be together. I know you need me. Do you know what it's like to be outside at night? There's this hum that is the sound of insects. One long continuous drone. If you listen hard enough you fall into the sound. It's all around you. You can't hear anything else. You become one with it, until it moves inside you, becomes a part of you. That's how we are together. I'll wait for you, Eleanor. I'm not going anywhere."

"I'll wait, too."

"We could get a farm one day. Or a house in the country. We wouldn't need anyone."

They were in the barn in back of William's house, where his father kept the horses. They were lying on a blanket over the hay, watching the light disappear from the rafters, and it was quiet except for the breathing, wheezing, and snorting of the horses. There were three. Each in its own stall, each exerting its own weight upon her. She felt the souls of the horses, all three of them inside her, kicking up their heels, forming a part of who she was in the darkness of the barn. They had come to the barn to get away from the house where his parents had gathered for dinner. They did not want dinner. They wanted to seek all the unknown places in each other.

"I have never been so close to anyone," William said. He took his Swiss Army knife from his pocket and pricked his finger until a bead of blood oozed out and he took her hand and he pricked her finger and they rubbed their blood and made a pact that they would never leave each other.

She liked being in the dark with William while the darkness slipped underneath their clothes and through their fingers and into their hair and in between the sounds of the horses who seemed to have quieted just then, until one slashed his tail against the stall. "Come here, Eleanor," William said. "Come closer. Isn't it beautiful in the darkness?" Eleanor felt herself being pulled further inside him, inside his privacy.

"I don't understand the world," William said. "Sometimes I feel it slipping through my fingers and I'm outside it, not a part of it, and I want to go out by the creek and listen to the rush of water."

When Eleanor was with William she was inside that missing place and he filled it with his breathing. With his need.

———

The day they said good-bye they were sitting on the bed in his room. It was the beginning of September. "I can't believe you're leaving me," William said.

"I'm not leaving you. I'm going away to school. I'll write you every day."

"I don't write letters."

She put her hand on his thigh, hoping he'd take it in his hand, but he was staring blankly out the window into the intersection of the quiet street. She gave William the Star of David necklace her father had given to her on her birthday. "Take it. This way you'll know that we are together even though we are apart. Put it on. It's my very best possession."

William's father opened the door while they were kissing on the bed, their legs and arms entwined together. "Get your lazy ass downstairs," Mr. Woods said. "No one listens to me in this goddamn house."

"Dad, calm down." He looked at Eleanor and the look said, *I'm sorry.* They followed Mr. Woods downstairs.

"Watch your mouth," Mr. Woods said. "And no one fed the goddamn dogs?" He kicked the empty tin dog dish in the kitchen. It went clanging across the tiles of the floor. "Where's your goddamn mother?"

"You have to leave soon," Eleanor said, after he left the room. "Promise."

"Give me a year," William said. "I'll figure it out."

"Let's go, Eleanor." William took her by the hand, out of the house. "I hate that motherfucker," he said, once they were in the woods behind the house and it was far away. They walked through the woods. William showed her some slabs of rock he was collecting. "I'm building a stone wall where no one can touch us." In the woods he wandered farther away from home.

He said he spent whole days taking stones from the ridge of a hill and making a wall so that a stream could fall in one direction.

Eleanor thought about his bruised eye the first day she had met him. "Does he hurt you?"

"Only you can hurt me, Eleanor," William said, and rested his head inside the cave of her chest.

"I don't want to leave you," Eleanor said again. William took out the Star of David that he had tucked inside his T-shirt. "You're not leaving me. You're only going away. You're inside this gold star pushed into my skin."

When she came home to visit she asked him repeatedly to visit her in New York. "I've looked into it," she said. "There are tons of schools in New York. If you get your science credits, you can apply to veterinary school like you said you wanted to." He was more comfortable around horses and dogs than people.

"I'm too close to them, Eleanor. At night I can hear the underside of things. I sometimes think I can hear wolves in the forest talking to each other. There's something I have to tell you. My father hurts her. I'm working for him, looking after some of his buildings. I have to keep an eye on her. I can't leave."

"I'll never hurt you. I'll come back. I promise. But you have to figure out what you want to do."

"I will."

In New York she lived in libraries and classrooms. Still she thought she could hear him when she wandered through the park, as if he were calling her over the top of the trees, repeating the same rhythm over and over into the air, *come back, come back*. She loved her classes, but she was torn.

She spent her summers with him, coming back to Chicago each June and returning to New York in the fall. When she was with him she got caught up in his latest passion, and it felt as if she had never left. One summer it was raising bees to make honey. Next, it was a vegetable garden he planted for his mother. Once Eleanor was home it would take a few days of adjustment and then she'd be glad to be back in the woods with him, touched by his purity and love for nature, happy not to have to explain herself, as she had to with her new friends in New York who were different, more full of themselves. Occasionally, when she was back in class, she felt an attraction to someone else. She'd be moved by the way one of her classmates analyzed a poem or a short story, saw something in it that was different than what she'd seen, but eventually the crush would disappear and she'd long for the visceral pull that connected her to William. But each year she felt a little further away from him, and knew she had changed. When she pestered him about his plans, he said he decided he wasn't going to college. He was looking into some kind of trade.

"I want to show you something, Eleanor," William said. It was the summer she graduated from college and they were at his mother's house while she was visiting her oldest son in Florida. "It feels like you've been gone forever." He took her into the woods, acres and acres of it, behind his house. He was in love with streams and cascades, a boy she wanted close to her heart, but she felt he could not fully reach her. She began to see frightening things in him. She could feel his body light up inside when she was in the room, the way fireflies light in the dark. But she was afraid of becoming his sole light keeper and attachment. He traveled farther into the woods, so that the brick colonial house became smaller in the distance, but he always seemed to come back to that house. She wondered why he could never find a way to leave it.

"I want to show you the stone wall. No one knows about it except for you." He had blue stone, flint, and beautiful white granite from a nearby quarry, and he was using the stones to build his own path, a little sanctuary in the woods. "I'm going to carve some kind of sculpture here after I finish it, to mark my place in the world. This is where I come to when I want to be alone with you." They spent the rest of the day laying the stones he had trudged through the woods. Watching how engaged he was when he worked made her hopeful again. He taught her how to make a stone wall, how to lay each stone so the wall would not topple over. She liked the physical exertion, when all she had to think about was putting one stone upon another. She liked the familiarity of William's kiss and the way he held her hand, and how they could sit underneath a tree and not have to say a word to each other. It was only with him that she felt she could fully relax and not have to prove herself. She trusted his love for her. He found a tree he liked and scratched their initials into the bark, enclosing them with a wobbly heart.

"My father has left. He's living in one of his rental properties. It's better now. I can think. I'm thinking I might learn carpentry. Or stone work. You look good, Eleanor. New York must be treating you well. You must be doing okay without me."

She liked being back in the woods with William, but the years she had been away from home formed a wall inside her made of the stones of her own ambitions. She knew that he could not understand because he had no ambition of his own. And yet, she believed in him. *No, I'm not okay. You're the first person I think about when I wake up, and the last before I sleep. Why can't you get your life on track so we can be together?* "I'm okay," she said, a little impatiently.

After they came back from the woods, William took her up to his boyhood room (there were still posters of Mick Jagger and Neil Young on his walls) with low alcoves and a brown corduroy bedspread over the bed. "It's been four years. In all that time there's never been anyone but you."

She fell into his arms and they began to kiss. He wanted to get deeper inside her. His face was tense, filled with determination. He moved furiously against her, rocking the bed and the house that had been empty without her. When they finished making love, she recited a poem. "Why don't you leave," William said. "Go back to your books." He got out of bed and looked over at her. He looked tired. His hair was thin and had broken off at the ends. His shirtsleeve was ripped at the elbows. Dry mud was underneath his fingernails. She saw that something had changed. He was angry that she had left him.

"I'm not leaving. I don't want to go," she said. "You have to come back to New York with me. It's time. You don't have to worry about your mother anymore."

"I can't come to New York. I can't breathe in that city. There are too many people. That city would eat me alive." He came back to the bed and sat down. "Let's get married. I've thought about this. I know what I'm doing."

She leaned over and kissed his cheek. "That's sweet." Looking at him made her ache. But she was mad; she was the one who had to leave, because what else was she going to do? William could not seem to find a thread leading away from home. He could not seem to put anything into motion. His hair had come loose from its ponytail and was greasy near the part. The sparkle was gone from his eyes. She wondered if this was the way a person is supposed to look when he proposed.

"We could buy an organic farm. I could learn carpentry. Have a simple life."

"We don't have money for a farm. Not now. What farm, William?"

"I can't do this anymore." His eyes darkened. "Don't you see? I think about you in New York and I can't breathe. It's driving me nuts."

"So do you want to break up? Is that what you're telling me?"

"Break up what? What's in here?" He pointed to his heart. "No, I don't want to break up. I just don't want to see you anymore. Not until I figure it out."

"You will, William." She cried into his shirt, making the cloth on his shoulder damp. "But we have time. Why do we have to rush things?"

"What is time, Eleanor?" he asked, in a strange, absent voice. "I'm not kidding, tell me."

She had no answer.

7

She reluctantly let go of the dream of the forest, but not of William. Even when she was in her first months of graduate school she was convinced that eventually they'd be together, and that belief allowed her to feel closer to him, perhaps falsely, even though they were apart. She had been studying Keats's concept of negative capability, and she tried to live by its tenets: in uncertainty and contradiction, without grasping for resolution. She thought if she gave him space, he'd find himself. She forced herself to be alone. But throughout the fall semester her thoughts kept returning back to William, as if he were a song whose lyrics and rhythms she could not excise; she wanted to smell the damp woods in his hair and feel the crust of mud on his hands when he finished laying the stones. She called him but he wouldn't return her messages.

William looked after one or two of the buildings his father owned. He spent mornings helping his father go over the books, then collecting rents, and in the afternoons building his stone wall in the woods with his dogs. Before Eleanor left, she again encouraged him to go to veterinary school (because she did not think he could be content building stone walls), but he said he couldn't handle having to put an animal to sleep. "Even dogs should be in charge of their own dying," he said, in a peculiar not-quite-in-the-world voice. He sent her packages filled with tiny stones from the woods or dried butterflies, their wings held back with pins, but there were no letters. She sent him dried flowers and poems that expressed her affection. Still, he would not speak to her.

The stipend from the university wasn't enough to pay rent in New York City. She didn't have enough money to buy herself a new pair of boots if she also wanted to eat. Couldn't they just sell her one boot, and the next month she could buy the other? She saw an ad in the *Village Voice* for figure models, and the idea intrigued her.

She thought sitting for an artist might be a way to learn how to quiet her emotions and become attuned to her inner world. She called for an interview. She discovered, once she called, that the artist was Adam Weiss, a painter she had heard about. He was considered the bad boy of the art world. He said, "I'm looking for someone serious. It's not just about the body. Modeling takes concentration. It's about getting in touch with the artist." *Oh*, Eleanor thought. *Well, why not.*

On her way to meet him she stopped to look at herself in the reflection of a shop window. She wore a black beret and a camel hair coat she had picked up at a thrift shop, and had applied two quick lines of burgundy lipstick. Her blue eye looked muted. Her green eye was luminescent. She worried that her face showed signs of her loneliness. How did others see her? In New York she had a handful of friends she went to films or parties with. Sometimes they met for cheap dinners at the diner on her street and drank cup after cup of coffee; she went home buzzing with caffeine. But she was a private person who kept her thoughts mostly to herself. When she looked at her reflection, she was relieved to see that aside from her eyes and her brilliant red hair spilling out from her hair band, she looked fairly normal. She thought of those days and nights she sat in the easy chair in the sixth floor of the library by the window, watching the other students her age, trying to understand who she was in comparison to them, and wondering if looking too closely caused damage.

One striking couple she used to watch became the archetype. They came to the library nearly every evening and sat at the same table. They looked almost like twins, both with dark hair and small features and dimples in their cheeks, with premed textbooks spread out on the library's long shellacked tables. Inadvertently, one distracted the other and then, feeling the heat and liquid rush, the beautiful girl rose from her chair and put herself in her boyfriend's lap and they kissed unself-consciously, finding, it seemed, ways of touching they hadn't uncovered before, until one pulled away from the other, reluctantly at first, and then with more determination, and they turned back to their books, occasionally glancing up at each other and smiling.

She began to see the couple everywhere, kissing in the corridors of buildings, underneath trees on the college lawn, in the

Thalia Theatre where she went to see old foreign films. It was as if they were there for only one purpose, to show her what her life was lacking. Even when she was with William, she had always felt a distance, as if there were a hidden shadow dividing the two of them. She loved him but she realized he was not of this world.

Eleanor apologized for being late. She took a seat across from Adam Weiss at a little table in Café Dante. She noticed him carefully observing the contours and angles of her face. He looked too long at her earrings, a pair of pearl posts. She touched one and twisted it with her fingers.

"They're crooked. One earring is higher than the other."

She'd had her ears pierced with a pinch gun in a shopping mall when she was sixteen. This was the first time anyone had called her on the imperfection that had always troubled her. It was unnerving. He continued to observe her. An empty espresso cup was pushed to the side of the table.

"I don't mean to make you uncomfortable."

"I'm not uncomfortable." She was sweating.

"You mentioned on the phone you were a grad student?"

She explained she was in her first semester, getting her doctorate in literature. She had her paperback copy of *Anna Karenina* she brought to read on the train still in her hand.

"My father was a literature professor before the war. When I was a child, he read that novel to me in front of the fireplace." He took the book from her and opened it. " 'All happy families resemble one another, but each unhappy family is unhappy in its own way.' " He looked at her without breaking a smile. "What's unique about your family's unhappiness?"

"I didn't say my family is unhappy."

He slowly stirred his espresso.

"And your family?"

"I paint to forget about my family. But they turn up anyway." Adam brought the cup to his lips. "So you're reading Tolstoy? Are you as passionate as Anna?" He smiled slyly. "I like passionate women."

His body was too big for the small café table and he looked uncomfortable as he crossed his legs. He wore black work boots with paint splattered on them. She thought he was arrogant. *And you?* She wanted to ask. *Are you as reckless with women as Vronsky?* But she restrained herself and said, "Anna was seduced. It was Vronsky who was reckless with his passion."

The waiter stood over their table. "What are you going to have?"

"Mint tea."

"Mint tea in an Italian café? That must mean you haven't been to Italy." He stopped. "I'm sorry. A scholar of literature should go to Italy," he said, more gently.

His hair was thick and combed back behind his ears. His sideburns were slightly gray. His prominent nose was strong and noble looking. He sat with his legs crossed. His eyes gave no indication of his thoughts or emotions. He wasn't compelled to fill the quiet pauses in conversation. She couldn't tell whether she thought he was attractive or not.

"You're young," he said, breaking the quiet. "When you're my age you'll understand what kind of character Tolstoy had in mind for Vronsky. He's driven by his passions. He can't see clearly."

"And what about Anna? Should all women have to suffer because men can't see clearly?" Eleanor looked at the pastries in the glass cabinet, the cakes and Italian cookies, tiramisu, and Italian cheesecake, rows upon rows of sweet luxuries.

"We all have to suffer."

"But a person can decide when and how to act."

"This holds for Anna also. You can't blame only the seducer. Would you like a dessert?"

"No." She wanted nothing. She looked back at him.

"Do you really think we can control our passions?" he said, more gently. "Isn't that rather rigid?"

She looked at his hands. They were freckled with paint. At another table, a woman read by herself and sipped her cappuccino. By the window, a trio of young women were engaged in conversation. A man was writing in a notebook. The walls of the café, papered with panoramic photographs of Florence, had absorbed endless hours of conversation, of smells, of young women and men who had come to the café with heavy hearts and had left buoyed by the feeling of companionship and life the café's very walls inspired.

"I'm not rigid." Is that why her body was always clenched? Why her shoulders and neck ached? She had thought it was from studying in uncomfortable chairs. "You call it rigidity, but isn't it a question of morality?"

"This dynamic is good for my work." He put down his cup. "The role of the artist's model is to be a conduit to allow the artist to draw from her. To connect her energy to the canvas. It's a shared bond." He leaned over the table and looked at her closely.

She looked back unflinchingly.

"Will you be at ease being naked in front of groups of people? Art students who sometimes come into the studio to watch?"

"I'll be fine." Her hand was unsteady as she raised her cup.

"I once had a model who thought it would be no problem, but once she was in my studio and saw me gazing at her naked body, she ran out shaking and crying. Will you be able to take it?"

She nodded, barely able to swallow.

"I will know why you wrinkle your brow. The lines in your neck. The shape of your breasts. Does that disturb you?"

Her hands were in tight fists on top of her thighs. She felt slippery inside. "Are you asking me if I think I'm qualified for the job?"

"Even experienced models sometimes take on a personality change once their clothes are off. I've seen even the brightest become edgy and anxious. I've seen a model come in my studio thinking one thing about herself and finding out something else."

She struggled not to betray any emotion.

"You have the most enchanting eyes. The blue one looks joyful. The other aches. What did you say your name was again? Eleanor Cahn?"

She nodded, feeling a slight weakness inside.

"An artist's model has to work by the artist's schedule. She has to give in to the artist's whims. She has to allow herself to be subjected to the artist's process. Does that scare you?"

"Only if I don't like your work," she said, surprised at her own boldness.

After Eleanor accepted the job (she was intrigued by his arrogance), she went to the library and read some of the reviews of his work on microfiche. She discovered that he was thirty-eight. And that he was married. She noted that he had not mentioned his wife, nor had he worn a wedding band. His work was controversial. He had made paintings that were sensational, that, as he described in one interview in *Bomb,* were born out of intense anger. In one called *Provocateur,* a young boy stared unflinchingly at a naked woman old enough to be his mother. In another, a middle-aged man leered at a topless young girl combing her hair at the sink. In *Bearing the Weight of History,* a naked boy hid behind a Greek statue on the lawn of a manicured suburban estate.

Adam's studio was in Tribeca, in an old warehouse. The studio was drafty. Two long windows blocked with dark blue velvet drapes were on each side of the room. The concrete floor was splattered with dried paint. Stretched canvases were stacked against two walls. In the center of the room stood a long table made of a piece of antique pine. On the table sat jars of brushes and paint. It was private and intimate like a bedroom, except for balled-up oily rags on the floor. Next to the sink was a hot plate. Overalls hung on hooks by the door. A dirty pair of gym socks were bunched in the corner.

In spite of how frightened she was that she'd have to take her clothes off, Eleanor was mesmerized by the different colors of paint smeared on Adam's palette (how many colors of paint it was possible to create!), by the way he arranged his colors from the tubes in the same rainbow every time he set up his palette, by the dexterity with which he applied a color to produce a specific emotion on a canvas. At one end of the room was a daybed with a bolster that formed a backrest against the wall, and across from it stood a cranberry velvet chair, with matching ottoman, that was worn at the seat and looked like it belonged once in an old Tudor mansion. And in one window was a beautiful stained glass, making the room churchlike and holy.

"Let me tell you about a life room. It's the room in a university where models sit for students. The rooms vary from having an array of props to having none. Ideally a life room should have different boxes and pedestals, ropes and poles, that the model uses to extend her range of poses. Would you consider posing with a rope, Eleanor? Would you do that for me?"

"If that's what's required." She felt queasy.

"When I work with a live model in the studio we create our own intimate world of fantasy and imagination. Our own life room where anything can happen."

Adam dressed in white painter's pants and a white T-shirt. In the studio he looked bigger than he had looked in the café, broader, brutal looking. But his eyes were tender, slightly hooded. "I paint because the world is ugly. Your job is to make it beautiful."

He asked her to sit on the daybed. Her heart was beating rapidly. Could he hear it? Was he going to ask her to take off her sweater? He didn't say anything for a half an hour. How would she endure the silences? How could she be so still with another person in the room? She nervously brought the pearls she wore to her lip, rolled the strand around her neck.

Adam reached out and pushed her hand down gently. He made tea and offered Eleanor some dry biscuits from a box. "I want to look at your face. To see where it will take me. If you're frightened I won't be able to see clearly." How much is there to see, she wondered, but she kept quiet. "Painting is about isolating the moment, reflecting the world back to us. I have to find the right moment."

Another few minutes passed in silence.

"I'm interested in the relationship between men and women in my painting. I paint the middle class because they try so hard to hold the culture together. Because they're so tragic and mystifying." He spoke as if engaged in a long private conversation with himself.

"But aren't you middle class? I mean your parents?"

"That's not the point, Eleanor."

She sat on the daybed, playing with the string of pearls. Remembering the work she had read about on microfiche at the library, it seemed to her he was interested in young girls and boys, but she wasn't going to say anything. "I'm interested in exploring the hidden places, the secret of what draws men and women together, what repels us about each other."

She moved her body, trying to get comfortable. She couldn't find a position that let her relax. She discovered she was self-conscious watching another person staring at her. She was relieved he hadn't asked her to undress.

He peered at her from behind his canvas. "As a painter I see with my eyes first. When I begin a study, the model possesses my childhood, my struggles. My obsessions. The person you see on the canvas isn't the original subject anymore. She becomes my *métier,* my compass. She guides me. Slowly I allow myself to get closer, to close the distance."

A wave of anxiety washed over her.

"You've been hurt," he said. "I can see it in you."

She took a lock of hair in her hand and twisted it. His ability to scrutinize her made her uncomfortable. And yet she didn't *not* want to be in the studio with him. How did he know she'd been hurt? Was it etched across her face? Or was he being patronizing?

When she left his studio she was inspired and energized, filled with desire to create. She went back to her apartment and began to work on the essay she was writing, suddenly making connections in her head she had not dared before.

She went to Adam's studio early in the morning, and sat quietly on his daybed each day for a week before he started the first painting. He paced the room, adjusted the collar of her shirt. He scrutinized every angle of her face and body. She felt his eyes on her ankle, on the little stretch of skin that showed above her calf. He asked if she would take off her stockings and shoes. He looked at her behind his easel without drawing his brush. "You have the most amazing bones in your feet," he said. "I need to feel them in my hands so I know how to paint them."

When he was quiet, his eyes looked only half opened. Underneath were dark circles. On days when he looked particularly tired, it might take an hour or two before his eyes would begin to grow wide and searching. She had studied him for a week, while he was studying her, alone in the quiet of the studio. Other days he looked angry, or preoccupied, as if he had traveled far away in his memory. She learned how to gauge his moods, how not to take his moodiness personally.

Eleanor wore a navy blue skirt and a white blouse. Her pearls were tucked underneath her collar. Adam lifted her chin, just slightly, and then unbuttoned the first two buttons of her blouse so that the pearls were unleashed against her skin. She felt as if he'd taken off all her clothes.

Other days, as she sat on the daybed in Adam's studio, she felt pulled into the trance he got into when he worked, losing her own luster in the process. And she thought, *Do I have this in me? One day will it be possible for me to achieve in my own work what Adam is achieving in his—that perfect synthesis of who one is and what one sees?* She sat on the daybed with the sunlight slowly diminishing, feeling him study her until her mind grew so blank she nearly forgot who she was, and she felt a little sick inside. The alarm clock on his shelf went off. Adam painted by it. He said as long as he gave himself three full hours, he knew he'd gotten what he could out of that day. Later in the afternoon, he returned to the studio and looked at what he had accomplished. Sometimes he adjusted certain details. Other times he stared at the work, as if he were waiting for it to tell him what to do the next time he took up his brush. "The trick is not to take yourself too seriously, and to take yourself very seriously, both at the same time. If you don't think you can be as good as Rembrandt, why do it? Why even try? No one can be as good as Rembrandt.

The whole point in creating art is to find what you have to offer, what's special in your own soul."

She took in the whole of his body. The gray strands of hair that sprung out from his thick, black locks—she imagined he had had even thicker hair when he was younger—the way the hairs on his thick eyebrows grew in different directions, his slightly discolored tooth that was chipped at one corner, the muscles that formed in his arms when he moved his brush. He was beautiful when he painted. Some mornings he poured scotch into his tea or coffee and she smelled the liquor on his breath when he leaned over. She told herself he was a cliché: the drunken painter who puffed himself up. And yet, she admired that he showed up every day, striving for greatness.

She thought of him when she was alone in her apartment. What was his life like outside his studio? *He was so different from William.* She fantasized about his wife, about the parties she imagined they attended together, the gallery openings they frequented. She imagined them walking hand in hand throughout museums and galleries in Paris and other European cities.

Initially she was enthralled by the way he talked about painting. She had never been around a real artist. "What are you looking for when you look at me so intensely?"

"I like to capture figures that have the look of spontaneity, almost as if they're being illuminated in the middle of a conversation or after something devastating has happened, filled with the emotion of the moment. If you look closely at my work, study my paintings, inside them you'll find all you ever need to know about me. Each figure, each representation grows out of the former."

But he talked too much. He liked to give lectures on the films he saw, the artists he admired, what he considered sentimental or overexposed. He was judgmental, inflexible. When she grew bored with his monologues, he'd do something childlike and spontaneous. He asked her to take the subway uptown with him. It was a beautiful fall afternoon and he wanted to take a walk in Central Park. He wanted to see the color of the leaves. He had to see them, not to imagine them. He had to study the pigments, the fragmentation of color, the sky.

Once they were uptown he took her by the hand, sat her down on one of the benches. "Eleanor, I have a confession to make." She had been modeling for him for a month by then. "I'm attracted to you."

There was nothing she had revealed about herself that would draw his attention. It was the mystery in her that drew him. She did not trust him. "No, you're not," she said.

"I think about you all the time. You're behind every thought, every gesture. When I see a painting, I think of you. When I watch a movie, I imagine you in every scene. My world is clouded by you. You've blinded me. I'm Orpheus. I can't see if you're not in the room with me."

"I don't believe you."

"No, Eleanor. This is serious."

Back in his studio he instructed her to recline on the daybed, curved on her side. He wanted her to be staring directly at him for this particular pose. Because it was so unnerving, she distanced herself by thinking of the shape of William's body. She watched Adam work, but she thought of William. All those days she sat in his studio quietly thinking of another boy, she somehow must have willed Adam's interest upon her. Had she wanted him to be interested in her to see what it would be like to be free of William? She had sensed an attraction, had watched it unfold almost from the first day, but she had categorized it as a painter enthralled with his subject. She preferred it in that category, where it would not create any disturbances.

"I love your shoes," he said. They were an old pair of red Pappagallos. She thought, *He isn't attracted to me, he's attracted to who he thinks I am, for who he wants me to be, for the role I am serving in his studio, in his art. He's attracted to my shoes.*

"I'd be all over you if you wanted me to," he persisted.

"You're married."

"What does my marriage have to do with how I feel about you? Don't be naive, Eleanor. Marriage is not ownership."

"You can't say you're attracted to me and tell me that I'm naive." She had many rules. "You never ask me what I want or think."

"All behavior is dressing. I sit in the studio and I peel it away. Everyone is transparent. I see you." He took her hands and grasped them in his. "You alone are real to me. All this learned behavior. All the ways we are taught to think and feel, the boundaries we construct for ourselves. I want to be free of them." He twisted the cap off of a tube of paint. "It's all learned, how we are supposed to be, but it has no authenticity."

"But you don't know me."

"I know you."

"And the fact that you're married?"

"I didn't say it didn't matter. I said it has nothing to do with how I feel about you. Did you know you have these amazing yellow speckles in your eyes? Imagine the challenge it is to paint you."

She *did* like the way he looked at her, how he examined her with fixed attention. She saw that she could do anything she wanted and he would still want her. It was powerful knowing how deeply he wanted her, especially since she was in love with someone else. It made her imagine she was free of being hurt by him. His curious logic appealed to her. She wondered whether she could ever again live without the intense way that he looked at her.

He invited her to go to the opening of his show. She was nervous about meeting his wife, but when Adam introduced them, Mariana only nodded, as if she were bored with Adam's models, and walked away to talk with two other painters. She was an art historian from Romania teaching at Yale. Adam had given up his academic position once his paintings began to sell, though he still occasionally lectured. Mariana was the more practical minded of the two. She was petite and beautiful, with a cool air about her. She wore her short hair cropped around her heart-shaped face, and dressed that night in a short skirt with black tights and high heels and a Victorian high-collared lace shirt under a velvet blazer. She sipped a glass of wine, at ease with the other guests in the gallery. Eleanor watched as Mariana found Adam in the crowd and slipped her arm into the crux of his and wondered what it would be like to wake every morning next to him, to cook his meals, to wash his clothes.

The white walls of the gallery brought out the colors in Adam's paintings. They were paintings he had completed before she began to sit for him. She studied the work, located the narrative energy from one painting to the next. His colors—shades of blue, gold, and crimson—compelled her. She wanted to look at the paintings endlessly, the way one looked at a person with whom one was in love. They showed provocative subject matter, at once painterly and accessible.

In one, a boy was in his bedroom asleep, his mother sitting on the edge of his bed, smoking, in a cocktail dress and with thick nylon stockings. The painting conjured a memory of her own parents coming home from a cocktail party. She must have been the same age as the little boy. She looked more closely into the painting, and it was as if she stepped through a window and entered the canvas. Her own mother and father were fighting.

"Why aren't we enough for you?" her mother said. Or had she imagined it?

"I need to keep the people who are dearest away from me," her father replied. Eleanor pictured him wiping his brow with his hankie.

"And that Sheila Feinstein, what about her? You can't keep her away?"

Eleanor looked at the painting again. She smelled the dark odor of liquor on her father's breath when he came in to tuck her into bed. She had pretended she was sleeping. "What to do with this gift God gave me," he whispered. As a child she had failed to understand or connect the smell of the liquor on her father's breath with the behavior it provoked in her parents, but as she stared at the painting, she was back in her bedroom (her bed like the bed in the painting) wishing her parents would stop fighting. The next painting was a triptych. In one frame was an image of a woman, dressed as Eleanor's mother might have been years ago, in a tweed suit with a string of pearls around her neck. In the next frame a young girl sat in her bedroom reading. The painted eyes on the woman and the eyes of the child had the same shape and contour and the hollowed-out look of the eyes in a Modigliani painting. It was called *Twins*. Inscribed on the wrist of the mother in the painting was a serial number. In the last panel was the image of a tree with a car wrapped around its trunk. Another painting depicted a tranquil swimming pool where a boy floated in the pool on his stomach with his face in the water, leaving the viewer uncertain if he was alive or dead. The painting was called *Self-Portrait of the Artist as a Young Boy*.

She smelled the pungent scent that overwhelmed Adam's studio for the three hours she sat for him each day, a scent deep and muscular.

When she turned to acknowledge Adam, the heat and sweat of his body breathed on her skin. His smile illuminated his dark green eyes and his discolored front tooth, snug against the other whiter tooth. He was sunnier once he was out of his studio. Instead of baggy painter's pants and an oversized T-shirt, he was dressed in a black turtleneck sweater and black jeans. Eleanor experienced that strange disconnect of seeing a person in a setting different than usual. As she looked at him in a new way, no longer simply defined by her relationship to him as his study, she was overcome with admiration and another darker, more unpleasant and powerful feeling: that she wanted him. She quickly tried to bury the sensation.

"Relax," he said. "You're so tense." He placed his hands on her shoulders and massaged them. "I'm glad you're here."

She continued to study the paintings, particularly the haunting image of the young boy lying with his face half submerged in water.

"What do you think? Does he compel you?"

He moved closer, so that they were touching, nearly pushing her forward with the breadth of his body, and inhaled her perfume. She felt the tickle of his breath on the back of her neck. She thought she should not let her feet move from the wooden floor of the gallery or else she would fly forward into the painting. Adam lifted the hair from her neck and piled it into his hand, as if he were drawing it into a ponytail, and then he let it go. A chill ran down her back before he disappeared into the crowd.

At home in her studio apartment, she wondered whether she had felt Adam's groin push against her or whether she had imagined it. She flushed. She saw his paintings in her mind, that naked little boy alone in the tub. She ached with desire.

The next day in his studio she let him unbutton her blouse, and he painted her showing just the hint of her bra. She wore a kilted navy blue skirt and stockings. At the end of three hours, after the alarm went off, she dressed, put on her coat, and said good-bye. When she arrived home she felt she could still smell the fumes on her clothes from the oils in his studio. She thought of the canvases against his walls in various stages of completion. She undressed, sat on her bed in a tank top and underpants, and held the blouse she had worn in his studio to her face. She was supposed to finish a paper that was due that week, but she couldn't bring herself to work. She thought about Adam undressing her in his studio. The smell of paint intoxicated her. She remembered his words. "It's this strange twilight zone between rationality and unreason where the artist hunts," he had said, looking at her ravenously. His hands were rough and chapped from the strong soap he scrubbed with after he finished painting for the day, and they had been cold against her skin, sending a charge through her body. She held the longing inside her until it had reached its finest luster. In bed she thought about him a long time before she fell asleep. She felt a pain in her chest, as if it had cracked open just slightly, and her eyes filled with unexpected tears. She did not once think of William.

But William was in her dream, and in her dream she loved him the way she loved herself, so when he was gone she was missing. In the dream she felt vacant to herself, a stranger, and the long great tide of missing him formed a central artery inside her.

They were skating round and round in a large circle, feeling the wind tear at their face, and they circled the rink at least a hundred times—she had that many circles inside her with the boy,

that many hours of being next to him, absorbed in the circles they
made together, the thrust, thrust, thrust, glide, glide, glide of their
skates on the ice. They were holding hands and then William
pulled away from her and she felt confused, as if all the years of
their being together laying side by side in the dark like two com-
mas were over and she felt shame.

When she awoke from the dream, she looked in the mirror and everything was different. She told herself she couldn't work for Adam anymore. Her heart was committed to someone else. She was going home for Christmas, and she convinced herself that once William saw her again, they'd be back together. She took the subway downtown. She got off at the Spring Street station and walked briskly to Adam's building. She planned what she would say, keeping it short and simple. She didn't want to break up a marriage. She was going through something of her own. She was vulnerable. She had a life, and though it was mostly in her head, still it was her life. She didn't want to get involved with anyone. She didn't think it would be possible for her to continue working for him under the present conditions.

He buzzed her into the studio. He was still wearing the same clothes he had worn the day before, jeans and a torn white T-shirt. He was unshaven. He had slept in the studio that night. The smell of paint was inside and outside his body, mixed with his pungent scent—she didn't know how to describe it, like wet leaves?

"You didn't go home last night?" she asked.

"I camped out here. I wanted to be close to my work. I was looking at you all night, Eleanor." He pointed to the canvas. "And you? Did you sleep well?"

She propped herself up on the daybed and her mind went blank. She realized it took more energy to resist a person than it did to give in. She was leaving the next morning to spend

Christmas break with her mother. She told herself that she would continue to sit for Adam until he finished the series of paintings she had committed to, and then he'd have to find a new model. But she liked the way he looked when he had just woken up, his hair matted in the back, his sleepy eyes. Looking at him made her not want to go home anymore. She wanted to stay with him and not think about what faced her back in Chicago.

Even though she had refused to marry William, she thought he knew she was already married to him. It made her furious that he could not see what he needed to do and that she could not change him. She didn't want to think about him or her mother and her migraines. She didn't want to think about the piano that was no longer played.

"It's the artist's lot," Adam remarked.

She looked up at him, her face in a question.

"Empathy from a distance." He was cleaning some brushes in the sink. "To obsess on what you cannot have."

Eleanor reached for her coat.

"Have a good Christmas."

She reached to unlock the bolt on his door. He stopped, turned off the faucet, dried his hands on his pants, and handed her a present, a small box bound with a red velvet ribbon.

Her checks grew hot. "You didn't have to do that."

"Take it with you," he said. "Put it underneath your tree."

"But I'm Jewish," she said.

She called William once she was back in her own apartment to tell him she was coming home, sure that he would end his foolishness.

"We can't see each other, Eleanor. I have to do this. I have to prove it to myself."

"Prove what?"

"That I can live without you. Only then will it be possible for us to be together. Don't come home."

"I don't want to ever see you again," she said, trembling.

8

In Chicago, William was like a silent shadow next to her. She pictured him slipping his hand into the back hip pocket of her jeans. She heard him say her name, in that intimate way, filling her with a quick rush.

Her mother invited her best friends, Joan, Celia, and Carol, for Christmas. They formed their own foursome, a group of women from the neighborhood whose husbands had either abandoned them, or died, or divorced them. She learned from them that you could fill an entire lunch talking about fabrics for your couch or the color to paint your walls. She also learned that it was possible to survive disappointment if you chose to, or disappointment could put a dam in the middle of your life and you'd never be able to move forward. She learned that love could last a lifetime or a day, that there were all kinds of possibilities for losing or finding it. She learned that if you did not have faith, if you did not fulfill your dreams, they might hibernate in your head, creating such friction you couldn't lift it from the pillow. She learned to love the sounds of a piano reverberating through her house, and then the absence of sound. *Why won't he call me,* she imagined asking these women. *Why do I still care for him? Why can't I forget him?* But she knew she would put on her cheerful face and leave her questions to herself.

While her mother basted the turkey, she caught Eleanor up on gossip. Stephen Mason had moved back to town after dropping out of college. He doesn't trust institutions, Carol had explained. He wants to be a *real writer*. Her mother said he was working for his girlfriend's father, at one of the restaurants he owned downtown. She looked outside past the backyard at the empty plot of land where the playhouse had once been. Now it was filled with tangled weeds and dusted with a light snow.

Celia was telling stories about her divorce. "Since when is gaining weight grounds for divorce?" she asked. They had eaten dinner and were sitting by the fire, drinking coffee and still sipping wine. "If you were married to the son of a bitch, you'd gain weight, too."

Half listening to the conversation, Eleanor felt sorry for herself. She wondered why she had refused William's proposal of marriage. If she'd said yes, he would be just now coming to get her and she could forget her worries of always being alone like her mother, of whether she'd actually get through her orals and dissertation, or whether she'd eventually get a job.

It was the point in a dinner party when everyone senses it's approaching time to leave, but they also want to linger, to sustain that moment of pleasure where nothing is demanded from you other than to enjoy conversation with friends, slightly intoxicated by wine and cuisine and familiar sentiments. A tap on the windowpane of the front door startled her. Stephen Mason was standing underneath the awning. His coat was wet with snow and his face lit up when she opened the door. She was struck by the incongruities of his face: his chiseled cheekbones, his cautious but intelligent eyes, and the soft, slightly feminine wave of his hair, framing a masculine jaw. Looking at him made her think that people don't really change, they simply become more themselves.

"Merry Christmas." He handed her a bottle of wine and leaned over and kissed her on the cheek. "Hey, Eleanor. How come we never keep in touch?"

The comment surprised her. "I don't know."

"I thought I'd stop by and see if my mom was still here. Is it too late?" He explained that he'd had dinner with his girlfriend Chrissy's family.

"No, I'm glad you came," she said, surprised by her own words.

When he entered the living room, his mother brightened— the love of her life had walked through the door. "A house full of beautiful women," Stephen said. "I must have been a fool to have missed dinner. Seriously, it's good to be here," he said, looking earnestly at Eleanor's mother, then at his own mother, and then at Eleanor.

"We're glad to have you," Eleanor's mother said. "Look how happy you've made your mother. She says you're writing?"

Stephen explained an idea he had for a novel. Something about a guy who reconnects years later with a girl who used to live in the house in front of him. He went on to intricately describe the characters, catching Eleanor's glance as he spoke. Sort of like Pip and Estella in *Great Expectations,* he said. The girl is sophisticated and learned and the boy never feels worthy of her until he finally leaves home and proves himself. He described it as a twist on Thomas Wolfe's *You Can't Go Home Again.* "Sound familiar?" he said, and looked at Eleanor with a raised eyebrow and began to laugh. She liked his sense of humor. In the middle of his description—Joan said he should call it *Destiny*—Celia and Joan and Carol said they should call it a night. "Should I take this personally?" Stephen said, and the four women including Elizabeth broke into laughter, clearly charmed. Carol gathered her coat.

"Are you tired, Eleanor?" Stephen said.

"No. Not really."

"Do you mind if I stick around for a little while, then?"

"That would be nice," she said, noting in his eyes that same lost look he had when they were children. She was tired of hoping that William would seek her out. She was glad for Stephen's company. In fact, when she thought about it, she realized she liked being with him again. Eleanor did not follow everything he said but was surprised by his down-to-earth intelligence and daring. She was curious about him. She saw something in him that she felt she shared: a loneliness that inhabited the space her father had left. Her mother had bravely assumed the responsibility of Eleanor's care, but there was something vague and weightless about the way she moved through the world, as if she, too, had gone adrift. Earlier that night when her mother was setting the table for dinner, she'd accidentally taken down an extra plate, then put it back. Eleanor knew it was for her father. She still wore her wedding ring.

When the company left, her mother had said goodnight and went upstairs. Sitting beside Stephen on the sofa, Eleanor noticed Adam's wrapped present on the French desk in the living room, along with the present she bought for her mother. Though she had wanted to open it the minute she left his studio, she had refrained, as if she'd known that once she was in Chicago, immersed in memories of her past, she'd need something to remind her of her life in New York. She already felt far away from that life. Adam and the world he embodied seemed completely foreign to the quiet circumference of her small childhood world. She chastised herself for having entertained thoughts of becoming romantically involved with him, for dreaming that one day she'd lead a passionate artistic life. She told herself that she had imagined the intensity that had gone on in his studio, that it was simply the synchronicity between painter and subject that had intrigued her, and that outside the studio they were strangers. It seemed suddenly clear to her that for Adam she was an object, a subject for one of his paintings; he had no real desire to know who she was apart from how he could frame her to fit his own reality. It was silly to have endowed him with such power. She told herself that when she returned to New York she would put some distance between them and that she would focus on her own work. Adam was married.

"Eleanor, I'm glad you came home," Stephen said, knowing nothing of her thoughts. "Ever since we were kids I've felt like you're the only one who knows me. Do you know that I used to dream about you?"

"Really?"

"You didn't know that? I thought about you all the time. Even after I moved in with my dad. I wanted to call you a hundred times, but I didn't think you cared much for me."

"I cared," she said, suddenly realizing the truth of her words.

"I always liked being around you. You made me feel that it was okay to be sensitive. I don't have to pretend around you like I have to around Chrissy."

She looked at him carefully.

"I'm not kidding."

He explained that he was only working in Chrissy's father's restaurant for the money. "I have to get out of Chicago. I mean, how many more hamburgers can I flip? I want to make something out of my life. Chrissy doesn't understand what's at stake. Her father's dangling the keys to his business in front of her face. He manipulates everyone with his money. She doesn't get the writing thing. She thinks it's something I'm going to get out of my system."

"I didn't know you wanted to write."

"Yeah. I heard Ginsberg read from *Howl* once in San Francisco. It blew me away. He's the only poet who can write that 'the world is a mountain of shit' and get away with it. There was something about the rawness of what he was doing that I connected to. Same with Kerouac."

She'd never read Ginsberg or much of Kerouac, but she thought, compared to many of the pompous, entitled graduate students in her department, Stephen's passion for their work was refreshing.

"I don't think you really can come home again. I mean, and be the person you once were. That's why I need to leave Chicago, Eleanor. I don't like who I am here." They sat in front of the fireplace and watched the fire consume the wood. "I have ideas. But I can't do it in Chicago. I'm frozen here. All the memories. The pain."

She looked at him with recognition, thinking of her own parents. She knew exactly what he meant. She suddenly felt very close to him.

He was quiet for a moment. "Eleanor?" He paused. "What if I can't?"

"Can't what?"

He shook his head, not wanting to finish the sentence, and she let it go.

Outside it had begun to snow. From the window, it was a field of white. "You have to do what's going to make you happy. You can't live for other people," she said, thinking of William again.

"What about you, Eleanor? Are you seeing anybody?"

"Not really. There's someone here in Chicago. But we're really not together anymore. We're taking a break."

"I'd like to move to New York one of these days. I'm going to do it, Eleanor. I want it so badly I can taste it. I want to be a journalist. Travel the world. Write something so moving it will bring tears to your eyes. I have to turn this painful stuff inside me around. You know what I mean. Don't be surprised if I show up at your door."

He stretched out his legs and their thighs touched. She *did* know what he meant. It was the reason she had needed to leave Chicago, in spite of how painful it had been to leave William. The snow formed a ledge against the outside of the window, imbuing the house with a feeling of warmth and safety. She allowed herself to hold the calmness inside her. She looked at Stephen again; it seemed as if there was more he wanted to say. He exuded closeness and intimacy and invitation. He made her want to take his hands and bring them to her lips to relieve their coldness. But when she looked again she saw distance and study, hurt and promise and misunderstanding, and she didn't know if she could quite trust the way he absorbed her when he talked. It seemed practiced, intended to draw her further into the conversation so he could stay one step removed. She felt she had to be on her guard against it.

They sat in the darkness without talking. Eleanor leaned her head back on the sofa, closed her eyes, and tried to quiet her mind. His hand found hers, as if he'd understood and read what she was thinking, and for a moment she no longer felt the loneliness that had defined her life in Chicago. He stroked her hand as if he wanted to know her more intimately. She liked the feel of his hand touching hers, and felt herself shutting off all sensations save his touch. But then something about the feeling his touch inspired made her cautious again.

She wondered if Stephen was always alone, even inside himself, just like William. Some men were always alone and others were a part of the world, and she wondered why in the past she had given herself to the boy who was alone. Was she also like that? As she continued to hold Stephen's hand, the heat began to rise in her face, and she was aware that she wanted him to kiss her; it became uncomfortable sitting next to him. From the living room window, it was getting lighter. And as the sky lightened, the distance moved between them. She knew once he left she'd be alone again, and she felt the need to pull away in order to make space inside herself for his leaving.

"I like sitting here with you, in the dark," he said. "I hope this won't embarrass you. When I first saw you tonight I could barely speak. You've grown up, Eleanor. You look great."

He suddenly rose and gathered his coat and scarf from the chair where he had left them. The expression on his face changed. "Maybe it wasn't such a good idea to see each other," he finally said.

"Why?"

"It won't be the same. Still being here in Chicago once you're gone."

Eleanor walked him to the doorway, though she didn't want him to leave. He moved his face very close to hers. She thought for a minute he was going to kiss her, and she was surprised when he stopped. It made her draw further inside herself, instead of reaching toward him. It nearly made her turn her head when he said he was sorry he had to go, without any mention of whether they would see one another again. They said good-bye awkwardly, and she closed the door a little too forcefully after him, stunned that his leaving troubled her.

Long after Stephen left, Eleanor lay in bed thinking. She thought about his desire to be a writer and how he had seemed more open than she had remembered him. They seemed to share a bond. She watched the light of dawn slowly come into her bedroom, and she thought about how she wished he had kissed her. She almost felt the imprint of his lips on her own as she remembered how he had moved toward her and then stopped. Why had he turned away, just when she was opening herself to him again? Her disappointment and self-doubt turned into self-punishment. Perhaps she had not adequately expressed to him her own feelings, thinking he had intuited how she had felt. And her self-punishment turned to longing again, and it was inside this circle of emotion that she was caught. In the morning the grass was frosted, the branches on the tree that connected her house with his mother's sealed in a sheet of ice.

9

Inside the blue Tiffany's box Adam gave her that Christmas was a strand of beautiful black pearls. White pearls represented purity. Black pearls were seductive. She took them as a sign. When she returned to work the day after the new year, she flashed them outside her white blouse. She was sick of her midwestern self who grew up believing that she must be good and nice and reward anyone who approached her with a smile. She longed to be detached and indifferent and to command attention the way self-possessed, detached people did.

She was glad to be back in New York. Enough of the boy at home. She had called William, but he would not answer her calls. The entire seven days she had been in Chicago, she had hoped they would see each other. It was as if she had been testing him without having been aware of it, and the fact that he hadn't sought her out — if he truly loved her he would have — hurt her deeply. She convinced herself she had no other alternative but to forget him. She didn't want to think about Stephen, either. She wasn't going to romanticize their attachment. She had carried the evening with Stephen back with her on the plane, and then to her little apartment in New York City, but he had a girlfriend. She guessed that he had quarreled with Chrissy at her parents' house earlier that evening and had sought her out as a distraction; that supposition became her reality. She told herself that he must have been lonely that night, as she had been, and that her sudden feelings for him were a way for her to combat her feeling of loss over William.

Her mother had looked tired that Christmas. Eleanor sensed sadness in her routine: her small breakfast on the little table in the kitchen, a cup of tea, a slice of toast with jam, a piece of fruit as she sipped her tea and read the paper. Her migraines were more frequent.

"You have to move on," her mother had told her, when Eleanor admitted she wished William would call. There was a secret world inside her mother. You could hear it in the way she breathed and sighed, see it in the way she brought her fingers to her temple, suddenly, when she was washing the dishes. "Do you really think you can be in love with one person your entire life, even if you're not together?"

"Are you talking about William or Daddy?"

"It was a hypothetical question, Eleanor."

It was cold inside Adam's studio, but she didn't care. She was glad to be back to the life room, where something new was being created. Adam had an electric space heater he kept near the daybed, but the studio space was so vast and drafty that it barely warmed up. "Do you mind taking off your cardigan?" he said, once they exchanged pleasantries, after she had thanked him for the pearls.

She remembered afresh that morning how hard modeling was. Her neck began to hurt. She had to stop herself from rotating her head from side to side. Her foot fell asleep and she had to resist shaking it. It was a subtle art, to be able to open up enough to allow the artist to draw what was inside. Adam wanted more. He wanted an emotional exchange. He wanted an attachment.

"Tell me how you work," she said.

"When I initially coat the canvas, the subject is tentative. It's as though there is a screen, a distance between the artist and the subject. There's an aloof quality to the look in my subject's eyes, as if she is embodying my distrust, until I begin to know her better. As the painting develops I begin to see her clearer. She becomes my focus. My *raison d'être*. If I don't put everything I have in her, I see the falseness in the work. I look at the painting and it's not honest."

"How do you know what's honest?"

"We're all eventually transparent, Eleanor."

While Adam painted, she imagined the waves of the sea building and receding. She sat for nearly an hour without moving, her mind focusing on the imaginary drift of the sea and the current of Adam's gaze.

"You can't imagine how sexy it is having you in my head. All the hours when I'm painting and not painting your image is inside me."

She was startled.

"Your skin is soft. I want to paint it like velvet. And your hands. They're petite but strong. Are they your mother's or your father's?"

"My father's. I think." She tried to recall her father's hands. They were elegant, with long fingers that he had taken care to protect. They were hands with fingers that moved across a keyboard. She conjured her father's hands cupping her cheeks when he kissed her goodnight. She felt them against her skin as he fastened the Star of David around her neck. She held on to the things she remembered about her father to remind her that she was still his daughter.

It had been a long time since anyone asked her about her father. After he left, she and her mother learned through the postcards he sent that he had moved to Florida, then California, then cities in Europe; each time he wrote from farther away. "I'm listening to Wagner. To *The Ring,*" he wrote. "The music matches my mood, Eleanor. Listen to it. Feel my soul in the music." The summer Eleanor was fourteen, he was living in Miami, and he sent her an airline ticket to visit. The trip was a disaster. He lived in a hotel. She remembered the connecting door between their two rooms. From her own bed she could hear him twist the caps off of the miniature bottles of scotch from the minibar; the creak of the room service cart; and his long, convoluted business conversations over the phone. It was always those connecting doors she remembered, and the dark hallway in between, and her fear of crossing over the threshold into his room. If she were a painter, that is the image she would paint. The empty hallway. All night he listened to music by Chopin, Beethoven, and Mahler from a portable tape recorder. He never took her to see the beach. "The sun's too hot," he had said, his skin nearly white.

"Here, Eleanor. Listen to this. 'The Flight of the Bumble-bee.' I recorded it for you."

"But Daddy, it's a beautiful day."

"You go, Eleanor. I can't bear the brightness."

"I don't want to leave you, Daddy," she had said, and put on the headset to be closer to the language of her father's heart. A swarm of bees.

"You're pissed at your father, aren't you? You can talk to me, in here, when we're alone together. You can say anything."

"I worry about him. He doesn't take care of himself."

"Be angry. I'm giving you permission."

"My father writes me letters about his girlfriends. One wanted him to settle down with her in Florida. *In Florida,* he had written, as if it were the tundra. About another girlfriend he met in Paris, he said she wasn't passionate enough for him. He said a woman has to be slightly irrational. I hope you haven't taken after your mother. I mean, doesn't he get it? How it would make me feel? I really don't see the point."

"The point?"

"You know what I mean."

Adam put his brush on the table where he kept his palette. He moved toward her to adjust a strand of hair that had fallen in her face. "I do know," he said, in a warm voice. "Now may I unbutton your blouse?"

"I'll do it." Inside she was trembling.

"We need to get closer."

She stood very still as he unbuttoned the last two buttons. She felt the coldness of his hand on her chest. Slowly the blouse slipped from her shoulders, exposing her white cotton bra. *That was all,* she thought, wanting him to open other places inside her, wanting to be free of her wants.

He went back to the canvas. "When you're my age, you'll understand."

"Are you condescending to all your models?" She was twenty-three. She thought she understood perfectly.

He said nothing.

"Then you're happy?" She was thinking about the fact that he was married but didn't act married.

"I don't expect happiness."

He lifted his brush.

"I don't try to control meaning. I don't like to put feelings with labels on them in their own little boxes. As a painter you want to create a scene or moment that is so alive and complex that when someone comes to it they are shaken. Filled with their own associations."

"Are we talking about art?"

"Is there a difference?"

She watched the intensity in his face as he painted. She watched his jaw and the movement of his hand. If she put all her faith in what they were doing together, in the way he saw her and attempted to translate what he saw, then she did not feel simply herself anymore; she was a part of something other. She felt more confident, and with it came more freedom, as if she'd opened herself to express it.

He saw that she looked at him differently. She meant for him to see it. He put down his brush and knelt down before her in front of the daybed.

"You don't see it. Do you?"

"See what?"

He pointed toward the canvas. "See the look in her eyes. She drives me crazy. I want every man that looks at this painting to see it. A woman who awakens conflicting instincts to protect and conquer in every man who enters her unsteady field of force." He looked into her eyes, lifted her chin, and kissed her passionately. Her mother's loneliness, her consuming memories of William, her perplexing thoughts about Stephen—all of it vanished as she disappeared into the darkness of his kiss.

10

The flight to Paris began its descent. Eleanor was exhausted by her memories. It was as if they were in pieces, and by remembering them she was stitching the pieces together, arranging them like a patchwork quilt. She combed her hair with her fingers, raked through her purse for her tube of lipstick. It was eight in the morning, Paris time. By the time she arrived in the hotel, unpacked, and took a nap, it would be almost morning in New York; she could call home and hear her family's voices.

Michael was a loving father. The boys were well cared for and she knew she needn't worry, yet she did. She hadn't traveled abroad alone since she'd been married, and as she faced getting off the plane, she wished that Michael was with her. When they traveled as a family, Michael dealt with foreign currency and exchange rates, booked the hotels, paid for the meals. She tried to prepare herself for being alone in a strange hotel— no children running around the room, testing out the locks on the hotel door, flicking on the television, distracting her as she tried to get dressed.

She stretched her back and tilted her head to loosen the cramp in her neck. She thought about Michael again and hoped he had understood why she needed to go.

Outside the terminal she looked into the gray, bleak sky of Paris: Everything looked unreal—the way people dressed, the compact cars, the narrow road circling behind the terminal. She was across the ocean from her husband and sons and she felt strangely as if they did not exist, that the years in which they had become the central focus in her life were years that did not belong to her anymore but to a different woman. The thought frightened her.

She inched forward in the cab line, took a compact mirror from her purse, and stared at herself in the glass. She was the same person, with the same almond-shaped eyes of blue and green, small nose and mouth, and electric red hair pulled back in a ponytail.

Ahead in line a young couple was kissing. Eleanor looked at them the way she had once stared at the couple in the library. She, too, was a half of a couple, though, suddenly thrust into a foreign city after the long trip, she felt stripped of her attachments. She told herself she'd feel better once she slept. Yet, she kept glancing at the couple engrossed in each other, and she felt a strange ache.

She thought about her friend Jordan Klein, whom she had known since graduate school and who was one of her closest friends. She'd had a quick coffee with her the day before she was leaving. Jordan was tall and elegant, with straight black hair styled geometrically around her face. She had astonished Eleanor by telling her that she had taken a lover the last time she was in Europe. She had met him when she was on a Fulbright in Rome six months before. She said she hadn't planned for it to happen. That slowly they'd fallen in love. Eleanor had looked into her penetrating eyes, surrounded by eyeliner, and felt a surprising stirring of envy, even though part of her had disapproved of her friend. She had always thought that Jordan had a good marriage and now wondered how well she had known her. How well she knew anyone, really. When she'd asked Jordan whether she was happy, her face had brightened. "It's complicated." Eleanor's heart had gone out to Jordan's husband. Her daughter was the same age as Nicholas. She had a two-year-old boy. "I know I've disappointed you. I can see it in your face. I've been wanting to tell you for months." Jordan struggled to find the right words. "I didn't expect it to happen."

"But look what you're jeopardizing. Passion is transient."

"Or that's what we tell ourselves. Maybe it's because we haven't experienced the kind of passion that can withstand time that we doubt it. But what if you had a chance to experience it again? Do you think you could walk away?"

"This isn't a novel we're talking about. People in novels don't have their children to bathe and get ready for school." She was flustered. "Well, you know what I mean." She realized how empty her words sounded once she said them. She could tell that something had changed in Jordan. Jordan looked different.

Her face was flushed. Her eyes sparkled. She told Eleanor the details of the affair and how they'd met. "It's too late," she'd said, her eyes turning dark. "Even if I wanted to walk away, I'm not sure I could."

Jordan's bold nature had made Eleanor feel that she was too cautious and careful, a person who had stopped taking chances. "It's the most intense sex I've ever had. It's not just the sex. We connect. I've never felt so alive."

After coffee, on the way home, Eleanor stopped and sat on a street bench in front of a church. She sat still in one place, looked at the intricate building, at its masonry, its magnificence, to quiet the unrest.

She slipped into the back of a cab and told herself to stop thinking about Jordan. What Jordan decided to do was her own business. She told herself she'd call Michael as soon as she was in the hotel and she'd feel more herself. She looked out the cab window, and as they entered the city, the pale buildings with shutters on the windows, the gray sky, the small curving streets brought tears to her eyes.

The hotel was near the Boulevard Saint-Germain. The conference had reserved a block of rooms for the participants. Eleanor noted from the schedule that they were to meet for a brief dinner that night in the hotel. She was grateful for the hours in between to catch up on sleep. The hotel room was small, with a queen-size bed and a little French desk by the window, a reading chair and a lamp, and a tiny bathroom with a bathtub in place of a shower. She unpacked her toiletries and hung up her clothes. She was in Paris, and yet inside the quiet of her room she could have been in a hotel room in any city.

Yet a sense of unease washed over her. She missed her husband and children.

They came to her looking for their lost shoes, wanting her to cut the crust from their sandwiches, to bandage them when a knee was scraped. *Keep the light on, Mommy, I'm afraid,* the little one said. *Rub my back.* She collapsed on the hotel bed. She heard Noah's voice in her mind, pictured him slipping his hand in hers like he did when he thought no one was watching when she dropped him off at school. She thought of Nicholas's serious face. Who was she without their breaths, their wants and fears inside her? She turned over and reached out her arm, amazed that the space next to her was empty.

She had fallen asleep on top of the bedspread. When she awoke her head was heavy. She looked at the clock on the bedside table. Only a half hour had passed. She slipped underneath the cold, crisp covers of the hotel bed with the blue fleur-de-lis wallpaper, brought the unfamiliar white down comforter up over her shoulders, and tried to fall asleep again. The most seductive sleep was when she had too little time, and afternoon naps were always the deepest. She felt as if she were plunged into the darkest layers of her being. When she awoke it was as if she had experienced a lifetime. Her sheets were damp, her skin hot. Her dreams had been strange, though she couldn't quite remember them.

She looked at the clock. Two hours until she had to get up and greet the other conference participants at dinner. She lay in bed and thought about how long it had been since she had allowed herself the indulgence of sleeping past the hour of waking, past the sun rising, past the sound of the alarm, past the schedule of everyone rushing, and wondered how much she had missed.

She lay on the bed and watched the wind play with the long, sheer drapes, watched the light as it danced through the threads of cotton and made patterns on the honey-colored floor. The long flight the night before, the separation from her family, her convoluted dreams, and the sudden flood of memories that seemed now to come at her with new meaning, left her disoriented. She thought about how long it had been since she had allowed herself to remember her past. She felt unsettled, as if she didn't know who she was—the open, vulnerable woman from so long ago or the woman she was now, overscheduled, tense, and leading a conventional life she had not been fully aware she'd chosen. She took a bath to awaken fully. When she stepped out, she put on the hotel's white terry cloth robe and went back into her room to unpack. She smelled smoke and parted the curtains of the window. A fire was ablaze in the apartment building across from the hotel. She stood by the window watching the flames destroy the building. Glass shattered as the windows caved in. The smell was suffocating. She picked up the bedside phone and called the hotel desk. The concierge reassured her that they were aware of the situation and the fire appeared contained. The sound of fire trucks bled through the street, soon joined by police sirens.

The smoke wound into the French windows and she closed them, drew the curtains, and then she heard a voice inside her. *I'm glad it burned. I never liked that playhouse. Now I can see through our yards to your house without it blocking the view. I like knowing you're in the house in front of me, Eleanor. Sometimes I can't fall asleep until I see the light in your window go off.* The disconcerting memory ran through her mind again.

With some people it was better to leave well enough alone. She wished her mother had not given Stephen's mother the name of her hotel. She hoped he wouldn't call her. She vaguely remembered their last encounter, before she'd gotten married, when she had gone to visit him in Colorado. But she didn't want to think about it. It hadn't ended well, that much she remembered. She had not thought of him for years. And she didn't want to. Soon she would have to emerge from her room and greet the other guests in the hotel lobby, and she had to prepare herself. There were many steps to climb from her solitude of the last twenty-four hours. *He won't call anyway,* she thought. She put mascara on her lashes and combed her hair. Outside, the fire engines had departed. The air still smelled of something burning. Across the street the Paris light shadowed the beige bricks and soot-covered shutters of the burned facade. A spark from the debris danced in the air and extinguished itself on her windowsill.

PART II

May 4, 2002

My first morning in Paris is like being inside a dream. Everything is drenched in history; the streets are of a bright and cheerful narrowness, as if concealing something clandestine and private. Everywhere are children, parks, gardens, museums, palaces, and a grand cathedral. I imagine I'm in a novel in which some inevitable knowledge will be bestowed and that I, the heroine of the novel, have not yet fully comprehended it. I am keeping a notebook so that I will not forget anything. So that I will understand the nuances and not push away their meaning. I want to look at things closely. To see paintings and record what I recognize in them. I feel so alive.

As I walk the narrow streets and the long width of the avenues, every storefront entices me with its artistry: In the chemist's shop the bottles are arranged neatly and spaciously on glass shelves. The houndstooth combs and brushes and barrettes all of the finest quality. Each clothing shop has its own particular style and distinction, so unlike the shops in New York, where every shelf is crammed with the same merchandise. Everything is beautiful—the architecture of the buildings; the narrow, cobbled streets; the open markets; the painters and artists sketching along the banks of the Seine. The light.

This morning I took a walk in the Luxembourg Gardens. Even the wind carried with it a scent of the linden trees and lavender from the Parisian gardens. I watched the carousel and thought of the boys. I love all the small things, the shutters and terraces, the flower boxes in the windows, and then the grander mansions and museums, the energy in the cafés. Everything about the city exudes the feeling that art, literature, history is at the forefront of society. I walked past the Café de Flore with its red leather chairs and booths and square tables on the Boulevard Saint-Germain. Just down the street, Les Deux Magots, the two cafés separated only by a tiny, narrow street. I imagined Oscar Wilde, Joyce, Hemingway, Simone de Beauvoir drinking white wine or dry sherry at their open tables. The sounds of French conversation, with its lovely cadences and aristocratic sounds, the leisurely feel of the city, and its fashionable presentation stirs me. The women look aloof and flirtatious in their stylish dress. It's delicious being alone in a foreign country. Something has changed.

Why did I fear coming to this city alone?

May 5, 2002

At the Louvre today I saw a magical painting by Fragonard, *The Bathers,* and the painting has stayed with me. I love the freedom dramatized in it, the nude voluptuous women bathing in a stream, their frivolity and lightness. Adam would have loved the lushness, the embodiment of the rococo spirit, the spontaneous brushwork. The joyfulness, the delight in the body. Have I ever been that carefree?

I don't know why I am thinking of Adam so much, when I have not thought of him in years. It is as if he came into my life for a specific reason, to reveal to me the intensity and pathos that exists for those who create, or to unleash those desires inside me. Tonight dinner at a French café John Cloud heard about. He teaches at Princeton, and we have become friends. It's in the 11th arrondissement, close to the Bastille, on the Rue Saint-Sabin where they are famous for their cheeses and charcuterie. He heard it described as an artsy café that looks as if it might have been Bogart's just before he went off to Casablanca. You can sip coffee for five Euros standing or nine Euros seated at the dark red banquettes next to old wood tables.

May 6, 2002

Today I went to an inspiring lecture on *Anna Karenina* as the embodiment of the Russian view of human guilt and crime.

Afterward I wandered out to get a breath of air. It's always a jolt, when teaching or working in the library for hours, my mind focused on disentangling a thought, exploring a theory, to walk into the streets and witness the everyday: people shopping for their dinners, children skipping rope. I experienced that very sensation after stepping out of the lecture hall. It's as if I live in two separate realities. I love the linden trees in this city. The way they curve. The light gray color of their bark. I like walking the Champs-Elysées and admiring the Parisians in their stylish and elegant attire. I can be anyone I want to be here. No one knows me. It's that same feeling I experienced when I first moved to New York from Chicago. One can invent oneself in a new city. I imagine I'm inside a Henry James novel. Isabel Archer when she first embarks in Rome before everything begins to turn. The history. The glamour. The sensation of being a foreigner in a foreign land. The anxieties I struggle with at home, the small details of life, seem insignificant here.

There's this wonderful china shop I passed by twice. And in the window a beautiful painted pitcher. My eyes rested on it. The handle pale green, the body the color of cream. The lip of the pitcher a rich, seductive burgundy traveling through the mouth into the interior. An array of delicate hand-painted yellow crocuses—two dots of color in the middle of green buds—bordering the rim. The buds signify something about to break into blossom but forever frozen in that state of becoming, fired into the porcelain for eternity. I thought of Keats's "Ode on a Grecian Urn," the longing for the permanence of passion and beauty; to stop time before beauty becomes tragic. The flowers painted on the pitcher will never yield, will never fully be, but are always becoming. "What leaf-fringed legend haunts about thy shape . . . What men or

gods are these? What maidens loathe?/ What mad pursuit?
What struggle to escape/ What pipes and timbrels? What
wild ecstasy?" My mind keeps traveling back to the images
of the crocuses in their half state. Their deep, sensuous colors,
delicate buds, and the polished darkness inside the pitcher's
lip. I see promise in the pitcher. The painted buds trapped in
porcelain remind me that nothing remains the same. Not
even the bud of a flower.

I always knew I wanted to study literature, to become
a professor, a writer, to marry and have children. I never
imagined any further. What now? What does the middle
passage hold?

The little china shop is on the same street that I walk
daily from the hotel to the academy. Just today I've passed it
twice and each time I see the pitcher in the window my body
awakens to that invigorating feeling of almost becoming. If
objects speak, the pitcher says be present. Question. Listen. Is
it the foreignness and beauty of the city that awakens this
heightened sense of life?

Later this afternoon a lecture on the great French
masters—du Maupassant, Voltaire, Zola, Proust, and another
called the "Moral Ideal in the Works of George Sand."

May 7, 2002

It's a warm day today in Paris, and as the afternoon
descends, heat lightning penetrates the sky. Today I went
again to the Louvre with John Cloud. We stood in line to see
the *Mona Lisa*, and her queer, enchanting smile. How little
the painting affected me. I had seen her image everywhere,

on postcards, posters, in advertisements, on pens, and here
she was in the flesh. I kept staring, wanting to be moved. I
looked at the painting from different angles in the room, and
the *Mona Lisa*'s mocking, self-satisfied eyes followed me. I
kept hoping to find her enchantment, hoping to embody that
sensation of having come upon the painting for the first
time. Nothing. John says her name in Italian, *La Giocanda*,
means a light-hearted woman. I looked into her mercurial
eyes. It is antithetical to the human condition to expect
wholeness. The best one can hope for is solace in the
spiritual realm, not the carnal, she seemed to say as if
ridiculing me with her roaming eyes. I told John and he
understood what I was saying, without me having to explain
it. I could hear Michael. *A painting can't talk, Eleanor.*

I thought of the pitcher in the window of the china shop
and those lines from Keats: "What mad pursuit? What
struggle to escape?"

I don't really miss Michael anymore, though I long to
see the boys. Why? I miss Michael's calm, steady voice, his
soothing presence (of course I adore him), but lately he's been
on edge and I think the break is good for us. I'm freer, more
myself without him. I'm glad to have the freedom to explore
this city solo, in spite of my guilt for relishing this time on
my own.

Phrases from yesterday's lecture on Tolstoy echo in my
mind. The scholar from Johns Hopkins quoted from *Anna
Karenina*. "In order to know love one must make a mistake
and then correct it." His thesis was that only out of suffering
comes transformation. When I look at the paintings all
around me I think of the years that a painter might have
spent toiling away on one masterpiece. Of the sacrifice of
the lived life that is at stake.

I took a walk by the Seine and again experienced that
peculiar feeling of traveling to places inside myself I've
forgotten; it's as if I've just awakened from a deep sleep.
When I look at trees almost in bloom I see, instead of their
entirety, the details, the nubs of buds on the crook of every
branch, the underside of the leaves that have already sprung.
The density of color in each flower.

We've already established our own clique. I'd heard
about John Cloud—read a book he had written on the
Romantics—and it was thrilling to finally meet him. He's
tall, over six feet, impeccably dressed, oxford shirts, blue
blazer, and tie; he's also possessed of a deadly sense of
humor. He has piercing eyes that are like seeing through
the depths of the ocean. During a reception last night we
stood in the back of the room, sipping wine and laughing. I
told him about the pitcher and how it reminded me of the
Keats poem. He mentioned that Keats was orphaned by the
time he was fourteen, his father died when he was eight;
once he committed himself to poetry there was urgency
about it, as if he sensed a foreboding of early death. John
considers the poem "Endymion" Keats's best work. He
believes that it expresses the poet's quest for an ideal
feminine counterpart and a flawless happiness beyond
earthly possibility. "That couldn't be a romantic notion,
could it?" I said, and we both laughed. We have the same
sense of humor.

Dan Fineman, another new friend, teaches at Brown. He's
considered the young, handsome savant. He has blond frizzy
hair to his shoulders. Wears blue jeans. Shirts it looks like
he's slept in. It makes sense that he's a Hemingway scholar.
In the same way that it makes sense that the Shakespeare

scholar seems Faustian with his perpetual sighs and wiry
gray hair. Dan wears a tweed blazer with leather pads at
the elbow. He makes brief appearances at lectures and then
disappears. John says he spends the rest of the afternoon
flying a kite along the Champs-Elysée. John says he could
have sworn Dan's been drunk since he'd stepped off the
airplane. He heard that Dan would pick out the girl before a
party began, and by the end of the evening she'd be there at
the exit waiting for him. I like John. He's passionate about
books. He's distant and reserved. He grew up in a formal,
uptight Connecticut family. But he has recklessness inside
him, something untamed. I can see it when he looks at a
painting or smokes a cigarette. There's passion and pathos
in him; things inside him waiting to be expressed. Perhaps
that is why we've become friends.

Then there's the poet, Phoebe Hogan, with her big
owllike eyes and thick black mascara on her lashes. She
talks from the side of her mouth. I can understand now
why poets get a bad rap. She talks in nonsequiturs. The
first night I met her she asked me if I happened to know
anyone in Portland. When I told her I didn't she explained
that she's giving a reading at the University of Portland
and she thought perhaps I knew someone I could tell. She's
terrified that no one will show up at the reading. Are poets
always that spacey or is it an act she's putting on? Later at
dinner she quoted lines from Szymborska, the extraordinary
Polish poet. Something about how we cling to poetry like a
banister.

Robert Nye is the youngest of the five of us. He's in his
late twenties. He's assistant professor of modern poetry at
Rutgers and is a father of a young son. Julie Hamilton teaches
at Smith. She's a good friend of Jordan's. They met at the

MLA when they were undergrads. She's tall and sexy and has bleached blond hair and a deep, husky voice.

We stayed up late drinking and smoking at the hotel bar. John went through a pack last night. He says he never smokes at home; his wife won't let him. I find myself smoking in Paris, too, though I rarely smoke at home. Again, it makes me feel slightly dangerous and reckless, not just the cigarettes but the feeling of anonymity and the endless possibilities it gives birth to.

At the bar John, who is rather reserved, at one point looked into my eyes. "One eye is light and the other is dark. They capture you." The comment touched me and I smiled. "I've been thinking about 'Endymion' ever since our talk last night. Do you remember the first lines of the poem? 'A thing of beauty is a joy for ever;/ Its loveliness increases; it will never/ Pass into nothingness.'"

"I studied that poem for an entire semester," John said. "Can you imagine writing a poem that would require such concentration?"

"Yes," I answered. It's that kind of concentration I've always found stimulating.

After a few evenings with John, Robert, and Julie, I realize how much I miss being around people who are more like me. Maybe it hasn't been such a good idea, sparing Michael dinners and parties with colleagues and old friends from graduate school. Michael says that most academics and artists are narcissists. But how are doctors and their egos any different? Our social world together has been mostly Michael's friends. Brian and his wife, Marcia. Sally and Rick and all the kids. I love being around all of them. We've gotten close. But Brian and Rick are doctors. And Sally and Marcia don't really read. We seem

to have little in common except our kids. When I first met
Michael it was such a luxury not to have to talk about my
ambitions, about art, literature. Before, I spent all my time
with my graduate friends or with Adam, having abstract
discussions, talking about academic pursuits, and worrying
about publishing, about whether I'd get an academic
appointment. Having to bear the jealousies, the egos, the
competition. When I met Michael it was like I was on a long
vacation from myself. I liked experiencing the world from
his more practical, sensible, down-to-earth eyes. His
presence seemed to quiet my questing, unsettled nature.
But here in Paris it is as if I'm resuming the life I led
before I met my husband. I wonder if the other people
in our group feel the same. Most of us are married except
for Julie and Dan.

The pulse of the world and its sensuousness keep pressing
up inside me—it's almost like a physical pain. I realize I often
feel so truly alone.

Confession: I caught Robert's eyes at the hotel bar moving
over my body, his look lustful and sexual. As he looked at
me I felt a growing strangeness—a flower opening petal
by petal, and underneath each petal was another layer.
Do women always feel exposed when men lust after
them?

Time to get some sleep.

May 8, 2002, 4:00 A.M.

I slept for maybe an hour or two and now I'm wide awake. I
can't sleep. Something about Robert's look has stirred me. I
dreamed about William. I can't remember the dream exactly,

only the feeling it produced. In the dream William and I were together again. I sensed he wanted me. And that I wanted him, too, and it made me happy. And yet, once I moved toward him, he turned away from me and I felt humiliated, as if I had provoked both his desire and his rejection of me. The dream left me feeling frightened and strange.

There was something about the way he looked at me in the dream. Saw through me. The look was almost superior. The look said he knew I wanted him and that I had blown him off, that I'd had my chance. It was punishing and seductive and brutal. And made me feel ashamed for my desire. It's as if he was in my dream to remind me that our time together so long ago has shaped me, has been buried under layers of other experience, and now must be brought to the surface. Understood. Is it the very fact that I remember him that leaves me unsettled? Perhaps it was that look in Robert's eye that made me dream about William. He had the sinister look of someone who desires what he knows he cannot have. I remember having left the table to go to the ladies' room to relieve the sensation. And yet I did nothing to provoke Robert's attention. My eye caught his. The way he looked at me made me feel naked. As if I had invited his stare. And yet I kept looking back. Is it desire itself that makes me feel ashamed?

Now I must write it down, seal it on paper. Adam explained how a painter seals a canvas with a layer of gesso, that gesso used to be mixed with rabbit-skin glue and that it is used to prime a canvas before a painter begins to paint with oils. He explained that oil rots fabric, hence the reason for priming it. That always seemed an interesting irony. That oil paint, the material a painter uses to create beauty, has the capacity to rot the fabric it is applied to. As if all beauty is capable of ruin. Perhaps an idea for a story or poem.

I want to write down *everything*. Later I can sort it out. Louisa May Alcott kept serious diaries, and from passages in her journals novels were formed. Tolstoy kept them, too. I can't imagine that the Brontës and Austen didn't, as well. Given the narrowness of their experiences they would have certainly drawn from them. James did. His notebooks are often keys to his work.

It's nearly dawn already. The light is peeking in through the curtains. Sleep.

May 8, 2002

I woke up tired and dark this morning. Barely made it to Julie's lecture called "The Forlorn Mistress in Literature." She opened with Marvell's searing "To a Coy Mistress." I thought she trembled. It was quite moving.

I went to the Louvre again after hearing Julie's presentation. I stood in front of *Woman with a Pearl* by Jean-Baptiste Camille Corot. The painting is said to echo both *Mona Lisa* and Vermeer's *Girl with a Pearl Earring*. There is the same enigma about the model, the same gaze, the same uncertainty as in da Vinci's *Mona Lisa*. The pearl is a dark, leaf-shaped ornament attached to a light veil on the woman's forehead. What captivates me about the portrait is not its nod to Vermeer or da Vinci but what Corot might have revealed to the model about herself she had not yet known.

I looked at myself in the mirror in the bathroom of the museum. My face was blurry and out of focus. I applied fresh lipstick. For a moment I couldn't distinguish who I was.

May 9, 2002, 3:00 P.M.

Just listened to a lecture on *Portrait of a Lady*. Excruciatingly
dull. But still, the lecture brought back the tragedy of the
novel in its entire remarkable splendor. How little Isabel
Archer knows herself at the onset; how in her desire to be
free and independent she loses her freedom; how her lack
of self-knowledge leads her into a marriage with the evil
Osmond. Another complex yet doomed heroine whose sense
of pride and duty traps her. I've read the novel a few times
and the ending still devastates. Why does she return to the
evil husband? James's novels always have the feeling that

life goes on beyond the pages. That we are only given a glimpse. The first time I read the novel I imagined that Isabel eventually leaves Osmond for Caspar Goodwood, and yet there isn't one piece of evidence in the body of the novel—I've scanned it endlessly—that should have allowed me to think that way. James understood that people are trapped within themselves. We make choices that make sense at a particular instance, but why should we expect that those choices should withstand the passing of time?

Tonight I'm having dinner with John and Robert and Julie. I'm shattered. I long for just a few minutes of sleep but my mind won't allow it.

May 10, 2002, nearly dawn

It is 4:00 in the morning. I can't sleep yet. I'm thinking of the night, of my new friends. None of the three of us, the three of us that are married, talked about our spouses or our children all evening. It was as if we all wanted to be free of our responsibilities and our pasts, to inhabit a foreign city, to experience, at least for a few hours, the thrill of being alive. Phoebe, who had decided to tag along, said she had to leave to wash her hair. It was midnight. She recited lines from *Midsummer Night's Dream*. She wears high-colored lace tops and velvet blazers, long swirling skirts, and lace-up boots as if she's stepped out of a Victorian novel or a Shakespeare play. Once she left, John called her loopy and we all laughed. At the bar John decided to do an imitation of a poet giving a poetry reading where each line ended in a question. "This poem is about trees along the Seine," he began. "It's called

'The Trees Along the Seine.' 'The Trees Along the Seine.' It was inspired on my walk along the Seine through the trees. Here it goes. My poem called 'The Trees Along the Seine.' He paused. " 'The Trees Along the Seine?' " We were howling. He's right. Poets tend to read with that tic of ending a line with a question. Julie turned to me after the laughter died down. "It's hard to believe you have kids, Eleanor," she said. "I can't picture you as a mother."

The night seemed to move slowly, as if in slow motion, but I couldn't seem to break away and retreat to my room. I remember tugging at the end of my skirt that had hiked up just slightly over my thighs, once I caught Robert looking at my legs. I told John and Robert an anecdote about Professor Reynolds, our chair, and while I was talking I was thinking about what it would be like to kiss John. Writing this down, sealing it into memory, feels like an act of betrayal. Perhaps writing always feels like a betrayal. The hair clip that held my hair seemed suddenly too tight, and I opened its clasp. I told everyone at the table that the greatest thrill of our chair is when he finds spelling or grammar errors in published papers. He came into my office and showed me an article with two or three spelling errors that a full professor in the department had published in a journal. He was gleeful. "What does it mean to want to humiliate others, to want to be superior?" I said to my friends. "Professor Reynolds went to boarding school, then Harvard, was raised in a privileged world. He thinks spelling errors mean you're not intelligent." Everyone laughed. Did I really want to kiss John, or was I a little lonely away from Michael and in need of attention? What if I had allowed it? What harm could it have done, here in Paris? Is it good to keep yourself in check? To be constantly

in control of every thought, every feeling, every emotion?
Jordan and I had a philosophical discussion about morality
after she told me about her lover. She thinks it's immoral to
withhold. To deny oneself the possibility of love, no matter
the cost. She'd prefer to take the risk than to live in the
limitations of self-denial and regret. She pointed out how rare
it is to truly connect with another person. I looked at John.
Was I attracted to him? This is crazy. Would I feel the same
way if Michael were here? Of course not.

We stayed up drinking until last call. We trashed our
departments, gossiped about mutual friends, analyzed movies
and books. There was an edge to the conversation, a charge,
a current between us. After the bar closed, we drifted to the
lobby and lingered at the landing, as if we were wondering
in our collective unconscious what was going to happen, who
was going to pair off with whom. Once I climbed the stairs to
my room I even fantasized. John might be tender. Robert, shy
and sweet. Dan had come into the bar later. He likes women
who surround him and draw him out. I'm the opposite. I'm
always waiting to be drawn out. He's the kind of man you
could easily sleep with for the night, and then shrug it off the
next morning. But I have never been able to be casual about
sleeping with men. I told myself to stop thinking about them.
I brushed my teeth, poured myself a glass of bottled water,
took two aspirins, and got into bed. But instead of making me
sleepy the alcohol acted as a stimulant. I tried to sleep, but it
was hopeless. Before I turned on the light and reached for my
pen and notebook I was thinking that each person is like a
puzzle, filled with different pieces, conflicting tensions and
opposing characteristics shaped by particular events and

experiences, and that our behavior is predicted by these
pieces, lost in our memory or buried because we don't want
to remember them. My mind is filled with so many thoughts.
Only in writing do I seem to be able to quell the anxiety that
has overtaken me. Earlier in the day a scholar from Brown
quoted from the child psychologist, D. W. Winnicott, that the
poet, like the child, needs "a field of privacy to rest where the
self cannot be exploited." The idea of the lecture was about
the tension between the need to communicate and the need
to remain hidden. Fascinating.

May 10, 2002

It is only my sixth day in Paris, but the richness of emotions
it has inspired makes it seem an eternity. John Cloud gave an
astonishing lecture on Keats this morning. I sat in the first
few rows and was in awe of his intelligence. His calm yet
arresting demeanor. He lectured on "Endymion." He read the
poem in its entirety first, and hearing those first lines again
sent a chill down my spine. He quoted Keats, who said he
wanted in the long poem to capture the moment when the
imagination is healthy but the soul is in "ferment, the
character undecided, the way of life uncertain." After the
lecture I thought about what he'd inferred about the
Romantics. Whether indeed anxiety was born out of desire
in need of being expressed.

I climbed half the Eiffel Tower with Dan after the lecture
and then escaped back to my room for a short break (he
wanted to go out for cocktails! And it's not yet noon). When I
looked down at the Champs-Elysée I felt as if my life was still
waiting to unfold. While climbing the steps I thought about

the boys and how much they would have liked to climb them. How Noah would have raced to the top. I bought them postcards and snow globes with the tower inside. I thought of the people I love who are no longer in my life. Is it because I am alone and away from home that I reflect on these things?

I dreamed about my father last night. In Paris even my dreams are rich. Dramatic. I woke with the desire to record the dream, but I haven't had time until now. I haven't thought about him intensely in years. In my dream he appeared almost like a suitor. He was the father I remembered from my childhood. He looked innocent and sweet and vulnerable and not yet beaten down by the world. We were together in a boat and my father was rowing me down the river and it was a beautiful day and along the river a line of clapboard houses glowed pink in the rising sun. The stillness of the morning rested on the top of the water. The trees—oaks and huge maples, beeches and sycamores—bent toward us in their entire intricate splendor. They formed a kind of avenue as the rowboat passed, and their leaves sailed slowly into the air and onto the surface in ones and twos. As the sun rose, the clouds parted. In the dream it was hot and I unbuttoned the first buttons on my blouse. My father smiled at me as if I were a cherished object, as if he adored me. The dream seemed to happen in slow motion. I could feel my father looking at me with adoration, and it created a sensation of warmth and safety inside. The dream brought back what my father told me about his own childhood. I remember a line from Tolstoy. "Happiness is given to me from the beginning, drunk with my mother's milk." I knew as a child that I was loved. That I was cherished. It is what has sustained me. Even after my father left, I knew it. "This is what it was like in the old country," my father said, in the dream. "There were trees and forests, Eleanor. You could run forever in the forests and never be afraid. My mother wore a scarf around her beautiful hair so it wouldn't get caught in the wind." Or were those words he once told me that I've only attributed to my dream? Do people speak to us in dreams?

In the dream my body filled with the warmth of his eyes, with his love, and when I awoke I was bereft, so lost, it was as if I were in the middle of the river in that very boat, alone without a paddle. I didn't want to get out of bed.

Writing this I remember in detail the last time I saw my father, and it is essential I write it down. Not to forget. I'm afraid of all the things I've already forgotten, of all the moments I've cherished or that have disturbed or provoked me that I won't remember. It's been too painful until now. Strange how strong memories are. We were at the airport. Daddy was on his way to Europe. It was the first time he let me meet one of his girlfriends. He sent me letters describing them in detail, but he kept them all away from me. He was making a connecting flight. Her name was Gina. She was sexual and too young for him, and her presence startled me. I felt as if I were years older than she was, though I'm sure I was wrong. My father had that stupid, sheepish, I-can't-help-who-I-am look on his face, the look that said *I know what I've done to you, I know what I've done to your mother. I know I'm weak.* I wanted to hug him. He called a week before and asked me if I would bring Nicholas and the baby. Why did he want to meet his grandsons in an airport before connecting flights? Was it so he could quickly disappear

again? I remember when he called to tell me he wasn't
coming to Nicholas's bris. *Daddy, do you know what the word
means? It means covenant,* I wanted to say. *You're missing the
ceremony of the day my son forms his covenant with God.* But
I said nothing. I didn't want to alienate him or hurt him. I
knew he knew he was disappointing me. Michael says that I
expect too much from people. "Look at it from your father's
side. He's scared, Eleanor. Can't you see that? He knows
he's failed you and he doesn't know how to fix it. He isn't
capable of fixing it." Michael's right. He's sensible about
these things—it makes me hate him. I want him to rage
against my father.

   I remember that the morning I went to see my father at
the airport I bundled up my son. It was winter. January. I put
a few diapers and bottles in my purse, hailed a cab, and we
went to LaGuardia. I thought about pulling Nicholas out of
school, but I decided against it. How would I explain it to
his teacher? His grandfather will only see him in airports
between connecting flights? My father and Gina were
waiting for us at the United Airlines VIP lounge. My father
was drinking scotch on the rocks. His eyes were watery.
Daddy, it's the middle of the morning, I wanted to say. *Daddy,
it's not even noon.* I looked at Gina, and I wanted to say,
What are you doing, letting him drink at this time in the morning?
He looked smaller. Slightly hunched over. There was a
light brush of whiskers on his chin and underneath his
cheekbones. He hadn't shaved. Gina was sipping white wine
and smoking. She was wearing tan panty hose. They looked
cheap. "I know what you're thinking," my father said when
Gina excused herself to powder her nose. "'She's a shiksa. My
father only dates non-Jews.' You don't have to say it. She's
nothing like your mother, Eleanor. She's happy all the time.

Have you ever been around happiness, Eleanor? It makes you
feel as if you have to be near it all the time or it will vanish.
It's like a butterfly you chase but can't capture." Gina was in
love with my father. It was written all over her face. She was
bragging about him, telling me about the companies he was
looking to invest in. I've heard about these companies all my
life. Companies that manufacture water filters, a company
advertising for space in airports, a company involved in
herbal teas. I nodded. I looked at my father's hands. What
happened? How did he lose his ambition for his music? How
does that happen to a person? Once I asked why he never
played anymore. He said it awakened too much desire. He
has so few pleasures other than drinking and women and
even now those pleasures seem like curses to him, as if he is
destroying himself further with his pleasures. I thought his
music would save him, but I was wrong. How much do I
really know about my father? I remember that Noah was
asleep in his Snuggli on my chest. I noticed that my father's
hand (his fingers still long and elegant and well taken care
of) was on Gina's thigh and Gina was laughing. The drinks
made them happy. They were going to Amsterdam. My
father was checking out a small music publisher of some
sort. Gina had never been to Europe. I wanted to remind my
father that he had never taken me to Europe, though he had
promised he would several times. "Eleanor," my father said.
"Look at you." Quickly I saw myself take to him again, saw
myself become protective and possessive. When he embraced
me, I smelled the smell of my father and I felt myself slide
into it. I was nearly in love with him, forgetting all his faults
and failings.

Noah woke up. I took him out of the harness. My father
stared at him. His eyes watered. They were smiling and

crying at the same time. His look said, *This is what you're running away from, you shmuck. This beautiful baby. This life.* He hunched over. He was a mess. He took out his handkerchief and patted the perspiration from his forehead. He could not hold my son in his arms.

I've never really ever understood my father. I need to remember so I have a story about their grandfather I can tell to my children. If I think about him too long I want to cry.

The anger always began once he left, when I realized that I might not hear from him for months, maybe years on end. It rose inside me like a wave. It took me weeks to recover. In my mind I recalled everything he said and didn't say. I realized that for him once we'd parted, he'd fall back into his life. That he had learned how to tuck his fatherly instincts away.

Now that I've recorded the dream, I don't want to think about him anymore. I want to go back outside and walk along the Seine and then stop in an outdoor café and have an espresso and feel the pulse of the city surround me. I want to hold my sons in my arms. I wonder, is it the act of writing itself that releases so many memories?

Later I'm going to hear a lecture on Shakespeare titled "The Tragedy of the Human Soul."

May 11, 2002

It is 11:00 in the morning in Paris. I've just left the Louvre with John. We stood in front of a painting by Delacroix, the wonderful, complicated *The Baroque of Dante*.

Adam loved Delacroix's work. He was moved by the somber, dramatic use of the canvas and the dense execution he said was borrowed from Michelangelo or Rubens. He told me it was that kind of painting that could make you want to give up your career as a painter. Delacroix was only 24 when he painted it. It was wonderful to finally see it, instead of seeing the reproduction in a book. John and I sat on a bench together and looked at it. In the painting the tender hand of Virgil is leading Dante through hell as the damned souls of the Florentines writhe in the water, struggling to get into the boat. John saw Delacroix's work as an absolute manifesto of Romanticism. The poet leading Dante through darkness. I thought as I looked at the painting that at some point in life we all have to journey through the past to reclaim our future.

"What is your darkness?" John asked. I've only known him for a few days, but it seems as if we've known each other longer. *My father*, I wanted to say, but I kept quiet.

———

In spite of not wanting to think about him any longer, my father has been with me all morning. Something about that last dream. Do children always carry the pain of their parents? It was my father, in fact, who—though he would certainly have no knowledge of it—sealed my fate with Adam. I met my father at a bar shortly after the Christmas Adam had given me the black pearl necklace. It was one of his rare visits in New York. I hadn't seen him in two years. He was in town for a meeting and wanted to take me to dinner. I put on a nice dress and heels and the black pearls and met him at Tavern on the Green—he loves expensive restaurants, expensive hotels, expensive suits. He wore gold cuff links. He was waiting for me at the bar having a cocktail (when wasn't he having a cocktail?). He told you things you didn't want to know when he drank, details about his girlfriends, which ones he walked out on, which ones made him feel good, that sort of thing. I had no idea how long he had been sitting in the bar when I walked in. He was distracted. "Eleanor," he said, when he saw me. "You've grown up." I sat next to him and he ordered me a Kir Royale. He told me the best Kir Royale he ever had was in Paris in Harry's Bar. Perhaps I'll have to go to Harry's and have one in honor of my father. If you hadn't known we were father and daughter you would think we were two people, maybe even a couple, slightly in love. We were going to have dinner, and my father was going to take me to the philharmonic. I rarely went to concerts. I couldn't afford them and I was delighted. But shortly after I sat down at the bar he explained that we couldn't have dinner after all, something had come up; he had to take the 9:00 plane back to Miami. I tried not to look disappointed. No matter what, he was going to get up in a few minutes and leave and I didn't know when I'd see him again. He asked me about my mother. "I see her when I look at you," he said. He always asks about her but he never has the patience to hear how she is. He touched my hair. He fingered my pearls. He touched the skin on my wrists. He asked me if I was in love. William and I had broken up. There was no one and I said so. I didn't want to talk to him about Adam. He told me that my face was glowing. That he didn't believe me; there must be someone. He was distracted. He played with a book of matches. He asked me what I was doing over the summer. He told me that he could tell I was happy. That he'd done the right thing by leaving us. "I'll take you to the south of France. We'll rent a house, anything you want," he said. "You'll come. Everything will be fine. I'm going to rent a piano. I'm going to go back to my music. We still have our chance. See, it's okay," he said, touching my hair and squeezing my hand a little too forcefully, like he always did every time he saw me.

He was between girlfriends. He always looked slightly unhinged when there wasn't a steady woman in his life. He was wearing an elegant navy suit with a paisley tie and a crisp shirt. Daddy always dresses beautifully, no matter if he'd just lost his shirt in a business deal. But his eyes had that sad look in them. His face made me want to take care of him.

I was worried about him. I was afraid he was in debt again or had nowhere to go. I remembered how my mother told me how she'd learned they were in debt. She had gone to use one of her credit cards and it wouldn't go through. She went to the bank to withdraw some cash from their account and discovered that everything was gone. Daddy hadn't a penny to his name, only our house that he'd saddled with a second mortgage. My mother was furious that he hadn't told her how bad off they were; apparently he'd lied about things not even worth lying about and things he shouldn't have lied about. How he used one loan to pay off another or how when he said he was working late he was in another woman's apartment having a cocktail. He was into grandiose schemes and investments. His philosophy was that if you threw enough darts against a wall eventually one would stick. My mother said she would forgive him. They'd start over again. He could teach piano lessons. She didn't care. It was okay. She understood. "I don't want you to understand," she told me Daddy said.

Before he left me at the bar of Tavern on the Green he reached in his pocket and handed me two $100 bills and said he'd plan that trip to France. (There was never a trip.) He looked tired. I asked him if he was eating. "Look at me," he said. "Is this a face you have to worry about? Lighten up, Eleanor. Don't be so serious." He reached back into his wallet and left a few bills at the bar. "Men don't like it when women fuss all over them," he said. "Daddy, it's okay," I said. "No, it's not okay, Eleanor. None of it's okay."

He lifted my chin up to his face the way he had done when I was a little girl. I thought about the story he had told me about his parents in Hungary, about how he'd lost everything, how his entire childhood was wiped out, erased. He planted a kiss on my forehead. "Daddy," I said. "No, Eleanor." "Daddy," I said again. "Please." I told myself that maybe something really had come up and he had to get back to Miami. How would I ever know? How would I know anything about his life? He didn't ask me about school, about how I was getting along in New York. *Daddy*, I wanted to say, *look at me.*

Only in writing this am I making all the connections. I miss my boys but I'm glad I'm here on my own and have the time to write. It's a beautiful day in Paris. I've just been to the

Louvre. And still I can't forget my father. The memories keep unfolding.

It was after I saw my father that I felt a burning desire to see Adam. I felt if I didn't see him I couldn't exist, the desire was that powerful. After Daddy left I stayed at the bar and ordered another drink. Most of the clientele at the bar were older men, my father's age. It wasn't a young person's place. A man sat next to me. His hair receded on each side of his face, making an island in the middle of his forehead. He wore shiny gold jewelry, a thick bracelet around his wrist, the same color gold square ring on his left hand, and a similar ring with a diamond on his pinky finger. I let him buy me another drink and listened and laughed when I was supposed to, though I don't remember really listening. I heard the quality of his voice but not the words he was saying. As the evening wore on he touched my arm when he spoke to me. I excused myself to find the ladies' room and went down the back staircase. I took a coin out of my pocket, put it in the pay phone, and dialed Adam's number. Mariana answered. My heart jumped, but it was too late to hang up. I asked for him. Her voice was icy. She said he wasn't home. That he was rarely home. She asked me not to call there again. I went back upstairs and thanked the man who had bought me a drink and left the tavern. I began walking uptown to my apartment and then I turned around and decided to take a cab to Adam's studio. I was a little wasted from the drinks, but I knew what I was doing. I thought about Mariana sitting in her apartment. I thought about her petite, heart-shaped face. She was an exile from another country and Adam was the reason she was in America. He had gone to Romania on a Fulbright. Some of his paintings were being shown in Prague, and he took advantage and decided to look up a Romanian painter whose work he admired. He met Mariana and they

fell in love and she came back with him to the States
and eventually got a job at Yale. The country was under
Communist rule then. I think it must have appealed to the
romantic in him, saving a woman from the cruelty of a
regime, giving her hope in a new world, the cruelty of a new
regime (his). I thought about Mariana and Adam in the cab,
but my own desires and needs were more important. Thinking
about Mariana seemed to fuel my urgency to see Adam.

How did Mariana know it was me on the phone? We had
never spoken. My stomach was queasy. I remembered how
titillated I grew in his studio just a few days before, when he
unbuttoned my blouse and kissed me—the almost sandpapery
imprint of his lips on my own. I took off my leather gloves
and brought my fingers to my lips, leaned my head back
against the seat, and wanted him to kiss me again.

He told me he was in love with me that day. He told
me that I was all he thought about. That my innocence was
refreshing. I'm not sure I believed him. He sat down next to
me on the daybed and we kissed and I let him hold me. "I
fantasize about you," he said. The thought felt private and
seductive and it half thrilled me and half made me ashamed.
Was I in love with him? I always thought I was still in love
with William, that William would be the only boy I could
ever love, that I was still saving myself for him.

In the cab ride I thought about being in the studio with
Adam. I thought about how I listened as Adam explained to
me his relationship to art. How painting was all about light.
"You must learn to watch for it," he said. "How it brightens
and withdraws and changes direction. Learn about it when
you wake up in the morning. When you are eating your
breakfast, getting dressed. You learn to know how it will
make you feel and whether you can enter the dream of it
when you work. Whether it will be good for penetrating

inside." I liked being in the light under Adam's watchful gaze.
I thought about how everything he did was passionate, even
the way he reached for an orange in a bowl on the table and
peeled it open and the room filled with the intense, fresh
scent. He detached one segment from the orange and popped
it in his mouth, and as I watched, I could taste the juice in my
mouth. He took another slice in his hand and fed it to me,
and I tasted the orange on his finger on my lips.

In the cab I thought about the quality of his voice, the
inflections as he spoke. I remembered the last time I had been
with him. I looked at his fingers, his calloused, brutal-looking
hands. He had kissed my neck, lifted up my blouse to stroke
my bare skin, and I was irritated by the softness with which
he approached me. I knew I had to be very careful around
him, that I had to be sure of myself, and I wasn't sure at all
what I was doing or even if I wanted to sleep with him. His
touch was like the feel of sand on my skin at the beach. I
rose. I was going to be late for class. I told him I couldn't do
it. I left Adam's studio filled with nostalgia for something I
could not claim. Once I was in class I heard his words again.
"I've been looking at the spot above your breasts all night,
just this one tender spot," he had said and then he kissed my
chest lightly with his lips. I wondered if I had made a mistake
by saying no. If I'd ever have the chance again, and the
thought preoccupied and disturbed me.

When I returned home that evening there were three
messages on my machine. All of them were from Adam. He
had to see me again. He couldn't work. I was all that he
thought about. In the last message he said it wasn't fair, that
I was torturing him. *But you're married. You're the reason*, I
thought and even as I thought it a part of me questioned my
own logic. I did want Adam, but he was married. I didn't
understand what it meant. But after I had drinks with my

father at Tavern on the Green, I was overcome with a burning compulsion to see Adam again, and in the cab I was overcome with anxiety. I had not seen him in a week. I couldn't see anything else in front of me. Images of my father sitting at the bar, holding his scotch, the glass sweating on the cocktail napkin, stayed with me and I wanted to forget them.

When I arrived at his studio it was nearly 11:00 in the evening. "Balthus said 'to paint is not to represent, but to penetrate, to go to the heart of the secret,'" Adam whispered in my ear. Jesus, fucking God, who cared about Balthus? I wanted him to undress me. Adam was on top of me, kissing me. I wanted him to bear his weight over me so that I could no longer see any object in the room. I did not want him to be gentle, I wanted him to be brutal and I told him so. He hadn't shaved in a few days and I felt the coarseness of the bristles on my skin when he kissed my neck. "Harder," I said. I was still struggling with the fact that he was married, and the struggle was part of the way that we made love. I felt him touch me everywhere, how eager he was to work his hands and face and tongue over every part of my body. I didn't touch him back. I only kissed him. I wanted him to do whatever he wanted with me. It was very seductive to be made love to that way, to give up all control; it seemed that I had spent so much of my life trying to control my emotions. He spoke in one long litany about how long he had waited, how long he wanted me, and I was wrapped inside every word. I had the ridiculous notion that I could stay there forever, that there would be no light the next morning to draw me out, reminding me of those we had betrayed.

After that night I was even more conscious of how I had become an object in one of his paintings that he wanted to pore over and turn into something of his own. It was

seductive to be studied so closely. I thought I would learn
something about the way that a man could love a woman
by studying Adam's obsession with me. I did not understand
that love can also objectify. When I began modeling for
Adam I was twenty-three, in my first year of grad school.
He seemed fascinated with me in the same way Balthus was
fascinated with prepubescent adolescent girls. Adam studied
what I wore daily, when I came to model for him, as if to see
what he might steal for his work, what might enhance his
compositions. As a candidate for a doctorate of literature I
understood that nearly every subject, every theme had been
appropriated by writers. Love, betrayal, death, loss—it was
all already explored, pummeled, dissected. It was the way
in which each writer imbued his subject with his own
personality and voice and originality that made a work of
art singular. I suspected the same was true of painting. I had
no idea how he saw me until he allowed me to look at the
series he was working on. He worked on four or five canvases
at once, and when he first exposed the work to me it was
disconcerting to see my image distorted in those canvases. He
saw me as innocent, as a young woman covering up her own
sexual appeal. Was that who I was? Am I still that?

 In the first canvas I was wearing a white blouse buttoned
to the neck, the kind of blouse a schoolgirl would wear as
part of her uniform. I often wore a pair of shoes that looked
like black ballet slippers, and he had included those shoes in
the painting, had intensified them by his use of brushwork
and light so that the eye immediately fell to the shoes. It was
as if the girl in the painting (me) was trapped in the wardrobe
of an adolescent, and yet, unlike the girls in Balthus's work,
the girl in the painting was shapely. Underneath the painted
white blouse you could see the shape of her breasts and their
erect nipples. It unhinged me to look at the painting, at the

woman who was me, and not me at all, and after we had slept together, I looked at Adam differently. I was looking to understand myself in his work. I was uptight, nervous, I trusted no one. I watched how he painted, saw the intensity and frustration he brought to his work, witnessed his patience and concentration. When he was frustrated he snapped at me and accused me of purposely trying to sabotage his work if I were fidgety or lacked concentration. He said that if I did not learn to sit still I wasn't to come back, that he would find a new model to make famous.

It was from Adam that I learned that no matter what happened, what he had lost or suffered, it would eventually be translated into his work. To create, one had to live fearlessly. What does that mean? Have I been living fearlessly?

I thought of Adam as a person of great power and of myself as sensitive and intelligent, but was not yet certain what I would be able to achieve in my work. I admired Adam's singular vision. He was going to paint no matter what the cost. It possessed him more than anything. Was I like that? Am I still?

I remember all this sitting under the beautiful Parisian sun, with the modern sculpture in the courtyard that looks like a jungle gym. Thinking about it, about Adam and my father, has freed me somehow. What if I had never come to Paris? Would I have remembered it all? Is memory a blessing or a curse?

May 12, 2002

At the Louvre yesterday I was enchanted by a painting by Correggio, *Venus, Satyr and Cupid*. Correggio bathes his bodies in a glowing light. The bodies are soft and sensual. He catches Venus in a state of pure abandonment, a symbol of carnal love. I remember looking at the painting with John, and my entire body blushed. The painting brought tears to my eyes. I put the postcard of the painting by my bedside, and it is the first thing I saw when I awoke.

It's 7:00 A.M. The light is just barely touching my window. Today I present the paper. I'm suddenly nervous. I've worked on it for months; the *Yale Review* has accepted it for publication. But when I think about the paper's thesis, I'm unsure. By choosing Levin as the hero of the book, have I been too harsh on Anna and the passion she represents? Is it because I witnessed what my father's leaving did to my mother? Because of how much both of us suffered? Is it because of my own past mistakes, when I could not control my own passions, that I sympathize with Levin's moral view of love? I'm stricken with remorse, as if I've betrayed a dear relative, a friend, or a lover. Yes, Levin's wholesome love for Kitty is wonderful. But have I discounted Anna's depth of feeling?

I looked out the window. The breeze carried with it little tufts from the blooming linden trees. Their potent smell has overpowered all else. I showered, dressed, drank my coffee,

and ate the croissant I had ordered up to the room, still filled
with unease. Why?

I just got off the phone. I hadn't expected a phone call
so early. I assumed it was John or Robert or Julie asking if I
wanted to walk over to the Sorbonne.

But I was wrong.

It was Stephen Mason. I'm stunned. I hadn't really
thought he would call. My palms are damp. "Eleanor, is that
you? I didn't want to miss you," he said. His voice was thick
and raspy. It has not changed.

I look at the small clock on the nightstand. Study the
hands slowly ticking off the seconds. Time marches on. It is
8:00 o'clock in the morning.

"I can see your hotel from where I'm staying, Eleanor. It
reminds me of when we were kids and I could see into your
bedroom window." Hearing his voice transported me to when
we were kids. *I didn't feel anything inside me when the playhouse
burned. It took away all my feelings. Do you ever feel so much you
think you can't breathe?*

Had I awoken a half hour earlier I would already have
been out the door, on the way to the Sorbonne.

We agreed to meet tomorrow for a late lunch. Once I
heard his voice it was impossible to say no. He said he's in
Paris writing a travel piece and that he planned to spend the
day at the Louvre. I feel a peculiar mix of excitement and
anticipation. Am I making a mistake by agreeing to see him?
How strange to be in Paris at the same time. I'm sure it is the
sheer coincidence of being so far from home in a foreign city
that prompted Stephen to call after all these years. I tell
myself that there is no harm in seeing an old friend from
home. But I can't help wonder why he wants to see me now

and why I have accepted the invitation. Is it because I still want to know what came between us so many years ago?

I have to brace myself. I want the presentation to go well. I don't want to think about anything else.

May 13, 2002, 2:00 A.M.

I want to record everything that happened today, though it is late and I'm tired and slightly intoxicated. It is as if a weight has been lifted off my shoulders. The paper went very well. Questions were asked, a heated debate ensued. Perhaps I had indeed read my own insecurities into the paper and that was why I had begun to doubt it. Apparently I am one of the only women not completely sympathetic to Anna. Helen Heifetz from Barnard defended me, saying that Anna was the embodiment of both good and evil but that Levin is ultimately the hero of the novel. He chooses the spiritual world over the carnal. Those who had disagreed seemed to be provoked by my presentation all the same. I'm still high from it all.

Not really thinking, I went to the window at the end of the hall and called Michael on my cell phone. It was 8:00 o'clock in the morning in New York. I knew he would be at the hospital doing morning rounds. He is usually cheerful in his doctor mode when I call him at work. You can hear the confidence and satisfaction he derives from his work, from the love and regard of his patients, in his voice. He asked me how it went. I told him that it went well. The audience seemed to love it. "Of course they did," he said. I don't know why I called him.

The comment seemed to dismiss the nervousness that I had expressed over presenting the paper and the days of toil that had gone into writing it, though I knew Michael wasn't trying to be smug. I heard in his voice that he was glad it had gone well, glad that it was over. I knew he was anxious to finish up. We never did well over the phone. I asked him about the boys and particularly about Noah. "Noah's fine," Michael said. "He isn't a baby anymore, Eleanor." The comment stung.

Noah is sensitive. I worry about him. He's particularly thin-skinned at school. There is a boy in his class named Joshua whom he worships. They had been inseparable for months, and then, out of the blue, Joshua stopped being friendly to Noah and began to hang out with another boy. Noah came home each day from school and gave me a report on it, on whether Joshua had played with him or not. The more Joshua ignored him, the more Noah longed for the boy's attention. I told Noah that children are fickle. That the best thing he could do was to ignore it, but he was completely obsessed. Then one day he was flying a kite in the park and stopped to unwind the string. He looked up at me and said, "Love is like a string attaching one person to another. If you cut the string it will be gone. You'll feel really bad." I asked him if he was talking about Joshua. He looked up at me strangely. "Joshua didn't cut the string," he said. "I did. Look at how high my kite is flying." He had found, completely on his own, a way of dealing with Joshua's rejection.

"You're still angry," I said to Michael, because I did not want to let the hostility I heard in his voice go by unmentioned. I told him that it was important that I came to the conference. That I was halfway across the world and anxious about my children. Michael apologized for snapping at me and reassured me the boys were fine. "Has it been hard on you, that I'm gone?" I said, more gently. I heard the

estrangement in his voice (*who are we when we are not together,
Eleanor?*), his need for me to detach from my own interests
and make him the focus. In his wish that the paper was
received well was also the wish that the paper did not matter,
because my world at home beside him and the children
should be paramount. And it did matter.

I was anxious to hang up. Even though a part of me
understood Michael's reaction, speaking to him had slightly
punctured the high of the lecture. There was a lunch. We
planned a trip to Notre Dame and a dinner that night.

My new friends in Paris are more able to appreciate what
I have accomplished, which makes me feel, perhaps falsely,
that we are close, though I know very little about any of
them, only the details I have gleaned from the days we have
spent together.

Did I call Michael because I subconsciously knew he
would be edgy, that he would make me feel that by pursuing
my own ambitions I'm somehow betraying him? Did I call
him so that out of anger at him I might allow myself to feel
less guilty?

Julie's loud. I didn't initially find myself at ease around
her. I wonder whether we'd be friends if we had not been
forced together in a foreign city, had she not known Jordan.
She is the kind of woman who feels more comfortable, closer,
with men. It makes sense that she and Jordan are friends. I
don't have the feeling that she has many close friendships
with women. It has taken us a few days to warm up to each
other. She and John knew each other in graduate school, and
I feel slightly left out of their more intimate rapport. When
we'd first met, both standing in line waiting for a cab, Julie
took a paperback, some trashy novel from her bag, and began
reading. I thought she was reading to avoid conversation, and

it took me a few attempts at small talk to get her to warm up. I wonder if my controlled exterior (my hair coiled back in a twist) threatens her, the fact that I have children. My life must look conventional and safe to her. I need to show her that I'm vulnerable, to make her feel less threatened. Unmarried women in their late thirties and forties can feel bitter and defensive around women who are married, even if they claim to not want to be married or to want children, and I sense that defense in Julie. Of course, married women are a little jealous of the freedom of unmarried ones. I asked her whether Dan had made his choice among the young assistant professors, meaning, had he staked out his girl for that night, and she laughed her deep, throaty laugh. I had broken the ice.

The five of us get on well, I'm convinced, because we're atypical academics. We bonded the first evening in Paris over a large table together at dinner. A discussion had ensued over a young scholar, Leo Swift, who had written a popular novel about Edith Wharton. Brenda Hedges called it rubbish. In the novel Swift adopted Wharton's style and tone. Brenda called it "faux Wharton." "My feeling is if you want to read Wharton, read Wharton," she argued. Julie jumped in. Apparently she knew Leo Swift and argued that it was a worthy creative effort. She loved the novel, and called it brilliant. She thought it a tribute to Wharton. "All good literature does not get written in a vacuum," she said, "Writers are constantly reinventing Chekov or Tolstoy or Dickens." John jumped into the argument to defend Julie. He, too, had known Leo from graduate school and thought he was exceedingly bright.

I was interested in the discussion because I've thought of writing a novel, a modern version of *Anna Karenina*, but I've been too consumed with the children and my teaching. I'm tired of academic papers. I'm hoping by recording these thoughts in my notebook I'll be more in touch with my vision and ideas for when I'm ready to write.

I told my new friends about the book I want to write and we talked about it at length, and I realized then that I had never articulated the desire to anyone, not even Michael, and just talking about the book made me feel as if I were acknowledging a lost part of myself.

John rubbed his chin in contemplation. He confessed that he was a closet poet. He had written poems for years, ever since college. I looked at him differently once he said it and had a desire to read some of his work. I suddenly wanted to understand something about John I thought would only materialize in his poems. We talked about what fueled an artist. I expressed my theory (not a new one, I'm afraid) that it was childhood trauma and loss; the need to re-create a lost world. Robert wondered whether genius was inherited, biologically based, that surely all of us had experienced some kind of trauma and yet we were not all artists. Dan said he wanted to get drunk. That's all he remembers wanting for as long as he can remember, and we laughed. "I went to graduate school for purely rebellious reasons," he said. Otherwise, he'd be stuck working in his father's law office. I brought up Elizabeth Bishop. Her father had died when she was eight or nine and then her mother had been institutionalized for mental illness. Julie reflected that Bishop's work was cold, technically perfect but devoid of feeling. "But it's repressed feeling. It's the tension between her desire to disclose and not disclose that makes her poems emotional," I said.

By the time we finished the first bottle of wine, I began to feel tired, but I didn't want to go up to the room yet. We had moved our party to the hotel bar by then. A few minutes later our conversation was interrupted by a Tolstoy scholar, Professor Talbot, chairman of the Comp Lit Department at UCLA. Apparently, the fire I had witnessed in my room that first day might have been an act of terrorism by an as-yet unidentified group. The fears that had mounted since 9/11 came back instantly. We stayed up drinking. None of us wanted to be alone.

I remembered the fire, how it consumed the apartment across the way, and I thought that none of us were ever safe, that our lives were threatened daily by forces we couldn't control, and the best we could do was to find serenity in the moment. I longed to hold my sons, to make sure that they were safe.

I tried not to think about the strained conversation I'd had with Michael after I'd given the presentation. I'm in Paris, for God's sake. We're all tighter having spent many nights together. More relaxed in each other's company. The erotic tension between all of us is visceral. Julie has been flirting with John since our adventure at Notre Dame. Robert continues to stare at me. I felt him watching me when I was talking to John and Julie, looking at me when I sipped my wine. Is he waiting for a signal? What does he want from me? "It's always the woman who makes the first move," Jordan had once told me. Robert is sweet, but even if I were single, I'm not really interested in him in that way. What am I talking about? Of course I'm not.

Robert said my paper hit on something personal for him.

We talked about love and the idea that the self cannot be complete unless someone reflects who you are back to you, unless you've established that deep connection. Otherwise we are alienated, unknown to ourselves. As he spoke I thought about the earlier conversation I'd had with John about Keats's longing for a feminine counterpart in the poem "Endymion."

Robert asked if passion makes us stronger or whether it diminishes us.

"Eleanor and Rob are getting too serious," Dan said. "Would someone pour them another glass of wine? Passion gets me into trouble," he said. "That's as deep as it gets." Quite frankly, I was relieved. Robert's direct questioning made me uncomfortable. Again, I had begun to feel that there was something incomplete about my paper, and I wanted to forget it.

All evening I watched how Robert had attempted to control himself. Earlier in the evening after one or two drinks, he tried to abstain from drinking more. At one point he said he was tired, yawned, and remarked that he should go up to his room. It was close to midnight by then. Dan pleaded for him to stay for another drink. An hour or so later I saw him look at his watch again, noticed the ambivalence in his face because I felt the same way, pulled between two poles. Had he been thinking of his wife? Her name was Claire. She was a professor of anthropology at Rutgers, where they both taught. Robert had described her as quiet. "She's British, you know. She has no needs."

"Does passion make us stronger or does it fuck us up?" Robert asked again. The more he seemed to drink, the darker and more serious his countenance. "Come on, Eleanor, I need to know." He was drunk. "Claire and I went to college together," he explained about his wife. He said she was the first person he fell in love with. "Does that mean I'm supposed to feel passionate about her forever?"

I looked at Robert and told him that my paper was about a novel. I told him that when it came to real life I was in the dark.

I wondered whether Robert wanted to kiss me.

We stayed out late drinking, went dancing, and then resumed the party in Robert's hotel room. The quiet and claustrophobia—the hotel rooms are so small in Europe—inside Robert's room made me tired. Dan brought along a young grad student he had met at the disco. She was French. Her name was Genevieve. She had danced in a little circle by herself, enraptured with her own body. The two of them sat in one chair The rest of us were sitting around a small table. I felt the same feeling of discomfort I'd experienced the first time we went out drinking together, but this time I felt closer to the group, more connected, and I tried to relax. John had pulled the desk chair forward. After a scotch, Dan and Genevieve began to kiss in the chair, then got up and said goodnight. I was slightly envious of their ability to be intimate in front of others, showing that desire isn't something to be ashamed of. John said he didn't think we'd be seeing Dan at breakfast, and we all smiled.

I moved to sit at the edge of the bed. Robert got up and lay down on the bed beside me. He asked if we minded if he turned off the lights. We could crash on the queen bed, if we wanted to. I thought I should go to my room but I didn't want to be alone. John rose and said he should get to bed, and then he poured himself another finger of scotch, fell back down on the bed, and closed his eyes. His body was next to mine and if I had been single I might have reached out to touch him.

Earlier in the night at the disco I had watched John as he sat uncomfortably at the bar, drinking a glass of beer and smoking while the rest of us danced. His eyes followed me as

I began to loosen up on the dance floor. I could see in the way he looked at me that he wanted to relinquish himself, to let go, but he couldn't. He was caged inside himself. I understood it. I was usually too uptight to let myself go, but it was the combination of the excitement of the paper and being in Paris among no one who really knew me that released me. Later I joined John at the bar and tried to start a conversation (I hated to think of him alone, alien to himself, drinking more to estrange him further from the world) but the music was too loud, and I was grateful not to have to try too hard. I felt strangely as if I had deserted him by dancing, that we had served a certain role for each other—we were the two older, wiser onlookers in the group and I was breaking the rules.

Julie watched as John rose to leave and I saw a grimace of disappointment in her face. And then her face relaxed when he lay back down. She filled the water glass that had been in Robert's bathroom with another ounce of scotch. She lay down on the bed and began talking about a man she had been involved with, the chair of her department. She told us he was married. They'd slept together a few times and then he began seeing a graduate student and she had to go on pretending it didn't bother her, seeing him in faculty meetings, running into him in the department office. Robert suggested she go on the job market.

"And let that fucker ruin my career? Let him win?" She took a sip of her scotch and looked back at us. Her eyes moistened. "I'm still in love with him," she remarked. Her voice quivered. She cast her eyes down and sank into a private place within herself. We all grew silent. "It's so stupid," she said.

By then the mood had shifted, as if the intoxication of the night only seemed to show us how we had longed to let

go and now we were returning back to ourselves, alone and
separate.

After Julie revealed that she was in love with her
chair, I thought of her differently. She'll never marry.
She'll always see herself as a seductress, the other woman to
a man. She had fallen into the role and it had come to define
her personality. It was too late. She did not know how to
re-create herself apart from being a woman who had been
disappointed. I thought about how helpless we are to change.
How our ways of being get hardwired into our personalities.

To offer comfort I confessed to a time I had been with a
married man, with Adam, and saying it out loud, it occurred
to me that I had never told anyone about the affair before,
that it had dwelled inside me, had become almost dormant,
like a silent child living within me. At that time I had told
myself that Adam and Mariana had been unhappy, otherwise
he would never have fallen in love with me. I blamed Adam
for what had happened between us. After the affair had
started, something had shifted between Adam and myself that
needed to run its course. No matter how often over the years I
had dismissed Adam's infatuation with me as a middle-aged
obsession, no matter how much I had denied the truth of my
own feelings for him, of how I had damaged his marriage,
we had shared a real connection. By revealing the affair to
Robert, John, and Julie I was suddenly exposed to them as
a complicated, compelling woman and not the woman I
appeared to be on the surface. The mature, settled wife and
mother, the academic. Something has been brewing inside
me and I can't look away from it any longer: I see myself as I
truly am, rife with deep, complicated desires, a woman who
might never be fully content, who will always want more
attention, more connection and adventure. I see that I have
married a less complicated man not only because it allows me

to be whoever I want but maybe because it scares me less to
be around someone who will never really understand me. I
want to discount the thought, to stuff it away where my other
uncomfortable thoughts live. But it is no longer possible.

I took another sip of the scotch. The liquor burned my
throat as it went down. I looked at the three of them. I feared
I had let loose something in my personality, that I had said
too much and that in the morning when I saw them at
breakfast I would not be able to look any of them in the eye.
None of us would be able to. We had revealed too much of
ourselves and we could not take back what we saw. Robert
also made a confession. His father was sexually compulsive.
He had slept with women he didn't know, women he'd pick
up in bars, in restaurants, in hotel lobbies. He said his father
confessed about it when he left his mother. Robert said he
felt the compulsion. He worried that he had married too
young. He married his first girlfriend. He loved her. He
couldn't imagine his life without her, but he constantly
looked at other women. He'd had a flirtation with a young
professor in his department, but it had ended badly. The
woman had grown tired of it. The relationship had reached
beyond the level of flirtation and Robert had been afraid to
take it one step further and the woman had accused him of
leading her on.

"Maybe you're really in love with your wife and you're
afraid," I offered as counsel. "Maybe you're afraid of real
intimacy. Maybe what we think of as too familiar is really
too intimate?" I said. Or something to that effect.

"Maybe intimacy and sex are incompatible," Julie argued,
in her deep, hoarse, woman-of-the-world voice. She had
taken off her boots. Her feet with her painted toenails
underneath their sheer stockings, slightly crinkled from
her boots, looked exposed.

"Maybe I just don't want to fuck my wife," Robert said.

"I've never fucked a man I've respected or even liked," Julie said, rolling on her side. I like how she says what's on her mind. How definitive she is. "They're all assholes." We laughed. We doubled over and laughed until we cried.

"I just want to get fucked," Robert said. "I'm a guy, aren't I?"

We laughed harder. Once our laughter died out, silence fell over the room. I looked at Robert and I saw what he was thinking. There was a glint of relief in his eye. The moment had passed. We were four friends again. We wanted to imagine that we might seduce each other, pair off, whatever people did at conferences away from their spouses and loved ones, but we were impotent to carry it out. Julie yawned. "I'm out of here," she said. "We'd better get a few hours of sleep or we'll be ruined tomorrow."

John rolled over and moaned.

I picked up my bag from the chair where I had left it and said goodnight to Robert and gave him a light hug. I kissed John on the cheek. I unlocked the room with my key, took off my clothes, and slipped into bed without washing up or brushing my teeth. The light had just begun to reveal itself, slowly, shyly, as if resisting the darkness. Once in bed I took out my notebook—how wonderfully clandestine it felt—and began to write this just before the light crested.

May 14, 2002

I awoke to the telephone ringing. My wake-up call. I was so tired I fell back to sleep. When I awoke again it was 11:00. I had arranged to meet Stephen for lunch at noon. I regretted wasting the morning in Paris lying in bed. Stephen was supposed to pick me up at the hotel. We planned to walk and then find a place to eat. I have not permitted myself to think about him since he called the day before, but I wonder as I write this whether the fact that I was supposed to see him had colored the entire evening. I asked room service to bring up a pot of coffee and a croissant and took a bath. A slight hangover dulled my head. I stayed in the bath, letting the spray from the hand-held nozzle pour down over my head until I felt revitalized. And as the warm water released the tension in my body, I began to cry. This extraordinary emotion (was it longing?) began days ago, and has been growing inside me all week, perhaps since I boarded the plane, increasing during the growing intimacy I have felt among my new friends. I'm writing this fully dressed now, staring at the clock, waiting until it is time for me to go downstairs to greet him. Why have I agreed to see Stephen? What does it matter what took place between us so many years ago? I tell myself to take Stephen at face value. Not to analyze his intentions. It isn't as if I've forgotten that a long time ago we had confided in one another, had revealed ourselves to each other. I simply don't want to indulge in those memories any longer. Whatever was between us happened years ago and has nothing to do with our present lives. And yet, the fact that my mother mentioned him to me the night before I was leaving had already set loose memories and sensations from my mind's dark corners. Is it the very fact of knowing I might see him that has allowed me to remember William and Adam so vividly?

How much have I changed since we had last seen each other? I put on lipstick, outlined the rim of my eyes with a thin line of eyeliner pencil, and brushed mascara on my eyelashes. I let loose some strands of hair from my barrette.

I changed outfits two or three times, trying on everything
I had packed, and then ended up wearing the one I had
started out with. I'm acting like a schoolgirl. I am no longer
a teenager (why do I still feel like one?) or even a woman
in her twenties. I am a thirty-eight-year-old mother who
has carried and birthed two children. The scar from the
caesarean section I'd had with Noah forms a smile on my
bikini line. When I touch it I remember the sensation of the
boys inside me before they were born. I still carry an extra
tuck of flesh in my tummy from the pregnancies. My hips
and breasts are bigger, my figure more womanly. But inside I
am still the young, impressionable girl from childhood. This
is what unnerves me. I wish I could concentrate on having
fun and enjoying reconnecting with an old friend. And yet,
I've never been the kind of person to just have fun.

Last entry, inside the cabin of Air France, #18,
en route to New York

The movie has begun and the flight attendants have returned
to their little kitchen in the back of the plane. The lights are
dim. Every passenger is either asleep, tucked into his or her
separate self, heads leaning against windows, or thrown back
against chairs, or behind headsets. It turns out that John and
Robert are on my flight. We are dispersed throughout the
cabin, and I'm grateful not to have to talk to anyone. The
airplane floor is a mess of fallen blankets and discarded
shoes. Before I return home I need to record my encounter
with Stephen. He's still taking up my energy, my serenity, my
space. I'm going to write our encounter exactly as I remember
it. So that no one can take it back.

———

When I saw Stephen standing outside the hotel lobby
waiting for me I almost didn't recognize him. His hair had
receded, revealing a wide forehead. As a boy he boasted a
mass of unruly, wavy hair, and when I looked at him it was
as if I could still see the crown of it surrounding him. His face
had something tender and angry about it. He wore a pendant
around his neck, in the shape of a cross. It was tucked under
a soft pale yellow shirt. He wore khakis and hiking boots.
He looked broader than I remembered, as if he had been
working out. I still pictured him as boyish, troubled, with
his motorcycle helmet in his hand. He was carrying a leather
backpack over one shoulder. I looked at his browned arms. He
looked youthful, though his hair was beginning to gray at his
sideburns. I don't want to admit that his physical presence
still unnerves me. But it does. He's gorgeous and still has
those penetrating, not quite knowable eyes. Is it vanity that
has been our sole attraction all these years? When he smiled,
I noticed that one of his two front teeth was chipped. When I
asked him about it later he said he was in a drunken brawl
over a girl, and that he'd lost the nerve in the tooth. He said
he didn't want to fix it. He wanted to remember the fact that
he still had it in him to fight for someone. His face lit up
when he spoke. He wore a gold stud in his left ear.

He embraced me when we said hello, and we stepped
back, looked at each other, smiled. "It's been a long time.
Eleanor, all grown up," he said.

We roamed the narrow streets together. It was a beautiful
day, and as we walked it was as if we were revisiting all the
paths and valleys where we had known each other, though
neither of us had to say it. Everything was in bloom. I could
look at him and not feel attracted to him, not be drawn into
his pain, to the little boy inside him who needed my comfort.

For a writer he seemed uncultured, not bookish (did he ever read?), though I was surprised as we walked how much of the history of the city he seemed to know. I felt myself getting caught up in his manic energy.

Stephen told me about the article that brought him to Paris. It was a piece on the rise of Napoleon for a new men's magazine that he described as a cross between *GQ* and *Rolling Stone*.

"Did you know that Napoleon was only thirty when he entered Paris and crowned himself Master of France?" he recounted, proud of his knowledge, as we walked along the Seine toward the Louvre. "He established peace with the Vatican and revived the entire city." As he spoke, he motioned with his hands. He was dramatic and theatrical. I caught the same look in his eye that he flashed as a boy when he sang "Eleanor Rigby." I was attracted to how passionate he was about his work. He spoke about it with confidence and maturity. I'm proud of him. He never finished college. He went for two years to the University of Colorado and dropped out. He wrote scripts and pieces for magazines and painted and built houses to make money. I'm glad that all his hard work seemed to be paying off, that he was now a respected journalist.

Occasionally, as we walked, our arms brushed. I almost tripped on the cobbled streets in my heels, and he reached for my arm to help me catch my balance.

"Eleanor Cahn!" he exclaimed. He stopped to look at me. "In fucking Paris." We both laughed.

He asked me if I remembered playing strip poker in his playhouse. He said something about my being leagues ahead of him, even then. He paused. He was clearly trying to revive our closeness. He turned me toward him dramatically. And then asked me whether I had any Kleenex in my purse.

I looked at him strangely. He said he just wanted to find out if I was still a babe. "Mothers always keep Kleenex in their purses. You know. To wipe the snot from their kid's nose."

I pulled out a purse-size box of Kleenex and showed it to him. "So if I'm a mother I can't be a babe?"

"You can, Eleanor."

I was certain it was a line he gave to many women. I was on to him. On guard.

Was it kismet or mere coincidence that we found ourselves in the most romantic city together? At one point my thumb reached for my wedding ring, and I shamefully turned the stone inside the palm of my hand. In Paris, at that very moment, I committed to taking him at face value. He was in Paris writing an article on Napoleon for a magazine, and this had nothing to do with me. It was as if I was meeting him for the first time, and I was simply drawn to his energy and creative nature. The attraction was still there. I was warm and slightly agitated in his presence. His physicality was bold and sexual. It was the first thing that defined him; that charged energy that I had felt and had pushed away the very first time we were alone together in my childhood bedroom when I was not yet thirteen.

He continued talking about his work, about the piece he was writing. His face lit up when he spoke. He was on his own, unattached. He could travel around the world if he wanted to. I had wanted to live in Europe after I finished graduate school. It represented longing and possibility, a kind of permanent hunger. I had wanted to spend my time with writers, painters, and musicians eating and drinking in cafés. I imagined living in a drafty artist's studio with a primitive kitchen, a table where none of the dining chairs matched, a

small desk to hold my portable typewriter. Paris represented
that lost possibility. What had changed all that? Was it
because of my mother's insular suburban existence, my
father's wayward life, that I had chosen the safe road and
married? Was it merely that I was face to face with someone
who had chosen a different path that made me question my
own? I took the barrette out of my hair and it came tumbling
to my shoulders. For a minute I wanted to stop in a doorway
of one of the apartment houses with the Parisian blue
shutters and knock on the red door, and like Alice in
Wonderland magically enter into its inhabitants' lives, go
down that tunnel and never return.

Why had my mother never remarried? Why had
Stephen's mother never remarried? Even my mother's friend,
Celia, who had enough money to travel the globe if she
wanted to, confined herself to her small but elegantly
decorated apartment. Occasionally my mother and her
friends fantasized about starting up a new life in a new city,
the way one can dream of one's future when one is inside a
prison, but by the end of a week or a month the fantasy
deflated into routine, weekend trips to the flea market,
dinners out every week. Since my father, there hadn't been
another man in my mother's life. Her headaches had been
getting worse. I finally had convinced her to go to the
Migraine Clinic. The last time I was home for a visit she told
me about it. We were sipping tea from her best china cups
in her kitchen. I remember looking at the missing button on
her cardigan. I remember thinking that my mother made
beautiful clothes for other women but she barely thought of
herself. She told me that the first appointment at the clinic
was with a psychiatrist. She said she told him about us.
About me and my father. She said she told him her headaches
were like a hammer banging inside her head. She had to

rate the pain on a pain scale of one to ten. She said they
fluctuated from an eight to a nine when they were at their
very worst. It was the first time my mother had ever talked
to a psychiatrist. "I was frightened," she said. "To bolster my
confidence I wrote little notes to myself on a piece of paper
I put in my pocketbook. 'You're beautiful,' I wrote in large
letters. On another I wrote, 'Joseph still loves you.' I didn't
want to forget. I didn't want to think my life has been a lie."

I looked at the missing button on her cardigan and said
nothing. Was it fantasy that sustained her all these years or
had my father's love been enough to fill her for a lifetime? I
told Stephen that I believed the hammer beating inside her
head was caused by her longing for my father. But to my
mother I had only asked if she knew she was missing a
button on her sweater. She thanked me. She said she didn't
ever want me to hide anything from her. She always wanted
to know the truth.

Before I left that day she opened my father's armoire
looking for the letters he had sent her. She wanted to read
one or two to me, as if to convince me that he still loved her.
She still kept his sweaters and clothes in the armoire, and
when she opened its drawers it was like his essence swept
into the room. A soft smile broadened on her lips and her
hand reached toward her cheek and she dreamily stroked her
face before a current of grief washed over her. She took out
of the envelope one of my father's letters and read it to me.
"Dear Elizabeth," one of the letters said. "I still remember the
first day we met. We were wandering in the garden outside
the music school. I can still remember the smell of your
shampoo."

I was filled with two contradictory thoughts. I wanted to
tell my mother that I understood. And I wanted to rage at her
for not having the courage to move on, for continuing to love

a man who could not give her what she needed. And these two contradictory emotions, I understand now, have defined all my own relationships, my desires. I doubt whether I have ever quite understood what it is that I need or want. I have always been too preoccupied trying to understand another person and what that person needs or wants to ensure that he will not leave me like my father did. Have I always been more comfortable in a state of resignation, like my mother? After being in Paris where everything around me was so alive, resignation no longer seems acceptable.

As we walked past the china shop with the pitcher in the window, I pointed it out to Stephen and we stopped and admired it. A wave of inexplicable fear washed over me as I studied the painted crocus buds. I was relieved when we continued walking.

Stephen seemed particularly careful of what information he divulged about himself, making sure, I thought, to paint the best picture. His rugged face was set in the expression of a combination of self-satisfaction and neediness. He seemed unsure and intimidated by me, but at the same time aggressively demanding. We walked side by side, and his arm brushed up against mine again. Our lives were again intertwining beyond my will, like strands of thread that formed a tough, unbreakable knot.

"I have to show you something," Stephen said. He took me to Sainte-Chapelle. In 1100 when Paris began to emerge as a great city, kings and bishops began building the churches, including Notre Dame. Sainte-Chapelle was completed in just two years. We waited in line looking at the exterior. I had read about the church in one of the guidebooks, and others at the conference had remarked that it was worth seeing, but from the outside the cathedral looked dim and ordinary.

We ascended the narrow spiral staircase used by the palace servants and entered the room with the fifteen stained-glass windows that glowed with Chartres blue, reds, and yellows. The walls consisted almost entirely of glass. I grasped Stephen's arm in astonishment. We sat down on one of the rickety wood chairs and looked around us at the panels on the glass that told the Christian story from the Garden of Eden through the apocalypse.

"I was here a few days ago and I was glued to the chair. I began to think how fundamental it all is. Adam and Eve. You know, the girl and the boy and desire. I've run from that my entire life."

I remarked that the artistry of the stained glass was astonishing.

"I'm not talking about art." He reached over so that he was looking directly into my eyes. "I wonder what it would be like to just stay with it. To not have to run away."

"From what?"

"We're the center of our own stories, Eleanor. You have to remember that."

At that moment what he said seemed to carry import. I found myself fascinated, drawn into his self-mythology. I looked up at one of the panels. It dramatized Eve alone in the garden and the serpent with the head of a man coiled around the tree holding out the apple, tempting her with forbidden knowledge. "What are you trying to say?"

"We only have one life, Eleanor."

"And?"

"You have to think about how you want to spend it. And who you want to be with."

He looked at me with that seductive, pleading look again.

I had the strangest feeling that he was trying to tell me something. Or had I imagined it? We sat quietly for a moment.

I thought now that I liked him better when he didn't talk. It seemed when he spoke that there was an agenda or subtext behind his words that I wasn't sure how to read. To lighten things up, I told him that I was glad I did not take a bite of the apple he offered me earlier, when we were waiting in line. He laughed.

The hairs on his arm almost touched my skin. We were sitting that close. His body radiated warmth like a furnace, and I felt as if we were inside a tiny jewel box with the windows all aglow. When the sun shone intensely the church was less gothic.

"I could sit here all day in the dark with you," Stephen said. "We could pretend it happened. That you and I are together."

We sat in silence and I pondered what he said, looked back at him, and we both smiled, in recognition of our past history coming more into focus.

After we left the church we settled in for lunch at a bistro with blue shutters on its open windows. I had been reluctant to sit face to face with Stephen, and when we sat down I studied the menu intently to avoid looking at him. The intensity between us made me uncomfortable. Then he looked at me. Said he couldn't do this. That he couldn't sit in a café with me on my last day in Paris. That it had to be more spectacular. He stood up and took my hand and asked me to follow him.

We left the café and stopped first at a wine and cheese store and then a market, and a butcher, all on the same street. Stephen bought garlic, peppers and tomatoes, and soft leaf lettuces; beef and sausages, fresh pasta, a loaf of peasant bread, wine, and cheese. He fondled one red apple after another from a pyramid of apples until he found four that

were to his liking. He took me to a drafty artist's studio that
he had rented for the month. In the main room was an old
pine table he used for a desk. On top were stacks of papers
and a laptop. I imagined him working at night at the desk,
his inspiration the grandness and history of the city. The
kitchen was tiny. I couldn't find the refrigerator. He cracked
open fat cloves of garlic, then chopped onions and sautéed
them with olive oil in an old rusted sauté pan. He made a
rich Bolognese sauce of such brilliance it smelled as ancient
as the city. He uncorked the bottle of wine and we drank
while I watched him cook. He moved around the kitchen
gracefully, theatrically. He tucked a dish towel into the waist
of his pants. I watched him chop the vegetables intensely,
but with precision, then move to stir the sauce. Occasionally
I looked at my watch, aware of the time passing. "You're not
going anywhere," he said. Around him you were swept up
with him, into his passion; even the way he cooked the
meal seemed orchestrated, practiced, a way of roping you in
closer. I knew I had to be careful as I watched him. He was
impetuous, impossible to live with but impossible to turn
away from. But as I began to get loose from the wine I told
myself to stop worrying. What harm were we doing? He
seemed different than when he was a teenager. More sure of
himself. Steadier. For a while I considered that perhaps he
had matured. That he was a capable, responsible journalist.

"How's married life treating you?" Stephen said, once
we'd sat down on the two unmatched wicker chairs that
surrounded a small café table. He cut me a piece of soft brie
and spread it on a crust of bread.

"We've been married almost eleven years." I pictured our
breakfasts reading the Sunday paper, the boys racing their
cars across the table knocking over the cereal boxes, but the

image faded in the Paris light. "Is there anyone in your life?" I asked.

"There was someone once. A long time ago." Again his response seemed practiced. He spun the tin ashtray that sat in the middle of the table with his finger. "I've always been attracted to sad women."

"Everyone has their pain."

"Hers is different. It sits inside her. You can see it in her eyes. She has these enchanting eyes," he said, staring into mine. "The sadness. It doesn't move. It's amazingly seductive."

"Maybe it's your own pain you see when you look at her." He was still spinning the ashtray. "Don't you miss it?" I asked. "Being in a relationship?"

"I miss the struggle." Then he stopped the ashtray and looked up. "What about your husband?"

"Michael is one of the happiest people I know."

"It doesn't get on your nerves? The happy stuff?" He fidgeted with the cell phone he'd placed on the table. Then he got up. Found a fat white candle burned almost down to its center and lit it.

I realized that though I was hungry, and though the Bolognese sauce was rich and satisfying, I couldn't really eat. Most of the pasta sat on my plate untouched.

"It's pretty quiet in my house," he continued without waiting for a response, watching the flame from the candle dance inside its wall of wax.

My eyes studied the details of the fleur-de-lis design on the Provençal wallpaper crackling and fading on the kitchen wall. Stephen looked as if he was thinking about what I had said. Everything I said seemed to make him curious, as if he were reading between the lines for clues. It was that keen interest and curiosity and attention that compelled me.

"So your marriage is good?"

"Yes," I said. "My marriage is good."

He looked at me more deeply, as if he doubted what I'd said.

"We're different," I said, wondering why I felt I had to defend my marriage to him, and left it at that.

He reached over the table with his fork and from my plate twirled a ribbon of pasta onto his fork. "You're not letting this go to waste, are you?" He consumed the rest of my pasta with relish. Then he took his hand and licked his two fingers and picked up the crumbs on the table with them and put them in his mouth, not wanting to leave anything untouched.

"I don't think you're really happy," he said. "You can't fool me."

I looked back at him, surprised by his words.

"I know you, Eleanor. I was the first."

He didn't look away from my face, and as he stared, he cut into the loaf of peasant bread with a sharp knife and accidentally sliced into his finger. Instinctively, I jumped up and grabbed a dishtowel to press against his finger. "Are you okay?" I said, nearly taking his finger and sucking it to stop the blood like a mother might do.

"I'm fine." I was standing over him, so close I could smell the scent of his body and the heat he generated. I was holding his hand, pressing the towel tightly against his finger. He looked into my eyes and lifted his head up as if he wanted to kiss me. "But you can still hold my hand."

The moment passed and I walked away thinking how protective of him I felt—just as if he were one of my boys.

Stephen made espresso in a tin espresso pot on the burner of the stove. He mentioned that an agent in New York had just taken him on and that the novel he had written was close to getting picked up by a publisher. The agent was getting him magazine assignments, too. "I may be spending a lot of time in your city," he said, almost a taunt, tipping the candle and letting the wax make white droplets onto the tabletop.

"That would be nice." I didn't take him seriously. I had listened to his dreams and fantasies before, but I was never sure how real they were. He said his life was in turnaround. He reached his open palm in the air and held it there for me to give him the high five. "We've done it, Eleanor. Two misfits from the Midwest. Did you think you'd ever make it out of Chicago?"

I wasn't sure exactly what he meant. I looked at him questioningly.

"Our pasts. We've escaped, Eleanor."

I thought to myself, *Do we ever?*

He described his novel scene by scene. "It takes place in Alaska. It's about snow. It's a cold book. It's about a man who can't let go."

I couldn't follow the logic to the story and my mind drifted. I found it difficult to concentrate on his exact words, to stay focused when he talked. When I looked at him carefully I told myself that I wasn't attracted to him. He was solipsistic. Self-indulgent. Provocative. Everything he said seemed to serve his own purpose. He talked the way he cooked, in a whirlwind of drama and emotion. "All I have is my work," he said. "I'm a shallow man, Eleanor."

I didn't know if I believed him. It seemed as if he felt what he did was vastly important. It cloaked how fragile he seemed. "I can't really be with a woman, until I'm on track." He looked at me. "I'm getting there," he said. His pants and shirt were perfectly ironed. He looked studied, like he had put

too much emphasis on his exterior, and it bothered me
despite how clearly attractive he was. There was something
still unformed about him, and I couldn't quite put my finger
on why it disturbed me. And why wasn't he married or in a
committed relationship? What he said about work sounded
like an excuse. He had said he wanted children, talked about
how much he loved them when he asked me about my boys,
told me that his best friend in Colorado had two, a boy and a
girl. "Man, when I see those kids I think about what I don't
have and it spooks me."

"You could have a child if that's what you want."

He looked at me strangely, as if it had never occurred to
him, or that no one had been bold enough to say it.

"I have to stay focused," he remarked flatly. He fidgeted in
his chair, leaned it back and forward, making it creak as it
rocked.

He realized he was talking too much about himself. He
stopped. I noticed the mattress on the floor and the blanket
curled at the end where he slept. I saw myself in his eyes'
reflection. I felt myself being sucked in closer, as if the rest of
the world outside us had vanished. The sound of the Citroëns
whirling around the corner from outside his window, the
chatter of French conversation through the narrow street as
people walked past, dissolved. I thought how we can have
so many lives depending on the person we are with, and
briefly wondered what that life would be like with Stephen,
imagined the two of us living in the drafty studio, face to face
with each other, inside the dramatic moment as once I had
imagined the two of us together, both working on our own
creative endeavors.

He asked me what I was working on. I said a study on
infidelity, to make it simple.

"Is that something you know about?"

I saw him look around the room and his eyes landed on the unmade mattress.

"In *Anna Karenina*. You know, Tolstoy."

He looked at me sheepishly. I saw the face of the boy I had once been drawn to but never quite understood. It was still underneath the facade he presented, and being with him, as uncomfortable as I felt, made me ache for the restless, passionate part of myself I had forgotten. As I write this I wonder if it's going to end, this desire for something more, or is it simply being in Paris that has awakened it and once I'm home it will be forgotten, and I find myself resenting Stephen, briefly, for having revealed to me this forgotten world.

"We could do it, you know," he said, his eyes again grazing on the mattress, and then he looked back down to the chopping board where he was peeling the apples to sauté with brown sugar and cognac. His entire body engaged in the endeavor.

"Do what?"

"You know."

"Are you trying to put the moves on me?"

He looked at me soulfully and then went back to the orchestration of the dessert, taking an apple in his hand and, with the knife, slipping off its skin. I was stunned by the boldness of my words. "I'm always putting the moves on you," he said, doing a sort of Fred Astaire turn in the middle of the kitchen. "You know me. It's just that . . ." He stopped, unable to finish the sentence. I wonder what would have happened had I not questioned him. Had I simply waited and not broken the moment. Would he have tried to make love to me?

"What?" I said.

"It's just that I've always found you so incredibly compelling."

I rose to find the bathroom. It was off the kitchen.

"Hurry up," he said.

I stared at myself in the tarnished mirror that hung over a small, cracked porcelain sink. My body was speeding up, moving ahead of myself. I needed to calm down. Was I the mother of my sons, wife to a doctor, a respected professor, or a woman on the cusp of forty, completely unknown to herself, who has kept her true desires locked up in a suitcase, the contents now spilling over? Or maybe I was just responding to the situation at hand. Wouldn't any woman suddenly alone and face to face with a man she'd once been attracted to feel the same? Did I want him, or was it simply the intimacy of his company that made me feel for a moment that I might have, had I not been married? I told myself not to get drawn in again. You're not that person anymore. He's self-absorbed. Unstable, I told myself. It occurred to me that my life must have seemed charmed to him, that for the first time I had the edge.

When I came out of the bathroom he was serving the cooked apples on small, mismatched, chipped plates. I thought to myself that it was wrong to be in another man's apartment in a foreign city and I wanted to flee. "I need to go soon," I said.

We ate the dessert in silence. I watched how Stephen savored each bite, how it seemed as if his insatiable appetite was sublimation for something I could not name. When we finished he piled our plates into the discolored sink.

"Do you need help?" I stood up.

"From you, Eleanor."

"I meant the dishes."

He said he didn't want to waste our last few hours together cleaning up. He wanted to go out again. To see more of Paris.

How vivid everything was in his presence. How alive and disordered everything felt. How wonderfully unsafe. The wine made everything around us seem as if it were coated in a soft film. I had to take his hand to keep my balance.

We walked again; it felt good to be out of the dim studio and in the freedom of the Paris air. And once outside, away from the intensity of being in a private space alone together, I felt I could trust him again. It was my last day in Paris and I wanted to buy something to take home with me. I had already bought presents for the boys and a beautiful shirt for Michael. We passed the shop again where I had seen the pitcher with the painted buds ready to break into blossom, sealed in the porcelain clay.

"It's delicate like you are." He shook his head as if something disturbed him, as if he were thinking of something he didn't want to say. "It looks vulnerable. But its constitution is sturdy. You have to have it."

"Do you think so? It's expensive." I had checked the price the day before and had been contemplating whether to buy it.

"Not when it is something you have to have. Not if its beauty possesses you. You can't walk away from something like that."

He bounced in front of me and opened the door to the shop. "Remember the woman I told you about? She's soft and open like you, Eleanor. She's cautious, but she still cares about me."

"You're not over her, are you?"

"She's still in my life," he conceded. "At least she is now."
He looked at me and gave me a smile that was more like a
question.

I bought the pitcher. It was expensive but Stephen was
right. It didn't matter. It had already begun to represent
something in my life as I suppose all objects finally do for the
person that possesses them.

On the way back to my hotel we stopped along one of the
bridges across the Seine and stood in an alcove overlooking
the dirty water. Stephen leaned against the stone wall of the
bridge and I stood next to him. I didn't know how to hold my
body. I looked at him more carefully. I saw him watching me,
too. The tension made us both uncomfortable. The desires
that had been with us so long ago were magnified. His eyes
stopped on my eyes, my lips, then traveled to my neck. As he
watched me I felt the brush of his lips on my skin, the warm
heat traveling up my spine, though he hadn't touched me. I
looked at his hands. His arms were open, resting on each side
of the wall next to him, and I felt drawn in the empty space
his arms made but I couldn't move. I felt awkward and
turned my body away. I reached in my bag and took out my
sunglasses and put them on, though the sky was already
darkening. He had beautiful, textured hands; the dexterity,
sensitivity, and depth of personality was apparent in his long
fingers and hard knuckles, and I thought of his hands even as
I turned from him.

He took out a small video camera and began to film the
activity on the Seine. The city was beginning to darken. He
pointed the camera at me and pressed RECORD. I know now
why Paris is called the City of Light. Everything around us

sparkled, even the reflection of light on the water. I touched my hair and smiled warily. I've hated to be photographed or videotaped, to be captured unprepared and exposed, ever since I had allowed Adam to use me for his study. Stephen stepped back, kneeled, and pointed the camera at me, zooming in, then pulling back. "That's enough," I said, reaching out my hand to block the camera.

He stopped a tourist walking by and thrust the camera forward.

"On your honeymoon?" the tourist asked, taking the camera from Stephen's hands. "You make a beautiful couple."

We both started laughing and our laughter severed the tension. Stephen put his arm around my shoulder, and we leaned against the wall like a pair of lovers and smiled for the camera.

He asked me about my father. I shrugged my shoulders. And then I began to talk about him. I wasn't prepared to, but Stephen was the only one who knew my father and understood my childhood.

I told him about the one time before I left home when my father came home to visit. He was on his way to Europe and made a stopover in Chicago to see us. My dream in Paris had made me remember it. I told him how there was still hope then that he might return for good. My father wore a nice suit and smelled of aftershave. When he walked in the house he held my mother and me. He hugged me too tightly, crushing my chest. He was trembling. He sat down. He looked around the living room, studying each object and piece of furniture as if he were holding it in his mind, calculating what he'd lost. It was awkward. He had little to say. He reached in the pocket of his suit coat and handed me a bottle of French perfume he'd purchased in a duty-free shop at the

airport. He went to the piano and lifted the wooden cover.
He took off his coat. He played Chopin's sonatas, closing his
eyes, moving his body. I watched his hands dance across
the keys and wondered how a man who could make the
sounds he made could walk away from such beauty. In our
house he seemed uncomfortable. He was formal and polite.
I was fourteen. He asked me if I wanted a puppy. One of the
partners in a business he had a share in was a breeder. I told
him no. I didn't trust my father. I did not want to accept any
more promises that might be broken.

My father sat down on the couch next to me. He took
my hands in his. I studied my father's fingers, his carefully
manicured nails, noticing how well he still took care of them.
When he lived at home he wouldn't use a hammer to hang a
painting out of fear that he'd accidentally miss and damage
his fingers. "Look at you," he said. I said nothing. "Look at
you," he said again. "Daddy," I said. "This is my daughter?"
he said with a question. I saw his chest begin to tremble. I
held him so he wouldn't break. "Look at you," he said again.
"You've grown up." "I know, Daddy," I said.

My mother lit up in my father's presence. She was
another person. There was a lift in her gait as she set the
table for dinner. She used the formal china. She garnished
our plates with parsley. She gave my father second helpings,
relished cutting him a piece of cake. "Your mother can still
cook," my father said. He turned to my mother. "Eleanor, your
mother was the prettiest girl in all of Chicago. At least she
was in my eyes."

I told Stephen how my mother and father flirted over the
dinner table. My mother told the story of how my father had
taken her to the philharmonic on their first date. My father
said he wanted my mother to see that side of him. "If she

didn't have passion for music then I would know," he said.
"Know what?" I asked. "Whether I could be in love with her."
"Daddy, she still likes music," I said, and he looked up at me
and grew quiet.

When my mother went up to clear the dishes, he followed
her. I saw him stand behind her at the sink, lift her hair,
and kiss her neck. I went up to my room to give my parents
some space. When I came back down my mother was in
the kitchen. I could see that she'd been crying. My father
promised that he'd be back. That he'd call us as soon as he
was in Europe. "You look tired, Joseph," my mother said when
they were saying good-bye. She brushed her hand along the
side of his face the way she had done when I was a child.
"How long can this go on?"

I walked my father to the door. He kissed his two fingers
and rubbed them on the mezuzah. "Eleanor," my father
said. "Daddy," I said. "Eleanor, I'm sorry," he said. "It's okay,
Daddy."

A week went by and we didn't hear from him. My mother
hovered near the phone. A month. Nothing. Disappointment
became a part of the way her lips formed words. I looked up
at Stephen.

"She still thought he was coming back," I said. "Can you
believe it?"

"Mom," I had said to her, "you know he's not coming
back." "I know," she said. "He's not coming back, Mom." I said
again. "You have to forget him." "How do you forget a man
like that?" she said.

Stephen looked at me and we both laughed. Just talking
about it seemed to make me feel lighter, relieved. "They're one
of a kind, our mothers," he said.

————

Then Stephen began to tell his story. He asked me if I
remembered when his mother left Chicago and he moved in
with his father. It was to be with another man, he told me.
"You can't imagine what it was like. To watch my father make
love to his young new wife, knowing my mother was all
alone. But she wasn't alone, Eleanor."

I touched his arm. I told him I was sorry and asked how
his mother was now. He said he's stopped asking how she is.
He knows the answer. "There's never been anyone else for
her," he said. "The thing with the other man only lasted a
few months. She's never gotten over my father." I looked at
him with recognition. Stephen told me he knew I would
understand. He said I was probably the only person he knew
who would ever understand what it was like to know that no
matter what you did it would never be enough to make your
mother happy.

Stephen leaned back on the bench where we sat. And I
thought that he was right. That we shared that bond. And it
occurred to me that it was the very thing Michael had never
understood about me. "Your blue eye is very dark," he said.
Sweat pooled on my back from the sun's heat. Perspiration
dripped down my spine. I smelled Stephen's scent as we sat
on the bench. A couple, assuming closeness between us, sat
down on the empty space next to me, forcing me to move
closer to Stephen. Our arms touched. We watched birds swoop
down and graze across the water.

He took out a pack of matches from his pocket and lit
one; I watched it spark in his hand, watched how the flame
enchanted him, watched as it extinguished the minute it hit
the ground. Stephen leaned over closer, so that his chest
brushed mine, to tell me that there was an eyelash on my
cheek. He gently took it off with his finger and asked me to

make a wish on it. I can't even write here in this journal of my most private thoughts, what I wished for. It's too painful.

He told me that when he was in Colorado he was having trouble with a disk in his back. He wasn't getting work. He explained that he got addicted to Vicodin. "I kept taking them to relieve the pain, and then once the pain was gone, it was another kind of pain they seemed to numb." He said he never wanted to be in that kind of shape again. I said I was sorry. He said he was happy for me, for my life, and all that I'd accomplished.

I thought about the time years ago in my mother's kitchen when Stephen told me his parents were separating. After he left that night I looked out the window of my bedroom into his house. When I was upstairs in my bedroom I saw his entire house, the whole expanse of it, each light turned on. I saw the shadows of Stephen and his mother and father move through the house. That night I understood his loneliness, or perhaps I projected my own loneliness on to him. Perhaps he'd been happy.

I asked him if he was okay now. And he said he had to be careful. That he had to stay focused. He looked at me with a question in his face. There was always a question in his face, as if he was looking for affirmation. There was something compelling about his disclosure, as if he was asking me to get inside the hard wire of his brain and untangle it for him. I felt a maternal connection to him. What I'd sensed earlier in the day, that I hadn't been getting the clear picture of Stephen's life, that he deliberately left things out, was correct. He only now began to come into focus. "You and me are one of a kind," he said. "I've always known that about us."

I was a married woman. I had two children. I suddenly resented being put in the same category as Stephen. We were nothing alike. I said it was getting late. I was eager to get

back to the hotel. His behavior was puzzling. As usual my
inclination was to get too involved. I had always felt that
Stephen kept his fair share of secrets and the secrets had
made me think about him too closely. Now I wanted to be
free of him. Too often he made me uncomfortable, made me
feel that it was my responsibility to help him somehow. On
the way back to the hotel we walked in silence. He clasped
my arm and stopped me before we arrived at my hotel.

He told me that I looked really great. He looked at me
deeply as if he were trying to establish a connection again.
There was something I didn't trust in his eyes again. I could
almost read it. *I can still have you,* his eyes said. I stared back
at him firmly. If I gave an inch there was no turning back.
But it also struck me with the force of revelation that there
was a part of me that did want to be led away, and I had to
caution myself against it.

I asked him how he expected me to look. Something
about whether he expected I would look like a middle-aged
housewife. He looked at me soulfully and said, "That's not
you, Eleanor. That could never be you."

I pictured my children tucked into their beds, brushing
my fingers across their foreheads the way they liked. It was
what calmed Noah when he was worked up. I pictured myself
slipping my hand in the crook of Michael's arm and walking
down an avenue as we had done when we'd first married,
looking inside the shops, imagining the future we would
have together, the life we would build that seemed to stretch
before us like an endless, empty road. I had to tell myself that
that life still existed. Until Michael entered my life, I'd been
pulled in places I didn't understand, had done things I
regretted and had been ashamed of. Being with Michael
had canceled out the ways I'd trespassed. I found purity and
goodness in him that had moved me. He was the opposite of

my father. Of Adam. Of William. He would never leave me. I
knew that when I married him.

"But will he be enough for you?" my mother said when I
told her that Michael and I were engaged. In the years that
we'd been married that comment occasionally floated to the
surface of my mind and then I just didn't think about it. Only
now, flying miles away from Paris, am I remembering my
mother's remark. I know I should put down my pen and
sleep, try to rest before we land, but I have to record it all.
There are things I need to reconsider, and by writing them
down, the past seems to come to me with more clarity. I
thought that Michael embodied all the characteristics my
mother held dear. He could provide a good home, a family.
He was generous, kind, and reliable. "I still think about the
years I had with your father." "After he left you?" I was
angry. "What about those years?" "He has music inside him,"
she said. I told her that he had squandered it. "He wasn't
made for this world," she had countered. I told her she was
wrong about Michael. That he was never going to leave me.
"You never know what's going to happen in life," she said.
She asked me if he made me happy. "Daddy made you
happy," I told her.

We were in my mother's kitchen talking. I remember how
I looked out at the back of the Masons' house. I could see
through the still skeletal branches of the tree to the roof, the
brick chimney, the white shingles. Was Stephen a better
match for me? The last time I had seen him we had been in
our twenties. We had never really talked about a future
together, though it existed in the air between us. But the
minute I walked back into my mother's house I pushed the
thought away. I saw my mother wiping the table and putting
away the dishes. Everything seemed perfectly clear. I didn't
want to have her solitary life, and I knew by marrying

Michael that I was choosing a path different from the one she had chosen.

When we reached my hotel it was almost 7:30. The evening came on, and as the light receded I already began to long for what was lost of the day. It must have dawned on both of us simultaneously that we were saying good-bye, that the moment had come to a close, that we might not see each other again. What kind of relationship could we have in the present? Could Stephen and I really be friends? I doubt either of us had a chance to process what our encounter meant, and I wanted to ascribe what had happened between us to fate so as not to be accountable.

We stood in the lobby. Stephen was beside me. I could not see him—I didn't want to see him—but I sensed his presence next to me. I was aware of his every movement as I fumbled in my purse for the key, among my wallet, cosmetics, loose pens, and scraps of paper, and I realized I was avoiding how I would say good-bye to him. I realized that we had never once talked about our severed connection, and I regretted it. The fact that I was married and had my own life allowed me to be more free and open than I had ever been before with him. Now part of me wanted to stay attached. Another part of me wanted to flee to my room so that I could begin to quiet the feelings that our confessions had unleashed.

I found my key and for a second I wondered what would happen if I invited him up to my room, as if what had transpired between us all those years ago was just starting to be remembered, as if I were a woman without attachment, and I saw in his eyes that he was waiting for me with anticipation. It was as if both of us were certain only in the moment in which we were to part that something momentous had happened between us that we could not understand. His eyes pleaded with me. I should have turned away, but I did not.

I am not the kind of woman who is unfaithful to her husband. That kind gravitated toward my father.

My mind is going to overflow. He rested his hands on the bare skin of my exposed upper arms and it sent a shiver through my body. We looked at each other and I realized then that Stephen was not going to kiss me and that I was not going to kiss him. We smiled shyly and laughed. "I guess it's time," I said. All the emotions of being young, of finding someone you were attracted to, came back, and I realized how strange it was to feel that way again, how difficult it would be never to experience that tingling sensation of being hyperaware, so vibrantly alive. In my smile I felt my face coming to life and was suddenly embarrassed. I turned to look down, then laughed, and I heard Stephen laughing, too, and our laughter broke through my embarrassment.

Stephen told me it was good to see me so happy. It had been great to see me.

I took out my card with my university address and office number and handed it to him. He made some comment about the fact that now we were going to exchange business cards as if we were beyond that convention, and reached into the back pocket of his wallet and gave me his card in return. We said good-bye and hugged. When his hands were around my waist and then my hips, my body was wet with perspiration. When I touched his back to hold him it was warm against my palms. I was shaking a little. I looked up into his eyes and he kissed me on the lips. I did not protest. The scent of his body rose to my nostrils. It was salty and dark like earth, the same as I had remembered it. His fingers slid down my hips and touched the piece of skin between my skirt and my shirt that had risen when I lifted my arms to embrace him. I was terribly hot and the heat of Stephen's body so close to my own made my heart move violently in my chest. I closed my eyes to drown out what? Feeling? Fear? It was more complicated than fear. There was an edge to it. I sensed my own weakness rising in me. It was weakness born when promise is suddenly snatched back and you are left hungering for something you don't quite understand, and it was that particular weakness that only he inspired in me. Or at least I thought so then.

I stepped back after our lips brushed. It was too intense. Stephen stepped back, too, and looked at me shyly, and I saw the boy in him again. We both smiled and I walked away holding his card in my palm. Once I reached the elevator bank and looked back at Stephen I was stunned to find him still standing where I had left him, watching me walk away. For a moment I wondered whether I should go back and say good-bye again, but the part of me that was girlish and shy took over and I stepped into the elevator. By then my body was so filled with adrenaline I could barely think. My cheeks flushed. It was as if everything was happening so fast and I needed to slow it down so I could digest it and know how to act. After I had unlocked the door to the hotel room I had a premonition that Stephen was going to come back for me, that he was in a moment coming up the tube-shaped elevator and would soon be in front of my door, and I opened it and stepped out to look for him, but the narrow gray carpeted halls with their soft lavender walls were empty. I stared down a long corridor of absence. I went back into the room and sat immobile on the foot of the bed. I needed to begin packing. My plane was leaving later that night. But I was paralyzed. I unfolded myself onto the bed and lay down thinking I had made a grave mistake. There was something inside Stephen he wanted to give me, or something I needed from him, something we needed to say to each other, and we had let the opportunity pass. How would it have hurt if I had invited him up to my room? If we had ended the unrequited journey? Would I now be able to relax? I didn't want to leave Paris. I didn't want to return home. Did that mean I had no home now, other than these four walls in a hotel room painted a light Parisian blue? My room with the little French desk that now held my belongings, my folders and books and notebooks, the armoire filled with my clothes and the delicate pitcher. These were all I would need in the world. My own quiet. It had been so long since I'd felt this way.

Tears filled my eyes and moved down my cheeks. It was easier and more familiar to long for what I could not have than be in its presence, and my tears seemed to release some of the tension that had formed a knot in my body. I was surprised by how long I needed to cry. How bereft and lost I was. I thought as I began to pack that I'd never move beyond those feelings. Suddenly I was glad that I was leaving Paris, that I had to quickly finish packing and catch my flight, otherwise I'm not sure what I would have done. Once I had calmed down and settled myself against these overwhelming feelings, I was compelled to write it all down, this journal of what had transpired in Paris, lest it be forgotten. It was an urge almost like hunger. I couldn't wait until I had taken a cab from the hotel, checked in at the airport, found my seat on the airplane (it seemed an eternity) so that I could take out my notebook and pen and make sense of things. And now what? Will I be able to return to my life unharmed?

PART III

11

Eleanor walked with John and Rob to the baggage claim and through customs. They were tired and barely spoke. In expectation of returning home to their individual families, each had retreated back into themselves. They looked at each other tentatively, and then parted with quick hugs and promises to keep in touch. John slipped into the car he had ordered. Irrationality, grogginess, separation anxiety—whatever it was, she didn't want him to leave. She watched him through the window of the limousine as he lit up a cigarette, and then the limousine pulled off, taking him away to his suburban home in New Jersey.

It was early morning, the sky pink beneath the darkness. Slowly the dawn accepted the break of day and the light shifted. She smoothed the creases on her skirt, accumulated from ten days in Paris.

When she turned the key in her apartment door, her sons and husband were asleep in their rooms. A lovely light was cast in the apartment, half dark and half light—that semidark when objects just begin to emerge with clarity. As she quietly walked down the hallway to the bedrooms, she heard Noah's sigh as he turned over and Nicholas's thicker breathing. The warmth and press of light through the curtains filled their rooms, and for a moment she could not tell which bed she wanted to enter first.

She caught her reflection in the mirror in the hallway. Nothing about her had changed. She had seen the tougher, severe, more complicated look in women who had followed their passion. She just looked tired.

She couldn't help herself. She awoke the boys first, sliding next to Noah in his bed and kissing him, then Nicholas. She took in their individual smells that had become a part of the way she breathed. They couldn't seem to get enough of her. Noah sat in her lap, where he had come to join her, touching her dangling earrings. Nicholas sat next to her on his bed, clinging to her, touching her hair, reaching for her hand, in his excitement to have her home forgetting his need to separate. "Mommy, I missed you," he said, hugging her. Noah wanted to know how high the Eiffel Tower was and whether she'd actually climbed all those stairs. Michael stood in the hallway of the boys' room, yawning, in only his boxer shorts.

"My, my, look what the cat dragged in," he said, his voice not yet awake. He reached for her and she stood up and fell into his arms, taking in the warmth of his body. "Aren't we glad Mommy's home," he said to the boys.

Noah and Nicholas talked excitedly, trying to outshout each other. She tried to stay in tune to all that they said, not wanting to miss anything, feeling herself slowly come back to life in their presence. Michael said he would make pancakes for the occasion. The boys ran to help him. Noah liked spooning the batter onto the skillet and watching it begin to bubble and Nicholas asked if he could flip them if he promised to be careful. She reluctantly let them go and went into her bedroom to change out of the spent clothes she'd worn on the plane, happy to discard them in the hamper.

Breakfast was full of chatter and excitement. Noah poured too much syrup over his pancakes, making a lake on his plate. Though another day she would have scolded him, that morning she kept quiet. Nicholas spilled his orange juice. Michael loaded her plate with more pancakes than she could eat, and before he sat down, he reached over and kissed her again, clearly happy that she was home. Noah refused to eat, jumping up and down, touching her with his sticky hands, until he had opened his presents. She indulged him and went into the hallway to fetch her suitcase. They loved the hand-painted trucks and trains, the French books and stuffed bears she had brought home. "Will you read it to us in French?" Noah asked, holding a French version of *Goodnight Moon,* remembering how she had read him the English version when he was little. She showed them the postcards she'd collected. Michael appreciated the handwoven blue shirt and the Hermès tie she'd picked for him. He tried the shirt on over his T-shirt, then put on the tie, and the boys laughed since he was still in his boxer shorts.

She was truly happy looking into her children's bright, laughing faces. She observed Michael's cheerful smile, noting how her presence seemed to fill them with contentment. Noah told her he had looked out his window every night to see if he saw her plane coming home, and she put him on her lap, kissing the top of his hair, remembering how when the boys were both babies she couldn't seem to get enough of them, their physical bodies producing in her their own kind of hunger. "He actually thought he could see you out the window if he kept watching, Mommy," Nicholas said. "I told him that the plane wouldn't actually fly over New York City, but he didn't believe me. What an idiot."

"Nicholas, don't call your brother an idiot," Michael said.

Eleanor looked at Michael, realizing how hard it must have

been for all of them to be pulled out of their comfortable routine by her absence, and she felt guilty for having enjoyed her trip, for being so caught up with her new friends that she'd even, at times, forgotten them completely. "How were they?" she asked, clearing the table. "Did they really miss me terribly? Was it hard for you?"

"We managed," he said. "But you owe me." He looked at her sardonically and smiled. "I'll cash in later." He came behind her at the sink and pressed up against her when she was cleaning the breakfast dishes and the boys were playing with their new toys in the living room. Then he went into the dining room to check his phone messages.

After she cleaned up the kitchen, she went to unpack. She held in her hand the blouse she had worn on her last day in Paris and brought it to her face, unable to quite let it go. It smelled of the lavender perfume in her hotel room. As she unpacked, she felt herself back in Paris again. She checked her pockets and in her light jacket she found Stephen's card. Unthinking, she brought it to her lips, then folded the clothes into a shopping bag to take to the cleaner. She took out the notebook she had kept in Paris, slipped Stephen's card inside, and tucked it into the top drawer by her bedside table. She turned the key, locking the drawer.

Filled once again with a quick rush of euphoria, she carefully unpacked the pitcher she had bought in Paris. She took it into the living room to show Michael. She remembered Keats's poem, thought of John, and smiled. She thought about the lines from the end of the poem, how the speaker becomes aware that the lovers shown on the urn are in fact "far above . . . all breathing human passion." The poem's speaker relishes the happiness of the urn's world, where spring is permanent, where the melodies from the piper are "ever new," and where love is "forever warm."

Michael was at the dining room table looking at slides of animal heart tissue through his microscope. She was slightly disappointed that he was already back to his work, but she decided not to bother him, realizing that in her absence his own work must have suffered. She looked out the terrace window, opened the doors, and stepped out. The clouds were pillowed over the trees in the park.

"The sky is so beautiful today," she said, coming back inside. Michael was still looking into his microscope, making notes on a pad next to him. "I think we should take the boys to the park. When I was in Paris I thought of them every time I walked through the Luxembourg Gardens. We have to remember that life is gorgeous." She looked over his shoulder where his eye was pressed over the lens. "We can't miss any of it. Isn't it strange how one day you can feel closed off to the world, and then the next day everything feels possible?"

"I was in the pathology lab all week," he said, glancing up at her, sensing something was different. "I've been looking at animal cells while you've been traipsing all over Paris."

She looked at him, slightly hurt, but decided to let the comment go. "But what about when you leave the hospital? You have to start noticing things. The sky on the way home at dusk. The way the gray slowly creeps in."

"I usually think about my patients on the way home." Michael glanced up at her, raising his eyebrows suspiciously. Then he put his eye back to the microscope.

"Look what I bought in Paris." She showed the pitcher to him and told herself she was willing to accept the imperfection of her own capacity for human love and connection if only she could reach him for a moment. She put it next to his microscope on the table.

"It's nice," he said, barely raising his eyes from the lens.

"These buds. They remind me that everything is on the brink of becoming if we want to believe it's so."

"It's nice," Michael said again, looking up to adjust the magnifying lens.

"You don't see it, do you?" She wished for him to see what she saw, to share it with him.

"What?"

"How beautiful it is."

"Give me a minute, Eleanor. You've been to Paris but life has been going on here. This slide I'm looking at. There's an anomaly."

She left the dining room to find the boys, trying not to allow herself to feel disappointed. He did not want to see that anything about her was any different since it was not a difference they had experienced together, and the realization both frustrated and moved her. The boys were still in the living room playing with their new toy trucks and trains. She put the pitcher safely on her dresser in her bedroom, where it would not be harmed. When she climbed into bed later that evening she opened a book, but her eyes kept wandering back to the pitcher. Throughout the day things had seemed a long way off. They had all decided to go to the park. The boys brought their Rollerblades and Eleanor and Michael had followed behind them holding hands. Later in the day the boys went off on playdates; Michael worked while she took a nap. They ordered Chinese food for dinner, too tired to cook. She had lived the hours as if experiencing the day from a great distance, unable to bridge the disconnection she experienced being back home. She told herself she was just tired. Jet lag. She looked at the pitcher and imagined again what the buds would look like if they burst into being. She remembered stopping to look at the pitcher with Stephen and the lunch he made for her in his studio, how her hand pressed over his cut finger to stop the blood from flowing.

Michael turned off the light, slipped the book out of her hand, and reached for her. "You haven't told us anything about anyone you were with in Paris. The other people at the conference. Who you hung out with. What you did."

"I told you and the boys about everywhere I went. Everything I saw." She caught her own defensiveness, examined it, and realized that she hadn't wanted to say a word about what the trip had meant to her, afraid to articulate her feelings.

"But you seem so secretive."

"I'm not secretive. I'm just tired. Can I tell you more about the conference tomorrow?" She adjusted her eyes to the darkness and reached out to touch him.

"Of course you can," he said, tenderly. He turned her toward him. "I miss you."

"But I'm here."

"Physically you are." He snuggled up next to her. "But it's like you're not here, really."

"I'm here," Eleanor said again, tucking her face into his chest. Unexpected tears burned her eyes as she slowly relinquished herself to his body.

In the morning everything looked different, colored by her trip to Paris. She went about her routine dividing her time between teaching at the university, her writing, and her boys. She picked them up from school, took them for playdates, spent time with them at home before their dinner and their baths. Sometimes she took them out for pizza when Michael was working late. While at the university she looked forward to coming home, to the peace that descends on a house when children are absorbed in their rooms and Bach or Beethoven is playing on the CD player (it was a miracle, her boys and the happiness they gave her—she did not for a second take any of it for granted), but the minute she was in the comfort of her home, near that place of serenity, she found herself longing for the solitude of her office at school. She wondered why.

She experienced an urgent desire to get beyond her daily tasks, so that she would have the hour or two she needed for her imaginative life that had blossomed in Paris. But once she was alone she was paralyzed by a strange kind of fear. She was living her life day by day but she was absent from it. She couldn't seem to heal the division she had felt in bed with her husband the night she returned, even though their bodies were so close.

Her vision and sensitivity were heightened. She could tell which couples were connected, which couples were still in love by the way they looked at each other. On the subway she watched a man squeeze his wife's arm, saw another woman rest her head on her lover's shoulder. She watched the way friends of theirs kissed each other on the cheek or lips at dinner; at a cocktail party for new residents at the hospital she noticed Brian, a partner in Michael's practice, stop in the middle of a house full of guests to embrace his wife. At the party Eleanor tried to engage their friends in conversation, but she kept drifting off alone to look out the window. Sally and Marcia had wanted to hear all about Paris, but she found herself tongue-tied when she tried to explain how meaningful the trip had been, how important it was to be on her own, and instead told them about the wonderful food she'd eaten and the fashionable shops, knowing that's what they'd want to hear. In the middle of their conversation Brian came behind Marcia again and kissed her neck. She watched how the two made eye contact, seemingly perfectly in touch with the other all evening, and it filled her with loneliness. She found Michael talking to one of the new residents and his young wife. At first Eleanor tried to enter into their conversation, but found she couldn't connect and retreated inside herself; eventually she wandered off to find the bathroom. She didn't understand what had happened, why she felt so empty.

Her son Nicholas was performing in a school play. They scurried about the house, getting showered and dressed. Nicholas was too nervous to eat his typical breakfast of two waffles and instead grabbed a granola bar from the kitchen cabinet. Noah had a meltdown. They had run out of milk and he couldn't have his bowl of cereal he had every morning and he refused the bagel, the waffles, and the granola bar Eleanor offered instead. "Nicky gets what he wants but I don't get what I want," he said, and ran to his room and plunged his body dramatically against his pillow.

"Not everyone gets what they want," Eleanor said.

In the bedroom she heard something crash. She went to find out what happened. The boys followed behind her. Michael looked at Eleanor sheepishly.

"I'm sorry, Eleanor. It was an accident. I'll make it up to you." He explained that his arm accidentally knocked over the pitcher as he was rushing to get dressed. It was broken into three large pieces on the floor.

She put her hand over her mouth. She couldn't speak. She thought of the mornings in Paris when she had walked by the pitcher. She thought about how the buds of the crocus were brought to life in her imagination. It was as if he had smashed her dreams. How could he have been so clumsy? So unaware? She was about to say something and then her eye caught Michael's apologetic eyes. She looked at her husband again. She looked at her beautiful boys. She was trapped inside her love for them.

"It was just an accident, Mom," Nicholas said, standing beside Michael.

"You can glue it." Noah ran to get the adhesive from the desk drawer.

"It's okay," she said. "Daddy didn't break it on purpose." She kneeled down, retrieved the pieces, and glued the pitcher back together. If you looked closely you could still see the scar, like a wound down its cheek, from where the porcelain had cracked. She knew she had to hurry to get the boys to school on time but instead she sat down at the foot of her bed looking at the pitcher, remembering how it had moved her in the shop window, as if willing it fully whole in her mind. Its damaged beauty filled her with melancholy.

She pulled herself away and packed up the boys' backpacks, coaxed Noah out the door, and they hailed a cab. She and Michael took a front-row seat in the school lunchroom where the assembly was held. Nicholas beamed on stage. Still she couldn't stop thinking about the broken pitcher.

Michael sat in the wooden chair next to her. He put his arm around her chair and squeezed her shoulder while their son performed. They turned to look at each other proudly. She moved her hand from her lap to rest it in Michael's hand. He took it in his mechanically. She nearly wanted to extract it, and then realized how silly she was to expect her husband to make love to her whenever they touched.

Her heart was beating too quickly. She couldn't quite sit still, uncomfortable against the hard surface of the wooden school chair. She thought about the pitcher again, surprised by how much it bothered her that Michael had broken it. *In the company of my children is where I'll draw sustenance,* she told herself, trying to calm down. She had been under the illusion, since Nicholas had turned ten and Noah seven, that she was suddenly freer, that her boys needed her less. She watched Nicholas recite his lines, looking directly into her face for approval. She told herself there was nothing she would need more than Nicholas's face picking hers out in the audience or Noah's little hand reaching behind her neck when she lifted him for a hug. All other desires she could stuff in the hidden drawers of her mind the way she shifted winter clothes to the back to make room for her light summer things. And yet something had opened inside her, leaving her slightly exposed. It was like suddenly prying open a window that had for years been sealed shut with paint.

After the assembly, Nicholas's teacher, Miss Nightingale, stopped for a moment to say hello. "How's Nicholas doing at school?" Eleanor asked, feeling suddenly disconnected from his life.

"He's been a little off. But nothing to worry about. He was upset you weren't at the last soccer game. After he scored a goal he looked for you and crumbled when he couldn't find you."

"I was away for work. I've been to all Nicholas's games."

"I wouldn't worry. He just needs a little encouragement."

She and Michael walked to the subway. Eleanor saw him checking his pager. She was still disturbed about Nicholas. She could forget that underneath his confident exterior he was vulnerable. Sometimes he needed just to catch her eye in the bleachers to build his confidence when he was on the field. "Do you think my trip was hard on Nicholas?"

"He's fine. And besides, you're home now. I have to work late tonight. Brian and I are getting closer to developing the stent I've been talking to you about. "

"Couldn't you get someone else for tonight? Nicholas will be disappointed. You know how he counts on our dinners together on Fridays."

"Eleanor, this is big. It could save countless lives."

She tried to shrug off her worries about Nicholas once she was in her office. Her editor called to ask if she would expand her paper into a new book. She should have been elated, but the paper still nagged at her. She said yes. She did want to expand it, and yet she wasn't quite sure. She wrote to John—since returning from Paris she'd kept in touch with John, Julie, and Rob through e-mail—and tried to articulate what she felt her paper lacked. He wrote back that he always felt that he'd outgrown each paper, once it was either published or presented, and she felt better. She was happy she'd caught him on e-mail. She wanted to expand her thesis on the nature of love as a completion of the self in *Anna Karenina* by using other works of literature and thought she would start by rereading parts of *The Inferno*. "Do you think it is through love and our relationships with those we know intimately that we become the person we were meant to become," she asked, startled by her words once she'd typed them. "If that's the case, I'm in trouble," John responded.

The phone rang. She looked at her watch. It was already noon. It was one of her graduate students whose dissertation she was advising. They quickly made a time to meet. The phone rang again. It was Stephen Mason, slightly out of breath.

He was calling from a pay phone at Charles de Gaulle Airport. "I wanted to make sure you got home okay," he said. It had been at least three weeks since she'd been home from Paris. "It was great seeing you, Eleanor. Do you mind if I call you when I'm in New York?"

She tensed. "Of course not." She rested the telephone receiver back in its cradle and sat motionless in her office chair, surprised that the phone call had shaken her.

She closed her copy of *The Inferno* on her desk. Dante had become remote. Memory seemed as powerful as any piece of fiction and she lost herself in it again. What one remembered, filtered through the gauze of time, felt as if it had happened to someone else, was about another character, another person; one couldn't possibly be the person who had been so ignorant of what was to come.

12

She tore open the envelope. William sent her a fossil of a dragonfly inside one of the stones he'd uncovered building his wall, and wrapped around it was a note saying that he missed her and needed to see her. She was nearing the end of her first year of graduate school. She explained to Adam that she would continue to model for him but that she was going back to try again with William. Besides, he was married. She booked a ticket to Chicago for a weekend, happy that William was finally ready to see her.

"I knew you'd come." William was in the backyard letting the dogs run free. "Eleanor, your hair smells so pretty," he said, embracing her.

He saw his role once his father left, the last child at home, to take on the responsibilities of the house and keep his mother company. He divided his time between his mother's and his own apartment in one of the buildings his father owned. He took Eleanor into the woods to see the progress of the stone wall, and the minute he smelled the fresh air, his face brightened as if the world had not yet pressed against him. All the laying of stone and the time he spent riding his horse had given more heft to his body.

"Do you know there's life in a stone, Eleanor? It takes on the memory of a place." He reached down and handed her a piece of the stone that had broken off the larger rock. She looked at the pine leaves on the ground and branches that had fallen. In the air was the moisture before rain. It was cool and she wrapped herself in William's arms to keep warm.

"It's so nice to be with you like we used to," William said. "Words are never adequate. I loved you before words. When I looked at you that first day on the rink I knew. You see things in me I don't have to express. Our words are these stones. I'm glad you came back."

The next day he took her to his dim apartment that bordered a slum.

"I don't like it here, William," Eleanor said. "I don't feel safe. Do you have to live here?"

"I'm sorry. We don't have to stay." He considered for a moment. "It's why they call him a slumlord. He takes their money and lets the place go to shit. They have nowhere else to go. It's why I can't leave. What do you think I've been doing all year?"

She looked at him.

"I made out a system. I take what I can off the top of the rents each month without him knowing about it and I fix stuff for them. Mrs. C. doesn't have hot water. Mr. B. in 5C has busted windows. Sometimes I can't sleep trying to figure it all out."

"You look tired." She put back into place a lock of hair that had fallen over his eye.

"I'm just stressed. I have things to take care of, Eleanor. I can't let them down."

On the night before she was leaving William cooked dinner for her at his mother's house. She wanted to tell him about how intense and interesting modeling for Adam was, about the paper she was writing, but she refrained, thinking he'd be jealous of the life she had without him. The meat was tough and she kept chewing it. "It's great that you are trying to help those people. But what about you, William?" she said, worried about leaving him to the woods and the apartment downtown.

"I have responsibilities here." He pulled out a piece of paper from his pocket. He shoved it across the table. It listed each apartment in the building, who needed what done, what repaired. "Sometimes when I brush my teeth I want to go next door and give my toothbrush to one of those kids with rotted teeth."

"You're good, William."

"Eleanor." He stopped and looked at his half-eaten steak. "I wish there was an alternative universe, where none of the rules apply."

"I know what you mean."

"The world creeps in little by little and sometimes I don't weather it well."

"Promise me you'll take care of yourself," she said, when they hugged good-bye in his driveway. "Don't try to do so much."

"Look, a falling star." She looked up and saw another fall. "That's one thing you can't see in that city. Think of me when you go to Central Park, Eleanor."

"When do I not think about you?" she said, holding on to the sleeve of his coat.

William said he had met a man on the streets of downtown Chicago who was trying to save his soul— a born-again Christian—when he came to visit her in New York a month later. The born-again convinced William that the end of the world was coming, that if he did not redeem himself he would go to hell. "It's strange," William said. "I mean to me hell is right here on earth." He said the man told him that if he embraced Jesus he would understand the puzzle of darkness and light. William had a curiosity for things and explanations not of the earth, and he knew how to listen.

They were lying on her twin captain's bed that also served as a couch in her one-room studio. "It made me think," he said. "I don't understand why we're here. I don't mean in this room. I mean cosmically. I mean why are we *here*? I don't like to think about it, but it's there, that question. Are we supposed to wake up every day and do the same thing? Eat, go to work, sleep? What's the point when there's cruelty? What's the point when people next door don't have enough to eat? It's always haunting me, that there's evil in the world. I don't understand the way the world operates. I don't want to spend my whole life making money doing something I don't like so that I have a bigger house, a bigger television."

"We're here to be good people, William. You have to find your passion."

"You're my passion, Eleanor." He took her hand and held it like you would a valuable present and then kissed it. "I have my dogs and the woods where no one bothers me and I have you, what else is there? I wish we could go far away. Live in the woods, sleep underneath the trees. Eleanor, do you think there are trees in heaven?"

It was dark in the room. Outside, in the hall, she heard a congregation around the pay phone, talking about keg parties and cramming for exams. She squeezed his hand. "Let me finish school. We'll figure it out then," she said, thinking maybe that William could never leave the woods. She suddenly felt ashamed of all the hours she spent in Adam's studio when it was William who needed her. Her eyes adjusted to the darkness, and in the dark she could see the shape of William's arm as he lifted it toward the ceiling and stared at his hand.

"Do you ever look at your hands and feel that they don't belong to you? Like they are not your own?"

"Yes." She lied to reassure him. "Of course."

"Hold me, Eleanor."

"What's wrong? Tell me."

"Sometimes I can't figure a way out of my own head. I can't stop thinking about how I'm going to get it all done. The electrical. The hot water when winter comes." Her eye wandered to the crack underneath the door and the stretch of light. She heard a sound of an animal in agony. She thought it was a dog or cat out her window. She had never heard William cry before.

"You're stressed. You have to calm down." She tried to breathe strength into William's neck. She held him and they fell asleep like brother and sister without making love. The eagerness to touch, to kiss, to be close to each other's bodies had distilled into something more urgent.

In the morning she took William to the synagogue on 88th Street to consult the rabbi. "Something's wrong. You're not supposed to believe in Jesus. You're Jewish, for God's sake. " Even though she wasn't really religious, and barely went to synagogue, she woke up with the idea that William was in some kind of philosophical crisis and it was the only idea that made sense. "You can seek God, but he's a loving God."

But when they arrived at the door to the rabbi's chambers, William changed his mind. "I'm not going through with this. I'm okay, Eleanor," he said, when she was about to knock. "I don't feel so bad today."

There was a spark of light back in his eyes. He didn't seem so anxious. "I don't want to do this. Come on, I'm leaving tomorrow to go back home. You and I need to be together."

Before they left they took a peek into the synagogue. Eleanor's eye caught the everlasting light on the bema. "Look. God is watching us. He's taking care of you."

All the leaves had fallen off the tree on Broadway. It looked stark and naked. They walked back to her studio apartment. She looked at him in his wool sweater, and the bulk of him reassured her. William picked up a burnt-red leaf from the ground and pressed it into her palm. "It's the color of my heart."

She took it in her hand and put it in her pocket.

"You're okay now, aren't you?" Eleanor asked in the morning as William stuffed his work clothes into his duffel bag. "I wish you didn't have to leave."

They sat on the edge of her bed. William coaxed her down on the mattress and looked into her eyes. "It's okay," he said. "Do you hear the trees outside the window making love to the wind? Remember the sound. I'll be inside it."

They went to Broadway to hail a cab. Going to a fancy Ivy League University, studying literature — she spent days in her room smoking cigarettes, drinking instant coffee, and analyzing lines of poetry — and modeling for Adam seemed meaningless when she looked into William's searching, down-to-earth eyes the color of the forest. She had begun to believe that what mattered most was living through literature and art. She didn't live comfortably in the world the way that other people did. But what if she was wrong? Watching William, she told herself that she might give up her ambition. That she'd drop out of graduate school and go back to the woods and simplify her life. As they said good-bye on Broadway, the wind biting their faces and sending up swirls of garbage and papers from the street, she held on to the lapels of his coat. She looked in his eyes. "I'll be home soon. Hang in there. It won't be long now."

William stopped and pulled her closer to him. "You have to know it isn't your fault. You have to promise me you know that."

She didn't know what he was talking about.

"Promise." A cab stopped and pulled over. The white light on top of the roof of the cab went off. She said nothing.

"Promise me, Eleanor. This isn't a joke."

"I promise," she whispered into his coat. She thought he was referring to the fact that she had left him to go to college. She stood by the side of the street, watching as he climbed in the cab, until it was long out of sight.

She collapsed on the bed in her room. She looked at the red leaf he had given her that she had placed on her dresser. It was curling up at the edges.

13

Eleanor looked at the clock. It was 2:30. She thought about William's words again. *My hands, Eleanor. They don't feel like my own.* She looked at her own hands. Sunday she had slipped out to get a manicure to revive herself when the boys were at the apartment next door for a playdate, and though she admired the soft sheen the polish left on her fingernails, when she looked at her hands again, for the first time she thought she understood what William had meant. She put away her copy of *The Inferno* and closed her notepad, filled with the sense that something was coming unhinged. She packed up her belongings into her book bag and went to fetch Nicholas and Noah from school. She took in the scents of spring, noticed the daffodils still in bloom in the median running down the middle of Park Avenue, saw the buds on the trees, their narrow dark arrows about to blossom. It had been a long winter in New York and the flowers and trees were late beginning to bloom.

Nicholas was on the steps anxiously waiting for her. He hugged her hips. How quickly her children could snap her out of a mood. He wanted to have a playdate, and she let him run off, though she suddenly didn't want him to go.

Noah's class was coming out of the school building. Eleanor saw Noah's shiny black hair. He was carrying his square Batman lunch box. She walked in on a conversation between two of the other mothers about the spring fair and plans for the summer. You could be a banker, an academic, a stay-at-home mom, an actress, and none of it mattered when it came to talking about children. She liked the selfless bond she shared with other women as they arranged playdates, gossiped about their children, smiled at each other as their children came running out the school doors.

Eleanor let her son direct her to the playground. She watched Noah climb the jungle gym with his typical ease and spring. She marveled (still) that he was her child. She measured the miracles of the world by her children's small but meaningful accomplishments. When Nicholas learned to read she had to remind herself not to take his intelligence, his health, his beauty, his empathy, any of it for granted. She reminded herself how once she had wanted a child so badly she could taste it, because she did not want for one minute to think that her children wouldn't be enough to sustain her. She sat on the mound of lawn overlooking the playground and contemplated the children. She remembered that Stephen had called her earlier that day and she smiled.

She let Noah play in the playground until the other mothers and babysitters began to gather their charges to head home. As they walked toward the subway, she talked him through the minutiae of her day. The routine of knowing exactly where she was and what she did when they were apart calmed him. She began with conferences with students, the fracas with a faculty member, what she was reading or teaching, and as she spoke she reflected that the trip to Paris was finally behind her. For many nights since returning she had found her mind wandering back to the fixed look in Stephen's face as he stood on the bridge over the Seine. She thought if she continued to remember Stephen that day on the bridge she would never be able to sleep or rest peacefully again. She reminded herself that that night after she had seen him she felt as if a chasm opened and how eventually the feeling passed.

Noah loved to take the subway. Eleanor thought his enthusiasm for it would eventually wane and that it would turn commonplace, but it hadn't yet. Sometimes he was the conductor. Other times he was Spiderman and the bad guys were in one of the cars and he'd have to figure out which car before they arrived at their stop.

When they stood on the platform waiting for the train, even though he was seven, she still feared he'd jump out and fall in front of the tracks. She insisted that he stand behind the yellow line, holding her hand. He sometimes traveled so far into his imaginary play that he could block out the world around him. "All it takes is one misstep, one minute of not paying attention," she had warned him. He looked up at her with annoyance in his eye. "I'm not a baby, Mommy."

They waited for the train. Eleanor noticed a woman at the end of the platform in her early thirties with long blond hair, wearing a skirt and a colorful scarf tied around her neck. She was walking back and forth, pacing between two columns. She was used to seeing agitated homeless people pacing back and forth, but this woman did not appear homeless. She stopped close to the edge of the platform and then walked back against the wall. She looked up. It looked as if she'd been crying. A blotch of mascara was underneath one eye. Eleanor tried to catch her gaze in sympathy, smile, but the woman stared through her, seemingly absorbed in her own thoughts. Eleanor turned away to give her privacy.

Noah tugged on her hand. The train was approaching. She heard a cry and instinctively pulled Noah against her body to hide his eyes. The train hit something. The wheels screeched on the track, and the train came to an abrupt halt. Eleanor continued to hide Noah's face, making her body a shield. Commotion filled the subway station. She looked toward the end of the platform for the woman. She was gone. Had she imagined her? People began screaming. Police officers flew down the stairwell. Everyone shoved to get through the turnstiles. Eleanor gripped Noah's hand and pushed through the crowd converging near the exit. She was anxious to get her son above ground. She turned to walk him toward the stairway, holding on to his hand so tightly she thought she felt his knuckles crack. Again, the blare of ambulances reverberated inside her eardrums. As she mounted the stairs she looked back again, hoping to catch sight of the woman with the blond hair in the ascending crowd.

14

She ran the bath for the boys. She scoured the refrigerator for what she might prepare for dinner. She intended to pick up some fresh vegetables to make with pasta, remembering that Michael was not coming home. Nicholas arrived from his playdate and threw his backpack on the floor in the hallway, then kicked off his shoes in the middle of the kitchen. She yelled at him to pick up his shoes. It had been too much and her son's smelly gym shoes were in the middle of her kitchen and he had run off to play with his action figures. The laundry she had forgotten to fold that morning was all over the kitchen counter in piles. It was recycling day and she hadn't wrapped up the newspapers. There was no milk in the refrigerator. There was no pasta. "Nicholas, get in here and pick up your shoes," she shouted. He didn't hear her. "Get in here and pick up your shoes," she said again. There were smudges on the glass in the kitchen cabinets, handprints on the cupboards, piles of mail overflowed from its basket. "NICHOLAS!" she screamed. Her hands were shaking. "It's okay, Mom," Nicholas said, gathering up his shoes. "No, it's not okay," she said.

"I won't do it anymore," Nicholas said, standing in the kitchen with his tennis shoes in his hands. "I promise."

She looked at his face and softened. "It hasn't been a good day," she said. "Sorry I yelled at you."

Her son stared at her strangely, clutching his tennis shoes against his chest before he went to his bedroom.

Her objective was to get the boys to sleep so that she could retreat to her study. She was filled with the sensation that she was being punished for the transgressions in her mind. Perhaps she had willed the accident on the subway platform—if it was an accident. Had she been missing the clues and signs about her own life all along, the way she had missed the clues about William? She heard his voice in her head. *Why are we here in the first place?* The vacant eyes of the woman on the platform stayed with her. How she saw past Eleanor, how we always see past each other if we don't pay attention. How we can see even past ourselves.

She went into the kitchen to pour herself a glass of wine. She flicked on the evening news. The newscaster referred to an incident that had happened on the Number 5 train. The camera zoomed in on a photo of the woman. It was the woman on the platform. Her name was Monica Wilson. She was thirty-eight years old. She had been released from Paine Whitney, a psychiatric hospital where she had been admitted for suicidal depression. Her husband was a prominent media mogul who had started divorce proceedings months before the accident; they had two small children. There was strong reason to think it was a suicide. Eleanor tried to piece together what had happened on the subway platform. She had sensed the woman's unease, but she had no reason to believe she was suicidal. When she went to her wallet to pay the pizza deliveryman, her hands were shaking. She thought of Anna Karenina as if she had become a real person, a friend she had known and lost. She thought of how her passion for Vronsky had made her abandon her husband, her son, the society that kept her grounded. How she had, without will or reason, dug herself into a hole. She thought of her on that snowy St. Petersberg night with no alternative other than to throw herself before the train. What did it feel like for the world to be narrowed down to one throbbing pain inside you? What did it feel like when your only recourse was to end the pain?

She needed to get the boys their dinner. She needed to sit next to them while they ate their slice of pizza with carrot sticks and drank their glasses of lemonade. She would let them play for another half hour. Then she would read them a story and get them securely tucked in their beds. She had allowed disorder, a sense of panic to overtake her all day, and she told herself that she must temper it for the sake of the boys. Noah was only seven. She had to weigh whether to tell him the truth—because he'd eventually hear about what had happened on the subway platform—against her instinct to lie to him, or at least only tell him the partial truth. In his mind everything was simple. The world was still ordered in two ways, right and wrong, good and evil.

After she had gotten him into bed, after he brushed his teeth and she had read him a chapter from *Treasure Island,* he said, "Mommy, it was that lady at the end of the platform, wasn't it?"

"Yes, darling."

"She didn't listen. Didn't she know she wasn't allowed to step over the yellow line?"

"She must have forgotten. It must have frightened you. I'm sorry."

"It wasn't your fault, Mommy."

15

The key turned in the lock. From the crack of light in the hallway she saw Michael walking toward the bedroom and smelled the familiar antiseptic soap from the hospital on his skin as he approached. He undid the buttons on his shirt, sat at the foot of the bed, and untied his shoes.

"Hard day?"

"You're still up? I thought you were sleeping. Why are you lying in the dark?" He flicked on the little light on the bureau. She was fully dressed on top of the made-up bed.

"You look tired."

"Martin Fisher passed. We were doing a cardiac catheterization to identify the blockage. When we began the angioplasty the arteries were stiff and brittle. There was more than one blockage."

"I'm sorry."

"We didn't know how bad it was until we opened him up."

"I know how much you liked him." His back was to her. She touched his arm tenderly. "How do you keep on course?"

"You do everything you can. But sometimes the heart's already too damaged. It's humbling to realize not everything is in your power."

She had come to know the signals when Michael wanted to talk or be distracted. She had learned that whenever a patient died he did not necessarily need to talk about it. She watched him take off his clothes, hang them on hangers, so that his jacket and pants seemed like the shape of his former self, and wondered what was inside him when he left the pressures of the hospital behind, when he wasn't taking care of her or the boys. Why she couldn't access him; why he felt to her like a stranger.

"It's late. How come you're still awake?"

She told him about what had happened on the subway.

"That sounds horrible." He yawned. "Aren't you going to get undressed? Let me help." He helped her take off her jeans and unbuttoned her sweater. He slipped his legs between hers. "I'm sorry you and Noah had to see it." He ran his hand under the back of her camisole. Sex for him was an elixir. It helped to release the tension stored in his body. It was the way he got close. He needed Eleanor's body, though sometimes she wished he had other ways to connect.

"I can't get that woman's face out of my head."

Michael took his hand away from her waist and rolled over. "How did Noah handle it?"

"He was frightened."

"She must have been very disturbed." Unable to relax, he reached for the remote. The television screen came to life.

"Because she wanted to kill herself?"

"Eleanor, anyone who throws herself before a subway train isn't well."

"But maybe she hadn't wanted to die. Didn't she know that it would pass? That she'd eventually get to the other side? She had two children."

"If she didn't want to die, I'd assume she'd have chosen something less violent, less irrevocable." He roamed through the channels, then, unappeased flicked off the television. "I don't want to fight. I'm tired."

"Are we fighting?"

"Thinking about it isn't going to get you anywhere. We didn't know her."

"I witnessed a woman kill herself today. I can't stop thinking about those poor children." She looked at him. "I'm sorry." She remembered he had lost a patient.

"Come over here. Please," he said. "I have my rights, too, you know."

She moved closer to him and put her arms around him, longing to be able to connect. "Have you ever lost your bearings?"

"I'm not like that, Eleanor. Are we talking about the woman who died today?"

She thought about the dirty pavement of the subway platform stripped of nearly all natural light. About what must have been the last thing that woman might have seen: men carrying briefcases, a teenager looking at the text messages on his cell phone, the image of her holding Noah's hand, and what she herself had stepped away from—the gleaming subway tracks—waiting for the train. She thought of the light through the long tunnel signaling the train's approach. Had she ever wanted to die? There were hours in her past she was anxious, or at a loss, not knowing how to stop her restless mind, but not knowing how to ask for what she wanted. Did she know what she wanted? But usually her despair slowly dissipated once she pushed herself out of bed, out of the house and into the brightness of the day. No, she never wanted to die. She wanted to learn how to live with contradictory emotions and longings, with all the passion inside her. She thought of the train growing louder, how Noah clapped his ears closed against the shrill of it. In her mind she imagined the woman's feet in her boots moving toward the yellow line, saw her skirt rise up slightly, the wind on her face from the train's approach.

She clung to Michael as if she had fallen over the edge into the darkness of the rails and he was saving her from the approaching train. She made love to him fiercely, wanting something from him she didn't quite understand. Afterward she curled into his damp, sleep-filled warmth until she woke up uncomfortable, with a crick in her neck. The feeling of unease and emptiness remained.

16

Mrs. Woods greeted Eleanor in the reception area of the hospital, and tears filled her eyes when she went to hug her. She had called to tell her that William was in the hospital, and Eleanor had taken the first flight in. Mr. Woods was watching the television in the waiting room. He looked like he'd been up all night. His clothes were slightly crumpled and the back of his hair matted where he had fallen asleep against the back of a chair. He stood up when Eleanor walked in. "He'll pull himself together," he said, his voice tensing with emotion. He patted

Eleanor a tad too forcefully on the back. "He's a little mixed up right now."

William looked pale and tired. He was wearing a hospital gown, robe, and a pair of white sports socks and pulled an IV pole as he came to the waiting room to find her. The last time she saw him she was putting him in a cab on the streets of New York City more than a month ago. "Please be okay," Eleanor said, pressing her face into his neck, hugging him with all her might. They walked slowly back to William's hospital room and lay down together on the hospital bed with its perfect corners. His hair had lost its shine. "What happened?" she finally asked.

"I kept thinking about what that man said about Jesus and hell and not being saved and I started feeling funny. It was like being so far down in your head you don't know how to climb out. I forgot my name. Where I lived. I looked at my hands and my face in the mirror and they were not my own. I couldn't leave the apartment. I realized that a week had gone by, and I hadn't eaten or done anything that I could remember. I picked up the phone and called an ambulance."

"But what happened? I don't get it," Eleanor said again.

He looked at her blankly. "I'm worried about the dogs. Will you make sure they get fed?"

"Of course I will. Whatever you want, William."

Eleanor went to the hospital every day. She sat in the lobby when William went to group, and had his private sessions with the doctor, and then joined him in his room when they brought in his lunch and supper. She picked up the tin lids and said, "Today you're having turkey and mashed potatoes," and she moved the tray close to William and watched him try to eat. They watched television together. Eleanor held his hand. She looked at him for signs. The doctor called it depersonalization. What did it mean? That William was not a person anymore?

That he had no self? She said nothing. She kept looking for William in his eyes, but the anger and spark had vanished. *Why are we here in the first place? I wish there was an alternative universe we could live in, Eleanor. When I'm building the wall I think about it. About where we could live where no one will harm us.* She thought about those words looking at the grayish hue to his skin.

He stayed in the hospital for a month. When he was released, he went to his mother's house to recuperate. Eleanor went with him, sleeping in one of his older brothers' empty bedrooms. She called the chair of her department and explained the situation. She'd have to make up her work when she returned. During the day she sat next to him on the couch in the family room and held his hand. His loyal dogs were at William's feet. It was like they were in high school again, only they were in their twenties, living together in his mother's house. "Eleanor, you're holding my hand too tight," William said. "Can you let go for a second?" The days passed this way. It was so quiet they could hear the leaves shudder, the dogs whimper, and the cats meow.

"You have to go back to New York," William said, after another three weeks had passed.

"I'm not going back."

"You can't stay here and watch me."

"I'm not leaving."

"Stop looking at me that way."

"Where are you?" She pulled him by the shirt. She was angry. "You're not in here anymore." She pointed her finger in his chest.

"I'm right here. This is me now."

She moved closer to him on the couch.

"I can't breathe, Eleanor. I have to do this on my own."

"What about the wall? Who's going to finish it?"

"I'm not strong enough." He looked at her, his eyes sad and lifeless. "You're crushing me."

"I'll go back." She touched his arm. "If you promise it will help you get better."

"The only thing that will make me feel better is if you go on with your life. You have to do this for me."

Was the pain in her body William's or her own?

"William took the dogs out today." "William went to work." "William ate beef stroganoff for supper," Mrs. Woods said, with forced cheeriness when Eleanor would call from New York to get a report on his state of mind.

Eleanor went back to the synagogue to see the rabbi. "My daughter," the rabbi said, "the mind is fragile. You have to have faith in God and what God has willed." She didn't mind being the rabbi's daughter. She left his chambers and sat in the synagogue, watching the light fight its way through the stained glass. She began to pray. It was what she understood one did when there was nothing else to be done.

17

Her neck itched. The daybed in Adam's studio was hard. To avoid scratching her neck she thought about the paper she was writing on *The Inferno*. Virgil takes a journey through darkness. He doesn't know who he is or what his life means. She thought of William walking through the woods, circling the fields, the dogs trailing after him. She thought of the stone wall.

The wall had come to define the life they had together, who they were with each other, the way each stone began to fit, stone by stone, next to each other, securely, without mortar, over time molded to each other, forming a barricade against the world.

"What's in your head, Eleanor? Where are you?" Adam looked up from the canvas.

"I'm right here."

"What are you thinking about? You seem distant."

"I'm thinking about William." She had told Adam about what had happened. Ever since she'd reconnected with him she insisted that their relationship be platonic. In a way she'd always wanted to know whether she and Adam could be friends— whether their connection was real and not just sexual. He said he understood, he would try and restrain himself, but sometimes he weakened. She found herself torn, too. In her heart she was loyal to William, but she was beginning to feel more her true self with Adam. And yet she didn't completely trust him. "I don't know how to reach him anymore."

"I can't bear disconnection."

"Did you always feel disconnected from Mariana?"

"I married her because I never expected connection. This way she could never disappoint me." He left the canvas and sat next to her on the daybed. "Where were you last night? I tried to call you."

"I should be asking where you were."

"I'm freer than you are, Eleanor. My erotic life is here with you, not with my wife. Being married makes me love you more than if I were single."

"That's convenient."

"If I wasn't married I would expect more from you. This way we can be equal. You don't have to put groceries in my refrigerator. I don't have to pay your bills. There's no hierarchy between us. If I paid for your dress, then I own it when you're wearing it. It becomes harder for you to refuse me. You feel you have an obligation when you're married, that you owe your life to someone even when you no longer feel the same attraction. Let me explain it another way. If you sacrifice your own work time to come home and make me dinner, I've deprived you of something. It's a cruel institution, marriage."

It was weirdly convincing logic. She thought about how even though William had asked her to leave so that she could get back to her life, she was still in love with him. Love wasn't a choice.

"You can't come into my studio wearing your vintage lace tops and blue jean skirts and red sandals looking like a teenager. You just can't do it. You can't let me get close to you and let me smell your perfume and then pull away. It's killing me."

"Adam, I have to finish this paper."

"I can't keep looking at you and not want you next to me."

"But you promised."

"Cancel the conference. Stay with me."

She agreed to meet him back at her apartment after her meeting. It took too much work to say no. She thought about the time she had spent in his studio watching him work, modeling for him, and how complicit she was in his work. She was flattered that it was she he picked to immortalize. Even though she was his "study," she felt like a partner in his work.

Adam drank a beer on the bed and listened to Bob Dylan while she continued to work at her desk. She could hear his heavy boots—paint-splattered in dots and slashes over the leather—walk her floor. He stood behind her chair and massaged her shoulders.

"Adam, I told you I have to finish this paper. It's due tomorrow." She was struggling with it. Even its title was proving burdensome: "The Tension Between Morality and Eroticism and the Quest for Selfhood." In the paper she showed how desire for goodness and darkness were equally strong. "Do you think there are only two true objects of human love: God and the self?" she asked. "I mean, the self as man. Do you think that if we decide to love man over God then we are essentially doomed?"

"Why are they exclusive?"

"We can decide to love God over man, but if we forgo God and decide to love only man, to love only carnally, to exist only in pursuit of the flesh, then does that mean we are perpetual sinners?"

"What are you struggling with?" Adam asked, still impatient with her to finish. "Your desire for me and your devotion to William?"

She looked at him.

"Without darkness there can be no goodness. Man has to sin in order to be redeemed."

"So are you saying that what we're doing together is a sin?"

She thought of William. His sickness was a manifestation of a struggle inside him. He belonged to the forest. She wanted to lead him out of the darkened woods. But how? Was it ever really possible to reach another person? She didn't want Adam. She was devoted to William.

"You can fight desires but they still exist inside us. If I make love to you in my mind, am I still unfaithful? And does it make a difference? Didn't I sin against my marriage those weeks in my studio when I thought about touching you and my need to be close to you? I'll teach you about sin. Then you can decide if you'd rather worship God or the body." He tried to kiss her. "Or maybe you'd rather be with a boy rather than a man."

He lifted the hair off her neck. His breath smelled like beer and onions from the hamburger he had eaten earlier in the night. He wanted to touch her. She moved away, and as she did she caught him staring at her with an almost sinister expression.

"I need you, Eleanor." He cornered her again while she was at the sink filling up the kettle. He pressed his body into her back and kissed her neck. She was aroused by his desire for her, but she was tired of playing the part of the prepubescent lover. She was in her twenties. It occurred to her as he was trying to seduce her that this was central to his art. It would allow him to go further into his pathos, into his shame and desire, and by traveling further, it would allow him to push further into his work. Suddenly his desire for her repulsed her. It was purely carnal. How could she open herself to someone so foreign to her own nature? Adam was sophisticated and worldly and solipsistic. She was a girl from the Midwest in love with a boy who knew the name of every insect and bird but did not know how to navigate his own heart.

"I can't do this, Adam." She wiggled out of his grasp. "I told you. I'm back with William."

Her bottle of perfume was sitting on the windowsill. Adam looked at the blue cobalt bottle and seized it. He put it in his pocket and walked out of the apartment. "Find a new job," he said, under his breath. Or did he say, "Find a new guy?" She wasn't sure, and she continued to wonder once he had left. Her eyes focused on the windowsill where the perfume bottle had once stood. She conjured an image in her head of Adam in his studio opening the perfume and smelling it, and then smudging together colors from paint tubes to form a muted disturbing color, then taking the brush to his canvas, transforming his anger and desire into the texture of his subject's hair.

He was too complicated. Everything he wanted from her seemed for his own benefit. She thought about William. He was the opposite. She opened the window. The drone of traffic was suddenly absent. She listened again. She heard the creak of the tree on her street when the wind pushed against it. She picked up the phone. It had been over a month since she had last seen him.

"It's good to hear your voice, Eleanor."

"I wanted to call you a hundred times."

"I've been working again." He grew quiet. "I'm back at the apartment."

"Why?"

"The motherfucker moved back home. I can't live in the same house with him. I don't trust him, Eleanor."

"But it's too soon." She paused. "I just wish you didn't have to live there." Eleanor thought about that dark apartment bordering on the ghetto.

"Can you believe she took him back? After what he did to her? I have to live here, Eleanor. Who else is going to look after these folks?"

She took the phone and lay down on the couch. *This is good, William is talking again,* she thought. "How are the dogs? Bear? Scout?"

"They're good. But they're going to die."

"William, I'm coming home. I need to see you. Are you building the wall again?"

"I don't have the strength to lift the stones."

"I'll help. If you wait for me."

18

S he couldn't get the shape, touch, voice, image of him out of her system. They had that kind of telepathy with each other. She knew that the minute she looked into his eyes everything would be fine even though they'd been away from each other for more than a month. She surprised William and came in a day earlier than he expected. Usually she spent the first night she was home having supper with her mother, but that night she asked if she could borrow the car. She fixed herself up, putting on a skirt, the blue one with the white flowers, and a blue sweater that William liked her in. She fixed her hair the way he liked, taking the two front pieces and putting them in back with a clip, slipped in her favorite dangle earrings.

She drove downtown, parked her car in the apartment complex where William lived. Once she got out of the car, she pulled her long coat closer to her body out of fear, telling herself she had to get William out of that place. It was after 6:00, pitch black. The wind was tough. In the lobby, Eleanor told the security officer that she was here to see William Woods. She asked if he would let her up without buzzing so she could surprise him, and he went ahead and let her. She remembered exactly what floor William lived on, what apartment number. The door was locked. She knocked on the thick steel. There was no answer. She pressed the buzzer and then pounded on the door again.

But she had seen William's pickup truck. It was parked next to where she had parked her mother's car. Maybe he was taking out the garbage or tending to a problem with one of the units in the building. She stood in the hallway for a few minutes and waited. Then she stepped back into the elevator, went downstairs, and asked the security guard if he had seen William. She looked in the mirror in the vestibule. She thought to herself, as soon as William sees me we are going to be okay. The security guard said he'd try to page him. When he didn't answer the page, the security guard accompanied Eleanor back up the elevator. She thought how strangely yellow his coloring looked under the fluorescent light in the elevator. She remembered that security guard's face as he proceeded to unlock William's door.

He suggested she wait out in the hall after he flicked on the light and smelled its stench. Eleanor couldn't wait. She followed behind him. The room looked as if it hadn't been cleaned in weeks. Dirty clothes were in a heap on the floor. A filthy towel was on the back of the kitchen chair. There were empty Coke cans, pizza boxes, newspapers stacked on the kitchen counters and piled on the floor and on the coffee table. It smelled awful. It was the sight of that room, the fact that he hadn't cared enough about himself to clean up, that made her angry. *William, why can't you take better care of yourself?* she thought. The security guard tried to usher her back out the door, but she wouldn't go. On the table was an empty vial of painkillers William's doctor had prescribed for a disk he fractured lifting stones for his wall.

William was slumped on the couch, his face pushed into the pillows, his back to her. She thought he was sleeping, even though the security guard tried to pull her away. "It's okay," she said to the guard. "I want to surprise him." *Nothing is wrong. William's sleeping.* She leaned over and kissed his cheek. It was cold. She put a blanket around him. He didn't move. "William, wake up. Get up!" she screamed. The record player nearby was still on. *Everyone's leaving. And sunny skies has to stay behind.* The needle was at the end of the record, scratching it. On the coffee table was the last letter she had sent him, telling him when she was arriving. Next to it was a brush filled with strands of his hair.

Days later she went to the woods by herself and sat on the stone wall. There was still snow on the ground and she sat in the cold to be close to William. She heard his voice in her head. *A dry retaining wall is constructed without mortar or adhesion. It depends upon the weight and friction of one stone on another for its stability. Nothing exists alone, Eleanor. There is always balance. The first stones can be laid six inches below grade. There is no elaborate footing required for a dry wall since the stones are not bonded together and will raise and lower with the frost. In laying the first layer, larger stones should be used. A line should then be strung along the wall as a guide to keep the rest of the wall straight.* She had watched him drag the stones from one site to another in a piece of heavy canvas. *It's about endurance. I think of it as battling with what pulls me down, what takes the life out of me, and then building something beautiful from it. This wall is ours. Remember. One stone on another.* She pictured the way he had pushed her to the ground and started kissing her neck. *Let me look at those eyes,* he said. *The blue one is brighter today, Eleanor.*

She picked up one of the lighter stones and laid it on the wall. The wall was perpendicular to a creek, and she heard the sound of the water moving through the stones, reminding her of the living world. *What happened to all the love letters I sent you when we were apart? Where are the letters, William? Nothing is private between two people.* She lifted one stone, and then another, placing each one on the wall the way he had taught her. *One life spirals into others. I thought God would protect you. But I made a mistake. You needed to watch yourself. To make your own covenant with God. Didn't I mean anything? Why, William?* She held the blue stone, his favorite, close to her chest before she threw it into the wall, shattering it into little pieces. *How could you do this to me?*

The air was turning moist. Darker. Clouds closed in overhead. Small animals scurried for cover. She could see the gleaming edge of a piece of red cloth in between two slabs of stone. It was the bandanna he wore around the crown of his head. She used it to wipe her eyes.

It's my life to do what I want with, isn't it, Eleanor? If I want to stay here in the woods, behind this wall? She stood up straight and stretched her back. *No, it's not okay, William.* Her muscles ached.

Her hands were crusty with mud. *What about us—the people who loved you? We sat around the linoleum kitchen table in your mother's house trying to figure out what would possess you to take your life. We talked about the coffin you built out of wood for the sick runt of your cat's litter. Your dad was there. He was crying like a baby. We talked about the amazing care that went into the way you built the wall. What went wrong? We talked about how you liked to run in the woods with your dogs, the way you juggled for hours at a time.*

She propped herself on the wall and let her legs dangle over one side. William was part of God; she listened for his mysterious echo in the woods. Nothing. Only the wind sighed through the dense trees. The shadow of a slender deer. A hundred sparrows crowded in one tree. It began to rain—a drizzle so light she could barely feel it. In time the rain quickened.

She hopped off the wall and picked up a fistful of dirt. *I know you can see me, William.* The rain soaked her hair and jacket. Her wet pants stuck to her legs. She shivered. In her memory she saw the shape of him scoop up a handful of earth. He held it in his palm and sprinkled it into her hand. *Here, take this dirt in your hands. See all the minerals and crystals inside it. There could be souls in this dirt, fragments of bodies. We're all inside each other.*

19

It was a Monday in June, and the halls were quiet as a morgue. Most of the students were away. She embraced her work with urgency. It was the only way she knew how to go on. She picked up her note cards where she had made some notes on *The Inferno* and reread them, still seeking answers.

Late in the day, Ursula, her assistant, handed Eleanor a pink message slip. Eleanor glanced at it before tucking it into her jacket pocket. She made a cup of tea, went into her office, and shut the door, grateful to be undisturbed. She looked again at the pink slip and studied the *S* of his name scrawled in Ursula's loopy script.

She pictured him as he looked in Paris standing against the bridge over the Seine. She crumpled the pink message slip into a ball and tossed it into the plastic receptacle underneath her desk.

She peered out her office window at the lawn between buildings where students congregated, at the still blossoming dogwood tree, at two young people by the tree embracing, unaware that she was watching. How passionately they kissed. She went out to the hallway, walked down the hall to the women's bathroom. In the mirror, one eye looked muted, subdued, the other was vibrant. She went back to her office and retrieved the crumpled message from the receptacle.

He answered on the first ring.

"Where are you?"

"Where are *you*?" he said.

"I'm in my office."

"I flew in from Colorado this morning. I had a meeting with my agent. I called you earlier, Eleanor. I thought maybe we could grab lunch. Now I'm at JFK on my way back to Colorado. Where were you?" he said, as if he had expected that she should be there the minute he had called. "You were supposed to be there." He cleared his throat to disguise the emotion in his voice.

"I went on a field trip with Noah's class. We went to Central Park."

"I may be spending more time in New York. I've been discussing a few story ideas with my agent. I have to tell you something."

"Go ahead."

"You've blossomed. You've taken on that kind of grace that comes with age and experience."

"Are you saying that I look old?"

"No. I'm saying the opposite. I'm saying you look sexy."

Her throat was dry. She coughed into the phone.

"One thing I know is that what I've learned about myself and love has been the longest and slowest lesson of my life."

The memories of what had happened between them hung in the silence.

"It has?"

"I haven't solved that part of the puzzle yet. But then, I've always been the late bloomer. When I'm in New York again, would you have lunch with me? I can't get you out of my head."

She laughed.

"What are you doing?" he said. "Right now."

"I'm on the phone talking to you and looking out my office window."

"Now I can see you," he paused. "Your eyes. They haunt me. Your red hair. I can remember exactly what you were wearing when I saw you in Paris. Eleanor?"

"I'm still here."

"I was so inept back in those days. I'm sorry if I hurt you."

There was static in the line. The call was breaking up. "I'm losing you," Stephen said. "I'll be in touch."

She sat in her chair.

For the next hour she went over each word, interpreted and weighed each nuance, even the pauses between words. She couldn't work. She packed up and left the office. Her cell phone rang; she answered and was startled to hear the sound of Michael's voice. He asked if he needed to pick up anything for dinner. It reminded her that she lived in two worlds and it was time for her to check in to the present.

Over dinner Michael mentioned a new resident who was working under him. The resident seemed worn down in the mornings, almost hung over. He wondered whether he had a problem. "He has newborn twins," Michael said. "He can't afford to be acting this way."

"What way?"

"Irresponsibly. He's a grown-up, Eleanor."

"Have you talked with him about it?"

"I told him he better get his act together," Michael said.

The rest of the evening floated by. It was the blue hour, when it wasn't quite dark. Her mind kept drifting back to her conversation with Stephen, and in spite of not wanting to think about him, she felt strangely disconnected and dreamy.

Later, she remembered the time when she visited him in Colorado. She was sure that now he would have an explanation for why he had abandoned her there. She thought that if she could frame everything just the way that it had happened, she could maybe find the meaning that had eluded her. But she did not want to think anymore about their past. By thinking about it, it was as though she was imbuing him with newer, more immediate significance than was appropriate. She wanted to forget him just as intensely as she longed to be close to him. And why was she thinking about him at all? She was married.

20

"Eleanor, I didn't expect to find you in Chicago," Stephen said. "I was looking for my mother. I thought she might be over here." His shirt was crumpled. He hadn't shaved. He looked tired. He dug the heel of his cowboy boot into the linoleum of her floor, leaving a scuff mark. "I've been driving for two days. I got on my bike and I couldn't stop. You ever have that feeling?"

He had lost a little of his boyishness. He had broadened

across the chest. His face had grown taut, and the long unruly hair he'd had when she saw him last was slicked back. Despite the fact that he looked tired, he was beautiful. The years had solidified him, so that his once boyish good looks had evolved into a cool, rugged charm. She hadn't seen him in more than a year, since Christmas of the year she started graduate school. He sat on one of the kitchen stools on the other side of the island where she was washing the dishes. She had come home in late August to spend time with her mother before school started. It had been months since William had died. He haunted every corner of the city.

"How long are you in town? My mother said you moved to Colorado."

"I'm not sure. Maybe a day or two. I can't breathe here. When I'm in the mountains I feel like I've been freed. Maybe it's the mountain air."

She sat on one of the stools in the kitchen next to him. He told her about some of the journalism pieces he was working on for an outdoor magazine in Colorado and that he was writing a novel. He described it as experimental.

"It's all about voice. When I'm writing I say the words in my head as if I'm talking to someone and I need them to listen."

"Really? When I'm working on a paper I don't really think about my audience. I'm thinking about my own obsessions."

After William took his life, Eleanor thought she'd never go on, that she'd never be able to sit with another person and care about their conversation. But there were days, even weeks, when she didn't think about William and then, out of the blue, the loss of him would seize hold and nearly paralyze her. Other times she'd think, *Okay, well, William's gone.* She had thought she'd never be able to sit next to a man again, but now she was talking to one. Her mother phoned to say she was working late. Eleanor invited Stephen to stay for dinner.

"They're getting old."

"Who?"

"Our mothers." He paused. "I wonder what my life would be like if they hadn't gotten divorced." He peeled the label of the beer off the bottle she had offered him, scratching the stubborn, gummy part with his thumbnail. It looked like something was bothering him.

"I think about that, too. What my life would be like if my father had stayed."

"She never wrote to me the time she was gone."

"Maybe she thought it would be better for you not to hear from her. Maybe she thought she'd only hurt you more."

He looked at her as if she had betrayed him.

"I'm sorry. I know it hurt you."

"My mother told me about it. The guy from high school. I used to see his pickup in your driveway when I came to visit."

"William."

Stephen rose and placed his hands on her shoulders. "I'm sorry. I know you loved him."

Tears burned her eyes. She didn't expect to cry. For the week she'd been home she felt William all the time. She let Stephen turn her around and embrace her. She realized how stiff her body had been in her effort to stay numb. He pressed his lips against the skin of her neck and her body softened. She lifted her head and they kissed on the lips. William kissed like a boy, clumsy and tense and in a hurry. Stephen kissed slow and long and carefully. "I've wanted to do that ever since we were twelve." He stopped for a moment and looked at her and shook his head, as if he were angry that he hungered for her before kissing her again. The kiss was partly sexual, partly tender, and emotional, and she pulled away from him, afraid of where the encounter was leading. She thought to herself: *I'm kissing Stephen Mason. I'm kissing the boy from the house in back of me who once lit his playhouse on fire!* She was sure as he kissed her that he had started the fire. She remembered his smile as they watched the playhouse burn and she thought to herself that maybe burning it was his attempt to let go of the past. And then she told herself she was being silly—of course the fire was an accident.

"What made you come all the way across country? Are you still in touch with your old girlfriend?"

"Chrissy? That didn't end well." He looked down and then perked back up. "I like to drive. Even if there's nowhere to go. You know. The feeling of not being stuck. Of moving. I thought I'd come see my mom. Sometimes I can't shake it. Her alone in that house all the time. And then once I get here I can't stand being around her." He glanced from the back window toward his house. The light was on behind the blind in his mother's bedroom window. "I should go," he said reluctantly. "You know, Eleanor. I'd really like it if you visited me in Colorado sometime."

He kissed her long and tenderly, and the kiss seemed to unlock unknown depths inside her that made her feel both exhilarated and frightened at the same time. They did not end the evening in platitudes. Stephen did not promise to call the next day, nor did she attempt to secure a promise. She assumed she would see him again before she left to go back to New York. There was something about the way that he looked at her that, though it stirred her, was also safe and familiar and left her with little doubt that he cared for her.

The next morning she drove her mother's car to the woods behind William's mother's house and then wandered until she found the wall. She purposefully moved the stones that William had stacked in piles, laying them one by one on top of each other until dusk set in. The stones had begun to change and shift over time, taking on more history, depth, and dimension. She heard his voice in her head, and the voice guided her: *Eleanor, lay the stones as they would lie naturally on the ground. The wall is one version of utopia. It can be whatever you want it to be.*

She wondered if God was in the wall, the same way he was inside each living creature, in each stone. She began to think of the wall as a work of art, a tribute to what she had lost. Adam said that all anxiety was a response to grief; that art was born out of anxiety. She understood what he meant. She didn't want to finish building the wall because finishing it would mean she was saying good-bye to William. After he died she had begun to think of him as a poet without a calling. She thought about the tenderness of his soul as she worked, how building the wall had been for him what words were for her, a need to organize thought and emotion, and it helped her to accept his death. She worked for hours at a time. Though she didn't smoke often, she bought a pack of cigarettes and smoked one for the sake of ritual when she was finished.

The wall could go on as long as she wanted it to; it could be a continuous thing, a relationship. It was always in her mind, behind her thoughts, giving more structure to her life. Every now and then she'd have a strong impulse to take the stones apart, one by one, so that she could keep building it and never finish.

Stephen was standing on the front stoop of her house when she returned. "Eleanor, I have to tell you something. I've been thinking about it all day. I haven't stopped thinking about you since the other night. I saw the light on in your house, and I thought 'This is why I came home.'"

She looked at him squarely. Was he serious? "But you didn't know I'd be here." She stared at the rawhide bracelet around his wrist, his boots splattered with dots of white paint from the housepainting and construction work he did to support his writing habit. She saw every flaw of his character in the way he raised one eyebrow to look at her. She thought of him at thirteen, then at sixteen, then just over a year ago at Christmas, and she began to lose her bearings.

"It's just so good to be with you again. I remember when we were kids. When your father was around. In the summer I could hear his piano coming through your open windows. I saw him playing and you and your mom listening on the couch. You all looked so happy."

"You remember that?"

"I've never forgotten." He studied her dirty clothes. "Hey, where've you been? You look like you've been playing in the dirt."

"I'm building a stone wall." She was disarmed by his openness and warmth. "Don't ask."

"I think it's a sign."

"A sign?"

"Yeah, you know what I mean. Both of us being in town. I think it means something. I can feel your energy when I'm with you." She let him kiss her again, slowly. "You know I stayed up half the night last night writing. Seeing you inspired me." He touched the small of her back.

"What is it with us? How come we don't stay in touch?" he asked.

"I don't know."

"Do you want to be close to me?"

"Do you want me to?"

"If you want to be close to me, there's something I have to show you."

She let him take her hand as they walked to his mother's house. Lilacs were in bloom. Sprinklers folded back and forth lazily over the lawns so lush they looked like paintings. The night before she'd asked him a lot of questions. He was trying to get started as a journalist. He wrote rock and music reviews for an alternative paper. He was working on a cover story about rock formations in the Colorado Rockies for a Denver magazine. He was working on a novel. But something about him didn't seem settled. He looked preoccupied; she couldn't put her finger on the reason.

They walked to the back door. She saw the tree up close, the one she had studied so often from her window. It looked wounded; the branches shot up like unkempt hair.

Stephen opened the back door to the house. He took her down to the cellar and opened a locker to an old pantry. Inside were dozens of empty jugs of wine. "She drinks."

"But all these bottles? Why?"

"You can't trust a drunk. Like every addict, she loves the glamour of deception."

"You never knew?"

"I wondered. But I guess I didn't want to know. I'm leaving today." He forced the keys to his bike in his pocket tight against his upper thigh. "She disgusts me." He retreated into the living room and slumped into the velvet cushions of the couch. "I don't want to be here when she gets home from work. It's what she does at night. Why she's so alone."

She heard him breathing heavily. She went to touch his leg, then pulled her hand back. She didn't know how to comfort him. She kept her hands folded neatly in her lap, trying to honor his private torment, seeing that his anger filled him with a kind of passion.

"I'm not coming back here."

"Come back with me to New York."

He dug a lighter out of his pocket, flicked back the ignite switch. He lit the flame. When it went out he flicked it back again. He flicked it on and off restlessly. "I've got things to take care of in Colorado."

"Then I'll come visit you. I've never been to Colorado."

"The mountains. Man, you have to see them to see how small we are."

"Do you want me to come?"

He pulled out of his funk. "I'll take you to the mountains. I want to be the first to see your face when you see how awesome it is. Yes, I do want you to come."

"I don't want you to leave yet. Come to the barbecue tomorrow. Then afterward you can go."

"I'll stay, Eleanor. But only for you. Then you have to promise you'll come see me in Colorado."

She felt excited when she awoke. Being with Stephen these last few days had made her believe once more in her ability to be touched by another person, and she carried that new hope inside like a gift.

A light summer rain cleaned their streets and broke the humidity, creating inside the house a sealed-off feeling of contentment. That night, with the air crisp and smelling of dampened grass, she thought that she could learn to accept William's death. She imagined his soul at peace, wrapped in the pines.

When the guests began to arrive she felt in her stomach the anticipation of seeing Stephen. When Carol came in the door she was sure that Stephen would soon follow behind her. She thought she saw his shadow approach but then overheard Carol explain to her mother that Stephen had left that day. Carol said he'd spent the morning with her, that she'd made him a big breakfast and they had drunk an entire pot of coffee. That by early afternoon he had become restless. "I thought maybe I'd done something," she said, "and then he came downstairs carrying the same duffel bag he arrived with, said he was going back on the road, that he had to get back for an assignment. Stephen's always been hard to pin down. I let him come and go as he pleases. I've learned not to expect anything from him." Her laugh was meant to hide sorrow. Eleanor stared at her, half angry and half feeling sorry for her. "Elizabeth, I should have called to tell you he wasn't coming. I half expected that he might turn around and decide to come back."

"Don't worry about it," Eleanor's mother said, giving Carol a hug. "At least you had him for a few nights. It's hard to see our kids growing away from us."

Eleanor distracted herself with superficial conversation. She was surprised by the unexpected emotion that rose inside her. She didn't understand what she had done that would have made him leave without at least saying good-bye to her. Had she misread the situation? She told herself that he couldn't bear being at home any longer and she shouldn't take it personally. When she went to sleep that night she could no longer recall the feel of his kiss or the solid weight of his fingers in her hand. She tried to picture him, but he had become vague and remote. She couldn't remember his voice. Maybe she had only imagined he had once touched her lips with his own.

21

After William died she had isolated herself when she wasn't studying, often sitting quietly in dark, cool cathedrals around the city. But once she saw Stephen Mason in Chicago that summer, something opened inside her. She needed to live again. She wasn't going to feel sorry for herself any longer. The fact that William had chosen death made her cling to life more profoundly.

She hadn't spoken to Adam since he'd walked away with her perfume bottle. His possessiveness seemed inconsequential in the face of William's death. What mattered was that she needed a friend. "I've missed you," she said when she called. "I committed myself to you. I mean to your work. I'm ready to come back to the studio." He had described their silent moments working together as a sanctuary in which they gave their presence over to a higher power; she needed to be inside his sanctuary. They agreed to resume their relationship as painter and model, barely missing a beat.

She thought about how he had once described the studio as a life room. "I tell my students to go in and find the meaning," he had said. "For each person it is different." Eleanor thought of the life room as one that was of endless length and endless breadth. A room filled with one's sole associations.

"I knew you'd eventually call," Adam said. "But it had to be you. You had to want me. You look different. Older." The canvases she had modeled for had sat in his studio unfinished since she had left. "They've been speaking to me. But I didn't know how to access their meaning until you walked in the door." She sat down on the daybed and took off her sweater. He began each of their sessions by playing Jascha Heifetz performing Bach's violin sonatas. "You look sad. Has something happened?" He was already behind the canvas, eager to work.

"It's William. He killed himself."

"The boy from home?"

She hadn't said William's name in so long that just talking about him filled her with unexpected emotion.

He put down his paintbrush. "I'm sorry, Eleanor."

"All the signs were there but I didn't see them."

"It's not your fault. You know that."

"It's okay," she said. It was still too painful to talk about. "Let's work."

She felt the pleasure of watching Adam; it was when she liked him most, when he didn't seem to need anything from her. She closed her eyes and held on to the image of him lost in his work and realized how much she needed distraction and how happy she was to be back in his studio. He moved forward to arrange her in the position he wanted. Then he reached for the buttons on her blouse and unfastened them. It was quiet in the room. She realized it was easier to be with Adam when love was not at stake.

"There," he said. "Don't move." He went back to his canvas. Eleanor watched Adam with his brush in his hand, looking at her. Her blouse was opened halfway, exposing her white lace bra. Adam continued to paint. He put down his brush and approached. "I want you to take off all your clothes this time," he said. She did what she was told, though as she did she felt almost shy. He went back behind his canvas and stared at her. She looked straight back, and as she continued to look she felt herself grow more powerful, more attuned to who she was. She nearly loved herself in Adam's eyes. He put down his paintbrush. He came to her. He kneeled down and put his face in her lap. "I've missed you, Eleanor."

Eleanor ran her fingers through his hair.

"You're not really here," he said. "I've lost you."

"I'm here."

Adam took a beer out of the mini-refrigerator. He came back to the window by the daybed. She covered herself with a blanket. He leaned against the wall by the window drinking from the bottle and smoking. "Mediocrity goes against everything I believe in. I need you to feel passionate. I need you to want me. Don't you find me attractive?"

"It isn't that."

"Then what is it? Is it because I'm married? Because if it is I'll leave Mariana. If that's what you want. You're all I've thought about."

"You don't get it, do you? It's not you."

"Then what is it?"

"It's because of William. I don't want to hurt you. I think we should be friends."

"I'll make you forget him."

"But you're still married." She felt that she should resist him. She wondered if it was her he really wanted or if it was because he couldn't have her. In the past he had told her that what was between them was completely separate from what he shared with his wife. But she wasn't sure she ultimately believed him. She remembered the ease with which Mariana conducted herself the night she had seen her at Adam's opening. Adam had described her as strong. He said that's what he had found attractive about her. I knew I could never be lost with her. But it's lonely, he had said, to be around a woman who is always self-contained. Who doesn't seem to need anything.

"I'm inaccessible to Mariana now, because of you, Eleanor."

"But is it right?"

"I don't know if it's right. But I can't live inside conventions. I'd rather be dead."

She was curious about Adam. She liked his mind. She liked watching him work, the caked paint on his clothes, in his hands and in his nails, the array of brushes and jars of paint that littered his floor. She liked the absorption and concentration he brought to nearly everything he did, even the way he stretched his canvas, a medium weave, not too much tooth, he had explained. He worked direct, using oil paint with no extra medium and no glazing, just a little turpentine. He liked to use the paint in its original consistency, not thinned and not impasto. But she often felt reduced to silence in his presence, and she worried about growing attached.

"Do you think Mariana knows we've been involved?"

"A woman knows when she no longer commands the attention of her lover. Unless she doesn't want to know."

Adam viewed his relationships with women novelistically. There was a quality of unreality about it, as if he were living in it and outside it at the same time. She didn't quite trust it. She told herself that she really couldn't take Adam away from his wife when she was sure that in the end it was his wife he would go back to. What good was she to another person, she asked herself. The one person she loved she could not save.

"I've been in love with you since the first day we met. You know that."

She let him slowly take the blanket from her hands. It felt so nice not to have to think about William, not to hear her own thoughts. She felt as if little pieces of herself were floating unhinged, free of attachment. At first she was passive, but a kind of passiveness with its own brutal force of resistance. She was allowing him to use her body, and allowing it to be used; humiliating herself. There was a strange power she derived from it, shaming herself, making sure that she was not seeking pure pleasure. She needed to be overcome by passion. She had to almost hate herself for allowing herself to be wanted. It had never been like that with William. "Our bodies fit perfectly," Adam said. She allowed herself to let go and gradually felt herself become less passive. She needed to be in control. She couldn't afford for anything to happen she wasn't fully aware of.

She kissed him back, drawn to the intensity with which he seemed to care for her, and felt as if all the defensive layers she had erected to protect herself were breaking. Though it was summer and the windows were open, no breeze stirred the dark leaves of the tree outside Adam's studio; she felt something other in the air, something as ancient and familiar as the scent of rain. Afterward she wept from the sheer emotion.

"There," Adam said, declaratively, when they were finished, as if he had truly conquered her, or had just finished a painting he had been agonizing over for months.

"Mariana asked me to move out," he announced some weeks later while they were having lunch at Fanelli's.

"I didn't tell you to move out," Eleanor said. "I don't want to get too attached." She was afraid to put too much stock in what was between them. She wanted him to want her but she did not want her attachment to become so deep that separation would be like agony.

"It wasn't my decision." He slipped off his shoe and rubbed his foot against her calf underneath the table. "But you're happy about it, aren't you?"

"I don't know."

Once they had moved out of the confines of Adam's studio they were on more equal footing. They talked about music, painting, and poetry. "The artist's world is different from the world other people inhabit," Adam said. "Artists need time and space. They need to be passionate and emotional and to not always make sense. Mariana never understood it."

"But maybe it's better for an artist to be with someone who is sturdy, who is in the world," Eleanor argued.

"I thought that once. But it's so alienating. People like you and me. We belong together."

That evening they had plans to attend a gallery opening of an artist Adam knew. Eleanor was wearing a skirt, ballet-slipper flats, and a summer blouse. Adam went into her closet and pulled out a pair of heels and a halter top and asked her if she would change. She complied, not thinking much about it until they walked in the gallery. "This is Eleanor," he said, introducing her to a circle of his friends, as if she were simply a girl out in the night to admire, another detail in the image he wanted to project to the world. She felt demoralized, as if she could never come into her own around him, as if she would always be viewed as his model. And yet, there was another part of her who enjoyed it, who loved being on view for others, like an adoring daughter looking up to her father for approval. She realized that she liked being with him. She had tried so hard not to like it. In one of his first paintings of her she was dressed in a white blouse. Everything about the portrait was schoolgirlish, Balthusian. In the last painting, the blouse on the figure was opened suggestively, and she had a bewitching smile on the figure, who was and was not Eleanor at the same time. The strand of pearls that had been in the earlier painting was ripped off the woman's neck and the pearls were scattered on the floor. At the very edge of the painting was the figure of a man, suggesting that it was he who had ripped the pearls from her neck. Some pearls still dangled on the strand around the girl's neck, dropping into her cleavage. It was brutal and seductive at the same time. The painting was composed so that the viewer's gaze went not to the pearls but to the look in the young woman's eye, which suggested that she was both taunting him and repelled by him. When she looked at the paintings it was like seeing herself transformed over time.

22

"They never liked Mariana. She's too cold for them," Adam said, when Eleanor asked what his parents thought about their separation. They were in his studio working. "She never wanted to go see them. She had no patience for them." He had explained that his father was once a renowned professor in Budapest. In America he owned a pawnshop. "They want me to be happy. My happiness seems to be their only ambition now."

"My father's parents never made it out of Europe."

Adam wiped his hands on his pants and went to a drawer in an old pine bureau in a corner of his studio. He took out a prayer shawl wrapped in cellophane. "My father gave this to me on my bar mitzvah. It was given to him on the boat over. He was sick. A stranger took it off his own back to keep him warm. He doesn't want me to forget."

"My father won't talk about his past. I can't imagine what they lost. How they survived."

"I've been trying to get my father to start writing, now that he's sold the shop. But he's stubborn. He says he's made his peace with the past, but I'm not sure."

Adam left the studio to get fresh bread for lunch at the bakery around the corner. Some paintings he was arranging for a new show were stacked in a corner. They were paintings he had done before she began modeling for him. Eleanor wondered why he hadn't yet shown them to her.

They were part of a series of a family. Around the dinner table sat a mother and father and a boy who resembled Adam, and hiding under the table, a young girl. All you could see of the girl were her legs sticking out from the damask cloth. The look on the parents' faces was anguished, as if Adam had found a way to drain his own sadness into them. On their wrists were serial numbers. Another painting was of a portrait of a young girl, wearing the same red tights and shiny shoes as the girl in the former painting. The girl had Adam's black eyes and curly black hair. Strangely, the girl bore a resemblance to Eleanor. Her look was unnaturally ethereal. When Adam came back, he saw her looking at it.

"I'm painting for my parents," Adam said, putting down the bag of groceries. "So it won't be lost."

"The girl in the paintings?"

"My sister."

"You've never mentioned her."

"She was killed in a car accident when she was twelve. The Weiss family's Greek tragedy."

Eleanor had thought the painting of the girl under the table was about Adam's isolation from his parents because the boy in the painting, almost ghostly, was staring into the canvas, oblivious to the other two figures in the composition, but she had read it wrong. It was the absence of the girl that had been the painting's focus, as if she would always be hiding under the table, always in the background. Eleanor thought about Adam's family and how it would feel to lose a child and a sister. Tears filled her eyes. She put her arms around him and hugged him.

"I want you to have the prayer shawl, Eleanor. Give it to your father. He should have something."

"I couldn't take that. It belongs to you. To your family."

"To my father we're all fathers and sons and daughters. All of us who are Jewish. Besides, you're my family now."

The prayer shawl was dirty white. Delicate light blue threads made a stripe in the cloth. She undid the cellophane wrapping and touched the cloth. She thought of the rabbi's words she had heard as a child when she went to synagogue on the high holy days.

The Lord said to Moses: Instruct the people of Israel that in every generation they shall put fringes on the corners of their garments and bind a thread to the fringes of each corner. Looking upon these fringes you will be reminded of all the commandments of the Lord and fulfill them and not be seduced by your heart or led astray by your eyes. Then you will remember and observe all my commandments and be holy before your God.

The afternoon had illuminated a corner of Adam's inner world. His continual need to layer his paintings with more paint was, to him, like bringing a lost world back into focus.

"Why didn't you tell me?"

"I paint for freedom from pain."

Eleanor tried to mention his sister and his paintings and what it evoked for her, but he wouldn't let her.

"Don't read me into my work. It makes me feel too exposed," he said, and then, as if realizing that he'd been harsh, he reached for her.

23

A gallery was hanging Adam's series of paintings, and he asked her to help him write the catalog for the show. The largest canvas was the portrait of his sister. She liked collaborating with him on the catalog and was happy that the upcoming show had raised his spirits. He accompanied her to poetry readings and lectures and she felt that he had become more a part of her world, too.

Mariana receded from their lives, though occasionally Eleanor felt her in the room with them the way history impinges upon the present, as if she were a presence peering in at them from a window. Adam was oblivious to everything but his canvas, as if his past was obliterated. But when she peered back at Adam, she recognized that no one escapes his past. There were too many days and nights, at least ten years, recorded in Mariana's and Adam's bodies. Once he had taken Eleanor to visit another artist's studio, a friend of his from graduate school. She built small boxes, little caskets with pillows inside that had the word "shamed" written on them in black ink. She was going to bury the boxes in Central Park. Eleanor understood wanting to bury shame. She still felt guilty for taking Adam from Mariana.

There was talk among Adam's artistic circle that Mariana

was seeing another painter. Adam and Mariana still kept in touch. One night when Adam was out, Mariana called.

"Tell him he needs to call his dealer in London," she said.

"I'll give him the message."

"I won't call again," Mariana said. "I can tell it makes you uncomfortable."

Eleanor looked up at one of Adam's early paintings he had brought with him when he moved out of Mariana's apartment. She felt diminutive next to it. She was sure the figure in the painting was inspired by Mariana. She could see a suggestion of Mariana's knowing, ironic eyes in the portrait. The canvas was divided by a wall. On one side of the canvas the woman sat in a chair. On the other side Adam's self-portrait sat in an identical chair, the two chairs back to back.

Once his show opened, his dealer arranged for Adam to give a lecture at Pratt and he invited Eleanor. After the lecture he went out drinking with some of the graduate students, and she tagged along. One of the students began talking about another recent show in a gallery in Soho that was garnering considerable critical attention. Adam hated the show and talking about it soured his mood.

"Tension is what gives a work its pathos," he said, holding court at the table. "You can't teach a painter about pathos. It's either in the work or it isn't." He said that when he was teaching he could tell on the first day of class which students had it and which students didn't, and it annoyed him that he had to waste his time with students who would never be artists. "What really pisses me off," Adam said, still raging, "is how these young punks can splash paint around on a canvas and think they've achieved greatness." It angered him that certain artists were more recognized than he was and that because he was still a figurative painter, he was out of vogue. Eleanor had learned to tolerate his rants. She saw them as a reflection of his commitment and his talent. She didn't try to fight with him anymore. But she was embarrassed at the way he was acting around students.

"It's because you're a purist that you take it so personally," she said, hoping it would pacify him. But as the night wore on he was getting increasingly drunk. One of the more earnest in the bunch asked him what his work was about. He said he didn't understand it. Adam thought for a moment. "It has its own language," he said. "Its own rationale. You don't ask a painter what his work is like. He can tell you about how he applies the paint, who his influences are." He grew solemn. She saw that he was struggling to think about how to describe his work outside the context of his own personal life, and the struggle made him angry. And he was drunk. "It's like fucking," he finally said, loud enough that everyone in the bar turned around to look at him. "My paintings are about fucking."

Eleanor left the bar and walked home alone.

She was late getting to his studio the next morning, and when she arrived he was in a foul mood, still drunk from the night before. After an hour, he took a razor and began to slash at the painting.

"What are you doing?"

"It's a piece of shit. I can't look at this garbage." He slashed at two other canvases that had been hanging on the wall for months in a state of half completion. She felt as if he were lacerating her own body.

It didn't take long to discover what was at the root of Adam's despair. A critic had savaged his show in the *New York Times*. He left her apartment and was gone all night. She went to find him in his studio the next morning, but the studio was empty. He was nowhere.

He came back to her apartment later the next afternoon, still drunk.

"When those motherfuckers assault your work it's as if they've stolen your soul." He went to the kitchen cabinet and took out a bottle of whiskey and sat at Eleanor's black-and-white flecked linoleum table with the crack down the center.

She put her hands on Adam's shoulders. She saw a defeated look in his eyes.

"Eleanor, I don't want you to take this the wrong way, but I need to do this now. When I'm like this you have to wait it out. You asked me once why Mariana and I never had children. This is why. I'm like this. I've been like this my whole life."

"And Mariana?"

"How did she deal with it? She knew that eventually I'd come around again. She knows that before I do."

"You're going to go back to her, aren't you?"

He looked up guiltily.

"She knows me, Eleanor."

She thought she saw his eyes tear up, but then it could have been induced by the alcohol or his nights of insomnia.

"What will I do without you?" he said.

"How can you miss what doesn't exist?"

"You exist."

"Only in your studio."

She wondered if anyone would ever look at her so intensely again.

24

The red light on her phone was blinking when she walked into her office. Stephen had called. "Eleanor, I'm coming to New York next week. Will you have lunch with me?" It was October. Five months had passed since she'd seen him in Paris.

She was unsettled by his last phone call, but of course she could have lunch with him.

She was writing the morning they were to meet and it was going well again. In the current chapter she was raising questions: Had Anna Karenina ever loved her husband? Had she loved him and had not known until she met Vronsky that her capacity to love was deeper than she had realized — so that once she met Vronsky it seemed as if she had never loved her husband at all?

As the chapter evolved, Eleanor had become more sympathetic to Anna. Anna had loved her husband but she could not reach him. She had accepted his aloofness and thought herself content until she met Vronsky. She was not frivolous or malicious. She had not married her husband vindictively. But if she did not open herself to Vronsky, she would have died inside.

When Stephen opened her office door she almost mistook him for one of her students. He had grown a goatee and was dressed in a tight black T-shirt and blue jeans. She was disarmed by his rugged physicality. They hugged awkwardly. He had come from a meeting with an editor at a new men's magazine. He had pitched a story about America's fascination with pilots, and the editor liked the idea and had assigned the piece. He wore a pair of black high-tops, the kind she would have bought for her boys.

Stephen took the chair across from her desk. She liked the sense of control and authority it created, having him on the other side of her desk. But she barely registered what he was saying, distracted as she was by his physical presence. He filled the room. As he spoke she studied a pendant that hung from his neck. He hadn't worn it in Paris. In fact, in Paris he had appeared more grown up, professional. He seemed different in

New York, less confident, less mature, and she was relieved to find herself less enamored. Or was she just telling herself that? He talked excitedly about the story he was going to write. He said that pilots were a symbol of sexuality and danger (she thought the conceit obvious, a cliché). His face was animated when he talked. He was going to interview pilots from several different airlines. He stood up and walked around her office, studied her bookshelves, picked up *Paradise Lost,* looked at the title, put it down.

"My God, Eleanor," he said. "Professor Cahn. Who would have thunk it."

She didn't know whether she was offended or not.

"You were always the smart one but you tried to hide it. You didn't like to make the rest of us feel stupid."

"Is that how you saw me?"

"You were one of those intense girls. I remember sitting at the table in your mother's house, listening to you. I was pretty obsessed with you then."

He picked up the framed picture of Michael and the boys. "These are your sons?"

She nodded. Her eyes went to the laces on his shoes. They were untied.

"Good-looking kids."

Watching Stephen hold the photograph of Noah, Nicholas, and Michael made her slightly queasy. Why hadn't she put the photograph away? She tried to remember whether she had told Michael she had seen Stephen in Paris. When she and Michael began to get serious with each other and had cataloged past lovers, she hadn't mentioned Stephen. There hadn't been much to say. Their relationship had never been defined. Surely she couldn't say they'd been lovers. She hadn't told Michael she saw him in Paris and that he had called her in New York and she was going to meet him for lunch. But there had been a moment when she considered telling him, almost had the words formulated on her tongue, and she nearly deceived herself into thinking she had.

It was raining outside; she could hear it slash her office window. It had rained for almost a week straight. She was cooped up, unsettled. She was sure if they had one streak of good, warm weather she'd find her center again. Stephen still held the photograph of her family in his hand. He stared at it again, and then resumed his pacing around the room.

"How's he doing?" he said. "Your husband."

"He's good."

"I never thought he was someone you'd be in love with."

She grabbed the photograph out of his hand and put it back on her desk. "Why?"

"I don't know. I thought you'd have gone for someone a little rougher around the edges. Or more poetic. Is he really happy all the time? You said that in Paris."

"He comes from a perfect family," Eleanor thought for a moment. "His parents have been happily married all these years. He gets along with both of them. He has two sisters he adores." She paused. "I know," she said, conspiratorially. "It's unbearably perfect."

"Not to mention, he's a doctor."

She nodded, suddenly caught up in the assumption he was making about how she and he were alike and Michael was different.

"Where do you live?"

"On Central Park West."

"Fancy."

"Not really."

"What kind of doctor is he?"

"A heart surgeon."

"How did you end up with a doctor? You never told me."

"You never asked." She thought for a moment. "You don't fall in love with someone because of his profession."

"You are what you do. Aren't you defined by what you do?"

"What are you saying?"

"I'm just trying to figure out how a doctor fits into your worldview."

"There's dignity in what Michael does. He saves lives."

He paused and moved the chair closer to her desk. "I know. But he's part of them."

"Part of who?"

"Of everyone we're not."

She looked back at him, not knowing if she heard him right, and if she did whether she believed in what he was saying.

"Enough about your husband," he said. "Grab your bag."

"We'll go somewhere around the corner," she said, asserting herself.

He pointed to his backpack. "I have other ideas. I packed us a lunch."

"But it's raining."

"There's this underpass I saw when I went running yesterday. It's by the reservoir. You can see the water. Don't worry. You won't get wet."

The rain came at a slant, soaking her dress, her stockings, her shoes as they went to hail a cab. This is crazy, she thought to herself. But she found herself caught up in Stephen's enthusiasm. Her umbrella that had barely protected her turned inside out. She dumped it in a garbage bin and stood under Stephen's umbrella and let him put his arm around her so she would not get wet.

On her way out of the gates of Columbia she passed Mark Zukovsky in a Black Crowes T-shirt. He stopped, looked at her and at Stephen, and then had the audacity to wink at her.

Once they got out of the cab at 72nd and Riverside, they

walked down the stairs to Riverside Park. "We could be in Paris again," Stephen said. Shielded by his big black umbrella, they gazed onto the water, watching the rain fall. They were the only two people along the walkway by the river. "Let's pretend we are." Stephen took her to a bench under the overpass where they could still see the water. "It was amazing seeing you in Paris. It was a wonderful fantasy to have you for myself in a place so far away from home." Overhead the subway occasionally rumbled and they could feel the vibrations. She felt slightly guilty for enjoying herself but then told herself she was not doing anything wrong.

Stephen talked about his work. About how difficult it was to be a freelance journalist. How he was bored by writing for outdoor and men's magazines and wanted to spend more time on his novel. He talked about moving to New York, only he couldn't afford the city without getting some kind of full-time job with a magazine or paper. "I've got the clips," he said, "but unless you're attached to a place, or have the right contacts, nobody really wants you." She got caught up in the dramatic way he moved his hands as he spoke. She realized how lonely she had been, because in that moment she didn't feel lonely anymore.

"Most of the writers in New York went to fancy schools," he continued. "Have you noticed that there are two kinds of people in the world, Eleanor? Those who have the right connections and those who don't? The thing is, I'm good. I know I am."

She nodded. She said it sounded like he was on the verge.

"I lost a lot of years." Stephen unwrapped a sandwich he'd made with mozzarella, sun-dried tomatoes, and pesto and handed her half. She remembered his addiction to pain killers. He looked at her for a reaction.

"I'm sorry. It's not something you need to feel ashamed of."

He raised his eyebrows affectionately. His lips turned into a half smile. "I knew I could count on you. I knew you wouldn't judge me. When I move to New York I'm going to try to get my novel published."

"You've finished it?"

"You never really finish a novel. It exhausts you finally."

"That's fantastic."

"It's either fantastic or it's a piece of shit. I don't know, Eleanor."

"Tell me."

"It's written in vignettes. I don't even know if it's a novel. I've read parts of it at bookstores and bars where they have readings in Colorado. They work as performance pieces. The audiences seem to dig it. I was trying for the moody masculinity of a Hemingway character and the boy-meets-road of Kerouac. But it's more poetic. All I know is that writing it makes me feel alive."

"I know how you feel. I couldn't live without my work, without novels like *Anna Karenina*. Sometimes I'm afraid to say anything about an essay I'm working on until it's finished."

"You're superstitious, too?" He looked at her seductively. "But does this mean you are not going to tell me what you're working on? I want to know everything about you."

She laughed.

"Maybe we could work on something together. It would be amazing to collaborate on something with you. What about a film adaptation of a book? I know about the world and you know about books. We could do something really sexy together."

"I don't know anything about how to write a script," she said, but caught herself enjoying the idea. She was curious about his novel. She wondered if he had talent and almost asked if she could read it. What was she doing? Had seeing him for lunch meant they had made a decision to be in each other's lives again? Seeing each other for a single time in Paris she could write off as curiosity, but meeting him again meant something else. She crossed her arms against her chest.

"If I hurt you in the past, I'm sorry." Stephen turned to her and reached for her hand. "You don't think I've forgotten, have you?"

"Forgotten what?"

"When you came to visit me in Colorado. Before you got married."

She could not summon any words. She was surprised he had brought it up. She had been touched by his intensity and earnestness, by his interest in her, but now he looked remote and she remembered that she couldn't trust him. She realized that she had been drawn in again and that she needed to put some distance between them.

It stopped raining, and as they walked along the walkway near the water, dodging the puddles, she wondered why he seemed so intent on wanting her back in his life. Once he was gone she'd be left with the same unanswered questions about their past. It came as a surprise to her that she could be angry at someone for almost two decades. She had to ask him.

"Do you have a second to sit down?" She pointed to a bench. The sun had come out, finally, illuminating the water and the blades of grass slick with rain, making everything sparkle.

"Sure."

"The time I came out to visit you. In Colorado. So you *do* remember what happened?"

"The poem. I still have it, Eleanor."

Her face flushed. She had forgotten about the poem. It was true. She had written him a poem.

25

It was a furnace inside her apartment. Her clothes were sticking to her skin. She couldn't breathe. Walking down Broadway the air was stagnant, heavy, as if she were parting it with her body. The sidewalk smelled of garbage and rotting fruit. Adam had left. Part of her was relieved. There was always a part of her that knew it wouldn't last. But she had gotten used to his presence in her life, her absorption in his work, his absorption in her. The isolation and loneliness made it impossible for her to think. She couldn't sleep. She went to pick up the phone. There was no one she wanted to call. And then out of nowhere she thought of Stephen and on a whim called him in Colorado.

When he picked up the phone she realized she was still mad at him. "What happened? You promised you'd come to the barbecue that night. You left without saying good-bye. You didn't even call me."

"I couldn't stay."

"But why didn't you call? You could have at least tried."

"You know why."

"But you promised."

"I'm sorry, Eleanor. I thought you understood why I needed to get out of there."

"But I thought I could count on you."

"You can. Do you still want to come visit me in Colorado?"

The cold Boulder air stung, and she felt nauseous from the elevation. She slung the strap of her black duffel bag over her shoulder and climbed the four or five steps to Stephen's door. She half expected he wouldn't be there when she showed up and asked the cab driver to wait in the driveway before taking off. Barefoot, in black jeans and a red flannel shirt, his hair soft and runaway, he greeted her. She had forgotten how attractive he was. But he looked tense. She doubted for a moment whether she should have come. His house had a simplicity that suited her. It was an A-frame, with big open windows facing the mountains. She had an image of him pensively at work, the mountains their own majestic inspiration.

"You didn't think I'd show, did you? It's written all over your face."

"Yeah?" he said, in a question. "I don't know. I'm just startled to see you in the flesh."

"Are you glad I came?"

"Eleanor, never ask a guy if he loves you."

"I didn't ask whether you loved me."

He took her duffel bag out of her hand and carried it upstairs. They both stood awkwardly in the center of his room without saying anything.

A double mattress was on his floor covered with a sheet and a royal blue nubby cotton blanket. Against the wall were propped two pillows, one without a pillowcase. Facing the bed was a tank for tropical fish but only one swam inside. He saw her looking at it. "It's a Chinese fighting fish. They're loners. If another fish is in the tank with it, one will try to kill the other."

She buried her head in Stephen's crinkled leather jacket as his motorcycle sped through a windy mountain pass. He parked the bike off the road and they hiked until they reached a secluded spot where the frame of a new house was being built. The concrete for the basement was poured. On top was built a barn-style frame. They sat in a field of wildflowers beside the unfinished house. Stephen picked a daisy. "She loves me." He tore off a petal. "She loves me not." He paused at the last petal. "You can't do that to me, Eleanor." He looked at her seriously. "You can't break my heart."

She stopped picking grass from the ground into a pile and looked at him. "I won't."

"You have to promise." He fell on top of her, crushing her with his weight. "You know I'm not like other people."

"I'm not either."

"You know it's because of what she's done to me."

"I know."

"See this house? Me and my buddies are building it for a developer. Follow me." He walked her through the layout, underneath the exposed beams. "This could be our house. Imagine our bedroom. And this is the living room. And here's the bedroom for our kids. Would you have kids with me, Eleanor?"

She smiled, reluctantly. "Is that what you want?"

"We have something between us no one can take away. You know me like nobody else. I bet you'd want a big kitchen. I'll build you a study on the third floor. You could write your books up there. This town is made up of people who don't fit into the rest of the world. That's why I like it here. A town of misfits."

"Are you trying to get me to move to Colorado?" Tears of delight filled her eyes. Suddenly it all made sense. Stephen was the man she'd been waiting for.

He took out a bottle of wine and two plastic cups from his backpack. They sat on the newly built wooden floor, which was covered with shavings. The air smelled of pine. Even the wine tasted of it. The western sky formed a ceiling over the open rafters.

"I write at night after the bars close down. Maybe that's why no one thinks my novel makes any sense." He laughed. "I'm obsessed with it, Eleanor. It's about a guy on the run. Searching for himself. That kind of book. It's set in Alaska. In the snow. I'm trying to do something interesting. I'm trying to write from my heart."

"I'd like to read it, if you want another pair of eyes."

He looked at her funny. "It would have to be pretty good before I'd show it to you."

"I think that's great, that you're obsessed. Your novel."

"I still have to figure out how to tap into it." He pointed to his temple. "Everything up here. It's got to go somewhere. Boulder's great. But nobody really cares what you do here. You wake up in the mornings and the beauty is awesome. You look out at the mountains and you think none of it really matters. It's like you disappear into all the beauty."

He ran one finger up and down the inside of her arm. "I mean, me and you, this is all that matters. I feel your loneliness. I know where it comes from." He tucked her hair behind her ears.

They put on their helmets. As they stood by his bike, Stephen slipped his fingers in the belt loops of her jeans.

"Do you think I could really do it? The conventional thing?" He looked back toward the unfinished house. "I think I could do it with you, Eleanor. Come on. We need to go before it gets too dark."

Country music drifted through the cowboy bar; the walls were studded with deer antlers. She took pleasure in being in a foreign place, in a new surrounding, in a world different from her intellectual life in New York. There was something dusty and stagnant about her academic existence. She wanted to embrace life. She felt the exuberance of the endless possibilities reflected in the openness of the mountain air. She could barely contain her happiness.

It wasn't one of the fashionable bars for tourists and ski bums. It was a hangout for townies and guys who worked the oil rigs. The back room smelled of stale beer. They drifted toward two empty stools near the pool table. A man at the bar was drunk. He talked loudly to another guy playing pool. Said he had wasted the whole day waiting for work at the rigs. Said his wife was going to beat the crap out of him. His face was leathery.

"I don't like having you here." Stephen was loose from drinking. His mood had shifted. "This isn't a place for you, Eleanor. You're too good for this place." He had that uneasy look she knew so well.

"What are you talking about? Colorado is amazing. The mountains. The fresh air. I love it here. Relax."

"You're too sophisticated for this place. This town is filled with a bunch of losers. I work all day with these guys. They're younger than me. They talk about girls, getting drunk, who they did it with the night before. This isn't a place for you."

"It's fine." She rubbed his thigh. "I like it here. I'm glad to be here with you."

"I wake up and think I have to do something substantial with my life. I have to get out of here. But the next day I get up and do the same thing. I haven't figured out yet how to support myself as a journalist. The work isn't steady."

"But you're writing. It takes time."

"Yeah. Time," he said, philosophically. His face relaxed. "Speaking of time, it's about time I did this." He leaned across the bar stool to kiss her.

Stephen lit the fish tank in his room. They sat on the edge of his mattress watching the blue Chinese fighting fish darting acrobatically through the pink coral. He seemed nervous. She touched his leg. "What's wrong?" She saw that same wanting-to-run look in his eye she noticed at the bar.

"I don't want to do this, Eleanor. It shouldn't be like this. I want to be sober when you and I make love. I don't want to miss any of it."

"I can wait."

They slid underneath the sheets still half dressed. The fish swam luminescent, transparent in its tank. Its mouth closed and opened against the glass.

"You're the only girl I've let into this house, you know."

"I don't believe you."

"It's true. I keep it locked up pretty tight."

His lips were rough and cracked, the skin broken through. She tasted blood when they kissed. He rubbed his hands over the curves of her body. But he suddenly stopped. "Crap," he said.

"Is something wrong?"

"It's not you. I can't do this, Eleanor."

"It's okay," she said, so as not to further his shame or hers.

He quickly got up and went to the bathroom. When he returned she pretended she was asleep.

In the morning the light pressed through the plastic blinds. What is intimacy, she thought, feeling the warmth of Stephen's body, except for the feeling of not being alone? She didn't care that they hadn't made love. She was glad to be close to him. She thought about his writing and his commitment to it: his desire to articulate his personal vision into a fully imagined world. She knew the risk he was taking. She pictured the unfinished house near the field of wildflowers. "I want to live in that house with you," she said. "Maybe I've had enough of New York."

"Really?"

She nodded.

"Stay in bed, Eleanor. I wish I didn't have to leave you, but I can't afford to lose the work. I'll make it a half day." He leaned over to kiss her and then found he couldn't leave. "See what you're doing to me." He reached for her again. "My mother came into my bed and slept with me when they fought." He turned over and pushed his body into her back, struggling against her. "She curled herself around me like this and cried into my pajama top. She thought I was sleeping. It made me never want to get close."

"You can be close now."

After he aroused her, he pulled away again. "It can't be like this," he said.

"Like what?"

"I have to go to work."

When she got up later she attempted to study. She looked out the window at the icy mountains, with their impenetrable dips and slopes. She thought about the night before, about the unfinished house and the dreams it inspired, and then she analyzed Stephen's odd behavior more carefully. He claimed he did not want to make love to her until he was sober. Did that mean he wasn't attracted to her? But it seemed as if he was. He said he was unsure of his future and whether the years he had put into his writing would actually amount to something. How could he make a commitment to her, when he was unsure of his own future? She told herself she needed to be patient. She was moved by his thoughtfulness and hesitation. It spoke to a certain integrity of character she admired. But why did he make that comment about her not belonging in Colorado? She rationalized. Like most men, he was afraid of getting close. It was up to her to make him feel secure and loved. It exhausted her to think about it, but she had grown used to the proposition, as if it were a duty she'd inherited.

In town she picked up groceries from the market with the thought that she would make dinner. She spent the rest of the afternoon and into the early evening cooking lasagna. She was happy, cutting up onions for the sauce, grating the flaky parmesan. She put on the radio, a soft country station. She straightened the kitchen, thinking about what it would be like to live with Stephen. Maybe she could get a teaching job in Colorado, work on her dissertation here. She'd encourage him to finish his novel. They could have a simple life in the mountains, days spent writing and teaching, long hikes along the hillside, nights making love. It was 7:30 in the evening. Strange that he did not come home or call. Suddenly, she realized that Stephen wasn't coming back. It was obvious. She had been a fool to trust him. All afternoon she had made up excuses, telling herself that he must have gotten caught up at work, or gone out for a beer, or maybe his bike had broken down. By the time she had prepared dinner it was 9:00 at night. It was odd being alone in a house that was not her own. When she looked outside it was pitch black. She couldn't see the mountains. She took the lasagna out of the oven and left it sitting on top of the stove. She was no longer hungry. She took one of the blankets off Stephen's bed and brought it downstairs to the sofa. She poured herself a glass of scotch from the cupboard.

Headlights illuminated the house, but the car passed. After the harshness of the first few swallows, the scotch became more palatable. Her mind entered a murky, disconnected state. At one point she convinced herself that Stephen had been in a bike accident and was lying in a ditch somewhere, but eventually she came back to reality. Why had she thought he'd be any different? When she awoke it was to Stephen's lips kissing her forehead. Dawn. He knelt on the floor in front of her. Slowly she came to full consciousness. She smelled the warmth of beer on his breath and then the overpowering odor of smoke—of someone who had been inside a burning thing. She pushed him away.

"Where were you?"

"There was a fire at the house we were building. The entire thing. It's gone."

"What happened?"

"They can't pin it on me."

"What are you talking about?"

"We went for a beer and when we came back to get our stuff the whole thing was in flames."

"You look scared."

"You have to leave, Eleanor. You can't stay. I can't do this."

"What have you done?"

She stood up and began to pack her things in her duffel bag. He watched her from a chair with relief in his eyes. It made her feel like slapping him, but she restrained herself. She thought about the house burning to the ground and felt a terrible loss.

She was unprotected on the back of his bike on the way to the airport, exposed to every danger, forced to trust him. She held on tightly to his jacket. The smell of smoke was in his clothes and hair. *This can't be happening,* she thought, still in a state of disbelief. She thought that at any moment he would stop the bike, explain to her what happened, take her back to his house. But he didn't.

When they arrived at the terminal, the plane was boarding. "I'll write to you. We'll be in touch." She said nothing. She stood in line to board the plane, trembling. He followed behind her and pulled her out of the line. "It's not you," he said, again. "Look at me, Eleanor." Though the comment was meant to comfort, it had the opposite effect. It was like a verbal assault. How could it not have been her?

She looked at him, perplexed, and shook her head.

The airline clerk reached out to take her ticket. Once in her seat, she panicked. She undid the buttons of her coat. She wanted to undo her seat belt, too, to walk back out to the reception area, find him, and make him explain. She was desperate to do so. But the door of the plane had shut and sealed her inside it. Had he started the fire? She pushed the thought away. It was impossible. She looked out the tinted glass window of the airplane into the gate of the terminal. He stood by the window watching as the plane backed onto the runway. It took her a long time before she could move her palm from the window. She was in love with him; maybe she had been since they were children.

26

"He looks like you did at that age." She pointed to a boy walking toward them along the walkway by the water.

"Except he has more hair on his head than I do." Stephen laughed. "Can you believe we were ever that young, Eleanor?"

"You left me alone in your house. You disappeared. You never tried to make me understand what got you spooked. What happened at that fire?"

He looked uncomfortable. His cheeks turned pink. "I don't remember it that way."

"You made me leave."

"For your own good. But I've never left you."

"You disappear. That's what you do."

"I don't disappear. I'm right here." He squeezed her upper arm as if to prove it. "Don't you see I've changed?" He moved closer to her on the bench.

"I'm not sure."

"Why did you have to get married?"

"Before I met Michael, why didn't you call? You could have called."

"I didn't know you wanted me to." He paused. "After what I did."

The tension between them was something visceral. "I can't believe I'm sitting here next to you," he said. He took her hand, brought it to his lips, and kissed it. "Our connection. I still feel it, Eleanor. Are you glad to see me? You look a little strange."

She smiled. She *was* glad to see him.

"I wish you could come with me."

She looked at him, stricken.

"I have to catch a plane."

She walked home slowly. Her mind kept going back to Stephen. She didn't want to judge him, but she had done so nonetheless. He was selfish. And then she rationalized his behavior, remembering the scars of his youth. She crossed the park and was walking up Fifth Avenue. *I've never left you,* she heard him say. She saw a sign. THIS IS GOD'S HOUSE. ALL ARE WELCOME.

She went inside the church. The tension of having been with him left her restless. She felt the erotic pull in her body. She sat down on the bench. The darkness of the church, the votive candles, and the smell of incense provided refuge from the world. She told herself none of it was really relevant. She was married with two sons. Stephen was on his way to the airport to fly away again. It was dark and cold in the austere church and she was uncomfortable sitting on the hard pew. She fought against the jumble of emotions until she was exhausted. She heard a voice inside her. *You don't have to save him. But is it him I'm trying to save, or is he saving me?* There was no answer.

27

S he was twenty-eight. Her mother hosted an engagement party for her and Michael. A few minutes before the party was to begin her mother announced that Stephen was in town and was coming to the party. This was going to be the first time she saw him since her visit to Colorado. She felt excited and nervous. *Why should I care that Stephen Mason is in my living room? He means nothing.* She realized she was still furious with him.

She walked down the stairs confidently in a skirt, lace top, and black heels and into the living room where the guests were mingling, thinking now she'd have her revenge, though she didn't like to think of herself as vengeful. She noticed Stephen, who was dressed in a leather sports jacket and cowboy boots. He needed a haircut. They drifted into their own separate conversations, but his eyes followed her around the room. She knew the way his mind worked and could already hear what he was telling himself—that she had sold out and was marrying the enemy.

She had thought she had the edge, but when she saw how animated Stephen looked describing an article that he was writing to one of his mother's friends, she felt herself weakening. She wanted to speak to him but instead sat down next to Michael, who was dressed elegantly in a tweed jacket.

Stephen still lived in Colorado. He was home for a short weekend. He was uncomfortable: Everything about his body language said he didn't want to be there. He sat down on the chair opposite her and made small talk with Michael over the fondue tray. His hands flickered with the knob on the flame. He skewered a square of bread and dipped it into the cheese and popped it into his mouth. He took the empty skewer and thrust it into the flame. Michael explained he was doing his residency at Lenox Hill Hospital. Stephen said he'd once spent a month inside an ER at a hospital in Denver doing some research for an investigative piece. The hot skewer was in his hand. He thrust it out at Michael as he spoke.

Eleanor never told Michael that there had ever been anything significant between them. There didn't seem to be anything to tell, though she had the feeling Michael sensed their attraction. He stepped away to refill their drinks. She glanced at Stephen. He was looking at the flame underneath the fondue tray. He took a cocktail napkin and let the fire burn the fringe, then blew it out before the napkin caught fire.

"I'm sorry I can't stay for dinner," Stephen explained to her mother. "You must be psyched that Eleanor is marrying an upstanding individual. A doctor. Doesn't everyone want that for her daughter?"

"I would expect nothing less from Eleanor," Elizabeth said proudly. "I only wish her father were here to see her. Celebrations make him uncomfortable. He's too emotional. Your father would be a puddle, wouldn't he, Eleanor?" Elizabeth said.

Stephen caught her eye. She looked away and began talking to another one of her mother's friends, but she continued to listen to Stephen's and her mother's conversation.

"No, I'm not seeing anyone," he said. "Do you know the first question a girl asks when you meet her? She wants to know what you do for a living. When you say you're a writer they look at you sideways. They think to themselves, 'This one isn't marriage material.'"

"How's the writing going?" her mother gently asked, as if she were afraid to hear his answer.

"I've had a few breaks but it isn't enough to make a living. I'm still painting houses and putting up aluminum siding. I go through these periods where I tell myself to forget it. The writing. That it isn't going to happen. I have to shake my doubts. Other times I know I have to stick with it."

"Of course you must, dear," Eleanor's mother said. "Where would we be if everyone were a doctor?"

Eleanor watched him skewer another piece of bread and dip it into the bubbling cheese. She looked at him again. He stared right through her. He went into the kitchen, taking his drink with him. She told herself she was lucky to have found Michael. She sat down next to him and locked her fingers within his. Stephen had peered back into the living room from the kitchen. He saw the gesture. Did she do it specifically to hurt him or was it to reassure herself? She was bothered that she still found him attractive and that she felt compassion for him. She rose to go to the bathroom. He went in the other direction to grab his coat. They met in the narrow hallway. The attraction was like an electric current connecting her body to his. How could she still be drawn to him? She looked at him for a moment and thought they might embrace. Stephen leaned against the wall and stared at her as if they were two teenagers flirting at a party. She saw in the way he looked at her that he knew he still possessed power over her, and the knowledge was enough fuel to get him through the evening. She thought that his anger would allow him to forget her. She stumbled on her high heel.

"You have something in your hair." He reached over and took out a crumb. As his hand slipped into her hair, she grew warm and flushed. "You're radiant, Eleanor."

He walked back into the living room and left her standing in the hallway. Once she regained her composure and followed him, she saw Michael stand up to shake his hand. Carol had reached over to kiss him good-bye. He gave Eleanor's mother a hug. He did not say good-bye to Eleanor. He placed his half-drunk vodka tonic on the coffee table in front of her. As he was walking out the door she looked at his glass—the ice had melted, the lime had absorbed the alcohol, and it turned soft and pulpy.

She slid next to Michael on the sofa. She sipped on her glass of wine, holding the globe with two hands so it wouldn't shake, and listened to Michael tell her mother about the studio apartment in New York they were renting. She was devastated that Stephen left but she resisted the impulse to go after him. Why should she? That was long ago. He was the one who left her. She was upset that he did not try to explain himself, and relieved at the same time that he hadn't. Carol sat down on the couch next to her mother. "When I told Stephen Eleanor was getting married and that you were having a party for her he drove all night to be here, Elizabeth. He knows how much you and Eleanor mean to me," Carol said. "You were the only friend who didn't judge me when I left town."

28

In her office the morning after seeing Stephen, she logged on to e-mail and sent a message to John.

To: JCloud@princeton.edu
From: ECahn@columbia.edu

John: Can you explain the significance of Plato's meaning of platonic love? It's for my new book.

To: ECahn@columbia.edu
From: JCloud@princeton.edu

E: Transcending physical desire and tending toward the purely spiritual or ideal.

To: JCloud@princeton.edu
From: ECahn@columbia.edu

So you're saying that physical desire impedes a higher spiritual quest?

To: ECahn@columbia.edu
From: JCloud@princeton.edu

I'm saying that Plato saw resisting sexual desire as a way to reach a higher spiritual plane. Marsilio Ficino, a Renaissance follower of Plato, used the terms *amor socraticus* and *amor platonicus* interchangeably to mean a love between two humans that was preparatory for the love of God. From Ficino's usage, Platonic came to be used for a spiritual love between persons of opposite sexes.

To: JCloud@princeton.edu
From: ECahn@columbia.edu

So you're saying that once platonic love is consummated it's no longer spiritual? That the reason platonic love is so intense is because of the tension of having never been consummated? The imagination continues to fuel the possibilities, perhaps idealizing the connection?

To: ECahn@columbia.edu
From: JCloud@princeton.edu

I'm saying then it's no longer platonic. It becomes something other. In fact, it may or may not be as powerful as spiritual love. The Romantics would say it was ecstatic love. When I think of unconsummated love I think of Dante and Beatrice. Of *La Vita Nuova*. Dante believed his love for Beatrice led him to the love of God. He met Beatrice when he was nine and idealized her. He believed it was through Beatrice that he was able to explore the self. That the exploration of the self is the exploration of truth. And that poetry was the vehicle for his exploration.

To: JCloud@princeton.edu
From: ECahn@columbia.edu

How's *The End of Romanticism* coming?

To: ECahn@columbia.edu
From: JCloud@princeton.edu

I think I prefer the Romantic period.

She smiled and logged off e-mail.

PART IV

29

Hi, Eleanor, I'm in Utah. The mountains are amazing. I'm
doing a story for *National Geographic*. I'm still thinking
about what you wore that day in Paris. That flowered, silk
skirt — were they rosebuds? — and your hair up in a twist.
I think both of your eyes looked blue that day. How's
everything in your world?

She turned off the computer. She went into the bathroom
down the department hallway. It was hot and muggy. September had been cool, but in the last week there had been another
heat wave. Tiny mosquitoes and gnats had flown inside the
mesh of the screen window and lined the inside of the sink,
drawn to the coolness of its white porcelain. She locked the
bathroom door and sat down on the window ledge for no other
reason than to enjoy the comfort and insularity the bathroom
provided.

I'm in Vermont, chasing after a Democrat for the Associated
Press. How's your Anna doing? Isn't that the character? The
one from the Russian novel? I can picture you in your office,
Eleanor. I know where to find you. That's what I think about
in bed at night. You behind your desk with your avalanche of
books behind you.

Fall was fading. Soon it would be winter.

It was the emancipation of summer, the freedom of beginning the day with only a light summer blouse and thin skirt, the openness of walking arm in arm in the park that had left her naked and vulnerable in Paris. She welcomed the spareness of winter; the thinner clouds, cool air. She longed to bundle herself up in thicker clothes for protection.

She began to look for Stephen's e-mails. He sent them from Internet cafés around the country. At lunch her friend Marcia confessed that she'd struck up an e-mail correspondence with an old boyfriend and that she had decided to keep it private from Brian. "Why would I purposely instigate a fight with him?" she said. "Besides, it has no impact on Brian."

"Is it because you're bored?" Eleanor asked.

"I don't think about it that deeply."

Hi, Eleanor. I'm doing an overnight in New York to see an editor. Will you be around on Saturday? I'm sending this to you from the airport cybercafé. Your pal, Stephen

Now he was her pal.

Michael was working at the hospital. Eleanor planned to take the boys ice skating. She e-mailed Stephen back and told him to call her on her cell phone. Maybe she'd invite him to go skating with them at the rink in Central Park. For twenty-four hours she thought about walking the path through the park with him in intimate conversation. But by the time she arrived at the rink with the boys, after she had laced up her sons' skates, said hello to another boy and his mother from the boys' school, the fantasy faded. How could she have entertained the idea of bringing Stephen skating with her boys? What was wrong with her?

She called Stephen's cell phone and left a message saying it wasn't going to work, that she was sorry to have missed him, that she hoped next time he was in town they'd have another chance. Afterward she felt more deeply connected to him, as if by not seeing him she had ensured that they would see each other at a later date.

> Eleanor, I'm back in Colorado. The mountains are so distant today, I can barely see them. I'm working on my novel. You're my ideal reader. When I'm writing, it's as if I'm writing to you. I see you in my dreams. Your comrade, Stephen

Now she was his comrade.

She woke up and didn't want to get out of bed. It was as if she were dragging herself out of layers of a complicated dream. Ever since the boys were born, she'd sprung out of bed as soon as they awoke. But it was different now. Everything was different. She wanted to fold back into sleep to quiet herself. She rationalized her way out of bed, telling herself that the boys and Michael needed her, they were part of her tangible world. Michael left for the hospital at the crack of dawn. The boys played quietly in their room while her mind struggled to float back from semiconsciousness. She slowly made out the objects on her dresser, her bottles of perfume and the broken pitcher from Paris, sealed back together with glue. She remembered buying the pitcher with Stephen. Even as she told herself what a child he was, there was a part of her that knew that it was the vulnerability in him she was drawn to.

At breakfast she helped Nicholas study for a math test. While he was looking at his flash cards her eyes drifted to the window.

"Mom, where are you?" Nicholas said. "You're not paying attention."

"I'm sorry," she said, bracing him by the shoulders. "I'm here. I won't leave you."

"I know you won't leave me. But could you help me study for my test?"

"Of course I will," she said, recovering. "I'm your mother."

The Wings of the Dove was the topic of discussion in her Henry James seminar.

"Kate Croy knows from the outset that she must have Denscher. She knows that money is the only thing stopping them and that she and Denscher could profit from Milly's dying. It's calculated, but Kate perceives her and Denscher's love as being of greater consequence. She sees it as nearly spiritual, essential, beyond anything. That's what allows her to betray Milly," Maryanne Foster said, looking at Ted Donough as she spoke, as if she were speaking intimately to him rather than to the class.

"Are you suggesting that James intended for her to be calculating?" Eleanor egged her on. Eleanor stared at the gold stud punched into the soft flap of skin underneath Maryanne's eyebrow.

"Of course," Maryanne responded. "Kate didn't realize that it would have consequences. That she couldn't control how another woman affected him."

"Well, one of James's themes *is* the cost of betrayal. But go on, Maryanne."

"Kate makes Denscher see that their only chance together is if he makes love to Milly. Kate puts the seduction in motion, calculates the outcome—Milly's fortune—but she doesn't anticipate that Denscher will grow to care for Milly. She's clueless. She believes their love is absolute. That's her failing." Maryanne confidently tossed back her dyed black hair.

"Failing?" Eleanor probed.

"She didn't realize that Denscher would fall in love with Milly's memory. That memory is more powerful."

Ted cut in before Eleanor could respond. "So are you saying that seduction here isn't really a calculation on the part of the seducer? That by remaining passive, the object of desire put the seduction in motion?"

"Of course." Maryanne tossed her head back, laughing.

After class Eleanor thought about the animated way in which Maryanne drew Ted Donough to her. Ted was completely absorbed. Eleanor was almost jealous of her freedom.

Stephen was on assignment in Gettysburg, Pennsylvania, when he called. He was writing a story on the reenactors of the Civil War. The phone call came just as she was going to pick up the boys from school. "It's like being inside a play," he said. "It's surreal, watching these people dressing up and fighting like there's a war still going on. What is it with people and their obsessions with the past?"

Silence.

"Eleanor, are you there? How are you? It's good to hear your voice."

She liked hearing his voice, too, but she was skeptical. "Why are you calling?"

"Do you want me not to call?"

"I'm not sure."

"I talked to my mother the other day," he said, in a voice full of sorrow. "She calls me on my cell late at night." Pause. "She's so miserable, Eleanor."

"Don't pick up the phone at night," Eleanor said, climbing out of her anger. "Why does she call so late?"

"Because she's lonely."

"Not because she wants to hear your voice? To hear how you're doing?"

"Eleanor. I thought we don't sugarcoat, you and me. We don't lie to each other."

She remembered once when they were kids, going over to the Masons' house to borrow butter for her mother. Stephen's mother sat at the round, six-person kitchen table. The back door was open and through the screen Eleanor felt the eeriness of catching someone sitting in privacy. Stephen's mother, dressed in a cool summer blouse and shorts, was nursing a cold drink. The heat made her face oily. Was she drunk? The overhead fan circled the air around the room. Eleanor felt a hint of it on her face through the screen, and thought about the long days and nights of unsaid words and unspoken longings churning in the air between its metal blades. As she talked to Stephen on the phone the memory of that day was still inside her, as if she were in that private kitchen, inside that unbearably hot house, as if she were somehow complicit. While Stephen's mother opened the refrigerator and gave her a stick of butter she saw Stephen standing in the doorway. He was bare chested, wearing pajama bottoms. He looked at her, as if he were saying, *This is what's it's like here, now you know, Eleanor. Now you can see.* Or perhaps he had only stared into the dark, avoiding his mother's gaze.

"Maybe you shouldn't be in touch with your mom for a while," Eleanor said. She held the phone against her ear in the office. She wanted to get off the phone. It made her feel guilty. She didn't want to be where he was taking her, back to her childhood, back inside whatever tangled nest lay between him and his mother. "It's okay to back away."

"But she's ill," he said. "She has no one."

"You can't be her caretaker. She'll survive with or without you."

"Tough love, you mean."

"Love is tough."

"Eleanor, I didn't mean to monopolize the conversation, talking about my mother. I didn't plan to talk about her when I called."

"It's okay. You don't have to apologize."

"No one else knows what she's really like. How's your mother, Eleanor?"

She thought of her own mother and knew exactly how he felt. After she put the phone back in its cradle on top of the desk, she felt compassion for him. She realized she didn't know where he was. He was unattached, a figment, a lost voice over the air waves. Was he in his car? In his hotel room? On the battlefields of Gettysburg, standing in grass? Why didn't she tell him not to call? She listened to the caustic language of birds outside her office window, floating over the treetops.

"There's someone else," Eleanor said, the next time he called, watching the shriveled flower on the geranium on her windowsill that had been vibrant all summer. It came out of her mouth as if she were talking about something as casual as the weather. There was a pregnant pause that she wanted to fill, but could not. Did she want him to stop calling, and couldn't tell him to, or did she want him to think that she was the type of woman who is adventurous?

"Oh."

"I mean, someone who is attracted to me. Who I'm attracted to. But we know it isn't going to go any further." She caught herself in her own lie and was making it worse.

Silence. The blank, empty silence of two people breathing into the phone. The awkwardness of how to fill it. Of what to say. The awkwardness of feeling too much.

"Who is he, Eleanor?"

"It doesn't matter."

"Falling in love has upset you."

"I'm not in love."

"It's the exhilaration. It makes you feel alive."

"We're just friends," Eleanor said.

"Of course we're friends. Eleanor, are you okay?"

"I'm fine."

"What about your marriage?"

"Michael? Michael's fine."

Noah came into their bed in the middle of the night and instead of getting up and insisting he sleep in his own bed, Eleanor let him wedge his body in between her and Michael. She didn't want to be alone with Michael or to have her body too close to his. She felt a dark force she could not control pulling her away from him.

Nicholas was still having problems at school. Twice his teacher had called home to tell Eleanor that he had acted out. He said "ass" when she had asked the students for new spelling words. He hit a girl in the playground. "Miss Nightingale is lying," he said, when Eleanor confronted him the next day. When she went to check on him later, hoping he'd be filled with remorse, he was in his room playing with his action figures.

"I'm not going back to school," he said later. "You can't make me."

"What happened? Tell me what's wrong." Eleanor kneeled down in front of him.

"Nobody believes me," he said. "I had to sit out for recess. Miss Nightingale didn't believe me."

"What didn't she believe?"

"That I didn't use the middle finger."

"Did you?"

"See. No one believes me."

She stared at him.

"If you and Daddy get divorced," he said, "I would want to live with Daddy."

"Why?" She tried not to show that the comment hurt her. She knew he was angry at her.

"Because Daddy does more fun stuff with me. But you lay with me before I go to bed." He looked up at her and smiled, fully aware of what he was doing. "Still, I would want to live with Dad."

"It wouldn't be your decision. Children don't decide where they are going to live. Their parents decide for them. Besides, Daddy and I are not getting a divorce."

"Do you think it's true, Michael?" Eleanor asked later when she was repeating the story to Michael.

"Of course he did," Michael said. "What's wrong with you? That's not something a teacher would make up."

"What's wrong?" Eleanor said. "What's wrong with our son?"

"You know," Michael said, standing before her almost lifeless.

"I don't know."

"You're not here anymore. You haven't been here for the last six months. Not for me, just barely for the boys. I don't know where you are. I don't feel good," he said.

"I *am* here. I've been consumed with my book. I'm sorry. I'll try not to think about it so much. You know how much I care about you and the boys."

She woke up in the morning in a panic, gasping for air. After she took the boys to school she went across town to the church on Fifth Avenue where no one who knew her might find her (her own synagogue wouldn't do), the church that said THIS IS GOD'S HOUSE. ALL ARE WELCOME. But there was yellow tape over the entranceway to the door. Construction workers were outside. They were not letting her in.

30

"Here's what you do with your new mitt. You put a ball inside it like this, and then you put it under your mattress and sleep on it." Eleanor listened from the living room as Michael was putting the boys to bed. "That way the leather begins to soften into the shape of the ball," he said, bestowing his boyhood knowledge on them before he turned off their light.

"Can you hear my heart, Daddy?" Noah said. Eleanor pictured him taking Michael's stethoscope and placing it against his chest, a routine Michael did with the boys before bed. They liked to listen to their heartbeat. Michael showed them how to take their pulse and blood pressure.

"I am your heart," Michael said. "Sleep tight."

After, he appeared in the doorway of their living room wearing jeans and a turtleneck, looking handsome and tired. Why did she feel so separate? She wanted Michael to force his presence upon her, to reconnect her, but instead he sat at his desk and put his eye over the lens of the microscope, retreating to his cells and their own insular language. If I don't force him to pay attention, he's not there, she thought. The paint was chipping along the moldings on her living room wall. The fabric on the pillow seemed faded. Or was it just her mood?

They went upstate to spend the weekend at Sally and Rick's house in the country. Marcia and Brian and their kids also went. They barely spoke during the car ride home. Nicholas played his Game Boy. Noah was stretched out on his back like a pharaoh, listening to music.

"What did you think of what Brian said at dinner last night?" Michael asked as they were driving home. "Goddamn it, Eleanor. Do you purposefully do that? Not hear me?"

"I was thinking about my work," Eleanor lied. She reached out to touch his thigh. Her eye caught the angry scowl across his face. She retracted her hand.

"You always think about your work lately."

"I'm sorry. What did you say?"

"When Brian was joking last night that Marcia has been so nice to him that he suspects she's having an affair. What did you think?"

"Do you really think that if someone's nice they're having an affair? That's silly."

"I don't know. I think there's something going on."

She thought what it would be like to tell Michael the truth. She knew she wasn't being fair. She had everything a woman could want, and yet she couldn't seem to stop what was overtaking her. Maybe if she explained it to Michael she could stop it. *Michael, I don't know how it happened.* She wanted to take his hands, which had healed many other bodies, into hers. *It's someone from my past. We reconnected again. He makes me feel necessary. It's like he's healing something.* But the words would not come forward. She watched him looking ahead responsibly, staying between the lines to avoid oncoming traffic, his sturdy hands carefully turning the wheel toward home. "Did you enjoy the country? You look so tired," she said, and kissed his cheek.

The boys fell asleep in the car. When they got home she carried Noah from the car. His legs curled around her waist, finding a secure spot, while his head leaned into her neck, and his fingers gripped the sweater on her back. She carried him blindly in the dark, navigating the shadows and corners in her house, knowing where each chair sat in the living room, each sofa, each lamp.

She watched Michael take off his clothes, wash his hands, and put on a pair of sweatpants and T-shirt. She looked through the open door of the master bathroom at their matching white robes hanging like phantoms. If only she could tell him something about her work and her thoughts, tell him about the unknown parts of herself and bring them to life with him, but she was mute. His refusal to step outside his anger, his refusal to penetrate her and she him, his belief that he was entitled to her happiness, her pleasure, and her well-being just because he was her husband—she could not understand or accept. They were like two beings at war with each other, and at the same time seeking comfort. "How's the stent coming along?" she said. "Any advancements on that front?"

"It's a work in progress. We have to go over these findings with a fine-tooth comb. We don't expect results overnight."

"I'm so proud of the work you're doing," she tried, retreating to the kitchen. Noah, having woken up, took her hand and dragged her into the living room where Michael was working.

"Tell Daddy you love him," Noah said.

"Of course I love him." Eleanor dried her wet hands on the front of her jeans.

"Tell him," Noah insisted.

"Noah, you're being silly."

Michael looked up at her, waiting, his reading glasses slipping down his nose.

"Of course I love Daddy."

She couldn't sleep. Or if she slept it was in that half-asleep, half-awake state where her mind was still active and present. She kept the bedroom door open, a habit they had fallen into when Nicholas was a baby so that they could hear him if he cried in the night. Through the open door she watched the pattern of light in the dark hallway that came from the dim light underneath Michael's microscope in the other room. The light danced off the walls, evaporated, bloomed into focus again. She thought about Michael. It wasn't his fault that he wasn't attuned to the same nuances as she. It wasn't as if she could understand the cells he studied underneath his lens. Why was it so important now that they speak the same language? When she had first met him it hadn't seemed to matter. Why did it now? She prayed for sleep to overtake her before Michael came to bed so she wouldn't have to experience their estrangement, but even though she closed her eyes when he entered the bedroom and slid underneath the covers, she was wide awake.

Michael, too, was restless. He tossed and turned, unable to get comfortable. He threw the sheets off his body, tortured by the airlessness that sat in their bed like another person prying them apart.

"You can open the window," she said, hugging his shoulder. "I don't want you to suffer. I can't sleep, either."

She wandered into the boys' room and slid in next to Nicholas.

"What about Daddy?" Nicholas said, when he found her sleeping next to him in his bed in the morning. "Daddy's all alone."

She began to have fantasies of God watching over her, though she had never considered herself to be a religious person. She felt God's presence when she was moved by the beauty of nature. But now she was frightened by the shift inside her. She imagined God watching over her to help her find her way, the way she had imagined her father had when she was still a young girl and he no longer lived at home. She told herself if she was present to every nuance of how she felt and of what she believed to be true and authentic, then she would survive the crisis within herself.

God must have orchestrated everything. He had sent Stephen to Paris to her. He was testing her faith in her beliefs and in her marriage. Their meeting seemed an improbable coincidence the more Eleanor considered it. She wondered if God was trying to bring her closer to her true nature.

She walked home through Central Park on her way back from school. It was snowing. A light dust of white covered the lawn and trees. She heard a voice from behind. Someone was singing an old gospel song. "Come bathe in the water with Jesus, come bathe in the water with Jesus. I saw the light from heaven come down." She looked around to follow the voice. A beautiful, large black man was walking through the avenue of snow. God was malevolent. He was teasing her.

She remembered sitting in the synagogue beside her mother on the high holy days. The seat beside them that belonged to her father was empty. *God's will is inside you,* the rabbi said. *It is written in the book of life. We know how many will die, how many will live.* Did that mean that everything was mapped out already, no matter how we chose to live, it would come out the same way eventually? Was this her destiny?

After she came out of the park and turned up Broadway, she stopped. To her right was a church and on the church was a placard. NEVER PLACE A PERIOD WHERE GOD HAS PLACED A COMMA. GOD IS STILL SPEAKING. She thought about it. God is giving me permission to explore, she reasoned. He doesn't want me to end the sentence.

When she arrived in her office, the red light on her phone was lit. She could barely swallow. "Call me, Eleanor," Stephen said on her voice mail. "I'm in New York. I've been here all week. I told you I'd be back." He had been in New York for a week and she had not known it. She imagined him wandering through the streets. She imagined him kissing her. It began slowly. In her fantasy no words were between them. He stood before her and lifted her head to his with his hand on her chin. Heat overtook her body. She snapped back to the piles of pink message slips on her desk. Outside the window, the wind was tangled inside the tree branches.

He was on assignment and was staying in an apartment on 57th Street. He had been in her city for a week and had not called her and within that week she must have thought about him hundreds of times. She would call and they would meet and that would be the end of this madness. There were things between them that had not been pursued, that had not been said, and they cut through her. He had come in and out of her life since they were children, and each time, it seemed with more significance. They had walked though an entire city nine months ago. *Almost a year of this,* she thought. Nearly a year and they hadn't touched on any of it. *What should I do,* she whispered to God, but she heard only the thumping inside her chest. Stephen had been in New York all week.

She grabbed her coat and walked to the grand church on 112th Street. She belonged to a large Jewish congregation on the Upper West Side. Services were held in different venues, in a synagogue on 88th Street, in a Presbyterian church in Alice

Tully Hall. God was everywhere. The synagogue had portable bemas and arcs. The torahs traveled.

If God existed, he would find her anywhere. She needed faith to help her understand her contradictions. It could not be a crime against God to follow her heart, could it? She heard Jordan talking to her about her affair with the Italian. *It was high style,* she had said. *If you're going to do it, my God, do it in style.* What did she mean? She had been too frightened to ask. She sat down in the front pew of the grand church and realized it was all very simple. She would not call him back.

The church was too big and hollow. She couldn't get comfortable. She looked at its stone walls and thought all it would take would be one loose piece and all the walls would come undone. It was drafty and cold. The images of Christ with blood spurting from his limbs frightened her. *We are all one under God,* she heard in her head.

Back in her office there was another message. "Eleanor, are you there? Where are you? How can I find you?"

The messages would stop if she didn't call. She resolved to never do so again. But the little red light on her phone continued to light up with his messages throughout the next few weeks. Each morning she checked. And she checked her cell phone constantly; each time it rang she looked at the number lit up in the little window screen on her phone. When she returned from teaching, she checked again. At night she went into the bathroom with her cell phone and dialed her office machine. "I'm in my apartment now," he said. "I'm talking to you overlooking the trees in Central Park. It's desolate in the park without the leaves, Eleanor. I'm sorry to leave all these sporadic messages. But when will I see you?"

She grew to depend on the messages but knew it was also better not to answer. Just to hear his voice and imagine him was enough. "I can't sleep at night with the sound of traffic at my window. I'm used to the silence of the mountains." There was something about her connection to him that felt poetic and necessary; or was it his elusiveness that made him seem that way? What she felt for him contained deep emotion and special tenderness for his weaknesses. He depended on her somehow, and it was impossible for her to turn away. She played the last message over in her mind, sitting with his voice, feeling it in the pit of her stomach until she didn't have to play it anymore.

Do you remember when we were kids? I used to
feel safe knowing you were in your bedroom. Your
window was like a lighthouse in the dark. Eleanor,
when will you call?

A student knocked on the door. They talked about his paper on *Jude the Obscure*. Eleanor thought about those children, dead in the small rented room where Jude and Sue had loved, unmarried by the laws of the state, of the church, and yet wed in spirit. She thought of the agony their love had borne. Over a century had passed, but things have not changed. Soon she would be punished. When she taught, Stephen receded from her mind almost completely. Only after she went through her daily routine and was in bed did she repeat the messages in her mind: *It's desolate in the park, Eleanor.*

The messages came about once or twice a week. "This city's crazy. I don't know how you live here. There's so much to absorb. So much to see. I'm in the bathtub. I did something to my back running yesterday. I thought about you as I jogged through Central Park. 'Eleanor would love the light this early in the park.' I saw you sitting on a bench watching me. I'm talking to you sitting in a bath full of ice. Leave me a time and place where you want to meet. I'll be there. It's cold without you."

Time in between each message was like a long-lost dream. When she heard the sound of his voice she saw the image of his house in back of hers, the boy in the playhouse dealing the cards, the tormented teenager on her mother's couch, the half-finished house in Colorado.

"I'm going to come find you," he said. "I know where your office is. I'm going to sit on those steps we sat on last time until I do. I have to see you, Eleanor. You know that. I've come to New York."

She visited the church daily. She sat on the same bench. She counted the rows each time until she found it. She came to be in the presence of something outside herself. When she left the church she felt almost released.

She walked up Amsterdam back to her office. Just as she was turning the corner through the gates she saw him. He was not a figment. He was before her in the flesh and blood.

"We're having coffee." He took her hand and gave her a superior smile. "You can't betray anyone over coffee."

"Is that what this is? Betrayal?"

"You look amazing." He was standing by the gate in a black leather jacket, waiting for her. "Besotted. I'm besotted," he repeated. He hugged her awkwardly. She did not look amazing. She was wearing Nicholas's baseball cap and her unwashed hair was tucked in a bun inside it.

"What are you doing here? You can't just be here." She wanted to punch him and cry from happiness both at the same time.

"You know why I'm here."

At a nearby Starbucks he explained he was staying in the apartment of his agent, who was in Los Angeles closing a movie deal. He was finishing up the magazine piece on pilots. They were considering making him a contributing writer at the magazine. If this happened, he could afford to stay in New York. He had interviewed pilots from several airlines. "Just last week there was this pilot on American. Once the plane was airborne he began proselytizing. 'Those of you who are not believers, let's take this moment to reconsider.' Can you believe it? These guys are powerful. Think of the lives they control. It makes you wonder."

She was in her judgmental mood. The piece on pilots sounded ridiculous. She had no interest in hearing about it. She tried to find other things about him that turned her off. She wanted to store them up so she could resist thinking about him when they were apart. When he smiled, she studied the silver fillings between his bicuspids.

"Did you know that women fantasize most about firemen and pilots? It's a control thing, isn't it? Women want to be saved."

"You are not the Messiah."

He looked at her strangely.

She was tired of hearing him talk, always listening to messages. She told him about the book she was writing that had grown out of the paper on *Anna Karenina* she had presented in Paris.

"I have an idea," he said. "The film script we are going to collaborate on should be about a woman who throws herself in front of a train for having an affair. Does that sound familiar?"

"That's ridiculous. I love that novel. And besides, it's been done."

"Eleanor, I know you do. You thrive on high drama."

She thought about how to defend herself. She stopped. There was no point.

"It's not a bad thing." He paused to consider. "It's just who you are."

"What about you? Isn't everyone emotional?"

"If that's the way you choose to live in the world."

"What if it's not a choice?"

"For some people it isn't." He reached across the table to quiet her fingers that had been fingering the sugar packets tucked in their wire container, but before he touched her he looked at her knowingly, as if saying, *I know who you are.* He took a sip of his coffee. "It's okay. I like that about you." He smiled. "Poor Eleanor. Your green eye is hazel today."

She watched the way his lips moved and the way the joints bent in his fingers. She watched the hollow in his cheek when it throbbed.

"I knew you before your husband did. I knew you when you were a girl wearing your hair in braids. I used to watch you." He pointed his finger at her chest. "I know what's inside here. I know what you're struggling with. You're trying to decide who you are. If you're like Kitty or Anna."

"I'm not so sure."

She thought about how often she must have sat by her window as a child, staring across at Stephen's window and longing to receive a sign from him that acknowledged her nights and days of desire. There was never a sign. Now he was sitting across from her at the table in the café and she had no idea why or what to do about it. She felt a chill. There was no word to describe what they were to each other.

"It isn't that simple," Eleanor said, thinking once more about *Anna Karenina.*

"What? What did I miss?"

"Why Anna killed herself. She was tormented. She couldn't bear the cost of having betrayed her family and society. And her son, for god's sake. She had lost everything." She paused. "She loved another man. That wasn't supposed to happen." She thought of the woman she and Noah saw that day on the subway platform who fell before the subway train. She pictured her vacant eyes and the unsettled way she held her body as she paced between the two posts on the platform. Did she die of love? Eleanor thought of everything she had witnessed that had transformed her. Stephen could not—did not—know her. She wanted to be sitting back in the church, in quiet, practicing restraint.

"You wouldn't understand it. You've never been married. You don't have a son."

His face was stricken as if she had physically hurt him. "What makes you think I don't understand? I'm a writer. I understand."

"So you're saying that because you are a writer you can read my heart?"

"That's exactly what I'm saying. My novel is about a girl. My agent is shopping it around." Eleanor pictured the novel wrapped up in brown paper like Michael's dry-cleaned shirts, tied with twine, being shopped from one publishing house to another by a messenger wearing a bicycle helmet. She berated herself for not listening properly because she knew once he left and she was alone, she would struggle to remember every word. She listened with one part of her while the other was trying to quiet her feelings. "It's about a girl who lived in front of this boy's house—their windows almost kissed. A girl that he lost. It's about a boy who only loved one girl his entire life and he didn't know how to tell her or how to be with her. He doesn't know how to do it. That's what my novel is about. It has no plot. It's about desire."

"Is it still set in Alaska?"

"Yes. Where it's always cold. The boy never gets warm."

"Why in Alaska?"

"Because it's fiction." He looked at her carefully. "I'm trying to learn. Don't you understand? It's why I'm here."

"Learn what?"

He reached for her hand. "How to be intimate, Eleanor."

Eleanor looked at the second hand ticking on her watch. She was in Starbucks. Her latte was lukewarm. Stephen's sweater had picked up crumbs from someone else's snack. He was real. He was across from her and not a figment of her imagination. She wanted to touch him to see if her hand would slip right through. It was five minutes past 5:00 and she was late picking up the boys from their after-school program, though she wasn't ready to leave.

"I have that poem you wrote for me, Eleanor. I brought it with me to New York. You know. The poem. Remember? You read it to me that first night. When we came home from the bars in Colorado."

She studied his eyes to see what was behind his words. She remembered how in Colorado she waited for him all night to come home. Had he really changed? "How strange that I don't remember it. Why did you bring it with you?"

He looked at his watch. "I have to get back to work, Eleanor. We'll talk more later. This piece. It's torturing me."

"You still haven't told me what happened that night."

"I've already told you it wasn't about you. I was afraid."

It was time now to go home to her life of making dinner and sleeping beside someone who had grown as distant to her as a foreign land; to a life of reading her students' wordy essays and watching her boys turn her living room into a *Star Wars* spaceship. She threw her unfinished latte into the trash receptacle and followed him out the door. Already she regretted what had happened. What had she gained in seeing him? Why had he insisted he see her? She walked briskly in front of him.

"Have you been to Café Luxemburg? I'm meeting an editor there for lunch. What about Michael's? Do you know the place? Have you heard of the Monkey Bar?"

"You know about the Monkey Bar?"

"Yeah, I'm having a drink there later. With an old buddy from Colorado."

She suddenly felt jealous of the life he was living without her. She imagined him and his friend going to bars and restaurants together. Maybe he would try to meet a woman. She didn't want to be his confidante — the person who showed him his true self so that he could be free to sleep with someone else. What was she doing to herself? She wanted him to go away.

They were approaching 89th Street where he would turn to head south. They reached the corner. He stopped and they hugged awkwardly. His elbow hit her in the ribs.

"I'll call you, Eleanor." Pause. "Eleanor? Please answer my calls. Don't avoid me. I need you." He stared into her eyes. "Are you okay? Your eyes, they look funny. You look so worried."

She looked at him, struggling to make sense of how he affected her. No words came. She was out of words.

"We're finally in the same city. It's happening, don't you see?"

They started walking in opposite directions. He stopped and looked back. She wanted to run to him but she kept walking. In her mind she knew he had stopped. She thought he would follow her. After a block or two she thought about chasing after him. She was surprised he wasn't following her. Already her mind was flooded with unanswered questions. Already she was sifting through the words to uncover the subtext, the clues. She didn't know where to go. She stopped at a newspaper stand to regain her equilibrium. She looked at the rack of magazines. Her eye hit on *Vogue*. She studied the sexy model on the cover and read the cover lines. SURRENDER TO YOUR MARRIAGE. HOW TO WORRY WELL. THE NEW ANTIAGING CREAMS. WRESTLING FREE OF YOUR DEMONS. She turned to walk back uptown to pick up her kids. Her mind was racing. She turned around again, certain he'd be behind her, out of breath, trying to chase her down. "This has to stop," she said, but he was nowhere to be found.

31

She logged in to her e-mail account.

> To: JCloud@princeton.edu
> From: ECahn@columbia.edu
>
> Explain the Romantic tradition. The emphasis upon emotion and expressivity in art, in the writings of Wordsworth, Keats, Baudelaire, the sense of marvel and curiosity, its intense focus upon a loved person. Explain to me its downfall. Why "The End of Romanticism?" I need to know. Yrs, Eleanor

> To: ECahn@columbia.edu
> From: JCloud@princeton.edu
>
> The Romantics reconnected emotion to all other important human faculties (cognition, perception, rational thought) in refreshing and complex ways. Tired of the exhaustion of reason, of truth, the Romantics embraced beauty. Under their pens, emotion — and especially passion — became the center of human existence. It expressed our most exalted state and a conduit to knowledge, morality, beauty, and meaning. At a certain point it couldn't sustain itself. Truly, John

To: JCloud@princeton.edu
From: ECahn@columbia.edu

Why?

To: ECahn@columbia.edu
From: JCloud@princeton.edu

Emotive expression changed into a quest for formal
experimentation.

To: JCloud@princeton.edu
From: ECahn@columbia.edu

The Romantic tradition gave in to emotion. The modernist
tradition turned to the cerebral. But surely some artists and
writers are still stuck in the Romantic tradition? How do
they fit into the culture? How does Romanticism have any
meaning today?

To: ECahn@columbia.edu
From: JCloud@princeton.edu

It still has meaning. Without it language and art is too cool.
Glib.

To: JCloud@princeton.edu
From: ECahn@columbia.edu

What's your definition of a post-Romantic?

To: ECahn@columbia.edu
From JCloud@princeton.edu

Post-Romanticism combines a romantic emphasis upon
beauty and passion with the modern and postmodern
emphasis upon originality and experimentation. The post-
Romantics would argue that without Romanticism there is no
art. One grows out of the other.

32

The boys were in their bedroom playing with the babysitter.
She should release the babysitter but instead she looked at
the pitcher from Paris sitting on her bureau. Her eye ran up and
down the seam where it had cracked. She rose from the bed to
look for the poem. Long ago, she used to write poems on her
typewriter, two sheets of paper with a carbon in between. She
found poems for William but she could not find the carbon
copy of the poem she had written for Stephen. She tore open
files, rummaged through her desk papers, opened old shoe
boxes stuffed with letters. It was as if she was looking for a
piece of herself and not just a piece of paper. Michael was out
of town at a medical conference he went to every year at the
end of February. Usually she hated it when he was out of town
but she was glad to have the house to herself.

She went into the boys' room to speak to Rachel, the teen-
age babysitter. Rachel wore a crown of braids around her head.
She was that age when she might write poems to boys and
Eleanor almost asked her but stopped herself. "Rachel, I have
to call one of my students. Would you mind putting the boys to
bed before you leave?" She kissed the boys goodnight and went
back into her study. She began searching again, pulling out old
college papers, poems she had stuffed in folders and drawers

and between her favorite books, but it was nowhere to be found. She went into the bedroom and closed the door. She couldn't stop thinking about the conversation she'd had with Stephen the day before. She still felt agitated. *What did he want from her?* She dialed Stephen's cell phone number.

"Eleanor?"

"What are you doing?" she asked once he'd picked up the phone.

"What's going on?"

"I'm married."

"If it makes you uncomfortable we don't have to see each other."

He was going to wiggle out of it. Her fury reduced her to silence.

"I was waiting for you to take the lead," he said, after a few seconds passed. "I know you're married."

"I can't talk about this now. Don't you understand? I'm at home."

"We have to talk about it sometime. I need you, Eleanor."

After they hung up she lay down on her bed and closed her eyes. She let Stephen's voice linger in her mind. *I was waiting for you to take the lead.* She lay down still on her back with her eyes closed. He was in the room with her. He was lying beside her and she became soft and open under his touch. She could feel his lips, first on her face, her forehead, behind her ears.

She got out of bed. She opened her top dresser drawer. She took out the prayer shawl and spread it over herself. She heard the rabbi's voice: *Looking upon these fringes you will be reminded of the Lord and fulfill them and not be seduced by your heart or led astray by your eyes.*

She took the shawl's tassels and braided them in her hands.

The next morning Nicholas walked into her room.

"You're different, Mommy."

"What do you mean?"

"You didn't even come in our room to say goodnight."

His words sliced through her. "I'm not different. I'm your same mom. I was working."

She went to the bathroom and brushed her teeth, trying to push away the meaning behind her son's words. But he was right. When she looked at herself in the mirror she saw someone she didn't know. She saw a woman capable of having two lives, two separate identities. She thought of her father. He had recently sent her his new cell phone number on a postcard from Spain. When she came out of the bathroom she called him.

"Daddy, this is Eleanor."

"Eleanor?"

"Daddy, it's me. I need to see you."

33

She and Stephen met in the park. Her stomach had been queasy all morning in anticipation, and she regretted that she had drunk that last cup of coffee. Why had she agreed to meet him again when she had resolved not to? The minute she had arrived in her office that morning the phone was ringing. She picked it up. "We have to talk," Stephen had said. "You have to meet me." She promised herself she would tell him to stop.

"I have good news," Stephen said, once she arrived. They were sitting on a bench near a stand of bare trees in the park. It was cold, but not too cold.

"I sold my book, Eleanor. After almost twenty fucking

years." He looked like he wanted to grab her but he restrained himself. "You know how it feels. All those years of working on it alone in a vacuum. The doubts. The fears. I put it away for three years and I couldn't even look at it. It was like a demon that possessed me. I used to think that if I hadn't spent all those years writing I could have been living my life. I couldn't stand myself. But I had no choice. I was compelled to do it."

Eleanor stared at him. She squeezed his arm with her hand. "I knew it would happen."

"This is the best day of my life." He beamed. He paused in thought. "Wouldn't it be great, Eleanor. Both of us writers. Both of us on the same page. Imagine what we could do together."

She couldn't stop smiling. They were so alike! The energy and self-satisfaction he derived from his work seemed to fill him the same way it did her. She understood what it was to devote years to something she wasn't sure would ever amount to anything. The nights she lay awake before presenting a paper, and then the intense feeling of gratification, like no other, once the audience responded.

"When I was writing my novel in Colorado I always thought of you, Eleanor. You were my audience. It was like I was writing to connect." He closed his eyes. "You didn't forget about me all these years. Did you?" He opened his eyes and looked up at her slowly, taking her in, layer by layer, as if he were undressing her.

"I did forget about you." It started to snow. She felt it lightly on her face. "You were not on my radar screen." She thought about the first year of her marriage. She and Michael found the top-floor walk-up of an old brownstone. It was a studio with a tiny galley kitchen that overlooked a back garden. Before they moved in Michael went to the hardware store to buy detergents to clean the apartment. When he came back he held a broom in his hand. "This is our broom, Eleanor," he said, smiling, panting after he'd walked up the five flights of stairs. He held it out to her. "This is our dustpan."

She looked at Stephen. Snow dusted the ground. "I wondered about you from time to time. But I brushed you away like snow from my coat."

"So you're saying I'm like snow?"

"Yeah. You come on strong and then you melt and evaporate."

"I think about you, Eleanor. Where does it come from? Your intensity? I was in love with it, but scared of it. I know your secret. Your emotional turmoil. I used to watch you through the window. That stuff doesn't go away. I should know," he said, as if he knew intimately the long hours of loneliness. "Our mothers. They are so much alike. I know what that does to a person. I know you better than you think."

She looked at him, moved by his words.

"I fucked up. I shouldn't have let you go that day in Colorado."

"You could have called me. You could have tried to be in touch."

"You got married. How could you have done that?"

"You didn't try to stop me."

"I wasn't ready until now. I thought there'd be time. I didn't know until I said good-bye to you in the hotel in Paris how much it mattered."

She looked at the swaying trees and at the snowflakes speckling the branches. "You're ten years too late."

"No one will ever know me like you, Eleanor."

"What are you telling me?"

"The attraction is still there, and you know it. You can't walk away from something like that."

"But you've done it so many times. What do you want me to do now?"

"You know what you have to do."

He took her hands and brought them to his lips. "I need to hold you, Eleanor. We should go to the Plaza."

"I bet you've used that line before." She looked at him more closely. He was wearing a zip-up sweatshirt with a hood and a cross or dagger, she could not tell which, dangling from his neck. Over his sweatshirt he wore a black leather jacket. "Is that why you came to New York?"

He looked down at his hands and then pulled his cell phone from his pocket to read a text message.

"Is that why you came to New York?" she repeated.

"Maybe." He zipped up his sweatshirt. "I came to New York because I had business to take care of. This is important to me, Eleanor."

"What's important? Your piece? Your novel?"

The snowflakes were bigger, denser. "Think what you want to think." He was distracted suddenly. "We should walk." She brushed the flakes off her coat but they stuck. They seeped into her thin coat. "I'm trying to see if I can do it," he said.

They both rose and walked slowly toward the gates to the park. Once they had walked out of the park and were standing at the corner, Eleanor felt as if she were inside a painting, walking through the park in the snow. She wasn't married. She had no children. There was no thought of anyone she might hurt. They were a couple walking in the park, hand in hand, inside a painting. They had betrayed no one.

Eleanor looked into his face. He was smiling. He was the man in her painting and not an intruder in her life. "I want something to happen," she said, not quite knowing what she was saying, and they went their separate ways.

34

She thought of nothing else, not her work, her husband, her children. She imagined foolishly that she was young. That she was without attachment and in that state it was as if what had started between her and Stephen so long ago was continuing. She told herself that if she let this opportunity with Stephen pass she was denying herself something important. Stephen had entered her life with purpose. If she continued to always do the proper, right thing then she would indeed be a good, proper person. But if she allowed herself to walk through the gates that led to the unknown she would find an important part of herself that had been cut off. Perhaps it was that very thing that might make her discover something extraordinary about herself she might not have known. Every once in a while she would think about the effect on Michael and the boys, but it was something she couldn't think about, had to purge from her thoughts. How could her love for them be separate from this other thing? How could she be so divided?

She could not deny that every part of her being was suddenly awake. She noticed the snow fall in a way she had never noticed snow before, attuned to the crystal edges, to the lightness and absorption, the perfect quiet. She knew she looked prettier. She didn't even have to look in the mirror—it was her inner being shining through. She had always thought she was invisible, that like Houdini she could slip through walls, make herself disappear. But now she felt fully visible. Yet her hair was still the same texture and length, her eyes the same colors. She had not lost or gained weight. She told herself that she should walk to Stephen's apartment. That she should knock on the door and announce herself and not walk away like she had years ago in Colorado when she had not stood up to him. She told herself that she should open her mind and stop censoring her thoughts. It was the most disarming and liberating feeling she had ever experienced.

She wanted to be near Stephen because being with him would be a natural extension of all the thoughts and desires and compassion she had felt for him since they were children. She thought that being with him would be like finding the other half of who she was, that there would be a union. She thought that by making him whole she would make herself whole, that being with him would seal something. That there was the possibility that Stephen would change her, that she could change him, that they could change the idea of each other, and that was not something she could dismiss. If she denied herself this chance she would deny herself the possibility of being with someone who she believed comprehended her deeply. Wasn't that denying life itself? She wanted to be near him. She had remembered the shape and feel of how they had kissed long ago. She wanted to be near him because she thought it would stop the restlessness that kept her up at night. She thought that by being near him her desire would end. She felt desire for him in her chest, in the tips of her fingers. She liked the way his mind worked. How full of emotion he was. It meant he was alive, that he was feeling something, even if the intensity kept him away from her. She thought if she could break through she would enter into some kind of kingdom that she had craved and had never had. The feeling she imagined was almost indescribable, not even depicted in the books she loved. Oh dear lord, if it were a ruse she was doomed. *Were we all, we who lived deeply, doomed?*

"I don't feel like myself anymore," Eleanor confessed to Jordan over lunch. She gave Jordan the history. "I don't know what we

278 • JILL BIALOSKY

are. He's someone from my past. Someone I knew a long time ago. Someone I'm not sure I even like or trust."

"And?"

"I can't stop thinking about him. And now he's in New York. We meet in the park. Or in a café for coffee. Nothing's happened. I'm not sure I even respect him. Can you be obsessed with someone you don't like? He wears sweatshirts and a pendant around his neck."

"Does Michael know?"

"Should I have told him?"

"That's not what I'm saying. What I'm saying is that something has happened. That's why you're anxious."

"Because I haven't told Michael?"

"Because you're keeping it a secret."

"Do you think Michael tells me about women colleagues, other doctors he sees at the hospital? Other women he has lunch with? Aren't married people allowed to have friends of the opposite sex?"

"But you're not friends."

"How did it happen with Luca?"

"You don't wake up one morning and decide you want to have an affair, Eleanor. I met Luca. That's how it happened."

"Were there others before Luca?"

She shook her head.

"What about Jonathan? Did you want things to end?"

"I wanted them to stay the same. I wanted my affair and my husband and my children. But once Luca and I fell in love it got more complicated. He wanted me to leave Jonathan. It drove him crazy that we couldn't have holidays together. That Jonathan and I were still friends."

"That's not what I want." Eleanor picked the anchovy out of her salad. "I don't want to lose my family. I want to make it stop."

"You're probably working out something deeper."

Eleanor began to shred her napkin.

"You know. Your relationship with your father. Your mother. Only you know what, Eleanor."

The napkin had become a castle of torn-up paper on the tabletop.

"You need to have an affair," Jordan said.

"No. You're not listening."

Eleanor stared into her haunted blue eyes. She seemed witchlike. A siren. "This isn't about my mother or my father. I'm not sure it's even about Michael. Stephen's awakening things in me. Before Michael I couldn't wait to get settled so I wouldn't have to feel this way anymore. I wanted to know who I was going to marry. I wanted my kids. But now if it weren't for seeing him again in Paris, I'm not sure I would have known it. It has to mean something, doesn't it? The fact that he showed up again. The fact that I've known him since we were kids?"

"Or the fact that he isn't your husband?"

"Don't do that. Stop making what I'm going through be about what you've gone through. I told you. I don't want to have an affair."

She looked at Eleanor closely. "You know what Freud said, don't you? There are no accidents."

"You mean it's about my childhood? Is that what you're saying?"

"Is that what you think it is?"

"I thought I could control it."

"You have to play it out."

Jordan wasn't pretty. Her eyes were arresting, but her face was too thin and oily. She had a somewhat tortured expression in her mouth and a geometrical haircut that made her look like she belonged in a different century. But she had a sexy body with big shapely breasts. Eleanor's eyes went to them the minute she saw her. She walked into a room slowly. The way she held her arms, how her legs turned out slightly like a dancer's when she walked, it was as if her body was saying *Look at me*. She wore clothes that played up her figure. Thin, gauzy things, low cut and cinched at the waist. She was the kind of woman who surveyed desirable men to see whether there was a vibe. Eleanor had noticed it of late. And yet, when they first met, Jordan was different. Was it midlife, marriage that had changed her? The news of Jordan's infidelity had traveled through the department quickly. He was a young Italian scholar studying the Italian Renaissance poets. It was a cliché.

"Luca is the first man who is more interested in pleasing me than himself," she said. "He thinks everyone wants me."

"Is that what you want him to think?"

"Desire is about power, Eleanor. I don't care what he thinks."

"What do you two do together? I mean when you're not in bed."

"We haven't gotten to that stage yet." Jordan took a bite from her tuna salad. She ordered the same thing every time they had lunch. She picked off the tuna and some egg and left more than half of her salad uneaten. Her antidepressants caused her to lose her appetite. She had been on a different medication that had taken away her sex drive and she had decided she'd rather have her sex drive than her appetite. "I don't want him to get too close." Jordan sipped her Diet Coke. "I don't completely trust him."

"Is that why you want him?"

She paused. She looked into her picked-over salad, deep in thought, and then up at Eleanor. "It's why he turns me on."

She did not know if she was jealous or whether she pitied Jordan. The need for intensity, to sacrifice to Eros at the cost of all else, was that not a death in itself?

She left the restaurant no more sure of anything.

She walked back to her office slowly. She thought of her boys. Had the love she had bestowed on them driven her further from Michael? She thought of the life she and Michael were providing the boys, of the commitment they both felt to them. But finally, even giving children a good home and security wasn't enough to make a person whole. She was still evolving in spite of being a mother. Why had she thought it would be enough?

She quickened her pace and with it her resolve: She would not seek him out again. It was her will triumphing over his. The sun shone on the black iron bars of Columbia's gates; she walked through feeling as if she had escaped danger by a hair's breadth.

35

To: ECahn@columbia.edu
From: JCloud@princeton.edu

Eleanor,
The Romantics were either in a state of exaltation or despair. Keats, Shelley, Wordsworth. Their poems express the universal longing for romance and its deep awareness that all romance — literary and human — depends upon incomplete and uncertain knowledge. Think of the self-deception of the speaker in Keats's "La Belle Dame Sans Merci" or "The Beautiful Lady Without Pity." I taught this poem today and every time I teach it I see something different. As the poem opens the knight is anguished, ill, lovesick. The knight has fallen in love with the enchantress at first sight. Yet his own words make us doubtful that he

sees her as she really is. Read the poem for me, Eleanor. Tell me if you agree. It's about love's delusion. Yrs, John

To: JCloud@princeton.edu
From: ECahn@columbia.edu

John: I read the poem. Some of the saddest lines in the language. "And I awoke and found me here / On the cold hill's side." It's so expressive of forlorn lovers. The knight believes she was his alone. His grandest deception. It isn't until after she lulls him asleep that he dreams that she has cast the same spell on others. How tragic, when one realizes one's been delusional. So in need of love the knight chooses an object. It could have been anyone. He might well have loved himself. Truly, Eleanor

To: ECahn@columbia.edu
From: JCloud@princeton.edu

Eleanor, yes, it could have been anyone — that's the heart of the matter. Your friend, John

36

She met her father at Kennedy Airport in the VIP lounge.
"Thank you, Daddy," she said, when she saw him sitting at the bar dipping his fingers into a packet of salted nuts. He looked at her.
"Eleanor, so good to see you."
"Daddy."

"This face," he said. Tears were forming in his eyes. He picked up her hands and held them.

"Daddy," she said. "It's okay."

He ordered her a glass of wine.

"How's Michael? How are my grandsons?"

"They're good."

"And this one? How is she? My little girl."

"I don't know, Daddy. Something's happening. I don't know who I am."

"You're my little halavah. My sweet." She remembered how he used to sing songs from *Fiddler on the Roof* in the house when she was a child. He used to call her his little bird. He made her listen to Bach's Suites for Cello. *It's the saddest music I ever heard. When I listen to it I think of my father and my mother and I'm overwhelmed by sorrow.*

"Daddy, I have something I want to give you." She opened her bag and extracted the prayer shawl wrapped in cellophane. "I've had this for years. I've wanted to give it to you. To tell you. But I couldn't."

"Tell me what?"

"There's a God. He exists. You've been running away for a long time. Why don't you go back home now. Mom is still waiting for you. You don't have to live in hotels and fly on planes and drink in lounges. Look. A friend of mine gave it to me a long time ago. Your father had one; this could have been his."

"My father's dead." He looked at the prayer shawl. He looked again.

"My father is dead, Eleanor," he repeated. "They're all gone. It's dirty. My father wasn't dirty."

"Take it, Daddy. I want you to have it. Don't you understand? We're all connected."

"I have to go now, Eleanor. I'm going to miss my flight."

"Daddy," she said. "Take it."

"Little bird."

"Mommy's waiting. She's been waiting all these years." She thrust the prayer shawl at him. "You have to go see her now."

"It's dirty, Eleanor. If there was a God would he make such filth?"

He tore open another bag of peanuts and they spilled onto the counter. "Listen, Eleanor." His hands were trembling. "I spoke to your mother the other day. She's the only woman who understands me."

"I know, Daddy."

"When this deal goes through I'm going to invite all of you to Europe. We'll rent that little house we always talked about. Your mother. She'll come, too. Have you listened to Casals perform the Bach suites? The recording I sent you? I wanted you to listen to the intensity of feeling Casals brings to the music. Now and then he makes a mistake and you get a sudden flash of the human element—that this is a real person playing and feeling this music."

"I don't want to talk about music, Daddy."

"The cello suites had been forgotten for almost 200 years. Until Casals rediscovered them again. In his later years, in exile from Franco's Spain, Casals refused to play in public, saying that he could not perform until Spain was free again. But in private the only music he would play was the suites. Don't you understand? It means something. People are not forgotten. We're all going to be together again. I promise. You believe me, don't you, darling?"

She shook her head in disbelief. She started to tell him that of course she didn't believe him, but before the words came out of her mouth she stopped. "Daddy?"

"Eleanor?"

"Are you taking your blood pressure pills?"

"There's no pressure in my heart, Eleanor. It's another one of your mother's myths."

37

She was absently drinking a glass of wine at a dinner party. "Eleanor," Marcia said. "Where are you?"

Eleanor thought she had perfected the art of being present and removed at the same time. Apparently she hadn't. In her mind she was replaying a scene with Stephen, and the dinner with Michael and their friends had receded to the background, had become the fiction.

"You're not having an affair, are you?" Marcia started laughing. Brian looked at Eleanor. "Brian, do you think Eleanor's having an affair?" Marcia laughed harder.

Eleanor took a sip of her wine. "Can you imagine me having an affair?" She looked at Marcia with slight contempt. Marcia, bored by being a stay-at-home mom, had lately been talking about dabbling in film. She wanted to use Brian's money to see if she could invest her way into a project. It irked Eleanor that she thought that all she had to do was spend some of Brian's money and she could make a film. That she could buy her way into art.

An awkward silence descended. Michael stared at her dead on, scrutinizing, the way he did sometimes when he thought she was completely absent. She had no appetite for her salad of tiny macrobiotic greens. He looked down and then up at her over his wineglass. *Where are you, Eleanor? Where have you gone?* the look said. *Why can't I find you anymore?*

After the appetizers, Michael continued to study her sternly, as if he had digested what had been said and was looking for imprints of betrayal on her body. His look said, *What are you doing? Why are you throwing away our life together?*

Eleanor met his eyes. She realized how lonely it was to be at Marcia and Brian's house with all of them thinking she was with them while she was actually inside her own mind with no way to be reached. She rose to go to the bathroom. Brian followed. Tenderly, he put his hand on the back of her neck. "Give your husband a kiss, Eleanor. Tell him you love him. Men need that. Michael's been under a lot of stress at the hospital."

She brushed her teeth, relieved to be home from the dinner party. She looked at herself in the mirror. She told herself to lie down beside her husband and will him to possess her mind. Their attraction to each other had to be there still, buried somewhere. She remembered the time they had first made love. Michael took his stethoscope and ran it along every part of her body, listening to her insides, her stomach gurgling, her heart beating, the pulse in her wrists, her neck, her chest. The stethoscope was cold but it eventually warmed to her body heat. He listened and probed but he did not speak. It was his way.

She slipped into bed and waited for Michael to come out of the bathroom. When he folded his body underneath the covers she reached over and touched his shoulder to pull him toward her. "I don't know what's happened to us," she said. "I'm sorry I seem so far away. It's just sometimes I feel as if I don't have anything to contribute when we're out with Marcia and Brian."

"Is that what it is? If that's it we don't have to see them anymore."

"I wanted to be like them. But I'm different. You and I. We're different."

"I'm still the same, Eleanor. You're the one who has changed."

She was stunned to hear him say it. She knew he was right and yet she didn't know how to define it or explain it. She wished she were like Marcia, who seemed absorbed in the details of her life, the things Eleanor cherished, too, her children, her husband, making dinners, going on vacations, but who didn't seem to need that much more. Was she like that once, too? It wasn't fair to Michael that she was different. Michael thought that all she needed was a good dinner at night, a glass of wine, the touch of his lips on her cheek when he kissed her. That it was enough to have their beautiful home, their beautiful children. *You're a doctor's wife, for god's sake,* his look said to her. *Look how much you have in comparison to others,* he said without speaking. He didn't know that it wasn't enough. That she was her father's daughter.

She couldn't get comfortable in bed. It was as if Stephen was inside her, tormenting her with a different kind of life he might provide if they were together. She turned and twisted, pulling the covers over her tightly. She knew she had too much heart and emotion. It was her fatal flaw. She would have liked to laugh at herself. Who wouldn't?

She turned her back to Michael as if to protect him from herself. He pulled her back toward him. *You're my wife,* his body said to her. *I want you whether you like it or not.* The desperation with which he needed her was sexy, and she did want him. But even after, she felt empty inside; lonely. When he finished he took the bedspread that was folded neatly at the foot of the bed and walked out to spend the night on the couch. She wanted to call him to come back but she was resigned to their separateness.

"Mommy. Mommy, Mommy," Nicholas called, his voice growing louder. "Mommy. Mama."

She looked at the digital clock, the numbers falling with a clunk. It was 3:00 in the morning. "I'm right here, Nicholas," Eleanor called.

"Mama, where are you?" he called in desperation. "I need to find you. Mommy, Mommy."

She jumped out of bed. Nicholas was in the kitchen. He was opening the door to the refrigerator and the light it gave off illuminated his face. His eyes were wide open like little *O*s but he was fast asleep. "Mama, Mama," he cried anxiously, as if he were searching for her and she had disappeared. She caught up to him.

"I'm right here, Nicholas." Eleanor hugged him close. But he was stiff. He would not embrace her. His sleep had stolen her from him.

She turned him toward her. She grabbed him by his biceps. "I'm here, Nicholas," she said. "I'm right here. Can't you hear me?" She tried to take his hand from the refrigerator door. Michael had woken up by then and stood in the hallway in his boxer shorts and T-shirt, looking tired and miserable.

"Mommy, Mommy," Nicholas called again.

"Mommy's here," Eleanor said, shaking her son. "You're walking in your sleep." She caught Michael's eye and for a second they stood there looking at each other, both fully cognizant of what they'd done. Conspirators against their children. What was between them wasn't just about them anymore.

Eleanor picked Nicholas up and held him in her arms. He was heavy, but she needed to hold him. "Mommy's here," she said again, and hiked him on her hips, wishing he was back inside her womb, so they could exist together inside their own tranquil bubble once more. She carried him back to his bed.

In the morning Michael went into the bathroom, showered, shaved, and dressed for the hospital. Before he left (she was turned into her bed feigning sleep) she heard him go into the boys' room. First he kissed Noah. Then he kissed Nicholas. She waited for him to come into their bedroom and kiss her good-bye the way he had almost every morning of their married life, but instead he walked down the hallway toward the door. She wasn't what Michael expected her to be and she felt ashamed. When she heard his key turn in the lock she didn't know whether she was grateful or whether she wished he had come to say good-bye. But the minute he left the house she felt free.

She walked to the university. The tension began to build inside her as she neared her office building. She worried that when she arrived at school there'd be a message from Stephen—she knew he would call her—and she didn't know if she had the power to resist it. Instead, she went to the synagogue on 88th Street. She found her way through the dark corridors to the rabbi's chambers where she had once tried to take William.

The rabbi was sitting at his desk when she walked in. He looked diminutive without the white robe he wore on the High Holy Days. He was wearing a white shirt and a tie and sneakers on his feet. A partially eaten corned beef sandwich was spread out on top of white wax paper on his desk. Next to it was a pair of glasses and a pile of opened books. His computer was on. His study reeked of the deli.

She introduced herself. "I'm intruding on your lunch hour. I can come back later."

"May I offer you half my sandwich? A pickle?" His head was nearly bald. He was tan. He must have gone to Florida or a tropical island over the holidays.

She started to get up. "I'm not hungry."

"Sit." The rabbi said. "One or maybe two inspired moments have come to me after eating a corned beef sandwich."

"I have a question." She looked at him tentatively. "Do Jews believe in the devil?"

"There is no devil." The rabbi paused. He carefully took a bite of his sandwich. He looked up at her and smiled with the wisdom of someone who knows. "Your name is Eleanor?"

She nodded.

"There's a snake, but there is no devil," he said, slyly waving a sliver of pickle.

"You mean the Garden of Good and Evil? What form can he take? The snake. Can he be human?"

"You have to solve the puzzle for yourself."

"So you're saying that everyone is tempted at one time or another in life? That I'm not alone? I know it happens in literature. But sometimes I get confused."

"Is that what you hear me saying?"

"I just want to know if the snake is human."

"It's whatever you think it is." She looked into the rabbi's watery, compassionate eyes. "You don't have to be afraid."

"I am afraid."

"The truth is, Eleanor, we don't know why certain things happen. Or what they are trying to teach us. Each of us has questions. We have to bring those questions to life, act upon them, contemplate their effect upon our lives. Only you know the answer to what is inside you."

"So you're saying that it is okay to have questions?"

"What I'm saying is that without questions there is no meaning."

"So you're saying it's okay to be in the dark?"

"God lives in darkness, too."

———

There was a message when she arrived in her office.

I'm polishing the last draft of the novel, Eleanor.
I've been meaning to call you but I've been working
around the clock. It has to be right. It's for us. For you
and me.

She cleared her desk of extraneous papers, laid notes for
the chapter she was writing on the table near the window and
tried to put them in some kind of order. She told herself that it
was okay, that she was capable of living in the world and in her
mind at the same time. She could live two kinds of lives. The
phone rang.

"Eleanor," the voice from the other world said. "It's you. In
the living flesh. I'm not talking to your machine."

"It's me."

"Everything is riding on it," he said, as if he were extending
the message he had left in her voice mail. As if he knew there
was never any intermission between the lags when they spoke,
as if it were one long endless dialogue beginning when they
were twelve.

"I'm sure it's great."

"No, you don't understand. If they don't like it, that's it. I'm
out of here."

"I don't understand."

"The jig's up. I can't live in this city without a decent ad-
vance. I can't afford it."

She was quiet. The things she planned to say, the questions
she had wondered about when they weren't together went right
out of her mind the minute she heard his voice.

"I'm reading from my novel tonight. Do you want to come?"

"Where?"

"At this bar downtown."

"I don't know if I can make it."

"My agent got me the gig. She's inviting editors. Media. I need you to be there, Eleanor. It's finally happened. If you come I won't be afraid."

"What are you so afraid of?"

"Of looking at you and having to turn away, having to deny myself the pleasure of being with you."

"You know that I can't see you—that's why you say this." Eleanor's eyes filled with tears.

"Let me tell you about this piece I wrote last year about Amazon surfers. They flock to Brazil every year around the full moon and the equinox to chase an endless wave. It develops when the ocean tide advances into the river basin, creating a giant swell that flows upstream for several hundred miles at speeds of 20 miles an hour. A Pororoca wave can be as high as 12 feet. Surfers go after waves half that size because it increases their chances for a long, blissful ride. That's what I do, Eleanor. I chase the story because when I'm inside a piece I'm not in my head anymore. I know you get it. You do it with words, too. Only your words are about literature. I have to see you, Eleanor. You're the only one who understands what I do."

She went to the reading at an East Village bar where they hosted a reading series. Next to the bar was a microphone and a podium and a bunch of people sitting at tables, drinking. She came in late and sat in the back, nursing a glass of wine in the dark, watching him, certain he couldn't see her. She liked being close to him when he didn't know she was there. When she wasn't causing anyone harm. She studied his cheekbones. She studied the way he gripped each page. She didn't know whether the book actually worked on the page, or whether it was his voice, and the intensity he brought to bear that seduced the audience—whether he was a true or a false poet. There was no question that he was a charmer.

When he read he was a different person. The words tumbled from his mouth. His eyes lit up—he was a brilliant performer. She overheard people whispering about him next to her. "He's good. He's like an actor. The way he can get inside the narrator's head. He's mesmerizing to watch."

A boy is wandering in Alaska. It's cold and the roads are long but he has to keep going. If the boy stops he knows it will catch up with him. He can't sit still. He has to be in motion. He goes into a bar when it gets dark and he orders a cold beer at the bar and he looks at girls. Their breasts. Their thighs. Girls that want nothing from him. He sits next to a girl with long hair and listens to her talking with her friend. He doesn't want to talk to her, he only wants to listen. He only wants to hear her light up her cigarette, the sound of the match, the smell of her cigarette smoke. The way the wind sweeps through her hair when she tosses it behind her shoulders. He wants to hear her laugh and stomp out her cigarette in the bent tin ashtray when she's done. He watches the way she curls her foot around the ankle of her other leg. He watches the way her skirt creeps up when she bends over the bar. He doesn't want to touch her. At night when he's back in the motel he fantasizes. She's on top of him, the girl in the bar. Her hair falls over his face. He looks into her eyes and sees the girl from his past, not the girl in the bar, but the girl he's running away from. And then he looks out the window into the square pane and into the darkness. And the cold snow.

When he finished the performance he sat on his stool and stared at the audience, clearly enjoying the attention. He glowed.

She saw how comfortable he was in the spotlight. After, he waited, expecting people from the audience to come up to him. One girl said, "Amazing performance."

Eleanor sneaked out before he saw her.

"It's you, isn't it?" Eleanor said. She called him from her office the next day. "The boy in the story. I saw your performance. You were great."

"You didn't think I had it in me, did you? Why didn't you see me after?"

"I liked being invisible. You've been around. There have been lots of girls, haven't there? Lots of women."

"There's been no one, Eleanor. It's all lies."

"Then where does it come from? It has to come from somewhere."

"It's because I can't. Don't you get it? I write because I can't. Why can't I see you?"

"You know why."

She opened the paper later in the week. She was drinking her coffee in her renovated kitchen with the Sub-Zero, steel cabinets, Viking range, and Italian tiles she and Michael picked together. On the first page of the arts section was an article about new venues for avant-garde readings in New York City. The reviewer had gone to the bar the night Stephen had performed. He called him a performance artist with a "chilling rawness." "His words evoke the Alaskan landscape. He's an existentialist, capable of pure poetry," the reviewer said. There was a picture of him holding the microphone, almost indecently. It embarrassed her. He embarrassed her. He had nothing to do with the tiles in her kitchen. He had nothing to do with the integrity of her life. And yet, she felt elated for him, as if she'd been a part of his achievement. She sat in the kitchen for a half hour staring at the photo. She wanted to call someone and tell them to read the article in the *New York Times*. *He's a nobody from Chicago, Illinois. He's a boy I used to know. Isn't it crazy?* But she said nothing. She told no one.

When she arrived in her office there was a message in her voice-mail box. "They want me to perform the novel as a one-man play. They read about it in the *New York Times*. It's some club where they showcase new talent. She's a genius, my agent. Can you believe this is happening, Eleanor?"

He had invaded her city, wandered through its streets, and even invaded her office. The *New York Times* piece had sparked interest. The media seemed captivated by Stephen and his performance. While taking a train to Princeton to give a talk, she heard him on NPR over her radio headset. The commentator asked him how much of the novel was his story. "It's everyone's story," he said eerily.

"Do you really think we're as alone as the character in your novel?" Terry Gross asked on *Fresh Air*.

"Loneliness is inevitable," Stephen said. "It's a force of nature."

His gig was written up in the *New Yorker*'s "Talk of the Town." In her graduate seminar the students were talking about him. "We went to hear this guy, someone Mason from Colorado, do this performance piece about Alaska at KGB. About a guy who is always running away from himself."

Stephen, the flavor of the week.

————

The messages started again. "Eleanor, did you hear me on *Fresh Air*? Now it's all about sustaining it. We have a publicist working on it. The *Tribune* is doing a story. Our mothers will see it. Are you with me, Eleanor? Are you following it?"

He called again at the end of the week when she was in her office. "I finally reached you," he said, breathless. "You can't imagine how hard it is. Not being able to call you at home. Not having you by my side through all this. Will you go to the club?"

"They're calling you the Prince of Loneliness. Saying your work is about man's inability to connect."

"Isn't it fabulous?" He paused. "Eleanor, is everything okay?"

"Everything's fine," she said. *The Prince of Loneliness.* She wanted to strangle him.

"You know that day, when we were in the park, before all this started? And you said you wanted something to happen?"

"Yeah."

"I tried calling you back right after we said good-bye. But I missed you. I got your machine."

"Why didn't you leave a message?"

"I don't know."

"But you always leave messages. What did you want to say to me?"

"You're married, Eleanor."

"It's only just dawned on you?" She looked out the window at the tree in front of her building, so ancient and formidable, its gnarled roots nearly popping out of the sidewalk. "I told you I can't see you. I'm not trying to hurt you."

"Everything is riding on this. This thing I'm doing in New York."

"Why do you keep leaving me messages? What is it that you want from me? You're the one who started this. I don't understand what you're saying to me."

"You're cute when you're angry."

"Don't do that. I'm serious."

"Meet me now," he said.

On the way to his apartment she felt excited. She had on one of her sexiest skirts, with heeled sandals, bare legs, and a tight-fitting blouse. She made a point of not tying a sweater around her waist, or changing into flats, or pulling back her hair too tightly, as she sometimes did when she thought she looked too provocative. But when she arrived at his building, entered the lobby, and gave the doorman her name she felt uncomfortable, wanted to turn around and leave.

When he let her into his agent's apartment where he was staying it looked as if no one lived there. It was a studio, with a galley kitchen in the living room. "She spends most of her time in Los Angeles," Stephen had told her. "She keeps her studio for her clients." In the living room was a black leather couch. By the window stood a steel table with an opened laptop on it. Next to it, a pile of papers and books. Behind the table was a steel refrigerator, on top were three cereal boxes—Raisin Bran, Special K, and Captain Krunch. She had the urge to put the cereal boxes in the refrigerator to keep them away from bugs.

"You like Captain Krunch? That's Noah's favorite cereal."

"Noah?"

"My son."

"You have kids. I haven't even met your kids." His face turned accusatory.

"You haven't devoted that much time to my life. This has all been about you."

"You haven't exactly invited me over."

"Did you want me to? Did you want to see Michael? Did you want to meet my boys? Would you like us to all have dinner?"

"We could have done it that way."

"Is that what you wanted?" She sat down on the leather couch.

"I'm just saying that it could have happened."

He sat down next to her and propped his feet on the coffee table. "It's nice to sit next to you, Eleanor."

She looked back at him with distrust. "Why are you being smug? You don't want to be accountable. Is that why you're doing this?" She was ready to walk out the door. She took her bag from the vestibule where she had left it. "I don't know why I came."

"Doing what? Is it a crime that I love spending time with you? Get back here," Stephen said, as she opened the door. His mood seemed to lift. "I was just playing with you. I don't want you to leave."

"No, you weren't. You were testing me."

"Look at it from my side. You have everything and I have little or nothing to offer."

"What exactly do you want from me?"

"You're all I've been thinking about since the last time I saw you. I've replayed it a hundred times. Imagined the two of us together. I want it so badly, Eleanor. But it isn't right. I couldn't live with myself. All the other times I only thought about you. I wasn't thinking about them. I see you in your office. I see you in Paris. I see how beautiful you are. And then I remember that it's not just you. I can't have it. None of it. That life is sealed off to me."

She put her bag down and sat on the couch next to him. The back of her bare legs stuck to the leather, and it hurt when she lifted one leg to cross it over the other. She stroked his arm. "I understand. I know it's hard." She felt herself sinking into the couch and tried to realign herself. She was claustrophobic. It was dark in the room even though it was in the afternoon. It smelled damp and musty, the way apartments do when no one lives there. It was a studio for people in transit, for people who wandered in and out of the city, tempting others with their aloneness. She felt uncomfortable in her heels and skirt.

He turned his body around to face her. "Can I hold you? I've wanted to. It's all I've dreamed about."

She put her arms around him. He held her tightly. She thought about kissing the back of his neck, but she resisted. She was trembling. He pulled back to look at her. He turned to her and kissed her, but it wasn't the kiss she remembered. His lips were stiff. He couldn't let go. She had thought about kissing him at least a hundred times since they'd parted in Paris. She imagined it as something with heft and power. But her fantasy did not match the reality of his hard, anxious lips, his inability to allow her to penetrate him. When she looked into his eyes they were not the eyes she remembered. Where was his thick boyhood hair? His innocence? Why was he holding back?

"I can't do this." He stood up and walked over to the galley kitchen and stood in front of the sink and looked at her.

"Do what?"

"I can't be with you."

In all her dreams she had imagined this moment, when they were finally alone together, not in her office, or in the park, or in cafés, but alone face to face, able to do away with their defenses. His words came like an assault. The minute he broke from the embrace and stood at the kitchen counter she realized that for nearly a year, without being fully conscious of it, she had been waiting for this moment; everything that had transpired between them was leading to it.

She looked back at him in disbelief. She felt as if he had punched her in the stomach.

"You can't do this," she said. "You can't extricate a woman from her life and then do this."

"What are you talking about?"

"You know exactly what I'm talking about."

"That ring on your finger. You come into my apartment looking that way. All dolled up. You can't do that, Eleanor."

"But you asked me to come."

"I have to be focused on my work. Don't you get it? If I blow this I go back to Colorado."

She could not say a word.

"You see how I live and you know how others do."

"Who cares the way other people live? And besides. Look what's happening. Your work is getting noticed."

"The good doctor. What kind of mattress does he sleep on?"

"This isn't about Michael," she said calmly. "It's about us." She spoke in the same comforting voice she used when she spoke to her boys, when one of them was upset or worried. But she didn't know if she believed in what she was saying. "Let's calm down. Let's think it through."

He looked at her strangely. "No, Eleanor. You have to leave. This isn't going to work. You have to go back to your life."

"My life? And what's this? Intermission?"

"Yeah, that's what it is. Don't you get it? I can't have you."

She held on to the edge of the sofa to steady herself. He walked over to his laptop, sat down, and began to log in. "I can't handle this right now, Eleanor."

"What are you doing?"

"I'm expecting an e-mail from my publicist."

"That's it?" The room was spinning.

"I'm sorry," he said. He turned off the computer. "I don't know what I'm doing."

Eleanor wanted everything to slow down so she could think. All she could picture was how lost she was going to feel the minute she left the apartment. She didn't know what to say, but she had to find the words to turn it around. She couldn't walk out of the apartment and be left like this. It was too late. Too much had happened. "What about what you said, about doing this for us? About you and me? What did you mean?"

"Eleanor, you act like I promised you something."

Her hand reached out. She thought she would slap him.

He sat down next to her. "You're married," he said again softly. "Don't you see? I could never give you what he can. What we have has to remain a memory. I can't feel good about this. Not with you. It can't be this way."

"How will we know what's possible if we don't try?" The words came out of her mouth unexpectedly. Was it what she *really* wanted?

"Eleanor, have you known me to have a girlfriend in all these years? This is me we're talking about."

As he spoke his body seemed to say, *Please don't walk away. Don't abandon me. Walk me through this.* "You could try," she said. He was making her say things she didn't even know that she wanted. But the fact that he was saying no made her say yes. She didn't know where this was leading but she couldn't turn away. He had sprung out of nowhere and she had wandered away from her safe, secure life. They existed outside of ordinary time.

"You want to play house with me? Is that what you're saying?" He paused. He smiled. What was he thinking? Dinners in her kitchen, nights underneath her covers? Mornings reading the *New York Times* on her couch? "Oh, Eleanor," he said. "Why did you have to get married?"

"Why did you have to come here to my city? You have to leave. You can't stay here."

Still in a state of disbelief, she stood up to leave. He pulled her back and put his arms around her. "You know I care about you. You know what you mean. We can remember each other. It's what I do at night. Maybe it's more powerful that way."

"Don't say those things. I don't want to hear them. I don't understand. How did this happen? It wasn't supposed to."

"Your green eye looks so sad. Don't do that to me, Eleanor. I can't take it. I'll call you. I promise. I have to do what's in front of me right now. You have to understand that. Let's let it breathe."

She slapped him across the face and walked swiftly out the door.

She rushed quickly up Broadway, still feeling the sting in her palm. A million little birds were inside her, flapping their wings, wanting escape. Was it possible that she was supposed to go home in an hour and cook dinner for her family?

It was late in the afternoon. She went home and climbed into bed. She couldn't remember the last time she had come home in the middle of the afternoon to do nothing except lie on her bed. She had orchestrated her life so tightly, where would there ever have been time? But all she could think to do was get into bed and wait for the rest of the day to pass. Was her longing for Stephen as real as it felt or just part of her own need to connect intimately, to be stirred again? It made her feel physically sick. The hours seemed to pass slowly. She listened to the traffic outside her window, the grind of construction, the shouts from the streets.

She went into the bathroom and vomited.

The phone rang.

"Eleanor?"

"Eleanor who?"

"Eleanor, it's your mother."

"Hi, Mom."

"You sound awful. What happened?"

"Nothing's happened."

"Everything's happened," her mother said. "I can hear it in your voice. Eleanor, a mother knows when something is wrong."

"It's my marriage."

"What's wrong, Eleanor?"

"You were right, Mom. It's all falling apart."

"Follow your heart, Eleanor."

"I don't trust it."

38

This is where you belong. Now you can rest, Eleanor, the girl thought to herself. She took off her jeans and slipped inside the sleeping bag with William. By the time she had slipped in, the boy was naked inside the bag and had turned his body to the wall. He was almost asleep. She spooned him and they lay like that for a while and then a familiar feeling of disappointment inflated inside her chest. William wasn't going to turn around. He wasn't going to reach out for her body, run his hands up her thighs, touch her nipples.

They weren't going to kiss. Had she said something, done something to make him turn away? Why couldn't she reach him? She slipped her hands between his thighs but he remained turned against the wall. Don't you love me? *she said.* Aren't I desirable? *He didn't answer.*

"Eleanor," Michael said. "Aren't you getting up? Aren't you going to take the boys to school?"

"I'm so tired. Can you do it this morning, honey?" She could not let go of her dream. Her body was leaden.

During the afternoon she stayed in her bedroom, playing

hooky from her life, canceling her classes and not telling her husband. She went to pick up her boys from school, made dinner for her family, sat patiently with her husband at night (she did not retreat to her study) while he looked into his microscope for cells no one else could see. The next day she did the same thing. She went in her bedroom in the middle of the afternoon, shut her door, drew the blinds against the oppressive light, and not one soul knew about it.

After dinner she asked, "Tell me about the heart."

"It's nestled between the two lungs in the center of the chest, behind the breastbone. Let me show you. It's right here," Michael said, rising and pressing his hand against her chest.

She fell into the foundation of his chest, the little cave where her head rested perfectly against his breastbone, and told herself this could be enough. She felt his arms around her, holding her tightly.

"It looks a little like an upside-down pear." He broke from their embrace and took a pear from the fruit bowl on the table. "Give me your knife. I'll show you. See this bottom segment?" He sliced it off. "It's about the size of a clenched fist. It weighs between 300 grams and 450 grams."

"What happens when it beats erratically? When it's in crisis?"

"Eleanor. Tell me what's troubling you."

She thought about how to explain what she was feeling. She didn't know how. "It's nothing," she said. "I promise."

That night Eleanor dreamed about her father. In the dream, as always, she was trying to arouse his interest. The dream was a little confused. She was presenting a paper in an auditorium. Her father was sitting in one of the front rows. She kept glancing at him during her presentation. His eyes were closed. He was sleeping. After the presentation colleagues and students in the audience surrounded her, but she was anxiously looking for her father, afraid that he would grow impatient and leave the auditorium before saying good-bye. When she looked at the seat where she had seen him sitting throughout the presentation, she discovered that the man wasn't her father at all, but someone else, a homeless person. He was still asleep in his seat, even in the bright lights, surrounded by soiled old plastic shopping bags. She panicked. He had to be there. There must be something she could do to find him. She scanned the audience, running her eyes up and down the lines of people already leaving. Where was he?

When she awoke she was lost and confused.

"Why is Mommy sad?" Noah asked.

"Because she's waiting for us to take her to the park like we do every Sunday and you're not dressed yet." Michael scooped Noah in his arms and took him back to his room. Eleanor listened to father and son laughing and talking. She was grateful to Michael for how good he was with her boys. He would never leave them.

39

She e-mailed John from her office on Monday morning.

To: JCloud@princeton.edu
From: ECahn@columbia.edu

Do you think it is obsolete to live in the Romantic tradition?
As a scholar, one lives inside their words, inside their ideas.
One takes delight in the intricacies of a fantastic poem, the
landscape of a tradition. But they pull one out of life,

somehow, don't they? The Romantics are visionary, in search
of the sublime. It can be exhausting. Yrs, indefatigably,
Eleanor

To: ECahn@columbia.edu
From: JCloud@princeton.edu

I agree. One can get weary of visionary poems and their high
rhetoric. Do you know John Clare's poem called "Mouse
Nest"? It's about the speaker coming across a mouse nest in
a field of wheat. He records what he sees. He does not turn
it into a transcendent moment. The concrete, down-to-earth
experience is the transcendent moment. Yrs, concretely, John

To: JCloud@princeton.edu
From: ECahn@columbia.edu

Have you ever had an experience that lifted you out of the
ordinary and left you confused, deeply rattled, ready to
change your worldview, to make you believe things you
hadn't dreamed of? Yrs, exaltedly, Eleanor

To: ECahn@columbia.edu
From: JCloud@princeton.edu

Eleanor, it's too tiring. I've given it up completely. Yrs, most
boringly, John

When she logged off she thought about Stephen again. She
was trying to get over her anger and stop thinking about him.
All weekend she had vowed to do so—but she was caving
in. She rationalized the cruel way he had acted that afternoon,
how in the middle of the conversation he had gotten up and

checked his e-mail. She thought about what he'd said about wanting to preserve her in memory and it touched her. She told herself he was panicked. Worried about his career. Afraid for his future. For her. She thought of him alone in the sterile studio apartment with those boxes of cereal on top of the refrigerator. It reminded her of her father living in one of his hotel rooms. She couldn't bear to think of him so alone. She called Michael from the office and said she had a faculty meeting that night.

She went to the club to see him perform. His name was in lights on the marquee, above the show's title, *The Sorrows of Alaska*. The stage was dark. The song "North to Alaska" came rushing through the speakers. She sat in one of the red booths in the back and watched.

The stage was set up as it was at the other bar—a stool and a microphone. He wore black jeans and a black cotton pullover that was stretched out at the arms and hung over his hands. He had replaced his high-top sneakers with a pair of trendy black leather square-toed shoes, surely purchased in Soho. He was beginning to look like he belonged in New York.

He was driving again. He was out of the snow, so to speak. It was April and the grass was still frozen, but it was beginning to turn green and everything around him felt like it was thawing. Surviving the long winter made him want to call her again. But the minute his fingers went to dial he wanted to board up the windows, shut all the doors. He had been estranged from her for ten years. What would she be like? How would she look? How would he feel when he touched her? He had put hundreds of miles, millions of grams of snow between them. He wanted to push her into the snow and make love to her in the coldest, wettest part of his being. The last time he had seen her she had arrived on his doorstep looking like some kind of lost soul who needed his nourishment. His heart ached for her when he saw her. She had lost weight. When he opened the door she asked if he was happy to see her. He wanted to get in his car, to drive as far away as possible, so that he would not be the person he knew that he was, the person who wanted to destroy her.

His words cut through her. She wanted to approach him and force him to tell her why he was in New York, why he wanted to destroy her. She was not a character in his novel. Yet, she preferred being there without being observed. If she moved any closer to him she was afraid of the harm he might cause.

She went one other night that week, after the boys had gone to bed, showing up after intermission. She thought if she went to the theater one more time, she'd work him out of her system. It was good to be in the dark with him, never having to see him or touch him, just watching, knowing he was okay.

He left her a message on her voice mail.

I know I behaved badly. Here's the deal. Listen. I remember your father. I remember watching him teach you how to ride a bike without training wheels. You were on the bike. It was pink and it had tassels hanging from the handle bars. You were screaming. I was in the playhouse watching you. I used to watch you as a kid, even when you didn't know I was watching. You were screaming because you were afraid for your father to let go of the bike.

And then you were tearing down the street on that bike. You were fearless. After your father left, I used to think to myself, "How could he leave that little girl?" How do you expect me to walk away?

The phone rang. She lifted her head to answer it.

"Eleanor, it's me."

"Who?"

"Your husband. Who did you think it was?"

"I don't know. One of my students. What is it?"

"I wanted to remind you not to forget to pick up those light fixtures we ordered for the kitchen. Eleanor?"

"I'm here."

"Do you remember the studio we lived in when I was doing my residency and you had just started teaching? Remember how brown water came out of the kitchen faucet? Remember how you used the bathroom for a study so you wouldn't wake me when I was working nights and sleeping during the day?"

"You said one day we would look back and laugh at how far we've come. I didn't care where we lived. I was so happy," she said. "You said any place we lived afterward would feel like a castle."

40

Eleanor went downtown, to the gallery hosting Adam's much-praised retrospective. She had read a review of it in *The New Yorker* that morning; the reviewer called it "haunting, deeply moving, and deceptively simple. The paintings strike the perfect balance between the collision of history and the personal." She felt driven to see it, as if it were some kind of sign that would help her understand who she was. The gallery was an open room with mahogany floors; its white walls were covered with his vibrant work. The show was called "Portrait of the Artist's Sister." Eleanor recognized her image in each of the ten paintings in the middle gallery room. It was the work Adam painted years ago when she had modeled for him. In one painting the figure was sitting Indian style in the middle of the bed, her arms tucked underneath her head and her chest thrust out. Eleanor remembered the torture of holding the pose.

The figure in the paintings had her eyes. Her hair. The shadows underneath her eyes, her cheekbones. She saw her own disturbing essence captured. In one painting she looked angry and ornery and tough. But her eyes betrayed a woman who was vulnerable and devoted. It was haunting to see herself exposed and then to realize that it wasn't her at all.

She was the only one in the gallery—it was still early, just noon. The series was about Adam's obsession with his sister who had died when she was twelve, on the cusp of becoming a woman. She noticed that in each figure of the girl the color in each eye is slightly altered, one green, the other vaguely blue. Adam captured in the girl the awkwardness of being a young woman, the duality of being a girl and a woman at the same time. Of wanting to be desired and wanting to be invisible.

She sat on the long wooden bench at the center of the empty room. It was quiet and comforting to be surrounded by the familiarity of Adam's paintings, by the woman who was like a lost friend from long ago. It was as if time stopped and she was inside the life room of her past. It crystallized in that instant, how everyone who had shaped and influenced her was dwelling inside her. They would never die. The life room was more than a physical space to occupy. It was as Adam had told her: a private room filled with her own memories and associations. She could reconstruct and transform the idea of herself in any way she chose by using her fantasies and imagination. The realization came to her, filling her with energy and excitement and surprising freedom as if she now had come closer to understanding what she was meant to do. *This is me,* she thought, looking at the images in Adam's paintings. *This is who I am.* She remembered Adam's hands as they made their slow way up her body and she felt a twinge of nostalgia for the intensity of their connection.

She heard voices in the next room and then footsteps. Adam appeared as if out of her dream of him. He had aged. His hair was gray, but he had the same arresting presence she remembered. His eyes had deepened. The skin around his cheekbones had melted away, making his face more angular. "Eleanor," he said.

"I read the review. I had to come."

"I've thought about you. I went to pick up the phone to call you hundreds of times. Have you forgiven me?"

"You weren't so bad." She smiled. "Well, maybe a little. I wondered if I would bump into you. But then I remembered how much you hated seeing your work hung."

"I see the mistakes. How it was built. Sometimes it takes me years before I can see a painting completely separate from the places in me it derived from." He stopped. "Eleanor," he said. "Still so innocent."

"I'm not innocent. I wasn't then, either. You were always looking too closely. That's what made me uncomfortable."

He sat next to her on the long wooden bench in the middle of the room.

"You inspired them, Eleanor."

"They're about your past."

"It was what I saw in you that gave me access. Don't twist everything so that you don't count. You know you do that, don't you?"

"How did you remember that about me?"

"Tell me about you now. I read an essay you wrote in the *Yale Review.* It made me so happy to see it."

"It grew out of the paper I was writing when we were together."

"So I was an influence?"

"It wasn't just about you."

He looked at her sheepishly. "And now? What are you working on?"

"I've started a new book. It's still too early to talk about." She paused. "I'm a mother, Adam. I have two sons. Nicholas and Noah. They're a work in progress." She laughed.

"And the boys' father?"

"He's a heart surgeon. And Mariana?"

"She puts up with me."

"Remember the prayer shawl you gave me? I tried to give it to my father but he wouldn't accept it. He won't forgive the past."

She looked up at the painting of the girl and her parents with the serial number carved into their wrists.

"Could you, Eleanor?"

"I suppose not."

"Before you go, there's another painting in the next room I want you to see." He took her hand and led her into another room, in which was hung a single portrait of a girl, with a strand of black pearls around her neck, looking out the window at a crowning tree.

"The woman's eyes. She looks so lost."

"She's not lost. She's you. Look what I've called it."

She moved forward to read the placard. "*The Interior Life of Eleanor Cahn.*"

He nodded.

"It's like she lives inside her head, away from the real world," she said.

"But that's how we all live, to an extent."

"She's okay, then?"

He smiled. He walked her out of the gallery into the outer room. "She's more than okay."

A petite woman with long blond hair wearing a short, trendy skirt, black tights, and high black boots fitted to her calves walked into the gallery and took off her sunglasses. Eleanor watched as Adam became transfixed by the young woman, his gaze never leaving hers. She hooked her arm into his.

"Eleanor, this is Vicki." Adam said, clearing his throat once he regained his composure. He took her thin, shapely arm and held it out and studied it carefully as if he were just about to paint it.

41

To: ECahn@columbia.edu
From: JCloud@princeton.edu

Eleanor, I tried to call you. It's Julie. She tried to overdose. She's in the hospital. I'm sorry to have to e-mail you something so disturbing. Remember that late night in Paris when Julie confessed that she'd been in love with Stratford, her chair at George Washington? He recently married the graduate student. Julie's in bad shape. Yours, John

To: JCloud@princeton.edu
From: ECahn@columbia.edu

John, I don't get it. Didn't she care about her work? Her students? How is it possible? That laugh of hers. That

deeply ironic wit. Explain how the balance can tip over.
Yrs, sorrowfully, Eleanor

To: ECahn@columbia.edu
From: JCloud@princeton.edu

Read Keats tonight. Think of "Ode on Melancholy." Read
Coleridge. "The Rime of the Ancient Mariner." Wordsworth's
"The Prelude." Shelley's "To a Skylark." Stay well, John.

She thought about Julie again. She was in a state of disbelief. Julie's life was privileged. She had a good job, people who cared about her, a home. She thought of Anna Karenina. A countess, a woman of high society, married to a respectable man, the mother of a young son. Tolstoy wrote his novel over a century ago and it still didn't really matter how you lived, or how much you had, if inside your life was in pieces.

Her message light blinked on her office phone. She hadn't noticed it when she first walked in. She dialed her voice mail. *You have three new messages.* The first message was from her department chair reminding her that there was a lunch next week for a potential candidate in the department. The second message was from Stacy Kern, one of her graduate students, saying she wanted to schedule a conference. A third message was from Stephen.

Eleanor, they killed the piece. I thought publishing in
this hip, cutting-edge magazine was going to be sexy.
The reality is, it's fucked up. It wasn't what they wanted.

His voice on the machine, stripped of its usual persona, held no inflection. The phone rang. She picked it up, knowing it would be him.

"What happened?"

"My agent said that the editor's vision for the piece and mine were too far apart. The bottom line is I failed to win them." He sounded dejected.

"I see this all the time. An editor writes the piece in his or her head before they ever read a word of it. Of course they're disappointed."

"I'm leaving at the end of the week."

"What about the show? Your novel?"

"It's had its run, Eleanor. It's over."

"You can't leave." She was so stunned by his leaving that she forgot her anger.

"I can't stay here." A beep on the line announced another call. "That's probably my agent. Hold for a sec." He came back on the line. "I have to take this call, Eleanor."

"Will I see you before you leave?"

He put her on hold.

"She thought we'd get more of a kill fee," he said when he came back on the line again. "The whole thing is fucked up."

"Why don't you take a few days and think this thing through? Aren't you being rash? What about all the publicity your show has gotten? Doesn't that mean anything?"

"I feel abused, Eleanor. I'm too much of a bumpkin to survive in New York."

"Writers get their pieces killed all the time."

"It's coming down."

"You're not being rational."

"I'm leaving at the end of the week. The show's over. I have to."

"Will I see you before you go?"

"Thursday," he said. "Dinner."

She was losing oxygen. She opened the window and sucked in the air. She was angry that he was leaving without any regard for how it affected her but she also felt sorry for him and worried. She had to do something. She looked out at the patch of grass between the two buildings, covered in shadows. She decided to go for a swim. She tried to swim at least twice a week in Columbia's pool. She locked her office door and walked over to the building. After changing into her bathing suit, she plunged under water and swam a length of the pool without coming up for air. *He's leaving.* She emerged and exhaled. She went under again. She thought of Julie in the hospital. She swam faster. *Julie's in bad shape.* She came back up again. She did thirty laps of crawl and twenty laps of breaststroke, then rested at the edge.

The thought hadn't entered her mind so clearly before but it suddenly seemed simple. *Stephen was waiting for her to seduce him. How had she missed that?* They'd sleep together and end the unrequited journey. The months that he had been living inside her since they'd seen each other in Paris—almost an entire year had passed—were making her physically ill. She had to do something to stop it. She turned and began another lap. If they slept together she could see what was between them. Perhaps the reason why he hadn't come home that night in Colorado was because she had let him go. She hadn't told him how much she wanted him; how she believed in him. It was she, in the end, who had walked away. Perhaps all along he had wanted to make love to her but he was insecure, afraid to hurt her. Or afraid of being close to her. She was the stronger one. Why hadn't she seen it from his side before? It was all her fault. She hadn't seen what he needed. She was too caught up in feeling hurt and rejected. She continued to swim harder, faster, sure that she was right and that she could make him see how much she needed him.

She rose out of the pool and grabbed her towel from its peg. She was buoyant—as if she were still floating in water: A weight had been lifted. In her mind she felt the touch of his hands on her body, the press of his lips and wetness of his mouth. There was no doubt in her mind that it would happen. She couldn't let him go. She had to find out what was between them. It suddenly seemed clear to her—she wasn't herself anymore. She was someone else. She thought that making love to Stephen would have no bearing on her life because what they had did not exist in time. He was the only one who could connect her back to something essential, and not allowing herself to give in would be like an act against nature. The fierceness of her desire for him was a craving for identity, a relief from loneliness. She saw him staring through her childhood window, seeking her out as his savior. She did not think about her husband or her children. They no longer existed in this sphere.

She walked home. She passed a church on Broadway and read the placard. REPENTANCE IS AVAILABLE TO HUMANKIND AT ALL TIMES. WHEN THEY RETURN FROM THEIR INIQUITIES REPENTANCE RETURNS TO THE HOLY ONE AND GOD FORGIVES THEM ALL.

She did her errands. The mad rush of hours, the activities that filled each day were only to keep her from thinking about Stephen. She wondered why she had kept herself hidden all these years, why she had been afraid. She was no longer afraid. Her body was filled with a pleasant rush of adrenaline. She was awake. Alive. She wanted to live her life passionately.

She slept that night. She hadn't slept well in weeks, worrying about Nicholas's sleepwalking. Michael looked tired and on edge. The night before they had driven home from dinner and a cab had almost smashed into them. Michael dashed out of the car and began bashing on the hood of the cab like some kind of crazy person. "What are you doing, Michael?" she said, when he came back into the car. "Are you trying to get yourself killed?"

"You noticed," he said, glaring at the road.

Michael slept on the couch. His excuse of being near the air conditioner made it easy to leave their bed for the quietude of the couch, where he could lay in his own sea of solitude. He seemed unable to bear the distance in their bed. And he didn't know how to reach her, or she him. Perhaps she feared the disappointment that would follow if she attempted to reach him and failed. She hated Stephen for illuminating the things she tried to pretend didn't matter in her marriage. When she came into the living room to get a book earlier that night, she saw Michael stare at her bare legs and then look searchingly into her face. It hurt that he still loved her.

She slept so deeply that she did not hear Nicholas stir. Then something awakened her. She sat upright in bed. She ran down the hallway and saw his bed was empty. She rushed in the bathroom, the kitchen. He was nowhere.

"Michael!" she screamed. "Nicholas's gone." The front door to the apartment was wide open. Nicholas had unlocked the door. Where was he? She ran into the building's hallway. Michael followed. Had he gone into the elevator? Taken the stairs? Had someone taken him? She couldn't breathe. *This is my punishment,* she thought. She was relieved to find him in the stairwell, lying asleep in a corner. "My poor baby," she said, as she helped him up. Her eyes met Michael's for a moment in that look of shared parental love. Michael took Nicholas from her and she followed the two of them back into the apartment.

"This has to stop, Eleanor," Michael said once he had put Nicholas back in his bed.

"He can't control it," Eleanor said.

"That's not what I mean."

"If you and Daddy get divorced," Nicholas said at breakfast, "I'm going to run away."

She looked at him in disbelief. Was she dreaming? "Nicholas, Daddy and I aren't going to get divorced. I told you that before."

"Then why isn't Daddy sleeping in your bed anymore?"

"Because he gets hot at night and I can't sleep with the air conditioner on."

"You shouldn't do that to Daddy," he said.

She felt a surge of urgency and panic; she had to make the anxiety stop. Her mind felt fragmented. She looked outside at the sky over Central Park. It was breaking apart and coming together, a sky of disjointed clouds. If only Michael could allow himself to see her so she wouldn't feel so shut down around him. Why could Stephen see that emotional center in her and not her own husband? Or had she fooled herself into thinking he had?

No matter how strongly her rational mind told her she had to put an end to it, it was impossible. She watched Michael make notes from the slides underneath his microscope, not aware she was in the room. If she didn't love him now, were all the years they had been together a waste? But it was never about not loving him. It was about the places inside her she did not know how to show him, because he did not have those places inside him. How could she explain what had happened when she was so in the dark herself? How could he understand how she suffered when from his point of view there was no reason to suffer? She put her arms around his neck and whispered in his ear that she loved him. He looked at her bewildered, as if she were a different person. She took the boys to school. She sat on the porch of the school after the bell had sounded, after all the parents had left to go to their respective offices or homes, and she called Stephen's apartment. He wasn't there. She tried his cell phone. He didn't pick up. She had a strange feeling that he had left without saying good-bye. She hopped in a cab and went to his apartment. She asked the doorman to ring him up. The doorman said that he had gone out earlier that morning. She began to walk the blocks of the neighborhood looking for him. Her cell phone rang.

"You called, didn't you, Eleanor? I saw your number on my phone."

"I need to see you. There's something I have to say to you." She looked at herself in the reflection of a Starbucks window. Was that her? Why did she feel such shame?

"Eleanor, I'm at the club. I'm packing up my stuff."

"I'll come. I'll catch a cab. Stay there."

"I'll meet you in front of the club. But I only have a few minutes."

When she climbed out of the cab her eyes fixed on him. He looked young and boyish, in his blue jeans and Converse sneakers and black T-shirt. Underneath the tiredness, his eyes brightened when he saw her. In his eyes she saw how much he needed her.

The workman was on a ladder changing the marquee. Slowly the letters that formed his name were coming down. Eleanor watched. Stephen looked up, too, and they looked at each other.

"I'm sorry."

"It was like a dream. This whole thing in New York."

"It was real."

"What is it?" Stephen said gently. "What is it that couldn't wait until tomorrow?"

"I thought you left." He was still here. She touched him to make sure.

"I told you we'd have dinner tomorrow."

"I didn't believe you."

"You thought I'd let you down?"

"Can we go somewhere private? I can't talk here."

They went to a courtyard in back of the club and sat on a ledge. It was dark and claustrophobic. The sun hadn't yet reached the narrow corridor between the buildings.

"I want to make love to you," she announced.

His mouth broke into a smile. She took pleasure in seeing him caught off guard.

"Is that what you wanted to tell me? Why you've been looking for me all morning?"

She nodded. She looked at him squarely. Her body was like a powerful engine. Her face flushed with exhilaration.

"When?"

"Now."

"I have to meet my agent."

"Then afterward. I'll come back."

He touched her wrist and played with her bracelet, moving it up and down her arm like he had done in Paris. Then he took her hand and twisted the diamond on her finger so it went back inside her palm. "You're so beautiful," he said. "Meet me at my apartment at 4:00."

They stood up to say good-bye. He kissed her. It was a kiss filled with force and hunger. She briefly lost consciousness except for the feel of his lips and the rusty taste of his mouth and the embrace of his arms around her. She thought about the time when she was a girl and she was in the playhouse and he wanted to kiss her and she hadn't let him, and it was as if she had been waiting for that kiss all her life. But once she drew away she also felt strangely unreal. As he walked her back to the sidewalk in front of the club a letter came crashing down from the marquee to the pavement. When they looked up, all the letters—Stephen's name, the title of his show—were gone. She looked back at him to see if he was still beside her. He bent over and picked up the letter *S* and then put the letter in his backpack.

"It hurts, Eleanor."

"What?"

"It's the end. I have to do something to make it stop."

"I'll help you." There was commotion on the sidewalk, a constant stream of traffic on the block. She stroked the light beard that had arisen on his cheek. "It's going to be okay," she said, before they parted.

She had three hours to kill. She decided to distract herself by going into shops downtown. Hats, trinkets, pottery—so many beautiful objects, yet none of them interested her. She stopped for a coffee, then took the subway uptown, still pulled by a force she could not name. When she emerged above ground her eye lit on a little shop on the corner called Hearts; on a lark she popped in and fingered satin and silk bikini underwear and decided to purchase a pair of black lace panties and a low-cut bra. *Is this really me?* After she paid for them she went back into the dressing room, put the lingerie on underneath her clothes, and discarded the old ones in the trash bin.

In Central Park she walked by the lake; it was a beautiful spring day. She looked at her reflection in the water. Gazing deeper, she saw the reflection of her mother, her father, the reflection of William, of Adam, of Michael, as if they were all rippling inside her. She saw Nicholas and Noah, the face of Stephen—he was the furthest toward the bottom. Her own self struggled to reach the surface, trapped under the confusion of so many forces, love and desire all fighting for space in the life room of her heart, and she thought of Narcissus looking into his reflection and knew that it was not himself he saw but all the others who were inside him.

She was so deep in her own reflection it was impossible to hear the bell ringing on the little girl's tricycle rolling down the path, and then it wasn't the tricycle's bell ringing but her own cell phone burning a hole in her jacket pocket. She looked at the number on the little band of screen on her phone; it was Stephen calling. Her heart beat madly, and then her body went cold. She let her voice mail answer the call and stood still by the lake. She steadied herself, walked away from her reflection in the pond, and sat down on the bench, pressing her feet into the ground. She wanted to be held. Finally, she called her voice mail and listened to his message.

> I can't do this, Eleanor. I think you knew this was
> going to happen. Goddamn you. You knew. Even
> though you asked, you knew. I've been thinking about
> it ever since you left. I can't do this. Come see me.
> Please.

She knocked on the door. He called out that it was open. When she entered the apartment he was at his computer. He didn't get up out of his chair to greet her. He looked defeated. The room was filled with packed boxes. He had brought what looked like his entire life with him. He *had* meant to stay in New York. He got up from the table and slumped on the couch.

"I didn't want it to have to end like this."

"It doesn't have to."

"Eleanor, what do you expect me to do? I can't make it here."

"Why do you always make the decisions that involve us?"

"Eleanor, this is about me."

For a moment she thought she hadn't heard him clearly. And then she understood. "It's remarkable. How you truly have no idea of the effect you have on others. Or else you pretend that you don't."

"What have I done? I've exposed you. Is that it? Because maybe what the good doctor gives you isn't enough. That isn't my fault, Eleanor."

"Why did you come here?" She understood he had no idea of what he had done by entering her life. He could only see what stood in front of him, as if his own needs blinded him. "Do you think because we haven't made love that you are without responsibility?"

"What do you want from me, Eleanor?"

"Did you mean everything you've said? All your messages? All the times you mentioned wanting to be with me? They were all lies?"

"This is me we're talking about. I don't do the conventional. I burn bridges. Of course I feel responsible. It's why I can't."

"But I told you I wanted to make love to you."

He peered into her face. His eyes traveled down her body, slowly, without apology, taking her in, and then he shook his head as if he were holding in his eyes what he could never have. "I would hate myself. I can't be there for you emotionally. I can't be your soul mate."

"But the whole time you've been here you've taken from me emotionally. It's what you've demanded. That I be here emotionally for *you*. There's only one thing we haven't done."

"I can't do that, Eleanor. If we did it once we wouldn't be able to walk away, ever. It's what I thought about these last hours. You know that. You don't think I'm in pain? Besides, we have made love."

She looked at him strangely.

"You know we have. Every time. You think I'm making this up. Come here." He pulled her up from her place on the couch by the arm. "I tell you the truth about me. What I've been afraid to admit to anyone. I tell you I'm a broken ship. That I simply can't and you think I'm giving you a line? You think I'm trying to hurt you. You knew but you didn't want to know."

"A broken ship? What are you talking about? I really hate you."

"Come here." He pulled her into the bedroom. "You don't hate me." The mattress was stripped from the bed and there were more unsealed boxes on the floor. He pulled her onto the mattress and then leaned over her. His eyes glazed with emotion. He nestled his face in the cave of her neck, and they held each other silently. For one moment the storm inside her was perfectly calm. And then he looked up. "Let me do this once. The right way." He kissed her with an intense passion, slowly, and then with more determination and then slowly again, lingering, unwilling for a brief time to let go. After, when she had come back to herself, she was surprised to see that they existed as two separate people and she was calm again.

He turned off the lights. He picked up his camera from the floor, the same video camera he had with him when they were in Paris, and sat next to her. He turned it on and she looked into the small screen. They were together in Paris, along the Seine, the lights of the city sparkling behind them. Stephen's arm was around her shoulders. They looked like two young people in love.

"This is what we have. It will always be with us. No one can take it away. I see how much you want me. How much you care for me. You know I feel the same. But it will have to be enough."

"It's your own vanity that stops you. Your fear. You can't see beyond it. Don't you see? You play this game of hide-and-seek. But I've found you out."

He looked at her deeply and with anguish, the way a man looks at a woman he desires but can't have. Or was it a look he had perfected over the years to conceal his inability to stay in the moment long enough to accept love and its inevitable pain? She didn't know what to believe. He had allowed himself to open up and be vulnerable, but he couldn't stay in that place for very long. She saw for the first time that what was between them *was* real and he had made the decision that he could not have it. "Don't take away what we have from us, Eleanor, just because I don't conform to your standards of what people do and don't do."

"But don't you see what's happened? I'm supposed to get up now and go back to my family? You're impossible," she said, staring at him in disbelief. "I do hate you. I wish I never saw you in Paris."

"You don't hate me. You know me. I'm going back to Colorado to do the same thing I've always been doing. That's what I do. And you are going to go back to what you always do."

"I *do* know you. But I thought you changed."

"I'm not where I want to be. I thought I was. But I'm not."

"They'll be other women, won't there?"

"They won't be you." He drew her closer. "It's not just me. You have to ask yourself why you're in this. You think it's all me."

She looked around the room at the packed boxes. At the manuscript in a stack on his desk. "You're going to publish your novel this year. Why doesn't that mean anything?"

"The editor fucked me over."

"How long have you known this?"

"My agent told me this editor wanted to buy my book. I assumed it was going to happen. But it turned out the publisher hated it."

"But what about all the publicity? The show?"

"The publisher said it was a performance piece. He nailed me on it. He used it against me. No one wants to read about a guy stuck in Alaska. A guy who can't move. A guy who is paralyzed. He said it was all angst with no transformation."

"But it's good. I heard you read from it. You'll find another publisher."

"The publisher said it has to be there. On the page. It can't just be a performance. Here, you take it." He picked up the manuscript and put it in her hands. "I don't want it in my house. It's a novel. It's not like it was real. I want to take that fucker and light a match to it. I'm a journalist. I see myself as an interpreter of reality. This slice. This is our reality. This is what we have together."

She flipped through the pages of the novel on her lap. She stopped on a page and read it.

Sometimes in his dreams he can still see her. It's snowing. The snow never quits in the winters in Alaska. It's the farthest north he can get and still he wants to travel farther, wants to some days walk through the cold white arctic and never come out again. He can see their windows when they were children. He can see the branches of their two trees forming an arc between their two houses. The branches of the trees are touching.

"You're in love with me. That's it, isn't it?"

He stood up and walked into the galley kitchen. He opened the refrigerator door, then closed it. He looked like an animal trapped in a cage.

"I'm not going to hurt you." The manuscript was on her lap. She felt the paper sticking to her bare arms as they rested on top of it.

"Eleanor, please. You think it's all me. What about you? What's in it for you?"

Her eyes filled.

"What?"

"You know."

If she could stop him from fleeing then maybe she could see what she had been missing. She took the manuscript and handed it back to him.

"No. I want you to have it. You have to leave here and not turn back." He looked at her as if she were dangerous. "You have to be the one to do it."

"I'm not coming back." She turned to him again and looked at him openly. "I'm so frightened."

"Why?"

"I'm afraid I'll never feel this way again."

"I have to leave, Eleanor." He stood up. "I have to go back to the club before they lock it up. I forgot something."

She put the manuscript in her book bag and slung it around her body. The weight of it made her topple. She went to the door and before she turned the knob she turned around and watched his face brighten for a moment. "Eleanor, wait." She stopped and looked back. "Of course I'm in love with you," he said. "That's never been the issue."

Once she got outside she realized it was hard to walk. Stephen's manuscript was weighing her down. She took it out of the bag. She sat down on a bench. The manuscript was on her lap. She held it against her body, against her chest, holding it until the wave of emotion passed. Then she put it back on her lap and released her hands from the bulk of it. She watched the wind take one page, then another. She watched the pages circling through the trees and into the street and whirl around the avenues like little paper birds. Pages and pages of words swirling in a vortex of their own making.

42

She walked home through the park. She had gone with Noah on a field trip to Belvedere Castle to mark the completion of his class's semester study of Central Park. She learned that the park's 843 acres of land included 150 acres of water, 250 acres of lawns, 136 acres of woodlands. She learned there are 26,000 trees and 270 species of migratory birds in the park. She learned the rock outcroppings in the park, a metamorphic rock called Manhattan schist, were approximately 450 million years old. She learned there are 8,968 benches, 36 bridges and arches, and 21 playgrounds in the park. She recited these facts in her head as she walked through the park to steady herself.

It was overcast. There was moisture in the air but she thought the rain would hold. Before she knew it she was off the path. She hadn't been paying attention. She couldn't think straight. Her lungs couldn't get oxygen in order to breathe. She kept walking so that her heart would return to its normal beat, so that she could breathe. The rain began to fall and she welcomed the feel of it. No one was in the park, as far as she could see. It was as if she were in the forest, and not in the heart of the city. Her heartbeat accelerated. She tripped over a rock. She realized she had been walking in circles; a fog had descended and she could not see. She stumbled over broken branches and stones as the sky lost its light. What if it grew dark and she couldn't find her way out? She recalled the stories she'd read in the paper of women killed while jogging in the park. What if she never saw her boys again? How could she have put them at risk? She began to run to beat the falling of night. She tried to search for the tower of the castle so that she could find her way out but the fog was too thick. She thought of Michael and her sons. She needed to see them. The branches on the trees hung low to the ground and almost slashed her in the face. It was raining harder. The path was slick. She began to fall. Her feet sank into wet grass. Where was the path? Why hadn't she been paying attention? She was panicked. She was soaking wet. She couldn't think. And then she remembered that she had her cell phone in her bag. She took out the cell phone and dialed Michael's number. He picked up on the first ring. When she heard his voice she took a deep breath. "I'm lost," she said. She was panting. "I was walking home through the park. I went to the castle and I kept walking and then it started to rain and I lost my bearings. I don't know how to get back."

"It's okay," he said. "Calm down, Eleanor. I'll tell you where to go. I know the park like the back of my hand."

"But it's raining. And it's getting dark."

"Tell me where you are. What do you see in front of you? The boys and I go there all the time. It's easy to get lost."

The firm sound in his voice made her heart quiet. She described what was around her. She described a mass of boulders and an old oak to the north. She thought she'd heard water. Was it the reservoir? She described the long curvy path. She began to walk up an incline. Rain was hitting her sideways. She was soaking wet. The path was treacherous. "I don't know how it happened."

"Just tell me what you see." He talked her through the mist, through the twisted trees, directing her toward the path. The panic began to subside. She saw the castle. "I see the steeple. I see the rounded dome with the high windows. I see the porch and the tower. It looks like a house. A house with light. The rain has stopped. I'm walking toward it. I know where I am." She was breathless. "I think I know how to get back."

"Can you hear me, Eleanor?" His voice was far away, nearly fading. "Eleanor, are you still with me?"

"I can hear you," she said, now that she calmed down. "Did you ever lose your way?"

"The park is tricky at night. It could happen to anyone."

She was glad to hear his voice and yet she still wasn't sure she wanted to leave yet. Or that she was ready to come home.

43

S he opened the door to her apartment.

"You're soaking wet," Michael said. "You frightened me. Are you okay?" He embraced her.

"Thank you for being there," she said, kissing him. "I don't know what I would have done."

"Of course I'm here." He moved a lock of hair hanging over her face so she could see more clearly what was in front of her. "Go change so you don't catch cold."

After she slipped out of her wet clothes and put on her robe she sat next to Michael in the kitchen watching a news story about a fire in a club on the Lower East Side. The camera panned to the street. She recognized the Chinese restaurant on the corner, the greengrocer across the street. The little court-yard in the back where they had spoken was consumed in a tornado of smoke.

Michael turned from the television. "What a fire," he said. "Eleanor, are you okay? You look like you just saw a ghost."

"I can't believe it. So it's real."

"Of course it's real. The building's in flames."

"It's true. No one can stop it."

"Stop what?"

"The destruction, once it starts."

"Eleanor, your hands are shaking. Are you all right?"

"How is Mrs. Greenfield?" She needed to separate herself from the blaze.

"She's in intensive care." He paused and looked at his wife. "We're in the prime of our lives, Eleanor. The heart gets older. It's a sensitive organ. It gets damaged. We have to treat it better. You have to learn to calm down."

"How's your heart?" she whispered, a little afraid of how he would answer.

"It's not in any imminent danger."

"Mine is a little messed up."

He took the stethoscope out of his jacket pocket and listened. "It sounds okay to me."

"It's quiet now. Other times I need to feel it throbbing or I can't get up in the morning."

She looked at his hands still pressing the stethoscope against her chest. She was still alive and breathing. She wasn't going to die.

44

"Julie's still in love with him," Jordan said, sitting across the table from Eleanor. "She's still in the hospital." Eleanor hadn't been sleeping or eating well since Stephen left the city. She kept looking at herself in mirrors, in reflections of the glass as she passed store windows, searching for a familiar shape in the glass. They were having an early dinner together. They had decided to try a new Indian place in the Village that had just opened. The food was spicy, but over dinner Eleanor discovered she had a voracious appetite.

"She was such a party girl," Jordan continued. Jordan and Julie had both gone to Yale when they were undergraduates. "At Yale she had the world at her fingertips. Everyone was in love with her. She was that kind of person. You wanted to be around her. She was a force of nature."

"How did she go off course?"

"All those years they worked side by side and she still harbored feelings for him. Imagine that kind of torture. I don't think it dawned on her that Stratford was no longer in love with her until she found out he was getting married."

"Poor Julie."

"Imagine losing yourself over a man," Jordan said. "What a waste. A man!" she exclaimed again. "Julie always had a low opinion of herself. She thinks a man is going to make her happy. A man's attention is the only way she knows how to value herself. But she'll survive."

"It's more than that. It must have started so many years ago. When she was a child. That kind of pain, the loneliness. That inability to fully connect with others. Stratford was only the catalyst. Or maybe she saw something in him she wanted to heal. And it obsessed her. That she couldn't fully reach him. It was like he had taken a piece of herself and she needed it back." Eleanor took a bite from the chicken curry. She tasted the lamb. "What's the spice in here?" Her face was getting hot. She was beginning to sweat.

"You know Indian food."

"You mean I'm not hallucinating?"

"You're so dramatic, Eleanor."

"I wish I never saw him in Paris. I was a conduit. Someone to reflect who he was back to himself. What do I do now? I'm different. I'm not sure I can go back." She poured herself more wine. She had realized, like anyone in the throes of love, that she had come to live for him, and now that he was gone she wondered how she would fill the emptiness.

She remembered the touch of his skin on hers when he held her arm and how he made her feel alive. *What's in it for you?* she heard him say to her, again and again like a mantra. She took a sip from her water. In spite of the pain, she was glad he was gone. He had seemed so right for her, but in looking back, she wondered if she had also credited him with more than he deserved. Still, she wasn't sure how to fill the opening he had left inside her. To justify her temporary insanity, she tried to tell herself that nothing had really happened. They had barely kissed. And yet everything had happened. What did it mean about herself? About her marriage? What would she do now? How would she sublimate her desires? Why couldn't she think of any models in literature for a woman who valued her family but who still had needs apart from them? She lifted the fork to her mouth.

"Maybe he was a conduit for you?"

"But why?"

"You were working something out."

"Then the person doesn't really matter? It could be anyone?"

"That's not what I'm saying. Maybe he fit the ideal of the person you've been longing for. Maybe you wanted to bring something back that you had lost."

"But what have I gained? What was in it for *me*?"

"Don't expect to have all the answers. Twenty years from now when all you have are memories you'll be glad it happened."

"But it was all in my imagination."

"Was it, Eleanor?"

She rose to go to the bathroom. It was perfumed with incense and decorated in Indian cloth and beads. It was one of those tiny bathrooms divided into two stalls. Inside the stall was its own sink and mirror. She was a little woozy from the wine. The smell of the incense made her nauseous, and she felt claustrophobic. She turned on the tap to cool her face but only hot water came out, steaming up the mirror. Only her two eyes of different colors—opaque now—appeared in the mirror's fog. She heard someone come into the bathroom and go into the other stall. She looked at herself in the mirror again, and she thought she heard a voice.

It was real. It wasn't a dream.

She sat down on the toilet. *What?* Was she hearing things? *Now you're free.*

Maybe the woman in the other bathroom stall was talking on her cell phone and she'd overheard the conversation. Maybe it was the heat. Maybe she drank too much wine.

She went back to the table.

"Are you okay, Eleanor? You look pale."

"I'm a little light-headed. I think it's the heat. Or the food." She sipped on a glass of water. "Jordan, do you believe in God?"

"The closest I've come to finding God is when I'm in bed with Luca."

"Then God is love, or passion, is that what you're saying? Or in your case, sex?"

"Life is different from a novel. In a novel you can freeze-frame reality. But real life is fluid. You don't know what is going to happen next."

"So what are you saying?"

"You can't control everything that happens to you. Would you even want to?"

45

She was surprised at how much she was able to accomplish that year in spite of how distracted she had been. Her book called *The Persistence of Passion* had just come out. Reviews were mixed, but one reviewer called it "provocative" and cited one of her favorite passages: "Why hadn't Tolstoy killed off Vronsky? Did Cathy in *Wuthering Heights* have to die? And Madame Bovary, married to the cold doctor? Couldn't Flaubert have had more of a heart for his characters?" At the end of the book she concluded that passion wasn't worth dying for. But there must be an alternative, she thought.

To: JCloud@princeton.edu
From: ECahn@columbia.edu

John, have you ever felt as if you'd been through a war emotionally? And yet nothing about your life had really changed?

To: ECahn@columbia.edu
From: JCloud@princeton.edu

I don't know, Eleanor. I think I'm just waking up. You know what Kierkegaard once said. "Life can only be understood backwards, but must be lived forwards."

To: JCloud@princeton.edu
From: ECahn@columbia.edu

What are you doing next week? Maybe we could meet to discuss the Victorians. You know, something light. Or perhaps we should skip the Victorians and move on to the twentieth century. I don't want it to be over.

To: ECahn@columbia.edu
From: JCloud@princeton.edu

What don't you want to be over?

To: JCloud@columbia.edu
From: ECahn@columbia.edu

The quest.

To: ECahn@columbia.edu
From: JCloud@princeton.edu

It's never over, Eleanor. You can count on it.

Eleanor decided she had to write a novel in which the heroine didn't have to die for her passions. She would be loyal both to her passions and to her responsibilities—a heroine whose past and present were not always at war.

She sipped her coffee, picked up her pen, and imagined what her heroine would look like. Perhaps she would have red hair and eyes that changed color. Perhaps not.

ACKNOWLEDGMENTS

I would like to thank André Bernard, whose faith in the project sustained me through its course. His confidence proved invaluable. I owe a great debt to Sarah Chalfant and Jin Auh for wisdom and support, large and small. Likewise, to Diane Goodman for her early support and encouragement during the formative stage of the book. Thanks also to the excellent Rebecca Saletan, Tom Bouman, David Hough, and the terrific team at Harcourt. I am lucky to have Lelia Ruckenstein as a sensitive reader and friend. Her thoughtful and astute comments through many drafts proved invaluable. Special thanks to Sanda Bragman Lewis, Deidre O'Dwyer, Martha McPhee, Dani Shapiro, and Helen Schulman. Thanks to Rony Shimony and Alex Shaknovich for their medical expertise; to Benjamin Nachtwey for opening his studio and allowing me to be a muse for one day; and to the Corporation of Yaddo for its generous support and pleasant quietude in which to work. And always, to David Schwartz and Lucas Schwartz for everything.

Jill Bialosky was born in Cleveland, Ohio. She studied at Ohio University and received an MA in Writing Seminars at Johns Hopkins University, and an MFA from the University of Iowa. She is the author of the poetry collections *The End of Desire, Subterranean* (a finalist for the James Laughlin Award from the Academy of American Poets), and, most recently, *Intruder.* Her poems and essays have appeared in journals such as the *Paris Review,* the *New Yorker, O, The Oprah Magazine,* the *Kenyon Review,* and the *Atlantic Monthly.* She is the author of the novel *House Under Snow* and, coedited with Helen Schulman, the anthology *Wanting a Child.* Bialosky is an editor at W. W. Norton & Company and lives in New York City.